PERFECT STRANGERS

For Now, Forever

and

The Welcoming

ALSO BY NORA ROBERTS

Hot Ice • Sacred Sins • Brazen Virtue • Sweet Revenge • Public Secrets • Genuine Lies • Carnal Innocence • Divine Evil • Honest Illusions • Private Scandals • Hidden Riches • True Betrayals • Montana Sky • Sanctuary • Homeport • The Reef • River's End • Carolina Moon • The Villa • Midnight Bayou • Three Fates • Birthright • Northern Lights • Blue Smoke • Angels Fall • High Noon • Tribute • Black Hills • The Search • Chasing Fire • The Witness • Whiskey Beach • The Collector • Tonight and Always • The Liar • The Obsession • Come Sundown • Shelter in Place • Under Currents • Hideaway • Legacy • Nightwork • Identity • Mind Games • Hidden Nature

Irish Born Trilogy
Born in Fire • Born in Ice • Born in Shame

Dream Trilogy
Daring to Dream • Holding the Dream • Finding the Dream

Chesapeake Bay Saga
Sea Swept • Rising Tides • Inner Harbor • Chesapeake Blue

Gallaghers of Ardmore Trilogy
Jewels of the Sun • Tears of the Moon • Heart of the Sea

Three Sisters Island Trilogy
Dance Upon the Air • Heaven and Earth • Face the Fire

Key Trilogy
Key of Light • Key of Knowledge • Key of Valor

In the Garden Trilogy
Blue Dahlia • Black Rose • Red Lily

Circle Trilogy
Morrigan's Cross • Dance of the Gods • Valley of Silence

Sign of Seven Trilogy
Blood Brothers • The Hollow • The Pagan Stone

Bride Quartet
Vision in White • Bed of Roses • Savor the Moment • Happy Ever After

The Inn Boonsboro Trilogy
The Next Always • The Last Boyfriend • The Perfect Hope

The Cousins O'Dwyer Trilogy
Dark Witch • Shadow Spell • Blood Magick

The Guardians Trilogy
Stars of Fortune • Bay of Sighs • Island of Glass

The Chronicles of The One
Year One • Of Blood and Bone • The Rise of Magicks

The Dragon Heart Legacy
The Awakening • The Becoming • The Choice

The Lost Bride Trilogy
Inheritance • The Mirror

eBooks by Nora Roberts

Cordina's Royal Family
Affaire Royale • Command Performance • The Playboy Prince • Cordina's Crown Jewel

The Donovan Legacy
Captivated • Entranced • Charmed • Enchanted

The O'Hurleys
The Last Honest Woman • Dance to the Piper • Skin Deep • Without a Trace

Night Tales
Night Shift • Night Shadow • Nightshade • Night Smoke • Night Shield

The MacGregors
Playing the Odds • Tempting Fate • All the Possibilities • One Man's Art • For Now, Forever • Rebellion • In From the Cold • The MacGregor Brides • The Winning Hand • The MacGregor Grooms • The Perfect Neighbor

The Calhouns
Suzanna's Surrender • Megan's Mate • Courting Catherine • A Man for Amanda • For the Love of Lilah

Irish Legacy
Irish Rose • Irish Rebel • Irish Thoroughbred

Jack's Stories
Loving Jack • Best Laid Plans • Lawless

Summer Love • Boundary Lines • Dual Image • First Impressions • The Law Is a Lady • Local Hero • This Magic Moment • The Name of the Game • Partners • Temptation • The Welcoming • Opposites Attract • Time Was • Times Change • Gabriel's Angel • Holiday Wishes • The Heart's Victory • The Right Path • Rules of the Game • Search for Love • Blithe Images • From This Day • Song of the West • Island of Flowers • Her Mother's Keeper • Untamed • Sullivan's Woman • Less of a Stranger • Reflections • Dance of Dreams • Storm Warning • Once More with Feeling • Endings and Beginnings • A Matter of Choice • Summer Desserts • One Summer • Lessons Learned • The Art of Deception • Second Nature • Treasures Lost, Treasures Found • A Will and A Way • Risky Business • All I Want for Christmas • Home for Christmas

2-IN-1 NOVELS BY NORA ROBERTS

Entanglements • Pride and Passion • Welcome Home • The MacGregors: New Beginnings • Western Stars • Irish Pride • Small Town Dreams • Heart and Soul • True Horizons • Graceful Hearts • Without a Doubt • Bright Stars • Heart of the Game • Summer Shadows • Blue Skies • A Christmas Promise • A Force of Nature • Meant to Be • Here's to Us • Danger Zone • Starlight • Moondance • Royal Secrets •

*Irish Secrets • Royal Destiny • Close to Home
• Playing with Fire*

Nora Roberts & J. D. Robb

Remember When

J. D. Robb

Naked in Death • Glory in Death • Immortal in Death • Rapture in Death • Ceremony in Death • Vengeance in Death • Holiday in Death • Conspiracy in Death • Loyalty in Death • Witness in Death • Judgment in Death • Betrayal in Death • Seduction in Death • Reunion in Death • Purity in Death • Portrait in Death • Imitation in Death • Divided in Death • Visions in Death • Survivor in Death • Origin in Death • Memory in Death • Born in Death • Innocent in Death • Creation in Death • Strangers in Death • Salvation in Death • Promises in Death • Kindred in Death • Fantasy in Death • Indulgence in Death • Treachery in Death • New York to Dallas • Celebrity in Death • Delusion in Death • Calculated in Death • Thankless in Death • Concealed in Death • Festive in Death • Obsession in Death • Devoted in Death • Brotherhood in Death • Apprentice in Death • Echoes in Death • Secrets in Death • Dark in Death • Leverage in Death • Connections in Death • Vendetta in Death • Golden in Death • Shadows in Death • Faithless in Death • Forgotten in Death • Abandoned in Death • Desperation in Death • Encore in Death • Payback in Death • Random in Death • Passions in Death • Bonded in Death • Framed in Death

Anthologies

From the Heart • A Little Magic • A Little Fate

Moon Shadows
(with Jill Gregory, Ruth Ryan Langan, and Marianne Willman)

The Once Upon Series
(with Jill Gregory, Ruth Ryan Langan, and Marianne Willman)
Once Upon a Castle • Once Upon a Star • Once Upon a Dream • Once Upon a Rose • Once Upon a Kiss • Once Upon a Midnight

Silent Night
(with Susan Plunkett, Dee Holmes, and Claire Cross)

Out of This World
(with Laurell K. Hamilton, Susan Krinard, and Maggie Shayne)

Bump in the Night
(with Mary Blayney, Ruth Ryan Langan, and Mary Kay McComas)

Dead of Night
(with Mary Blayney, Ruth Ryan Langan, and Mary Kay McComas)

Three in Death

Suite 606
(with Mary Blayney, Ruth Ryan Langan, and Mary Kay McComas)

In Death

The Lost
(with Patricia Gaffney, Mary Blayney, and Ruth Ryan Langan)

The Other Side
(with Mary Blayney, Patricia Gaffney, Ruth Ryan Langan, and Mary Kay McComas)

Time of Death

The Unquiet
(with Mary Blayney, Patricia Gaffney, Ruth Ryan Langan, and Mary Kay McComas)

Mirror, Mirror
(with Mary Blayney, Elaine Fox, Mary Kay McComas, and R. C. Ryan)

Down the Rabbit Hole
(with Mary Blayney, Elaine Fox, Mary Kay McComas, and R. C. Ryan)

ALSO AVAILABLE...

The Official Nora Roberts Companion
(edited by Denise Little and Laura Hayden)

PERFECT STRANGERS

For Now, Forever

and

The Welcoming

TWO NOVELS IN ONE

NORA ROBERTS

St. Martin's Paperbacks

NOTE: If you purchased this book without a cover you should be aware that this book is stolen property. It was reported as "unsold and destroyed" to the publisher, and neither the author nor the publisher has received any payment for this "stripped book."

This is a work of fiction. All of the characters, organizations, and events portrayed in this book are either products of the author's imagination or are used fictitiously.

Published in the United States by St. Martin's Paperbacks, an imprint of St. Martin's Publishing Group.

EU Representative: Macmillan Publishers Ireland Ltd, 1st Floor, The Liffey Trust Centre, 117–126 Sheriff Street Upper, Dublin 1, DO1 YC43, Ireland.

PERFECT STRANGERS: FOR NOW, FOREVER copyright © 1992 by Nora Roberts and THE WELCOMING copyright © 1989 by Nora Roberts.

All rights reserved.

For information, address St. Martin's Publishing Group, 120 Broadway, New York, NY 10271.

www.stmartins.com

ISBN: 978-1-250-38638-0

The publisher of this book does not authorize the use or reproduction of any part of this book in any manner for the purpose of training artificial intelligence technologies or systems. The publisher of this book expressly reserves this book from the Text and Data Mining exception in accordance with Article 4(3) of the European Union Digital Single Market Directive 2019/790.

Our books may be purchased in bulk for specialty retail/wholesale, literacy, corporate/premium, educational, and subscription box use. Please contact MacmillanSpecialMarkets@macmillan.com.

Printed in the United States of America

St. Martin's Paperbacks edition / August 2025

10 9 8 7 6 5 4 3 2 1

For Now, Forever

PROLOGUE

"Mother."

Anna MacGregor clasped hands with her son as he crouched at her feet. Panic, fear, grief surged through her and met a solid wall of will. She wouldn't lose control now. She couldn't. Her children were coming.

"Caine." Her fingers were icy as they tightened on his, but they were steady. Her face was almost colorless from the strain of the past few hours, and her eyes were dark. Dark, young and frightened. It flashed through Caine that he'd never seen his mother frightened before. Not ever.

"Are you all right?"

"Of course." She knew what he needed and brushed her lips over his cheek. "Better now that you're here." With her free hand she gripped Diana's as her daughter-in-law sat beside her. Wet snow clung to Diana's long dark hair and was already melting on the shoulders of her coat. Anna took a long breath before she looked back at Caine. "You got here quickly."

"We chartered a plane." There was a little boy

inside the grown man, the attorney, the new father, who wanted to scream out a denial. His father was invulnerable. His father was the MacGregor. He couldn't be lying broken in a hospital. "How bad is he?"

She was a doctor and could tell him precisely—the broken ribs, the collapsed lung, the concussion and the internal bleeding, which her colleagues were even now struggling to stop. She was also a mother. "He's in surgery." She kept her hand tight on his and nearly managed to smile. "He's strong, Caine. And Dr. Feinstein is the best in the state." She had to hold on to that and to her family. "Laura?"

"Laura's with Lucy Robinson," Diana said quietly. She knew well what it was like to hold emotions in. Slowly she massaged Anna's fingers. "Don't worry."

"No, I'm not." This time Anna managed the smile. "But you know Daniel. Laura's his first granddaughter. He'll be full of questions when he wakes up." And he would wake up, she promised herself. By God, he would.

"Anna." Diana slipped an arm around her mother-in-law's shoulders. She looked so small, so frail. "Have you eaten?"

"What?" Anna gave a tiny shake of her head then rose. Three hours. He'd been in surgery for three hours. How many times had she been in the operating room, fighting to save a life while a loved one agonized in these plastic waiting rooms, these cold corridors? She'd struggled and studied to be a doctor to ease pain, to heal—to somehow, in some way make a difference. Now, when her husband was hurt, she could do no more than wait. Like any other woman. No, not like any woman, she corrected herself, because she knew what the operating room looked like, what it sounded and smelled like. She knew the instruments, the machines and the sweat too well. She wanted to scream. She folded her hands and walked to the window.

There was a will of iron behind her dark, quiet eyes. She'd use it now for herself, for her children, but mostly for Daniel. If it were possible to bring him back with sheer desire, she would do so. There was more to doctoring, much more to healing, she knew, than skill.

The snow had nearly stopped. The snow, she thought as she watched it fall thinly, had caused the roads to be slick and treacherous. The snow had blinded some young man, caused his car to spin out of control, and crash into her husband's foolish little two-seater. Her hands balled into fists.

Why weren't you in the limo, old man? What were you trying to prove with that flashy red toy? Always showing off, always . . . Her thoughts trailed away, going back in time. Her hands unclenched. Wasn't that one of the reasons she'd fallen in love with him? Wasn't that one of the reasons she'd loved and lived with him for nearly forty years? Damn you, Daniel MacGregor, no one can tell you anything. Anna pressed her fingers to her eyes and nearly laughed. She couldn't count the number of times she'd said that to him over their lifetime together. And adored him for it.

The sound of footsteps had her whirling, bracing. Then she saw Alan, her oldest son. Daniel had sworn before he had ever had a child that one of his offspring would be in the White House. Though Alan was close to making the oath reality, he was the only one of her children who took more after herself than their father. The MacGregor genes were strong. The MacGregors were strong. She let herself be folded in Alan's arms.

"He'll be glad you're here." Her voice was steady, but there was a woman inside her who wanted to weep and weep. "But he's bound to scold you for bringing your wife out in her condition." Anna smiled at Shelby and held out a hand. Her daughter-in-law with the fiery hair and soft eyes was big with child. "You should sit down."

"I will if you will." Without waiting for an answer, Shelby led Anna to a chair. The moment Anna sat, Caine put a cup of coffee in her hands.

"Thank you," she murmured and sipped for his sake. She could smell it, strong and hot, feel it scald her tongue, but she couldn't taste it. Anna listened to the ding of the electronic pages, the quick slap of rubber-soled shoes on tiled floor. Hospitals. They were as much her home as the fortress Daniel had built for the two of them. She'd always felt comfortable in them, confident in their antiseptic halls. Now she felt helpless.

Caine paced. It was his nature to do so—to prowl, to stalk. How proud she and Daniel had been of him when he'd won his first case. Alan sat beside her, quiet, intense, just as he'd always been. He was suffering. She watched Shelby slip a hand into his and was content. Her sons had chosen well. Our sons, she thought, trying to communicate with Daniel. Caine with his quietly strong-willed Diana, Alan with his free-spirited Shelby. Balance was needed in a relationship almost as much as love, as much as passion. She'd found that. Her sons had found that. And her daughter . . .

"Rena!" Caine was across the room, holding his sister.

How alike they look, Anna thought vaguely. So slim, so bold. Of all her children, Serena came closest to matching Daniel's temper and stubbornness. Now her daughter was a mother herself. Anna could feel Alan's quiet strength beside her. They're all grown. When did it happen? We've done so well, Daniel. She closed her eyes for only a moment. She could allow herself only a moment. *You wouldn't dare leave me to enjoy it all alone.*

"Dad?" With one hand Serena held on to her brother; with the other, she gripped her husband.

"Still in surgery." Caine's voice was rough with cigarettes and fear as he turned to Justin. "I'm glad you could come. Mom needs all of us."

"Momma." Serena went to kneel at her mother's feet, as she always had when she needed comfort or conversation. "He's going to be fine. He's stubborn and he's strong."

But Anna saw the plea in her daughter's eyes. *Tell me he's going to be all right. If you say so, I'll believe it.*

"Of course he's going to be fine." She glanced up at her daughter's husband. Justin was a gambler, like her Daniel. Anna touched Serena's cheek. "Do you think he'd miss a reunion like this?"

Serena let out a shaky laugh. "That's just what Justin said." She smiled, seeing that Justin already had an arm around his sister's shoulder. "Diana." Serena rose to exchange an embrace. "How's Laura?"

"She's wonderful. She just got her second tooth. And Robert?"

"A terror." Serena thought of her son, who already worshiped Grandpa. "Shelby, how are you feeling?"

"Fat." She flashed a smile and managed to conceal the fact that she'd been in labor for more than an hour. "I called my brother." She turned to Anna. "Grant and Gennie are coming. I hope it's all right."

"Of course." Anna patted her hand. "They're family, too."

"Dad's going to be thrilled." Serena swallowed over the fear that had lodged in her throat. "All this attention. And then there's the little announcement Justin and I have to make." She looked at him, willing her courage to return. "Justin and I are going to have another baby. Have to insure the line. Momma"—her voice broke as she knelt down again—"Daniel will be so smug about it, won't he?"

"Yes." She kissed both of Serena's cheeks. She thought of the grandchildren she had, of those she would have. Family, continuity, immortality. Daniel. Always Daniel. "He'll consider it all his doing."

"Wasn't it?" Alan murmured.

Anna fought the tears back. How well they knew their father. "Yes. Yes, it was."

There was more pacing, murmuring, hand-holding as the minutes dragged by. Anna set her half-finished cup of coffee aside, cold and unwanted. Four hours and twenty minutes. It was taking too long. Beside her, Shelby tensed and deliberately began to breathe deeply. Automatically Anna placed a hand on the mound that was her grandchild.

"How close?"

"Just under five minutes now."

"How long?"

"Couple of hours." She gave Anna a look that was a little excited, a little terrified. "A bit more than three, actually. I wish I could've timed it better."

"You've timed it perfectly. Do you want me to go with you?"

"No." For a moment, Shelby nuzzled into Anna's neck. "I'll be fine. We're all going to be fine. Alan"—she held out both hands, wanting to be hauled to her feet—"I'm not going to have the baby at Georgetown Hospital."

He drew her up gently. "What?"

"I'm going to have it here. Very soon." She laughed

a bit when he narrowed his eyes. "Don't try logic on a baby, Alan. It's ready."

The entire clan clustered around her, offering help, advice, support. In her calm, efficient way Anna summoned a nurse and a wheelchair. With little fuss she had Shelby settled. "I'll be down to check on you."

"We're going to be fine." Shelby reached over her shoulder for Alan's hand. "All of us. Tell Daniel it's going to be a boy. I'm going to see to it."

Anna watched as Shelby and Alan disappeared behind elevator doors just before Dr. Feinstein walked into the hall. "Sam," Anna exclaimed and was on him in seconds.

At the doorway of the waiting room, Justin held Caine back. "Give her a minute," he murmured.

"Anna." Feinstein put his hands on her shoulders. She wasn't just a colleague now or a surgeon he respected. She was the wife of a patient. "He's a strong man."

She felt hope surge and willed herself to be calm. "Strong enough?"

"He lost a lot of blood, Anna, and he's not young anymore. But we've stopped the hemorrhaging." He hesitated, then realized he respected her too much to evade. "We lost him once on the table. In seconds, he was fighting his way back. If will to live counts, Anna, he's got a hell of an edge."

She folded her arms around her chest. Cold. Why were the hallways so cold? "When can I see him?"

"They'll be bringing him up to ICU." His hands were cramping after hours of delicate work. He kept them firm on her shoulders. "Anna, I don't have to tell you what the next twenty-four hours mean."

Life or death. "No, you don't. Thank you, Sam. I'm going to talk to my children. Then I'll come up."

She turned to walk back down the hall, a small, lovely woman with gray threading through her deep sable hair. Her face was finely lined, her skin as soft as it had been in her youth. She'd raised three children, worked her way to the top of her profession and had spent over half of her life loving one man.

"He's out of surgery," she said calmly, calling on the control she'd been born with. "They're taking him to Intensive Care. They've controlled the bleeding."

"When can we see him?" The question came from several of them at once.

"When he wakes up." Her tone was firm. She was in charge again, and being in charge was what she did best. "I'm going to stay here tonight." She glanced at her watch. "He may float in and out a bit, and he'll be better knowing I'm there. But he won't be able to talk until tomorrow." It was all the hope she could give them. "I want you to go down to Maternity and check on Shelby. Stay as long as you like. Then go back to the house and wait. I'll call as soon as anything changes."

"Mother—"

She cut Caine off with a look. "Do as you're told. I want you rested and well when your father's ready to see you." She lifted a hand to Caine's cheek. "For me."

She left her children and comfort to go to her husband.

He was dreaming. Even through the drugs, Daniel knew he was dreaming. It was a soft world full of visions, tapestried with memories. Still, he fought it, wanting, needing to orient himself. When he opened his eyes, he saw Anna. He needed nothing else. She was beautiful. Always beautiful. The strong, stubborn, coolheaded woman he'd first admired, then loved, then respected. He tried to reach out but couldn't lift his hand. Infuriated at his weakness, he tried again, only to have Anna's voice float smoothly over him.

"Lie still, darling. I'm not going anywhere. I'm staying right here and waiting." He thought he felt her lips on the back of his hand. "I love you, Daniel MacGregor. Damn you."

His lips curved. His eyes closed.

CHAPTER 1

An empire. At the time he'd turned fifteen, Daniel MacGregor had promised himself he'd have one, build one, rule one. He always kept his word.

He was thirty years old and working on his second million with the same drive that had earned him his first. As he always had, he used his back, his brains and pure guile in whatever order worked best. When he'd come to America five years before, Daniel had had the money he'd saved by working his way up from miner to head bookkeeper for Hamus McGuire. He'd also brought a shrewd brain and towering ambition.

He could have passed for a king. He topped six-four with a build bold enough to suit his height. His size alone had kept him out of a number of fights, just as his size had seduced some men into challenging him. Either way was fine with Daniel. He was reputed to have a temper, but he considered himself a mild sort of person. Daniel didn't think he'd broken more than his share of noses in his day. He didn't consider himself handsome, either. His jaw was long and square, and running along its right edge was a scar that he'd gotten when a loose beam had toppled down on him in the mines. As a sop to his vanity, he'd grown a beard in his teens. A dozen years later it remained, deep red and well trimmed around his face, blending with a mane of hair that was too long for fashion. The combination made him look both fierce and royal, which pleased him. His cheekbones rose high and wide, and his mouth appeared surprisingly soft in its cushion of wild red hair. His eyes were a deep brilliant blue that lit with humor and goodwill when he smiled and meant it, just as they cooled to frost when he smiled and didn't.

Imposing. That was one adjective used to describe him. Ruthless was another. Daniel didn't care how he was described as long as he didn't go unnoticed. He was a gambler who played the odds boldly. Real estate was his wheel, and the stock market was his game table. When Daniel gambled, he played to win. The chances he'd taken had paid off. And when they had, he'd taken more. He never intended to play it too safe, because with safety came boredom.

Though he'd been born poor, Daniel MacGregor didn't worship money. He used it, wielded it, played with it. Money equaled power, and power was a weapon.

In America he found himself in a vast arena of wheeling and dealing. There was New York with its fast pace and hungry streets. A man with brains and nerve could build a fortune there. There was Los Angeles with its glamour and high stakes. A man with imagination could fashion an empire. Daniel had spent time in both, dabbled in business on both coasts, but he chose Boston as his base and as his home. It wasn't simply money or power he sought, but style. Boston with its old-world charm, its stubborn dignity and its unapologetic snobbishness suited Daniel perfectly.

He'd come from a long line of warriors who had lived as much by wit as by the sword. His pride in his line was fierce, as fierce as his ambition. Daniel intended to see his line continue with strong sons and daughters. As a man of vision, he had no trouble seeing his grandchildren taking what he'd molded and building on it. There could be no empire without family to share it. To begin one, he needed the proper wife. Acquiring one, to Daniel, was as challenging and as logical as acquiring a prime piece of real estate. He'd come to the Donahues' summer ball to speculate on both.

He hated the tight collar and strangulating tie. When a man was built like a bull, he liked his neck free. His clothes were made in Boston by a tailor on Newbury Street. Daniel used him as much because his size demanded it as for the prestige. Ambition had put him in a suit, but he didn't have to like it. Another man dressed in the elegant black dinner suit and pleated silk shirt would have looked distinguished. Daniel, in either tartan or dress blacks, looked flamboyant. He preferred it that way.

Cathleen Donahue, Maxwell Donahue's eldest daughter, preferred it, as well.

"Mr. MacGregor." Fresh out of finishing school in Switzerland, Cathleen knew how to serve tea, embroider silk and flirt elegantly. "I hope you're enjoying our little party."

She had a face like porcelain and hair like flax. Daniel thought it a pity her shoulders were so thin, but he, too, knew how to flirt. "I'm enjoying it more now, Miss Donahue."

Knowing most men were put off by giggles,

Cathleen kept her laugh low and smooth. Her taffeta skirts whispered as she positioned herself beside him at the end of the long buffet table. Now, whoever stopped for a taste of truffles or salmon mousse would see them together. If she turned her head just a fraction, she could catch a glimpse of their reflection in one of the long narrow mirrors that lined the wall. She decided she liked what she saw.

"My father tells me you're interested in buying a little piece of cliff he owns in Hyannis Port." She fluttered her lashes twice. "I hope you didn't come here tonight to discuss business."

Daniel slipped two glasses from the tray of a passing waiter. He'd have preferred Scotch in a sturdy glass to champagne in crystal, but a man who didn't adjust in certain areas broke in others. As he drank, he studied Cathleen's face. He knew Maxwell Donahue would no more have discussed business with his daughter than he would have discussed fashion with her, but Daniel didn't fault her for lying. Rather he gave her credit for knowing how to dig out information. But while he admired her for it, it was precisely the reason he didn't consider her proper wife material. His wife would be too busy raising babies to worry about business.

"Business comes second to a lovely woman. Have you been to the cliffs?"

"Of course." She tilted her head so that the diamond flowers in her ears caught the light. "I do prefer the city. Are you attending the Ditmeyers' dinner party next week?"

"If I'm in town."

"So much traveling." Cathleen smiled before she sipped her champagne. She'd be very comfortable with a husband who traveled. "It must be exciting."

"It's business," he said. Then he added, "But you've just returned from Paris yourself."

Flattered that he'd been aware of her absence, Cathleen almost beamed. "Three weeks wasn't enough. Shopping alone took nearly every moment I had. You can't imagine how many tedious hours I spent in fittings for this gown."

He swept his gaze down and up as she'd expected. "I can only say it was well worth it."

"Why, thank you." As she stood, posing, his mind began to drift. He knew women were supposed to be interested mainly in dresses and hairstyles, but he'd have preferred a more stimulating conversation. Sensing she was losing his attention, Cathleen touched his arm. "You've been to Paris, Mr. MacGregor?"

He'd been to Paris and had seen what war could do to beauty. The pretty blonde smiling up at him would never be touched by war. Why should she be? Still, vaguely dissatisfied, Daniel sipped the dry bubbling wine. "Some years ago." He glanced around at the glitter of jewels, the sparkle of crystal. There was a scent in the air that could only be described as wealth. In five years he'd become accustomed to it, but he hadn't forgotten the smell of coal dust. He never intended to forget it. "I've come to prefer America to Europe. Your father knows how to throw a party."

"I'm glad you approve. You're enjoying the music?"

He still missed the wail of bagpipes. The twelve-piece orchestra in white tie was a bit stiff for his taste, but he smiled. "Very much."

"I thought perhaps you weren't." She sent him a slow, melting look from under her lashes. "You aren't dancing."

In a courtly gesture, Daniel took the champagne from Cathleen and set both their glasses down. "Oh, but I am, Miss Donahue," he corrected, and swept her onto the dance floor.

"Cathleen Donahue continues to be obvious." Myra Lornbridge nibbled pâté and sniffed.

"Keep your claws sheathed, Myra." The voice was low and smooth, by nature rather than design.

"I don't mind when a person's rude or calculating or even a bit stupid"—with a sigh, Myra finished off the cracker—"but I do detest it when one is obvious."

"Myra."

"All right, all right." Myra poked at the salmon mousse. "By the way, Anna, I love your dress."

Anna glanced down at the rose-colored silk. "You picked it out."

"I told you I loved it." Myra gave a self-satisfied smile at the way the folds draped over Anna's hips. Very chic. "If you'd pay half the attention to your wardrobe as you do your books, you'd put Cathleen Donahue's nose out of joint."

Anna only smiled and watched the dancers. "I'm not interested in Cathleen's nose."

"Well, it isn't very interesting. How about the man she's dancing with?"

"The red-haired giant?"

"So you noticed."

"I'm not blind." She wondered how soon she could make a dignified exit. She really wanted to go home and read the medical journal Dr. Hewitt had sent her.

"Know who he is?"

"Who?"

"Anna." Patience was a virtue Myra extended only to her closest friends. "Fe fi fo fum."

With a laugh, Anna sipped her wine. "All right, who is he?"

"Daniel Duncan MacGregor." Myra paused a bit,

hoping to pique Anna's interest. At twenty-four, Myra was rich and attractive. Beautiful, no. Even at her best, Myra knew she'd never be beautiful. She understood beauty was one route to power. Brains were another. Myra used her brains. "He's Boston's current boy wonder. If you'd pay more attention to who's who in our cozy little society, you'd recognize the name."

Society, with its games and restrictions, didn't interest Anna in the least. "Why should I? You'll tell me."

"Serve you right if I didn't."

But Anna only smiled and drank again.

"All right, I'll tell you." Gossip was one temptation Myra found impossible to resist. "He's a Scot, which is obvious I suppose from his looks and his name. You should hear him talk; it's like cutting through fog."

At that moment, Daniel let out a big, booming laugh that raised Anna's eyebrows. "That sounds as though it would cut through anything."

"He's a bit rough around the edges, but some people"—she cast a meaningful look at Cathleen Donahue—"believe that a million dollars or so smooths out anything."

Realizing that the man was being weighed and judged by the size of his bank balance, Anna felt a twinge of sympathy. "I hope he knows he's dancing with a viper," Anna murmured.

"He doesn't look stupid. He bought Old Line Savings and Loan six months ago."

"Really." She shrugged. Business only interested Anna when it involved a hospital budget. Sensing the movement to her left, she turned to smile at Herbert Ditmeyer standing with an unfamiliar gentleman, "How are you?"

"Glad to see you." He was only a few inches taller

than Anna and had the lean, ascetic face of a scholar, with dark hair that promised to thin in a matter of years. But there was a strength around his mouth that Anna respected, and he had a sense of humor it took a sharp wit to understand. "You're looking lovely." He gestured to the man beside him. "My cousin, Mark. Anna Whitfield and Myra Lornbridge." Herbert's gaze lingered just a moment longer on Myra, but as the orchestra began a new waltz, he lost his nerve and took Anna's arm. "You should be dancing."

Anna matched her steps to his naturally. She loved to dance, but she preferred to do so with someone she knew. Herbert was comfortable. "I heard congratulations are in order"—she smiled up into his dependable face—"Mr. District Attorney."

He grinned. He was young for the position but had no intention of stopping there. If he hadn't considered it bad form, he might have told Anna of his ambitions. "I wasn't sure Boston news traveled as far as Connecticut." He glanced to where Myra was dancing with his cousin. "I suppose I should have known better."

Anna laughed as they twirled around another couple. "Just because I've been out of town doesn't mean I don't want to keep up with what's happening here in Boston. You must be very proud."

"It's a beginning," Herbert said lightly. "And you—one more year and we'll have to call you Dr. Whitfield."

"One more year," Anna murmured. "Sometimes it seems like forever."

"Impatient, Anna? That's not like you."

Yes, it was, but she'd always managed to conceal it so successfully. "I want it to be official. It's no secret that my parents disapprove."

"They might disapprove," Herbert added, "but your

mother doesn't have any trouble mentioning you're in the top ten percent of your class for the third year running."

"Really?" Surprised, Anna thought it over. Her mother had always been more apt to praise her hairstyle than her grades. "I'll have to be grateful for that then, though she still harbors the hope that some man will come along and make me forget about operating rooms and bedpans."

As she spoke, Herbert turned her. Anna found herself looking directly into Daniel MacGregor's eyes. She felt her stomach muscles tighten. Nerves? Ridiculous. She felt the quick chill that raced down her spine and up again. Fear? Absurd.

Though he still danced with Cathleen, he stared at Anna. Stared at her in a way that was designed to make a young woman's cheeks flush. Anna stared back coolly while her heart raced. Perhaps it was a mistake. He seemed to take it as a challenge and smiled very slowly.

With a detached admiration, she watched him maneuver. Catching the eye of another man on the edge of the dance floor, Daniel gave a quick, almost imperceptible signal. Within moments, Cathleen found herself dancing in the arms of another man. Anna braced herself for the next step.

With the ease of experience, Daniel weaved through the dancers. He'd noticed Anna the moment she'd begun to dance. Noticed, then watched, then calculated. As soon as she'd glanced over and had given him that coolly appraising stare, he'd been hooked. She didn't have the stature of Cathleen, but seemed small and delicate. Her hair was dark and looked as warm and soft as sable. Her eyes matched it. The rose hue of her dress set off her creamy skin and smooth shoulders.

She looked like a woman who would fit easily into a man's arms.

With the confidence he carried everywhere, Daniel tapped Herbert's shoulder. "May I cut in?"

Daniel waited only until Herbert had relinquished his hold before he clasped Anna and swirled her back into the dance. "That was very clever, Mr. MacGregor."

It pleased him that she knew his name. It pleased him as well that he'd been right about the way she'd fit into his arms. She smelled like moonbeams, soft and quiet. "Thank you, Miss . . . ?"

"Whitfield. Anna Whitfield. It was also very rude."

He stared a moment because the stern voice didn't fit the quietly lovely face. Always one to appreciate a surprise, Daniel laughed until heads turned. "Aye, but I go with what works. I don't believe I've seen you before, Miss Anna Whitfield, but I know your parents."

"That's very possible." The hand holding hers was huge, hard as rock and incredibly gentle. Her palm began to itch. "Are you new to Boston, Mr. MacGregor?"

"I'll have to say yes because I've lived here only two years, not two generations."

She tilted her head a bit farther so that she could keep her eyes on his. "You have to go back at least three not to be new."

"Or you have to be clever." He twirled her in three quick circles.

Pleasantly surprised that for his size he was light on his feet, Anna relaxed just a little. It would be a shame to waste the music. "I've been told you are."

"You'll be told so again." He didn't bother to keep his voice low, though the dance floor was crowded. Power, not propriety, was his forte.

"Will I?" Anna cocked a brow. "How odd."

"Only if you don't understand the system," he corrected her, unsinged. "If you can't have the generations behind you, you need money in front."

Though she knew it was true, Anna disliked both forms of snobbery. "How fortunate for you society has such flexible standards."

Her dry, disinterested voice made him smile. She wasn't a fool this Anna Whitfield, nor was she a silk-coated barracuda like Cathleen Donahue. "You've a face like the cameo my grandmother wore around her neck."

Anna lifted a brow and nearly smiled at him. The look made him realize he'd said no more than the truth. "Thank you, Mr. MacGregor, but you'd be better off saving your flattery for Cathleen. She's more susceptible."

A frown clouded his eyes, and he looked fierce and formidable, but it cleared quickly, before Anna could gauge her reaction. "You've a cool tongue in your head, lassie. I admire a woman who speaks her mind . . . to a point."

Feeling aggressive for no reason she could name, Anna kept her gaze directly on his. "What point is that, Mr. MacGregor?"

"To the point where it becomes unfeminine."

Before she'd anticipated his move, Daniel swung her through the terrace doors. Until that moment she hadn't realized just how hot and stuffy the ballroom had become. Regardless of that, Anna's normal reaction with a man she didn't know would have been to excuse herself firmly and finally and walk back inside. Instead, she found herself stopping just where she was, with Daniel's arms still around her, the moonlight pouring over the flagstones and warm roses scenting the air.

"I'm sure you have your own definition of femininity,

Mr. MacGregor, but I wonder if you keep it in tune with the fact that we're in the twentieth century."

He enjoyed the way she stood in his arms and subtly insulted him. "I've always considered femininity a constant thing, Miss Whitfield, not something that changes with years or fashion."

"I see." His arms seemed to fit around her a bit too easily. She drew herself away to stroll to the edge of the terrace nearest the gardens. The air was sweeter there, the moonlight dimmer. The music became more romantic with distance.

It occurred to her that she was having a private conversation, one that might have been approaching an argument, with a man she'd only just met. Yet she didn't feel any urge to cut it short. She'd taught herself to be comfortable around men. She'd had to. As the only woman in her graduating class, Anna had learned how to deal with men on their own level and how to do so without constantly rubbing against their egos. She'd gotten through the first year of criticism and innuendos by staying calm and concentrating on her studies. Now she was about to enter her last year of medical school, and for the most part, Anna was accepted by her colleagues. She was perfectly aware, however, of what she would face when she began her internship. The stigma of being labeled unfeminine still stung a bit, but she was long resigned to it.

"I'm sure your views on femininity are fascinating, Mr. MacGregor." The hem of her dress skimmed the flagstone as she turned. "But I don't think it's something I care to discuss. Tell me, what is it exactly that you do in Boston?"

He hadn't heard her. He hadn't heard anything from the moment she'd turned back to face him. Her hair swung softly just at her white, smooth shoulders.

In the thin rose-colored silk, her body looked as delicate as fine china. The moonlight filtered over her face so that her skin was like marble and her eyes as dark as midnight. A man hears nothing but the thunder when he's struck by lightning.

"Mr. MacGregor?" For the first time since they'd stepped outside, Anna's nerves began to hum. He was huge, a stranger, and he was looking at her as though he'd lost his senses. She straightened her shoulders and reminded herself she could handle any situation that came along. "Mr. MacGregor?"

"Aye." Daniel pulled himself out of his fantasy and stepped closer. Oddly Anna relaxed. He didn't seem as dangerous when he stood beside her. And his eyes were beautiful. True, there was a very simple genetic reason for their shade. She could have written a paper on it. But they were beautiful.

"You do work in Boston, don't you?"

"I do." Perhaps it had been a trick of the light that had made her look so perfect, so ethereal and seductive. "I buy." He took her hand because personal contact was vital to him. He took it because part of him wanted to be assured she was real. "I sell."

His hand was warm and as gentle as it had been when they'd danced. Anna drew hers away. "How interesting. What do you buy?"

"Whatever I want." Smiling, he stepped a bit closer. "Whatever."

Her pulse accelerated, her skin heated. Anna knew there were emotional as well as physical causes for such things. Though she couldn't think of them at the moment, she didn't back away. "I'm sure that's very satisfying. That leads me to believe you sell whatever you no longer want."

"In a nutshell, Miss Whitfield. And at a profit."

Conceited ox, she thought mildly and tilted her head. "Some might consider that arrogance, Mr. Mac-Gregor."

She made him laugh with the cool, calm way she spoke, the cool, calm way she looked even when he could see traces of passion in her eyes. She was a woman, he thought, who could make a man wait on the doorstep with bouquets and heart-shaped boxes of candy. "When a poor man's arrogant, it's crude, Miss Whitfield. When a man of means is arrogant, it's called style. I've been both."

She felt there was some truth in his words but wasn't willing to give an inch. "Strange, I've never felt arrogance changes with years or with fashion."

He took out a cigar as he watched her. "Your point." His lighter flared, highlighting his eyes for one brief instant. In that moment, Anna realized he was dangerous after all.

"Then perhaps we should call it a draw." Pride prevented her from stepping back. Dignity prevented her from continuing what was, despite logic, becoming interesting. "Now, if you'll excuse me, Mr. MacGregor, I really must get back inside."

He took her arm in a way that was both abrupt and proprietary. Anna didn't jerk away, and she didn't freeze; she merely looked at him as a duchess might look at a dust-covered commoner. Faced with that serene disapproval, most men would have dropped their hand and mumbled apologies. Daniel grinned at her. Now here's a lass, he thought, who'd make a man's knees tremble. "I'll see you again, Miss Anna Whitfield."

"Perhaps."

"I'll see you again." He lifted her hand to his lips. She felt the soft, surprising brush of his beard across her knuckles, and for a moment, the trace of passion he'd seen in her eyes flared full-blown. "And again."

"I doubt we'll have much occasion to socialize, as I'll only be in Boston for a couple of months. Now, if you'll excuse me—"

"Why?"

He didn't release her hand, which troubled her more than she could permit to show. "Why what, Mr. MacGregor?"

"Why will you only be in Boston for a couple of months?" If she were running off to get married, it might change things. Daniel looked at her again and decided he wouldn't allow it to change anything.

"I go back to Connecticut at the end of August for my last year in medical school."

"Medical school?" His brows drew together. "You're not going to be a nurse?" His voice carried the vague puzzlement of a man who had no understanding of, and little tolerance for, professional women.

"No." She waited until she felt him relax. "A surgeon. Thank you for the dance."

But he had her arm again before she could reach the door. "You're going to cut people open?" For the second time she heard his laughter boom out. "You're joking."

Though she bristled, she managed to make it appear she was simply bored. "I promise you I'm much more amusing when I joke. Good night, Mr. MacGregor."

"Being a doctor's a man's job."

"I appreciate your opinion. I happen to believe there is no such thing as a man's job if a woman is capable of doing it."

He snorted, puffed on his cigar and muttered. "Pack of nonsense."

"Succinctly put, Mr. MacGregor, and again, rude. You are consistent." She walked through the terrace doors without looking back. But she did think of him. Brash, crude, flamboyant and foolish.

He thought of her as he watched her slip into the crowd. Cool, opinionated, blunt and ridiculous.

They were both fascinated.

CHAPTER 2

"Tell me everything."

Anna set her purse on the white linen cloth and smiled at the hovering waiter. "I'll have a champagne cocktail."

"Two," Myra decided, then leaned forward. "Well?"

Taking her time, Anna glanced around the quiet, pastel restaurant. There were half-a-dozen people she knew by name, several others she knew by sight. She found it cozy, safe and serene. There were times in the rush and fury of classes and studies when she longed for moments like this. There would be a way somehow, someday to have both in her life. "You know, the one thing I miss while living in Connecticut is having lunch here. I'm glad you suggested it."

"Anna." Myra saw no reason to waste time on polite chatter when there was news ready to break. "Tell me."

"Tell you what?" Anna countered, and enjoyed the flash of frustration in her friend's eyes.

Myra took a cigarette out of a thin gold case,

tapped it twice, then lit it. "Tell me what happened between you and Daniel MacGregor."

"We had a waltz." Anna picked up her menu and began to scan it. But she caught herself tapping her foot as the music crept back into her head.

"And?"

She shifted her gaze over the top of the menu. "And?"

"Anna!" Myra cut herself off as their drinks were served. Impatient, she pushed her cocktail aside. "You were out on the terrace with him, alone, for quite some time."

"Really?" Anna sipped her champagne, decided on a salad and closed the menu.

"Yes, really." With calculated flamboyance, Myra blew smoke at the ceiling. "Apparently you must have found something to talk about."

"I believe we did." The waiter returned, so Anna ordered her salad. Seething in frustration, Myra ordered lobster Newburg and told herself she'd fast through dinner.

"Well, what did you talk about?"

"I seem to remember one of the topics was femininity." Anna took another casual sip but wasn't quite able to conceal the anger that leaped into her eyes. Seeing it, Myra put out her cigarette and perked up.

"I assume that Mr. MacGregor has some definite opinions on the subject."

Anna sipped again, savoring the taste of the champagne before she set her glass down. "Mr. MacGregor is an opinionated boor."

Thoroughly pleased, Myra cupped her chin in her hand. The little veil attached to her hat fell just below her eyes but didn't conceal their enthusiasm. "I was nearly certain about the opinionated, but I would have bet heavily against the boor. Tell me."

"He admires a woman who speaks her mind," Anna continued, firing up, "to a point. To a point," she repeated with a quick unladylike snort. "That point stops wherever it conflicts with his outlook."

A little disappointed, Myra shrugged. "He sounds like any other man."

"It's men like him who see women as subsidiary to their manhood." Sitting back, Anna began to tap her fingers in a slow, steady rhythm on the white cloth. "We're fine as long as we're baking cookies, diapering babies and warming the sheets."

After choking on a sip of champagne, Myra swallowed. "My goodness, he did get under your skin in a very short time."

Deliberately Anna drew herself back. She detested losing her temper and reserved the privilege for something of real importance. She reminded herself that Daniel MacGregor didn't fit the bill. "He's rude and arrogant," she said more calmly.

Myra gave it a moment's thought. "That may be," she agreed. "But it's not necessarily a mark against him. I'd rather be around an arrogant man than a stuffy one."

"Stuffy he's not. Didn't you see that maneuver he pulled on Cathleen?"

Her eyes lit up. "No."

"He signaled to some man to cut in while they were dancing so he could cut in on Herbert and dance with me.

"How clever." Myra beamed approval, then laughed at Anna's expression. "Come on, darling, you have to admit it was. And Cathleen's much too involved with her own charms to have noticed." Myra gave a sigh of pleasure as her lobster was served. "You know, Anna, you should be flattered."

"Flattered?" She stabbed at her salad. "I don't see why I should be flattered that some enormous, self-important dolt of a man preferred to dance with me."

Myra paused to appreciate the scent of the lobster. "He's certainly enormous, and he may be a dolt, but he is important. And in a rough sort of way, he's attractive. Obviously, from the way you've brushed others off, you aren't interested in the smooth, sophisticated type."

"I have my career to think of, Myra. I don't have time for men."

"Darling, there's always time for men." With a laugh, she took another forkful of lobster. "I don't mean that you have to take him seriously."

"I'm glad to hear that."

"But I don't see why you should just toss him back."

"I have no intention of reeling him in."

"You're being stubborn."

Anna laughed. One of the reasons she was so fond of Myra was that her friend saw things clearly—her way. "I'm being myself."

"Anna, I know what becoming a doctor means to you, and you know how much I admire what you're doing. But," she continued before Anna could comment, "you're going to be in Boston for the summer, anyway. What's the harm in having an attractive escort who's obviously going places?"

"I don't need an escort."

"Needing and having are two different things." Myra broke off the corner of a roll and swore to herself she'd only eat half of it. "Tell me, Anna, are your parents still pressuring you about your decision to go into medicine? Are they still lining up eligible men to change your mind?"

"They've already lined up three potential candidates for my hand this summer." She had to convince herself to be amused and nearly managed it. "At the top of the list is the grandson of my mother's doctor. She thinks his connection to medicine might influence me."

"Is he attractive?" Myra waved away the question at Anna's scowl. "Never mind, then. My point is that your parents are going to continue to toss all of these men your way, hoping something sticks. But"—she added a bit of butter to her roll—"if you were seeing someone . . ."

"As in Daniel MacGregor."

"Why not? He certainly seemed interested last night."

Anna took the roll Myra had buttered and bit into it. "Because it's dishonest. I'm not interested."

"It might keep your mother from inviting every single man between twenty-five and forty over to your house for tea."

Anna let out a long breath. Myra had a point there. If just once her parents would understand what it was she needed, what she was striving for . . . *For your own good.* How many times had she heard that particular phrase? If she ever married and *if* she ever had children, those four words would never come out of her mouth.

Anna was well aware her parents had stopped arguing about her going to medical school only because they'd been certain she'd be out again before the end of the first semester. If it hadn't been for Aunt Elsie, Anna was aware she'd probably never have managed medical school at all. Elsie Whitfield had been her father's eccentric older sister—a spinster who had made her money, some said, bootlegging whiskey during prohibition. Anna could hardly fault her however the money had been earned, since Aunt Elsie had left her a legacy large enough for tuition and independence, with no strings attached.

Don't marry a man unless you're damn sure of him, Anna remembered Elsie advising. *If you've got a dream, go after it. Life's too short for cowards. Use the money, Anna, and make something out of yourself, for yourself.*

Now she was only months away from the dream—graduation, her internship. It wasn't going to be easy for her parents to accept. It would be harder still when they learned she intended to begin her internship at Boston General—and that she didn't intend to live at home while she was doing it.

"Myra, I've been thinking about getting my own place."

With the fork halfway to her mouth, Myra stopped. "Have you told your parents?"

"No." Anna pushed away her salad and wondered why life was so complicated when so many things seemed clear to her. "I don't want to upset them, but it's time. I'm a grown woman, but they're never going to see me as one while I'm living in their home. Also, if I don't make the break now, they're going to expect me to go on living with them after I graduate."

Myra sat back and finished what was left of her champagne. "I think you're right. I also think you'd be wise to tell them after it's a fait accompli."

"So do I. How would you like to spend the afternoon apartment hunting?"

"I'd love it. Right after some chocolate mousse."

She signaled the waiter. "Still, Anna, that doesn't solve the problem with Daniel MacGregor."

"There isn't any problem."

"Oh, I think you can depend on one. Chocolate mousse," she told the waiter. "Don't spare the whipped cream."

In his newly decorated office, Daniel sat behind an enormous oak desk and lit a cigar. He'd just completed a deal in which he'd bought the lion's share of a company that would manufacture televisions. Daniel calculated that what was now a novelty would become a staple in the American home in a matter of years. Besides, he enjoyed watching the little box himself. It gave him a great deal of satisfaction to buy something that entertained him. Still, his biggest project at the moment was revamping the teetering Old Line Savings and Loan to make it the biggest lending institution in Boston. He'd already started by extending two major loans and refinancing several others. He believed in putting money into circulation where it could grow. The bank manager was horrified, but Daniel figured the man would bend or find other employment. In the meantime, Daniel had some research to do.

Anna Whitfield. He knew her family background because her father was one of the top attorneys in the state. Daniel had nearly retained him before he'd decided to go with the younger, more flexible Herbert Ditmeyer. Now that Herbert had been elected district attorney, he might have to do some rethinking there. Maybe Anna Whitfield's father was the answer. He'd just about decided that Anna was.

Her family home on Beacon Hill had been built in the eighteenth century. Her ancestors had been patriots who'd started a new life in the New World and had prospered. The Whitfields were, and had been for generations, a solid part of Boston society.

Daniel respected nothing more than a strong lineage. Prince or pauper didn't matter, just strength and endurance. Anna Whitfield came from good stock. That was Daniel's prime prerequisite for a proper wife. She had a head on her shoulders. It hadn't taken him long to learn that; though she was studying something as odd as medicine, she was at the top of her class. He didn't intend to pass along soft brains to his children. She was lovely. A man looking for a wife and a mother for his children had to appreciate beauty. Especially that soft, creamy sort.

She also wasn't a pushover. Daniel didn't want a simpering, blindly obedient wife—though he did expect a woman to respect the fact that he called the shots.

There were a dozen women he could woo and win, but none of them had presented him with that little bit extra. A challenge. After one meeting with Anna, Daniel was certain she would give him that. Being pursued by a woman flattered the ego, but a challenge—a challenge fired the blood. There was enough warrior in him to look forward to the fight.

If he knew one thing, it was how to lay the groundwork for a takeover. First, he found out his opponent's strengths and weaknesses. Then, he played on both. Picking up the phone, Daniel kicked back in his chair and began.

A few hours later, Daniel was struggling with the knot in his black silk tie. The only problem with being wealthy, as far as he could see, was having to dress the part. There was no question that he presented an imposing figure in dress black, but he never stopped straining against the restrictions. Still, if a man was out to sweep a woman off her feet, he was ahead of the game if he did it in his Sunday best.

According to his information, Anna Whitfield would be spending the evening at the ballet with friends. Daniel figured he had his accountant to thank for talking him into renting a box at the theater. He might not have put it to much use thus far, but tonight would make up for all that.

He was whistling as he walked down the stairs to the first floor. Most people would have considered his twenty-room house a bit overindulgent for one man, but to Daniel, the house, with its tall windows and gleaming floors, was a statement. As long as he had it, he'd never have to go back to the three-room cottage he'd grown up in. The house said what Daniel needed it to say—that the man who owned it had success, had presence, had style. Without those things, Daniel Duncan MacGregor was back in the mines with coal dust ground into his skin and reddening his eyes.

At the foot of the stairs, Daniel paused to bellow, "McGee!" He got a foolish surge of pleasure at the way his voice bounced off the walls.

"Sir." McGee walked down the long hall, erect and unbending. He'd served other gentlemen in his time, but never one as unconventional or as generous as MacGregor. Besides, it pleased him to work for a fellow Scot.

"I'll need the car brought around."

"It's waiting for you outside."

"The champagne?"

"Chilled, of course, sir."

"The flowers?"

"White roses, sir. Two dozen as you requested."

"Good, good." Daniel was halfway to the door

before he stopped and turned around. "Help yourself to the Scotch, McGee. You've got the evening off."

With no change of expression, McGee inclined his head. "Thank you, sir."

Whistling again, Daniel went outside to the waiting car. He'd bought the silver Rolls on a whim but had had no cause to regret it. He'd given the gardener the extra job of chauffeur and had pleased them both by outfitting him in a pearl-gray uniform and cap. Steven's grammar might be faulty, but once he was behind the wheel, he was the soul of dignity.

"Evening, Mr. MacGregor." Steven opened the door, then polished the handle with a soft cloth after he'd closed it again. Daniel might have bought the Rolls, but Steven considered it his baby.

After settling himself in the quiet luxury of the backseat, Daniel opened the briefcase that was waiting for him. If it took fifteen minutes to drive to the theater, it meant he had fifteen minutes to work. Idle time was for his old age.

If things went according to plan, he'd have that piece of property in Hyannis Port by the following week. The cliffs, the tough gray rock, the tall green grass reminded him of Scotland. He'd make his home there, a home he already imagined in his mind's eye. There'd be nothing to compare with it. Once he had it, he'd fill it with a wife and children. So he thought of Anna.

The white roses were spread on the seat beside him. The champagne was cased in ice. He only had to sit through the ballet before he began his courting. He picked up a rose and sniffed. The scent was quiet and sweet. White roses were her favorite. It hadn't taken him long to find that out. It would take a hard woman to resist two dozen of them, a hard woman to resist the luxury he'd offer her. Daniel dropped the rose back with the others. He'd made up his mind. It would only be a short time before he made up hers as well. Satisfied, he sat back and closed the briefcase as Steven pulled up in front of the theater.

"Two hours," he told his driver, then on impulse picked up one of the roses again. It wouldn't hurt to start his campaign a bit early.

The scene in the lobby of the theater was one of glitter and silk. Long sweeping dresses in pastels contrasted with dark evening suits. There was a glow of pearls, a sparkle of diamonds and everywhere the feminine scent of perfume. Daniel wandered through the crowd, not so much aloof as preoccupied. His size and presence coupled with his casual manner had fascinated more than one woman. Daniel took this with a smile and a grain of salt. A woman who was easily fascinated would be easily bored. Wide mood swings weren't what a wise man looked for in a mate. Especially when the man was prone to them himself.

As he strolled through the crowd, he was distracted now and again and stopped with a friendly word or greeting. He liked people, so it was an easy matter for him to socialize, whether in the lobby of the theater or in the pits at one of his construction sites. Since he was first and last a businessman, he was comfortable talking about one thing while thinking of something entirely different. He didn't consider it dishonest, merely practical. So while he stopped here, paused there, he kept a sharp lookout for Anna.

When he saw her, he was struck just as hard and just as fast as he'd been at the summer ball. She wore blue—pale, pale blue that made her skin glow as white as new milk. Her hair was swept up and back with combs so that her face was unframed and more like his grandmother's cameo than ever. He felt a pang of desire, then something deeper and stronger than he'd expected. Still, he waited patiently until she turned her head and their eyes met. She didn't, as another woman might have, blush or flirt but simply met his stare with a calm, appraising look. Daniel felt the excitement and challenge of the game as he moved to her.

In a move that was too smooth to be considered rude, he homed in on her and ignored the group around them. "Miss Whitfield, for the waltz."

When he offered her the rose, Anna hesitated, then saw there was no polite way to refuse. Even as she took the rose, its scent drifted to her. "Mr. MacGregor, I don't believe you've met my friend, Myra. Myra Lornbridge, Daniel MacGregor."

"How do you do?" Myra offered her hand, carefully sizing him up. He looked her directly in the eye, his own eyes cool and cautious. Myra discovered that, though she wasn't certain she liked him, she respected him. "I've heard a great deal about you."

"I've had some business with your brother." She was smaller than Anna, though rounder. One look told Daniel she'd be formidable but interesting.

"That's not who I heard it from. Jasper never gossips, I'm afraid."

Daniel sent her a quick grin. "Which is why I like doing business with him. You enjoy the ballet, Miss Whitfield?"

"Yes, very much." She sniffed the rose involuntarily, then annoyed with herself, lowered her hands.

"I'm afraid I haven't seen many and don't seem to get the full impact." He added a rueful smile to the charm of the rose. "I'm told it helps if you know the story or watch with someone who truly appreciates ballet."

"I'm sure that's true."

"I wonder if I could ask you a great favor."

Warning signals flashed and made her narrow her eyes. "You can ask, of course."

"I've a box. If you'd sit with me, maybe you could show me how to enjoy the dancing."

Anna only smiled. She wasn't so easily taken in. "Under different circumstances I'd be glad to help you out. But I'm here with friends, so—"

"Don't mind us," Myra cut in. Whatever devil prompted her to interfere urged her further. "It's a shame for Mr. MacGregor to sit through *Giselle* without really appreciating it, don't you think?" Eyes wicked, she smiled at Anna. "You two run right along."

"I'm grateful." Daniel looked at Myra, and his eyes, which had been cool, warmed with humor. "Very grateful. Miss Whitfield?"

Daniel offered his arm. For one quick, satisfying instant, Anna considered tossing his rose on the floor and grinding it underfoot before stomping away. Then she smiled and tucked her arm through his. There were better ways of winning a match than tantrums. Daniel led her away, tossing a wink at Myra without breaking stride. Myra caught it and Anna's scowl with the same aplomb.

"Isn't it odd to hold a box at the ballet without being able to appreciate it?"

"It's business," Daniel told her briefly as they walked up the stairs. "But tonight I'm sure I'll get more than my money's worth."

"Oh, you can count on it." Anna swept through the doors and took her seat. Carefully she set the rose across her lap and allowed Daniel to remove the ivory lace wrap she'd tossed on as an afterthought. Beneath it, her shoulders were bare. Both of them became aware of how stunning the lightest touch of flesh against flesh could be. Anna folded her hands and decided to pay him back by giving him exactly what he'd asked for.

"Now, to give you the background." In the tone of a kindergarten teacher reciting *Little Red Riding Hood,* Anna told him the story of *Giselle.* Without giving him a chance to comment throughout the lecture, she went on with everything she knew about ballet in general. Enough, she thought, to put a strong man to sleep. "Ah, here's the curtain. Now pay attention."

Satisfied with her tactics, Anna settled back and prepared to enjoy herself. She couldn't concentrate. Within the first ten minutes her mind wandered a dozen times. Daniel sat quietly beside her, but he wasn't cowed. Of that she was certain. She thought that, if she turned her head only a few inches, she'd see him grinning at her. She looked straight ahead. She'd deal with Myra, she thought grimly, for boxing her in with a red-bearded barbarian. And she wouldn't look at him. She wouldn't, she promised herself, even think about him. Instead, she'd absorb the music, the color, the dancing of a ballet she loved. It was romantic, exciting, poignant. If she could only relax, she'd forget he was there. Deliberately she took five deep breaths. Then he touched her hand, making her pulse jolt.

"It's all about love and luck, isn't it?" Daniel murmured.

She realized that, barbarian or not, he understood and, from the quiet tone of his voice, that he appreciated. Unable to resist, she turned her head. Their faces were close, the lights were dim. The music swelled and crested over them. A little piece of her heart weakened and was lost to him. "Most things are."

He smiled, and in the shadowed light he seemed

incredibly virile, incredibly gentle. "A wise thing to remember, Anna."

Before she could think to resist, he linked his fingers with hers. Hands joined, they watched the dancing together.

He kept close during intermission, catering to her before she could prevent him. Somehow he maneuvered her until it was too late to make excuses and rejoin her friends for the last half. As she took her seat after the intermission, Anna told herself she was simply being polite by remaining in his box until the final curtain. It wasn't a matter of wanting to be there, or of enjoying herself, but of good manners. She managed to sit primly for five minutes before she was again caught up in the romance of the story.

She felt the tears come as Giselle faced tragedy. Though she kept her face turned and blinked furiously, Daniel gauged her mood. Without a word, he passed her his handkerchief. She took it with a little sigh of acceptance.

"It's so sad," she murmured. "It doesn't matter how many times I see it."

"Some beautiful things are meant to be sad so we can appreciate the beautiful things that aren't."

Surprised, she turned to him again with tears still clinging to her lashes. He didn't sound like a barbarian when he spoke that way. Somehow, she wished he had. Disturbed, Anna turned back for the final dance.

When the applause died and the lights came up, she was composed. Inside, her emotions were still churning, but she blamed that on the story. Without a sign that she'd been moved, she accepted Daniel's hand as he drew her to her feet.

"I can honestly say I've never enjoyed a ballet more." In the courtly manner he could draw out without warning, he brushed his lips over her knuckles. "Thank you, Anna."

Cautious, she cleared her throat. "You are welcome. If you'll excuse me, I have to get back to the others."

He kept her hand in his as they walked from the box. "I took the liberty of telling your friend Myra that I'd see you home."

"You—"

"It's the least I can do," he interrupted smoothly, "after you were nice enough to educate me. It made me wonder why you hadn't thought of going into teaching."

Her voice cooled as they walked down the stairs to the lobby. He was laughing at her, but she'd been laughed at before. "It isn't wise to take on responsibility for someone else without asking first. I might have had plans."

"I'm at your disposal."

She didn't lose her patience often, but she was close. "Mr. MacGregor—"

"Daniel."

Anna opened her mouth, then closed it again until she was certain she could be calm. "I appreciate the offer, but I can see myself home."

"Now, Anna, you've already accused me of being rude once." He spoke cheerfully as he maneuvered her to his car. "What kind of man would I be if I didn't at least drive you home?"

"I think we both know the kind of man you are."

"True." He stopped just outside the door, where a few people still loitered. "Of course, if you're afraid, I'll get you a cab."

"Afraid?" The light came into her eyes. Passion, fire, temper, it didn't matter. Daniel was learning to love it. "You flatter yourself."

"Constantly." With a gesture, he indicated the door Steven was holding open. Too angry to think, Anna stepped inside and was struck by the warm, sultry scent of roses. Gritting her teeth, she swept them into her arms so that she could sit as close as possible to the far door. It only took an instant for her to realize Daniel was too overwhelming to make the distance viable.

"Do you always keep roses in your car?"

"Only when I'm escorting a beautiful woman."

She wished she had the heart to toss them out the window. "You planned this carefully, didn't you?"

Daniel drew the cork out of the chilled champagne. "No use planning if you're not careful."

"Myra tells me I should be flattered."

"My impression of Myra is that she's a smart woman. Where would you like to go?"

"Home." She accepted the wine and sipped to steady her nerves. "I have to get up early in the morning. I'm working at the hospital."

"Working?" He turned to frown at her as he settled the bottle back in its bed of ice. "Didn't you say you had another year before you'd finished your training?"

"Another year before I have my degree and start my internship. Right now, my training also includes emptying bedpans."

"That's nothing a young woman like you should be doing." Daniel tossed back the first glass of champagne and poured another.

"I assure you, I'll take your opinion for what it's worth."

"You can't tell me you enjoy it."

"I can tell you I enjoy knowing I've done something to help someone else." She drank again and held out her glass. "That may be difficult for you to understand, since it is not business. It's humanity."

He could have corrected her then. He could have pointed out that he'd donated enormous funds toward setting up medical services for the miners in his region of Scotland. It wasn't something his accountant had advised, but something he'd had to do. Instead, Daniel focused on the one thing designed to make her furious.

"You should be thinking about marriage and a family."

"Because a woman isn't able to handle anything more than a toddler tugging on her apron while another's growing under it?"

His brow lifted. He supposed he should be used to the blunt way American women phrased things. "Because a woman's meant to make a home and a family. A man has it easy, Anna. He only has to go out and make money. A woman holds the world in her hands."

The way he said it made it difficult for her to spit back at him. Struggling for calm, she sat back. "Did it ever occur to you that a man doesn't have to make a choice between having a family or having a career?"

"No."

She nearly laughed as she turned to look at him. "Of course, it didn't. Why should it? Take my advice, Daniel, look for a woman who doesn't have any doubts about what she was meant to do. Find one who doesn't have windmills to battle."

"I can't do that."

She had a half smile on her face, but it faded quickly. What she saw in his eyes sent both panic and excitement rushing through her. "Oh, no." She said it quickly and drained her glass. "That's ridiculous."

"Maybe." He cupped her face in his hand and watched her eyes widen. "Maybe not. But either way, I've picked you, Anna Whitfield, and I mean to have you."

"You don't pick a woman the way you pick a tie." She tried to summon up both dignity and indignation, but her heart was beating much too fast.

"No, you don't." He found the sudden breathlessness in her voice arousing and skimmed a thumb along her jaw to feel the warmth. "And a man doesn't treasure a piece of cloth the way he'll treasure a woman."

"I think you've lost your mind." She put her hand to his wrist, but his hand didn't budge. "You don't even know me."

"I'm going to know you better."

"I don't have time for this." She looked around, frantic, and saw they were still several blocks from her home. He was a madman, she decided. What was she doing in the back of a Rolls with a madman?

Her unexpected jolt of panic pleased him. "For what?" he murmured, and stroked a thumb down her cheek.

"For any of this." Perhaps she should humor him. No, she had to be firm. "Flowers, champagne, moonlight. It's obvious you're trying to be romantic, and I—"

"Should be quiet for just a minute," he told her, and decided the point by closing his mouth over hers.

Anna gripped the roses in her lap until a thorn pierced her skin. She never noticed. How could she have guessed his mouth would be so soft or so quietly clever? A man of his size should have been awkward or overbearing when he wrapped his arms around a woman. Daniel gathered her to him as if he'd done so countless times. His beard brushed her face and sensitized her skin while she struggled to remain unmoved. Her fingers itched to comb through his beard, and she reached for him before common sense could prevent it.

Something hot and fierce leaped inside her. Passion she'd kept firmly controlled, strictly in bounds strained free to make a mockery out of everything she had once believed of herself. If he were mad, then so was she. With a moan that was part protest, part confusion, she gripped his shoulders and hung on.

He'd expected a fight, indignation at the least. He'd thought she might pull herself away and level one of those cool looks to put him in his place. Instead, she pressed against him and made his impulsive demand flare like a torch in high wind. He hadn't known she could peel away his control with such delicate fingers and leave him stripped and vulnerable. He hadn't known she would make him want with such gut-wrenching desire. She was just a woman, one he'd chosen to complete his plans for success and power. She wasn't supposed to make him forget everything but the feel and taste of her.

He knew what it was to want—a woman, wealth, power. Now, with Anna pressed to him, with the scent of roses filling his head and the taste of her filling his soul, she was all those things in one. To want her was to want everything.

She was breathless when they drew apart, breathless, aroused and frightened. To combat her weakness, Anna fell back on dignity. "Your manners continue to be crude, Daniel."

He could still see the dregs of passion in her eyes, still feel it vibrating from her, or himself. "You'll have to accept me as I am, Anna."

"I don't have to accept you at all." Dignity, she told herself. At all costs, she needed to preserve some semblance of dignity. "A kiss in the backseat of a car means nothing more than the time it takes to accomplish it." It wasn't until that moment that she realized they were parked in front of her house. How long? she wondered. If color surged into her cheeks, she told herself it was anger. She fumbled with the door handle before the driver could come around and open it for her.

"Take the roses, Anna. They suit you."

She only looked over her shoulder and glared. "Goodbye, Daniel."

"Good night," he corrected, and watched her run up the walk with the pale blue dress swirling around her legs. The roses lay on the seat beside him. Picking one up, he tapped it against his lips. The bloom wasn't as soft as she was or as sweet. He let it fall again. She'd left them behind, but he'd just send them to her in the morning, perhaps with another dozen added. He'd only begun.

His hand wasn't quite steady when he picked up the bottle of champagne. Daniel filled his glass to the rim and downed it in one long swallow.

CHAPTER 3

The next morning Anna was at work at the hospital. The time she spent there brought her pleasure and frustration. She'd never been able to explain to anyone, neither her parents nor her friends, the excitement she felt when she walked into a hospital. There was no one who would understand the satisfaction she gained from knowing she was part of it—the learning and the healing. Most people thought of hospitals with dread. To them, the white walls, glaring lights and smell of antiseptics meant sickness, even death. To Anna, they meant life and hope. The hours she spent there each week only made her more determined to be a part of the medical community, just as the hours she spent each week poring over medical books and journals made her more determined to learn everything there was to learn.

She had a dream that she'd never been able to share with anyone. To Anna, it was both simple and pretentious: she wanted to make a difference. To accomplish her dream, she had to devote years of her life to learning.

Working as a layman, sorting linen, dispensing magazines, she still learned. Anna watched interns drag themselves through rounds after snatches of sleep. A great many of them wouldn't make it to a residency no matter how high their marks had been in medical school. But she would. Anna watched, listened and made up her mind.

She learned something else, something she was determined never to forget. The backbone of the hospital wasn't the surgeons or the interns. It wasn't the administrators, though they dispensed the budget and made the policies. It was the nursing staff. The doctors examined and diagnosed, but the nurses, Anna thought, the nurses healed. They spent hours on their feet, walked miles of corridor each day. Whatever hat they were wearing—clerk, maid, cleaning woman or comforter—Anna saw the same thing: dedication, often laced with fatigue. The interns were run ragged to weed out the weak. The nursing staff was just run ragged.

It was then, the summer before her last year of medical school that Anna made herself a promise. She would be a doctor, a surgeon, but she would be one with a nurse's compassion.

"Oh, Miss Whitfield." Mrs. Kellerman, the senior nurse, stopped Anna with a brisk hand signal, then finished filling out a chart. She'd been a nurse as long as she'd been a widow, twenty years. At fifty she was as tough as iron and as tireless as an adolescent. Kellerman was as gentle with her patients as she was hard on her nurses. "Mrs. Higgs in 521 was asking about you."

Anna shifted the stack of magazines she carried. Five twenty-one would be her first stop. "How is she today?"

"Stable," Kellerman answered without looking up.

She was in the middle of a ten-hour shift and hadn't time for chitchat. "She spent a restful night."

Anna bit back a sigh. She knew Kellerman would have checked Mrs. Higgs's chart personally and could have given her exact information. She also knew Kellerman's opinion of the system. Women were meant to function in certain areas, men in others. There was no crossover. Rather than question Kellerman, Anna walked down the hall. She'd see for herself.

The blinds were open in Mrs. Higgs's room. Sunlight poured through and slashed brilliantly over white walls, white sheets. The radio was on low. Mrs. Higgs lay quietly in the bed. Her thin face was lined more deeply than it should have been on a woman not yet sixty. Her hair was thinning, the gray dull and yellowing. The spots of rouge she'd applied that morning stood out like fire on her pale cheeks. Though her color made Anna apprehensive, she knew everything was being done that could be done. At the end of each of her frail hands, Mrs. Higgs's nails were tinted deep red. It made Anna smile. Mrs. Higgs had told her once that she could lose her looks, but never her vanity.

Because the woman's eyes were closed, Anna shut the door quietly. After setting down her magazines, she walked to the chart at the foot of the bed.

As Kellerman had said, Mrs. Higgs was stable—no better, no worse than she had been for more than a week. Her blood pressure was a bit low, and she was still unable to hold solid food, but she'd passed the night comfortably. Satisfied, Anna moved to the window to draw the shades.

"No, dear, I like the sun."

Anna turned and found Mrs. Higgs smiling at her. "I'm sorry. Did I wake you?"

"No, I was dreaming a bit." The pain was always

there, but Mrs. Higgs continued to smile as she held out a hand. "I was hoping you'd come by today."

"Oh, I had to." Anna took a seat beside the bed. "I borrowed one of my mother's fashion magazines. Wait until you see what Paris has in store for us for the fall."

With a laugh, Mrs. Higgs turned off the radio. "They'll never top the twenties. That was fashion with daring. Of course, you had to have good legs and nerve." She managed a wink. "I did."

"You still do."

"The nerve, not the legs." Sighing, Mrs. Higgs shifted. Anna was up immediately to rearrange her pillows. "I miss being young, Anna."

"I wish I were older."

Mrs. Higgs sat back, weak, and let Anna arrange her covers. "Don't wish the years away."

"Not years." Anna sat on the edge of the bed. "Just this next one."

"You'll have your degree in the blink of an eye. Then there will be times you'll miss all the work and confusion you went through to get it."

"I'll have to take your word for it." Efficient and unobtrusive, Anna took her pulse. "Right now, all I can think about is getting through the summer and starting again."

"Being young is like having a wonderful gift and not being quite sure what to do with it. Do you know the pretty nurse, the tall one with the red hair?"

Reedy, Anna thought as she moved her fingers from the woman's wrist. She recalled from the chart that Mrs. Higgs wasn't due to have medication for an hour. "I've seen her."

"She was helping me this morning. Such a sweet thing. She's getting married soon. I liked hearing her talk about her sweetheart. You never do."

"I never do what?"

"Talk about your sweetheart."

There were a few tired-looking flowers in a glass next to the bed. Anna knew one of the nurses must have brought them in, because Mrs. Higgs had no family. Leaning over, she tried to perk them up. "I don't have one."

"Oh, I don't believe that. A lovely young woman like you must have a handful of sweethearts."

"They distract me when they line up at my door," Anna told her, then grinned when the older woman chuckled.

"Not far from the truth, I imagine. I was only twenty-five when I lost my husband. I thought, I'll never marry again. Of course, I had sweethearts." A little dreamy, a little sad, Mrs. Higgs stared up at the ceiling. "I could tell you stories that would shock you."

With a laugh, Anna tossed back her hair. The sunlight slanted across her eyes, making them deeper, warmer. "You couldn't shock me, Mrs. Higgs."

"I was a dreadful tease, I'm afraid, but I had so much fun. Now, I wish . . ."

"What do you wish, Mrs. Higgs?"

"I wish I'd married one of them. I wish I married one and had children. Then there'd be someone who'd care and remember me."

"You have people who care, Mrs. Higgs." Anna reached for her hand again. "I care."

She wouldn't give in to the pain, or worse, the self-pity. Mrs. Higgs gave Anna's hand a quick squeeze. "But there must be a man in your life. Someone special."

"No one special. There is a man," Anna continued in a cooler tone. "He's just a nuisance."

"What man isn't? Tell me about him."

Because the tired eyes had brightened, Anna decided to humor her. "His name is Daniel MacGregor."

"Is he handsome?"

"No—yes." Anna shrugged her shoulders then dropped her chin on her hand. "He's not the kind of man you'd see in a magazine, but he's certainly not ordinary. He's more than six foot, about six-three, I'd say."

"Big shoulders?" Mrs. Higgs asked, perking up.

"Definitely." She had decided to make him sound larger than life for Mrs. Higgs's sake, then realized she didn't have to exaggerate. "He looks like he could heft two grown men on each one."

Delighted, Mrs. Higgs settled back. "I always liked big men."

Anna started to scowl, then admitted to herself that her description of Daniel was better for Mrs. Higgs than the Paris fashions. "He has red hair," she continued, then waited a beat, "and a beard."

"A beard!" Mrs. Higgs's eyes brightened. "How dashing."

"No . . ." The image of Daniel came to her mind much too easily. "It's more ferocious. But he does have lovely eyes. They're very blue." She frowned again, remembering. "He tends to stare."

"A bold one." Mrs. Higgs nodded approval. "I could never abide a wishy-washy man. What does he do?"

"He's a businessman. A successful one. Arrogant."

"Better and better. Now, tell me why he's a nuisance."

"He won't take a simple no for an answer." Restless, Anna rose and walked to the window. "I made it very clear to him that I wasn't interested."

"Which has made him determined to change your mind."

"Something like that." *I've picked you, Anna Whitfield. I mean to have you.* "He's sent me flowers every day this week."

"What kind?"

Amused, Anna turned back. "Roses, white roses."

"Oh." Mrs. Higgs gave a sigh that was young and yearning. "It's been too many years to count since someone sent me roses."

Touched, Anna studied her face. Mrs. Higgs was tiring. "I'll be glad to bring you some of mine. They do smell wonderful."

"You're a sweet child, but it's not the same is it? There was a time . . ." Her words trailed off, and she shook her head. "Well, that's passed now. Perhaps you should take a closer look at this Daniel. It's never wise to toss away affection."

"I'll have more time for affection after I finish my internship."

"We always think we'll have more time." With another sigh, Mrs. Higgs let her eyes close. "I'm betting on Daniel," she murmured, and drifted off to sleep.

Anna watched her a moment. Leaving Mrs. Higgs with the sunlight and the magazine from Paris, Anna left, closing the door behind her.

Hours later, Anna walked out into the afternoon light. Her feet were tired, but her spirits were high. She'd spent the last part of her shift in maternity, listening to new mothers and holding babies. She wondered how long it would be before she'd be in on a delivery and share in bringing in new life.

"You're even lovelier when you smile."

Startled, Anna spun around. Daniel was leaning against the hood of a dark blue convertible. He was dressed more casually than she'd seen him before, in slacks and a shirt open at the collar. As the light breeze ruffled his hair, he grinned at her. He looked, though she hated to admit it, wonderful. While she hesitated, trying to gauge the best way to handle him, Daniel straightened and walked to her.

"Your father told me you'd be here." She looked so . . . competent, he decided, in the dark skirt and white blouse. Not as delicate as she'd looked in the rose or blue gowns, but every bit as lovely.

In a casual gesture, she tucked her hair behind her ear. "Oh. I didn't realize you were well acquainted with my father."

"Now that Ditmeyer's district attorney, I needed another lawyer."

"My father." Anna struggled with a surge of temper. "I certainly hope you haven't retained him because of me."

Daniel's smile was slow and easy. Yes, every bit as lovely. "I don't mix business with personal matters, Anna. You haven't answered any of my calls."

This time she smiled. "No."

"Your manners surprise me."

"They shouldn't, considering your own, but in any case, I did send you a note."

"I don't consider a formal request for me to stop sending you flowers communication."

"You haven't stopped sending them, either."

"No. You've been working all day?"

"Yes. So now, if you'll excuse me—"

"I'll drive you home."

She inclined her head in the cool manner he'd come to wait for. "That's very kind of you, but it isn't necessary. It's a lovely day and I don't live far."

"All right, I'll walk with you."

She discovered she was gritting her teeth. Deliberately Anna relaxed. "Daniel, I'm sure I've made myself clear."

"Aye, that you have. And I've made myself clear. So"—he took both of her hands in his—"it's just a matter of seeing which one of us holds out the longest. I intend for it to be me. There isn't any harm in our getting to know each other better, is there?"

"I'm sure there is." She began to see one of the reasons he was so successful in business. When he chose, the charm just oozed out of him. It wasn't every man who could lay down a challenge with a friendly smile. "You have to let go of my hands."

"Of course . . . if you'll take a drive with me."

The light came into her eyes. "I don't respond to bribes."

"Fair enough." Because he was coming to respect her and because he still intended to win, he released her hands. "Anna, it's a lovely afternoon. Take a drive with me. Fresh air and sunshine are good for you, aren't they?"

"They are." Where was the harm? Maybe if she humored him a bit, she'd be able to convince him to put his considerable energy elsewhere. "All right, a short drive, then. You have a beautiful car."

"I like it, though Steven pouts whenever I go out without him and the Rolls. Pitiful thing for a grown man to pout." He started to open the door for her then stopped. "Do you drive?"

"Of course."

"Fine." Daniel drew the keys out of his pocket and handed them to her.

"I don't understand. You want me to drive?"

"Unless you'd rather not."

Her fingers curled around the keys. "I'd love to, but how do you know I'm not reckless?"

He stared at her a moment then burst into delighted laughter. Before she realized it, he swung her up and in two dizzying circles. "Anna Whitfield, I'm crazy about you."

"Crazy," she muttered, trying to straighten her skirt and her dignity when her feet touched the ground again.

"Come along, Anna." He plopped into the passenger seat with a wicked grin. "My life and my car are in your hands."

With a toss of her head, she rounded the hood and took her own seat. Unable to resist, she sent him a coolly wicked smile. "A gambler are you, Daniel?"

"Aye." He settled back as the engine sprang to life. "Why don't you head out of town a bit? The air's fresher."

A mile, she told herself as she pulled away from the curb. Two at the most.

Soon, they had somehow gotten ten miles out of town and were laughing.

"It's wonderful," she called over the wind. "I've never driven a convertible before."

"Suits you."

"I'll remember that when I decide to buy one of my own." She caught her bottom lip between her teeth as she negotiated a curve. "I just might look into it soon. I'll be moving into an apartment closer to the hospital, but a car is handy."

"You're moving out of your parents' home?"

"Next month." She nodded. "They didn't object as much as I'd anticipated. I suppose the best thing I ever did was to go to college out of state. All I have to do is convince them they don't have to furnish it for me."

"I don't like the idea of you living alone."

She turned her head briefly. "That isn't an issue, of course, but in any case, I'm a grown woman. You live alone, don't you?"

"That's different."

"Why?"

He opened his mouth, then shut it again. Why? Because, although he didn't worry about himself, he'd worry about her. However, that wasn't a reason she'd accept. He'd learned that much about Anna. "I don't live alone," he corrected her. "I have servants." Smug, he waited for her argument.

"I don't think I'll have room for any. Look how green the grass is."

"You're changing the subject."

"Yes, I am. Do you often take afternoons off?"

"No." He grumbled a bit, then decided to let it drop. He could always check out her apartment for himself and make certain it was safe. If it wasn't, he could damn well buy it. "But I decided catching you at the hospital was the only way to see you alone again."

"I could have said no."

"Aye. I was betting you wouldn't. What do you do in there? You can't stick needles and knives in people yet."

She laughed again. The wind smelled delicious. "For the most part I visit patients, talk to them, pass out magazines. I may help sort or change linen if they need me."

"That's not what you're going to school for."

"No, but I'm learning nonetheless. Doctors or even the nurses can't give patients a lot of personal attention, simply because of a lack of time and too much volume. I'm free to do that now, if only for a short while. And it helps me understand what it's like to be there hour after hour, sick, uncomfortable or just bored. I'm going to remember that when I start my practice."

He'd never thought of it just that way before, but he did remember the lingering illness that had taken his mother when he'd been ten. He remembered, too, how difficult it had been for her to be confined to bed. The sickroom smell was just as clear to him now as the scent of the mines. "Doesn't it bother you to be around sick people all the time?"

"If it didn't bother me, I wouldn't feel the need to be a doctor."

Daniel watched the way the wind tossed her hair back away from her face. He'd loved his mother, had sat with her every day, but he'd dreaded facing her illness and watching her fade. Anna, young, vital, was choosing to spend her life facing illness. "I don't understand you."

"I don't always understand myself."

"Tell me why you go into that hospital every day."

She thought of her dream. Why would he understand when no one else did? Then she thought of Mrs. Higgs. Perhaps he could understand that. "There's a woman in the hospital now. A couple of weeks ago they operated, removed a tumor and part of her liver. I know she's in pain, but she hardly ever complains. She needs to talk, and I can give her that. It's all the doctoring I can do now."

"But it's important."

She turned to him again, and her eyes were dark and intense. "Yes, to both of us. Today she was telling me that she wished she'd married again after her husband died. She wants someone to remember her. Her body's giving up, but her mind's so sharp. Today I was telling her about you—"

"You talked about me."

She could've bitten her tongue. Instead, Anna carefully explained. "Mrs. Higgs got on the subject of men, and I told her I knew one who was a nuisance."

He took her hand and kissed it. "Thank you."

Fighting amusement, she increased her speed. "Anyway, I described you. She was impressed."

"How did you describe me?"

"Are you vain as well, Daniel?"

"Absolutely."

"Arrogant, ferocious. I don't know if I remembered to include rude. The point is, if I can sit and talk to her for a few minutes every day, bring a little of the outside world into her room, it makes it easier. A doctor has to remember that diagnosis and treatment aren't enough. Maybe they're nothing at all without compassion."

"I don't think you'll forget that."

She felt a tug at her heart. "You're trying to flatter me again."

"No. I'm trying to understand you."

"Daniel . . ." How did she deal with him now? She could handle the arrogance, the flamboyance, even the demands. But how did she deal with the kindness? "If you really want to understand me, you'll listen to me. Earning my degree, starting my practice aren't just the most important things in my life. For now, they're the only things. I've wanted this too long, worked too hard to be distracted from it by anything or anyone."

He trailed a finger down her shoulder. "Are you finding me a distraction, Anna?"

"It isn't a joke."

"No, none of it is. I want you to be my wife."

The car swerved as her hands went limp on the

wheel. Hitting the brakes, Anna came to a screeching halt in the middle of the road.

"Does this mean yes?" Because he enjoyed the blatant shock on her face, he grinned.

It took her another ten seconds to find her voice. No, he wasn't joking. He was insane. "You're out of your mind. We've known each other a week, seen each other a handful of times, and you're proposing marriage. If you go into business deals with this kind of abandon, I can't understand why you're not bankrupt."

"Because I know which deal to make and which to toss out. Anna"—he reached out and took her shoulders—"I could have waited to ask you, but I don't see the point when I'm sure."

"You're sure?" With a long breath she tried to control the chaos of emotions inside her. "It may interest you to know that it takes two people to make a marriage. Two willing, dedicated people who love each other."

He dismissed that. "There are two of us."

"I don't want to get married, not to you, not to anyone. I have another year of school, my internship, my residency."

"I may not like the idea of you becoming a doctor"—nor was he convinced she'd pull it off—"but I'm willing to make some concessions."

"Concessions?" Her eyes went nearly opaque with temper. "My career is not a concession." Her voice was entirely too calm, too quiet. "I've tried to be reasonable with you, Daniel, but you simply don't listen. Try to get this through your head. You're wasting your time."

He drew her closer, aroused by her temper, infuriated by her rejection. "It's mine to waste."

Not as gently as he had before, nor as patiently, he

crushed his mouth to hers. She might have resisted; he didn't know. In that moment Daniel was too absorbed by the needs churning inside of him, the emotions swirling through him, to be aware.

Her lips were warmed from the strong sun, her skin soft from whatever female magic she performed on it. He wanted her. It was no longer a matter of his choosing or his planning. Desire overwhelmed, enclosed and ruled him.

This is how she'd thought he would be: strong, demanding, dangerous, exciting. She couldn't make herself object, though she knew it should have been simple. Cold. How could she be cold when her body had so suddenly turned to fire? Unfeeling. How could she not feel the sensations racing through her? Despite all logic, despite all will, she melted against him. In melting, she gave more than she'd known she had. She took more than she'd known she wanted.

She'd want again. While her blood thudded frantically in her head, she knew it. As long as he was near, as long as she could remember his touch, she'd want again. How could she stop it? Why did she want to? There were answers. She was sure there were answers if only she could find them. It was logic she needed, but the weakness took over until she was lost in the power they made together.

When strength returned, it was entwined with passion. But passion, she could control. Fighting regrets, Anna pulled away. She straightened in the seat and stared directly ahead until she was certain she could speak.

"I'm not going to see you again."

The first prick of fear surprised him. Daniel shoved it away and turned her face toward his. "We both know that's not true."

"I mean what I say."

"I'm sure of it. But it's not true."

"Damn you, Daniel, no one can tell you anything."

It was the first time he'd heard her lash out in anger, and though she quickly controlled herself, he saw that her temper was something to respect.

"Even if I were in love with you, which I'm not," she continued, "nothing could come of it."

He twisted a lock of her hair around his finger and released it. "We'll just wait and see."

"We won't—" She broke off and jumped as a horn blared. A car bumped along beside them. The elderly man driving paused long enough to glare at them and shout something that was lost under the sound of his motor as he went around them and continued down the road. When Daniel started to laugh, Anna laid her forehead on the steering wheel and joined him. She'd never known anyone who could make her so furious, make her so weak and still make her laugh.

"Daniel, this is the most ridiculous situation I've ever been in." Still chuckling, she lifted her head. "I'd almost believe we could be friends if you'd stop the rest of this business."

"We will be friends." He leaned over and kissed her lightly before she could move away. "I want a wife, a family. There comes a time when a man needs those things, or nothing else is worthwhile."

She folded her arms on the wheel and rested her chin on them. Calm again, she stared off into the tall grass along the road. "I believe that—for you. I also believe that you made up your mind to marry and set out looking for the most suitable woman to fit the bill."

He shifted, uncomfortable. It wouldn't be easy to have a wife who could read you that well. But he'd picked Anna. "Why do you think that?"

"Because it's all business to you." She gave him a steady look. "One way or the other."

He wouldn't evade—couldn't with her. "Maybe so. The thing is, you fit. Only you."

Sighing, she leaned back. "Marriage isn't a business transaction, or it shouldn't be. I can't help you, Daniel." Anna started the car again. "It's time we went back."

He laid a hand lightly on her shoulder before she began the turn. "It's too late to go back, Anna. For both of us."

CHAPTER 4

Lightning snaked across the sky and thunder rumbled, but the rain held off. The night, though summer had barely begun, was almost sultry. Now and again the wind moved through the trees with no sound and no power to cool the air. Enjoying the heat and the threat of a storm, Myra stopped in front of the Ditmeyers' with a high-pitched squeal of brakes.

"What a dreadful noise." She flipped down the mirror on her visor to check her face. "I really must get that fixed."

"Your face?" Anna's bland smile was answered with easy good humor.

"Before it's over, certainly, but immediately, that nasty noise."

"You might try driving with a bit more . . . discretion," Anna suggested.

"Now what fun would that be?"

Laughing, Anna stepped from the car. "Remind me not to let you drive my new car."

"New car?" Myra let the door slam, then fussed

with the strap of her dress. "When did you get a new car?"

It must be the air, Anna thought, that made her feel so restless, so reckless. "I was thinking perhaps tomorrow."

"Great. I'll go with you. A new apartment, a new car." Myra linked arms with Anna as they strolled up the walk. The scent of their perfumes, one subtle, one flamboyant, merged. "What's come over our quiet little Anna?"

"A taste of freedom." Tossing her head back, she looked at the sky. It boiled with clouds. Excitement. "One taste and I've discovered I'm insatiable."

It wasn't a word Myra associated with Anna, except when it came to her studies. Unless she missed her guess, her friend's thoughts had strayed from her medical journals. Speculating, she touched her tongue to her top lip. "I wonder just how much Daniel MacGregor has to do with it."

Anna paused to lift a brow before she rang the bell. She recognized the look in Myra's eye and knew just how to handle it. "What would he have to do with my buying a new car?"

"I was thinking about the insatiable."

It was difficult to keep her face sober, but Anna managed to ignore the wicked smile Myra tossed her. "You're looking around the wrong corner, Myra. I've just decided I want to drive back to Connecticut in style."

"Something red," Myra decided. "And flashy."

"No, something white, I think. And classy."

"It'll suit you, won't it?" With a sigh, Myra stepped back to study Anna. Her dress was the color of the inside of a peach, very pale, very warm, with the sleeves thin and cuffed at the wrists. "If I tried to wear a dress that color, I'd fade into the wallpaper. You look like something in a bakery window."

With another laugh, Anna took Myra's arm again. "I didn't come here to be nibbled on. In any case, flashy suits you, Myra, the way it suits no one else."

Pleased, Myra pursed her lips. "Yes, it does, doesn't it?"

When the Ditmeyers' butler opened the door, Anna swept inside. She couldn't explain why she felt so good. Maybe it was because her routine at the hospital was becoming more and more rewarding. Maybe it was the letter from Dr. Hewitt and the fascinating new surgical technique he'd told her of. It certainly had nothing to do with the white roses that continued to arrive every day.

"Mrs. Ditmeyer."

Stout and formidable in lavender voile, Louise Ditmeyer came to greet both of her guests. "Anna, how lovely you look." She stopped to study Anna's pale peach dress. "Just lovely," she continued. "Pastels are so suitable for a young girl. And, Myra . . ." She swept a glance down Myra's vivid emerald-green silk. The disapproval was evident in her gaze. "How are you?"

"Very well, thank you," Myra said sweetly. *Silly old fish.*

"You're looking wonderful, Mrs. Ditmeyer." Anna spoke up quickly, well able to read Myra's thoughts. To keep her friend in line, she gave Myra the tiniest of nudges in the ribs. "I hope we're not too early."

"Not at all. There are several people in the salon. Come along." She swept along ahead of them.

"Looks like a battleship," Myra muttered.

"Then watch your mouth or you'll get torpedoed."

"I do hope your parents are coming." Mrs. Ditmeyer

paused in the doorway and took a pleased survey of her guests.

"They wouldn't miss it," Anna assured her, and wondered if anyone would dare tell Louise Ditmeyer that lavender made her look jaundiced.

Mrs. Ditmeyer signaled to a servant. "Charles, some sherry for the young ladies. I'm sure you two can mingle on your own. So much to do." With that, she was bustling off.

Feeling aggressive, Myra sauntered up to the bar. "Make it bourbon, Charles."

"And a martini," Anna put in. "Dry. Behave yourself, Myra. I know she's annoying, but she's Herbert's mother."

"Easy for you to say." With a mumble, Myra took her drink. "As far as she's concerned, you've got a halo and wings."

Anna winced at the description. "You're exaggerating."

"All right, just the halo, then."

"Would it help if I spilled my drink on the carpet?" Anna plucked out the olive.

"You wouldn't," Myra began, then gasped as Anna tilted her glass. "No!" Myra righted it with a giggle. "I'd forgotten how easily you take a dare." She took the olive from Anna and ate it herself. "I wouldn't mind so much if you spilled it on the dragon, but the carpet's too lovely. Poor Herbert." She turned to study the other guests. "There he is now, cornered by that didactic, man-hunting Mary O'Brian. You know, he is attractive in an intellectual sort of way. It's a pity he's so . . ."

"So what?"

"Good," Myra concluded. "Now then." She lifted

her glass to hide her grin. "There's someone I don't think anyone would call good."

Anna didn't even have to turn. The room seemed smaller all at once, and warmer. Warmer and charged. She felt the excitement, remembered the thrill. For a moment, she panicked. The terrace doors were to her right. She could be through them and away in an instant. She'd make an excuse later, any excuse.

"My, my." Myra laid a hand on Anna's arm and felt her tremble. "You've got it bad."

Furious with herself, Anna set her glass down then picked it up again. "Don't be ridiculous."

Amusement mixed with concern. "Anna, it's me. The one who loves you best."

"He's persistent, that's all. Outrageously persistent. It makes me nervous."

"All right." Myra knew better than to try to budge Anna from her course. "We'll leave it at that for now. But since it seems to me that you need a minute to pull yourself together, let's go rescue Herbert."

Anna didn't argue. She did need a minute. An hour. Maybe years. It didn't matter that she'd considered and weighed her reaction to Daniel and had judged it to be purely physical. The reaction remained, and it grew each time she saw him. She didn't care for the edgy excitement he could bring to her just by being in the same room, so she would ignore him and relax. It had always been possible for her to control the reactions of her body. Breathe slowly, she told herself. Concentrate on individual muscles. The strain in her shoulders eased. They were, after all, at a very proper dinner party surrounded by other people. It wasn't as if they were sitting in a parked car on a lonely road. Her stomach tightened.

"Hello, Herbert." Myra eased her way to his side. "Mary."

"Myra." Obviously annoyed by the interruption, Mary turned to Anna. As she did, Herbert rolled his eyes. Amused and sympathetic, Myra tucked her arm through his. "Put any good criminals in jail lately?"

Before he could comment, Mary sent Myra a withering look. "Really, you make it sound like a game. Herbert is a very important part of our judicial system."

"Really?" Myra arched a brow as only she could. "And I thought he just tossed crooks in the slammer."

"Regularly." Herbert quipped, his voice dry, his look solemn. He nodded at Myra. "I do my best to make sure the streets are safe. You should see the notches on my briefcase."

Delighted he could play the game, Myra leaned closer and batted her lashes. "Oh, Herbert, I simply *adore* tough guys."

It was, unfortunately, a fiendishly clever mimicry of Cathleen Donahue, Mary's closest friend. She sniffed and stiffened. "If you'll excuse me."

"I think her nose is out of joint." Myra looked wide-eyed and innocent. "Anna, what's your medical opinion?"

"Terminal cattiness." Anna patted Myra's cheek. "Careful, love, it's catching."

"Quite a performance."

Anna froze, then forced herself to relax. How could she have guessed that such a big man could move so quietly?

"Good evening, Mr. MacGregor." Myra held out a friendly hand. The dinner party wouldn't be boring after all. "Did you enjoy the ballet?"

"Very much, but I liked your act every bit as much."

Herbert greeted Daniel with a quick handshake. "You'll find that Myra's never dull."

Flattered and surprised, Myra turned to him. "Why, thank you." Going with impulse, she made up her mind on the spot. She loved Anna like a sister. She decided to do what she thought best for her. "I think I could use another drink before dinner. You, too, Herbert." Without giving him a chance to agree, she pulled him along.

With a shake of his head, Daniel watched her maneuver Herbert through the crowd. "She's something."

Anna watched her steam toward the bar. "Oh, she's definitely something."

"I like your hair."

She nearly reached a hand up to it before she stopped herself. Because she hadn't had the time to fuss with it after her day at the hospital, she'd simply pulled it straight back. She'd hoped to look sophisticated at best, competent at the least. Her face was unframed and vulnerable. "Have you been to the Ditmeyers' before?"

"You're changing the subject again."

"Yes. Have you?"

A smile hovered around his mouth. "No."

"There's a wonderful collection of Waterford in the dining room. You should take a look at it when we go in to dinner."

"You like crystal?"

"Yes. It seems cold until the light hits it, and then, there are so many surprises."

"If you agreed to have dinner with me at my home, I could show you mine."

She dismissed the first part of the statement as nonsense, but honed in on the second. "You collect?"

"I like pretty things."

The tone was clear. Her look was as direct and as calm as ever. "If that's a compliment, I'll take it for what it's worth. But I have no intention of being collected."

"I don't want you on a shelf or in a glass case. I just want you." He took her hand, tightening his fingers on hers when she would have drawn away. "You're skittish," he commented, and found that fact pleased him.

"Cautious." Without moving her head, Anna shifted her gaze to their joined hands. "You have my hand."

He intended to keep it. "Have you noticed how well yours fits into it?"

She brought her eyes back to his. "You have very large hands. Anyone's would fit into it."

"I think not." But he released her hand, only to take her arm.

"Daniel—"

"It looks like we're going in to dinner."

She couldn't eat. Anna's appetite was never large, which constantly made Myra grumble, but tonight it was nonexistent. At first, she'd thought it a trick of fate that Daniel was seated next to her at the long banquet table. But one look at his face and she was certain he'd arranged it. He made his way without problem through the seafood appetizer and the soup course while she nibbled for form's sake.

He was attentive, infuriatingly so, while all but ignoring the woman on his right. He leaned close and murmured to her, encouraged her to try a bit more of this, taste a bit of that. Forced by upbringing to keep her manners in place, Anna struggled for composure. Her parents were seated closer to the head of the table. From that direction she saw both speculation and approval. She set her teeth and tried to choke down beef

Wellington. It didn't take her long to realize there was speculation going on at other points of the table as well. She caught the smiles, the nods, the whispers behind lifted hands. Daniel was making it clear, publicly, that he considered them a couple.

Her temper, always so well controlled, began to heat. Very deliberately Anna cut a piece of meat. "If you don't stop playing the lovesick suitor," she murmured, sending him a smile, "I'm going to knock my wineglass in your lap. You'll be very uncomfortable."

Daniel patted her hand. "No, you won't."

Anna took a deep breath and bided her time. As dessert was served, she scooted her hand along the table and nudged. If he hadn't glanced down just at that instant, he'd have missed it and would have had a lapful of burgundy. He made a quick grab. The glass tilted the other way. Before he could right it, half the contents had splatted over the tablecloth. He heard Anna swear under her breath and nearly roared with laughter.

"Clumsy." He sent an apologetic look toward his hostess. "I've such big hands." Unrepentant, he used one of them to pat Anna's leg under the table. He thought, but couldn't be sure, that he heard her grind her teeth.

"Think nothing of it." Mrs. Ditmeyer surveyed the damage and decided it could have been worse. "That's what tablecloths are for. You haven't spilled any on yourself, have you?"

Daniel beamed at her, then at Anna. "Not a drop." As the buzz of conversation picked up again, Daniel leaned toward Anna. "Admirable and very quick. I find you more and more exciting."

"You'd have been more excited if my aim had been better."

He lifted his glass and touched it to hers. "What do you think our hostess would do if I were to kiss you right here, right now?"

Anna picked up her knife and examined it as though admiring the pattern. The look she sent Daniel was as tough as nails. "I know what I'd do."

This time he did laugh, loud and long. "I'll be damned, Anna, you're the only woman for me." His announcement carried easily down both ends of the table. "But I won't kiss you now. I don't want you trying your first surgery on me."

After dinner there was bridge in the parlor. Though she detested the game, Anna considered volunteering to keep herself occupied and in a group. Before she could manage it, she was urged along outside by a half-dozen younger people.

The storm still threatened and the moon was covered with clouds, but the air was freshened by the building breeze. As the rain crept closer, the wind began to dance around her skirt. There were lights placed strategically here and there so that the trees and the garden were bathed in a muted glow. Someone had turned on the radio inside so that music flowed through the windows. The group started out wandering aimlessly, then slowly paired off.

"I wonder if you know much about gardens," Daniel asked her.

She hadn't expected to be rid of him easily. With a shrug, Anna kept several of her friends in view. "A bit."

"Steven's a better driver than a gardener." Daniel leaned over to sniff at a fat white peony. "He's neat enough, but he lacks imagination. I was hoping for something more . . ."

"Showy?" Anna suggested.

He liked the word. "Aye. Showy. Colorful. In Scotland we had the heather, and the brambles were full of wild roses. Not the pretty tame sort you buy at the flower shop, tough ones, with stems as thick as your thumbs and thorns that could rip a hole through you." Ignoring Anna's murmur of disapproval, he plucked off a bloom and tucked it behind her ear. "Delicate flowers are nice for looking at, for seeing in a woman's hair, but a wild rose—they last."

She'd forgotten she didn't want to be alone with him, forgotten to keep within a cautious distance of her friends. She wondered what a wild rose would smell like and if a man like Daniel would rip it out or leave it in the brambles to grow as it chose. "Do you miss Scotland?"

He looked down at her, for a moment lost in his own memories. "Sometimes. When I'm not too busy to think about it. I miss the cliffs and the sea and the grass that's greener than it has a right to be."

It was in his voice, she realized. Mourning. She'd never thought it possible to mourn for land, only for people. "Are you going to go back?" She found herself needing to know and afraid of his answer.

He looked away a moment, and the lightning flashed, reflecting fast and sharp on his face. Her heart thudded wildly. He looked the way she'd always imagined Thor would look—bold, ruthless, invulnerable. When he spoke, his voice was quiet and should have soothed her. She felt only more excitement. "No. A man makes his own home in his own time."

She ran a finger down a fragile vine of wisteria. Just a trick of the light, she told herself. It was silly to be moved by a trick of the light. "Don't you have family there?"

"No." She thought she heard pain in his voice, pain

that went deeper than mourning, but his face was impassive when she looked up. "I'm the last of my line. I need sons, Anna." He didn't touch her. He didn't need to. "I need sons and daughters. I want you to give them to me."

Why, when he still spoke the outrageous, did it no longer seem so outrageous? Uneasy, Anna continued along the path. "I don't want to argue with you, Daniel."

"Good." He caught her around the waist and spun her again. The solemn look that had been in his eyes was replaced by a grin. "We'll drive to Maryland and be married in the morning."

"No!" Though it wounded her dignity, she tried to wiggle away.

"All right. If you want a big wedding, I'll wait a week."

"No, no, no!" Why it struck her as funny, she didn't know, but she began to laugh as she pushed at his chest. "Daniel MacGregor, under all that red hair, you have the hardest head known to man. I will *not* marry you tomorrow. I will not marry you in a week. I will not marry you ever."

He lifted her off her feet so that their faces were level. When she got over her shock, Anna found it an odd and not entirely unpleasant sensation. "Bet?" he said simply.

Her brow lifted, and her voice was cool as a mountain stream. "I beg your pardon?"

"God, what a woman," he said, and kissed her hard. The visions that came and went in her head swirled so quickly that she couldn't separate them. "If I didn't want to do the honorable thing, I swear I'd toss you over my shoulder and be done with it." Then he laughed and kissed her again. "Instead I'll make you a wager."

If he kissed her just once more, she'd be too giddy to remember her name. Clinging to dignity, she braced her hands on his shoulders and looked stern. "Daniel, put me down."

"Damned if I will," he said, and grinned at her.

"You'll be lame if you don't."

He remembered her threat with the wineglass. A compromise, Daniel decided, and set her down, but he kept his hands around her waist. "A wager," he repeated.

"I don't know what you're talking about."

"You said I was a gambler, and right you were. What about you?"

She discovered her hands were resting against his chest and dropped them. "Certainly not."

"Hah!" There was a dare in his eyes she found hard to resist. "Now you lie. Any woman who takes herself off to be a doctor, thumbing her nose at the system, has gambling in her blood."

And right he was. She tilted her head. "What's the wager?"

"There's a lass." He would have lifted her off her feet again if she hadn't narrowed her eyes at him. "I say you'll have my ring on your finger within the year."

"And I say I won't."

"If I win, you spend the first week as my wife in bed. We'll do nothing but eat, sleep and make love."

If he'd meant to shock her, he'd fallen short of the mark. Anna merely nodded. "And if you lose?"

His eyes were alive with the challenge, with the taste of victory. "Name it."

Her lips curved. She believed in making the stakes

high. "You give a grant to the hospital, enough for a new wing."

He didn't hesitate. "Done."

If she was sure of anything, it was that he would keep his word, no matter how absurd the circumstances. Solemnly she extended her hand. Daniel took it for the official shake then brought it to his lips. "I've never gambled for higher stakes, nor will I again. Now let me kiss you, Anna." When she backed away, he caught her again. "We've set the wager and named the stakes, but what are the odds?" He brushed his lips against her temple and felt her shiver. "Aye, Anna, my love, what are the odds?"

Slowly he skimmed his mouth over her skin, teasing, promising, but never quite meeting her mouth. His hands, at once gentle and confident, roamed up her back to toy with the sensitive skin of her neck, then retreat again to her waist. He could feel the instant when her body gave in to its own needs and to his. He could feel his own climb higher. But he continued slowly, effortlessly to seduce.

The thunder rumbled again, but she thought it was her own heartbeat. When lightning flashed, it was like the fire in her own blood. What was passion? What was need? What was emotion? How could she tell when no man had ever brought her any of those things with such intensity before? She knew it was vital to separate them, but they flowed together into one incandescent sensation.

This was beauty. As her body went fluid, she recognized it. This was danger. When her muscles went lax, she accepted it.

His mouth brushed over hers again but didn't linger. Frustrated, edgy, she moaned and strained closer. Did he laugh, or was it the thunder again?

Then the skies opened and rain poured over them. With a curse, Daniel swooped her off her feet. "You owe me a kiss, Anna Whitfield," he shouted. He stood a moment while the rain poured down his wild mane of hair. The lightning was in his eyes. "Don't think I'll forget." With that he bundled her close and ran for the terrace.

Was it any wonder she was distracted in the hospital the next day? Anna found herself walking down corridors, then having to stop and sort out where she was going and what she was doing. It worried her. It infuriated her. What if she had her degree, if she had patients and became so easily rattled? She simply couldn't permit herself to think of anything but her duties as long as she was in the hospital.

But she remembered the wild thrill of being carried in Daniel's arms through the pounding summer storm. She remembered, too, the way he'd burst through the terrace doors and sent the quiet bridge game into chaos by demanding towels and a brandy for her. It should have been humiliating. Anna had found it sweet. That was something else that worried her. Thinking of how Louise Ditmeyer's eyes had widened like saucers, Anna smothered a laugh. He'd certainly added spice to a sedate dinner party.

She spent the majority of her day in the wards, bringing books and magazines to the patients and talking to them as they lay in beds set side by side. Lack of privacy, Anna thought, could be as debilitating as the illnesses that had brought them there. But there was only so much room, so many doctors. She smiled a bit, thinking that the impulsive bet she'd made with Daniel would do some good.

With a glance at her watch, she realized she had less than an hour to meet Myra. Today, she'd pick out her new car. Something practical certainly, she reminded herself. But not dull. Maybe it was foolish to be excited over the purchase of four wheels and an engine, but she kept thinking of the long, solitary drives she'd take. She'd been speaking no less than the truth when she'd told Myra that she wanted freedom. She thought of it now and longed for it. Still, she couldn't leave for the day without stopping in on Mrs. Higgs.

Planning the rest of her day as she went, Anna made her way to the fifth floor. She'd take Myra out to dinner and splurge. There was nothing Myra would like better. Then maybe they'd drive out of town and give the new car a test. Some weekend soon they'd drive out to the beach and spend the day in the sun. Pleased with the idea, Anna swung through the door of 521. Her mouth fell open.

"Oh, Anna, we were afraid you wouldn't come by."

Sitting up in bed, eyes bright, Mrs. Higgs fussed with the edge of her sheet. On the table beside her was a vase of red roses, fresh, flamboyant and fragrant. Sitting beside the bed like a suitor was Daniel.

"I told you Anna wouldn't leave without coming in to see how you were." Daniel rose and offered her a chair.

"No, no, of course I wouldn't." Confused, Anna approached the bed. "You're looking well today."

Mrs. Higgs reached for her hair. The young redheaded nurse had helped her brush it that morning, but she hadn't been able to use a rinse for weeks. "I'd have fixed myself up a bit if I'd known I was having a caller." She looked at Daniel with nothing less than an adoring smile.

"You look lovely." He took one of her thin hands between both of his.

He sounded as though he meant it. What impressed Anna most was the fact that his voice carried none of the patronizing tone that so many people used when speaking with the ill or the old. Something flashed in Mrs. Higgs's eyes. It was both gratitude and pride.

"It's important to look your best when you have a gentleman caller. Isn't that right, Anna?"

"Yes, of course." Anna wandered to the foot of the bed and tried unobtrusively to read the chart. "The flowers are beautiful. You didn't mention you were coming to the hospital, Daniel."

He winked at Mrs. Higgs. "I like surprises."

"Wasn't it nice of your young man to come by and visit me?"

"He's not—" Anna caught herself and softened her voice. "Yes, yes, it was."

"Now I know you two want to run along, and I won't keep you." Mrs. Higgs spoke briskly, but her energy was flagging. "You'll come again?" She reached up for Daniel's hand. "I so enjoyed talking with you."

He heard the plea she tried so desperately to hide. "I'll come again." Leaning over, he kissed her cheek.

When he stepped back, Anna adjusted Mrs. Higgs's pillows and made her more comfortable with a few efficient moves. He saw then that Anna's hands weren't just soft, delicate things made to be kissed, but that they were competent, strong and sure. It brought him a moment's discomfort. "Now you try to rest. You mustn't tire yourself."

"Don't worry about me." Mrs. Higgs sighed. "Go have fun."

She was already dozing when they walked from the room.

"Are you done here for today?" Daniel asked as they started down the hall.

"Yes."

"I'll drive you home."

"No, I'm meeting Myra." As always the elevator was slow and temperamental. Anna pushed the button and waited.

"Then I'll drop you." He wanted her to himself, away from the hospital where she'd looked so efficient and at home.

"No, really. I'm meeting her a couple of blocks away." Anna stepped into the elevator with him.

"Have dinner with me tonight."

"I can't. I have plans." Her hands were locked tightly together as the doors opened again.

"Tomorrow?"

"I don't know, I . . ." Emotions churning, she walked out into sunshine and fresh air. "Daniel, why did you come here today?"

"To see you, of course."

"You went to see Mrs. Higgs." She continued to walk. She'd only mentioned the name once. How was it he'd remembered? Why should he have cared?

"Shouldn't I have? It seemed to me she looked only the better for a bit of company."

She shook her head, struggling to find the right words. She hadn't known he could be kind, not really kind when the gesture brought no gain. He was in business, after all, where there was profit and loss and accounts to be forever balanced. The price of the roses would have meant nothing to him, but the gift of them everything to Mrs. Higgs. She wondered if he knew.

"What you did means more at this point than any of the medicine they can give her." She stopped then and turned. He could see the swirl of emotion in her eyes, the steady intensity of feeling that locked on him, and demanded. Anna asked, "Why did you do it? To impress me?"

No one could lie to eyes like that. He had done it to impress her and had been damn pleased with the idea until he'd begun to talk to Mrs. Higgs. He'd seen a mirror of his mother's fading beauty and tired dignity. And he'd go see her again, not for Anna, but for himself. He had no way of explaining it to her, and no intention of exposing feelings that had been private for so long.

"The main idea was to impress you. I also wanted to see what it was about that place that keeps bringing you back. I still don't understand it all, but maybe I see part of it now."

When she said nothing, he stuck his hands in his pockets as they walked. This woman worried him a good bit more than he'd anticipated. He wanted to please her—he was surprised how much. He wanted to see her smile again. He'd have even settled for one of her cool, regal stares. Frustrated, he scowled straight ahead. "Well, damn it, were you impressed or not?"

She stopped to look up at him. Her eyes were cool, but he couldn't read them. Then she took him totally by surprise. She put her hands on both sides on his face. In her strong, unhurried way, she drew his face down until she could touch her lips to his. It was hardly more than a hint of a kiss, but it exploded through him. She held him there a moment, her eyes locked on his. Then saying nothing, she released him and walked away.

For the first time in his life, Daniel found himself speechless.

CHAPTER 5

Daniel sat in his office in the Old Line Savings and Loan, puffing on his cigar and listening to the long-winded report from his bank manager. The man knew banking, Daniel conceded, and he was a whiz with figures. But he couldn't see more than two feet in front of his face.

"Therefore, in addition to my other recommendations, I further recommend that the bank foreclose on the Halloran property. Auctioning this property off would cover the outstanding principal, plus, in a conservative estimate, yield a five percent profit."

Daniel tapped his cigar in an ashtray. "Extend it."

"I beg your pardon?"

"I said extend the Halloran loan, Bombeck."

Bombeck pushed his glasses up on his nose and fluttered through his papers. "Perhaps you didn't understand that the Hallorans are six months behind on their mortgage payments. In the past two months, they've failed to keep current with the interest. Even if Halloran finds work as he claims he will, we can't expect the loan to be brought up to date within this quarter. I have all the figures here."

"I don't doubt it," Daniel muttered, bored. Your work, he thought, should never bore you, or you lose your touch.

Drawing the papers out, Bombeck placed them on Daniel's desk. They were, as Bombeck was, tidy and assiduously correct. "If you'll just look them over, I'm sure we can—"

"Give the Hallorans another six months to bring the interest up to date."

Bombeck blanched. "Six—" Clearing his throat, he shifted in his chair. His neat hands worked together. "Mr. MacGregor, I'm sure your sympathies toward the Hallorans are admirable, but you must understand that a bank can't be run on sentiment."

Daniel drew on his cigar, paused, then blew out a haze of smoke. There was the slightest of smiles on his mouth, but his eyes, if Bombeck had dared to look at them, were cold as ice. "Is that so, Bombeck? I appreciate you telling me."

Bombeck wet his lips. "As manager of Old Line—"

"Which was about to go belly up one month ago when I bought it."

"Yes." Bombeck cleared his throat again. "Yes, indeed, Mr. MacGregor, that's precisely the point. As manager, I feel it my duty to give you all the benefit of my experience. I've been in banking for fifteen years."

"Fifteen?" Daniel said as if impressed. Fourteen years, eight months and ten days. He had the employment records of everyone who worked for him, down to the cleaning woman. "That's just fine, Bombeck. Maybe if I give this to you in different terms, you'll understand my way of thinking." Daniel leaned back in his chair so that the sun shooting through the window behind him turned his hair to fire. Though he hadn't planned it that way, he'd have been more than satisfied with the effect. "You estimate a five percent profit if we foreclose and auction the Halloran property. Have I got that right?"

Sarcasm skimmed over Bombeck's head. "Exactly so, Mr. MacGregor."

"Good. Good. However, over the remaining twelve years of the Halloran mortgage, we would see a long-term profit of, conservatively speaking, triple that."

"Over the long term, of course. I could get you the exact figures, but—"

"Excellent. Then we understand each other. Extend it." Because he enjoyed doing so, Daniel waited a beat before dropping his bomb. "We'll be lowering the mortgage rates by a quarter percent starting next month."

"Lowering, but Mr. MacGregor—"

"And raising the interest on savings accounts to the highest allowable rate."

"Mr. MacGregor, that will throw Old Line deeply in the red."

"In the short term," Daniel agreed briskly. "In the long term—you were understanding the long term, weren't you, Bombeck?—in the long term we'll make up for it with volume. Old Line will have the lowest mortgage rates in the state."

Bombeck felt his stomach churn and swallowed. "Yes, sir."

"And the highest rates on savings accounts."

He could almost see dollar bills flying away on little wings. "It will cost the bank . . ." Bombeck couldn't even imagine. "I could work up the figures in a few days. I'm sure you'll see what I'm trying to say. With a policy like that, in six months—"

"Old Line will be the biggest lending institution in the state," Daniel finished mildly. "I'm glad we agree. We're going to advertise in the papers."

"Advertise," Bombeck murmured as if in a dream.

"Something big"— Daniel measured with his hands, enjoying himself—"but distinguished. Why don't you see what you can come up with and get back to me? Say, by ten tomorrow."

It took Bombeck a few seconds to realize he'd been dismissed. Too dazed to argue, he tidied his papers and rose. As he walked out, Daniel ground his cigar in the ashtray.

Dim-witted, nearsighted dunderhead. What he needed was someone young, fresh out of college and eager. He could salvage Bombeck's pride by making up a new position for him. Daniel felt strongly about loyalty, and dunderhead or not, Bombeck had been with Old Line for nearly fifteen years. It was something he might just discuss with Ditmeyer. That was a man whose opinion Daniel trusted.

Bankers had to realize it was their business to gamble. It was certainly Daniel's. Rising, he walked to the window behind his desk and looked at Boston. At this point, his whole life was a gamble. The money he'd earned could be lost. He shrugged at that. He'd earn more again. The power he now wielded could fade. He'd build it back up again. But there was one thing, he was coming to understand, that if lost, couldn't be replaced. Anna.

When had she stopped being part of his master plan and become his life? When had he lost track of the deal and fallen in love? He could pinpoint it to the instant—the instant she'd taken his face in her hands, looked so solemnly into his eyes and touched her mouth to his. He'd gone beyond attraction, beyond desire, beyond the challenge.

His systematic courtship had been blown to bits. The blueprint so carefully drawn was in tatters. From that moment, he'd become only a man totally bewitched by a woman. So now what? That was one question he had no answer for. He'd wanted a wife who would sit patiently at home while he took care of business. That wasn't Anna. He'd wanted a wife who wouldn't question his decisions, but go quietly about making them into fact. That wasn't Anna. There was a part of her life that would always remain separate from him. If she succeeded in her ambition, and he was coming to believe she would, she'd have Doctor in front of her name before a year was out. To Anna, it wouldn't simply be a title, but a way of life. Could a man whose business made such demands, took such long hours out of his day, have a wife whose profession did exactly the same?

Who would make the home? he wondered, pulling his fingers through his hair. Who would tend the children? Better if he turned his back on her now and found a woman who'd be content to do those things and nothing else. Better, if he followed the advice she'd given him and chose a woman who had no windmills to battle.

He needed a home. It was difficult for him to admit, even to himself, just how desperately he needed one. He needed family—the scent of bread baking in the kitchen, flowers sitting in bowls. Those were the things he'd grown up with; those were the things he'd gone too long without. He couldn't be sure he would have them with Anna. And yet . . . If he found them without her, he didn't think they would matter.

Damn woman. He looked at his watch. She'd be nearly finished at the hospital now. He had a meeting across town in just under an hour. Determined not to let his life be run by someone else's schedule, he sat behind his desk again and picked up Bombeck's report. After one paragraph, he slammed it down again. Grumbling and swearing, he stalked out of his office.

She'd spent five hours on her feet. With a tired satisfaction, Anna thought about a long, hot bath and a quiet evening with a book. Perhaps she'd just soak and plan how she'd decorate her apartment. In two weeks she'd have the keys in her hand and rooms to furnish. If her feet weren't certain to object, she'd poke around a few antique stores now. With pleasure, she thought of the shiny white convertible waiting for her in the lot next door. The car meant more than the fact that she didn't have to walk home. It meant independence.

Taking the keys out of her purse, she jiggled them in her hand and felt on top of the world. Anna had never considered her ego very large, but when her father had all but drooled on the upholstery then demanded a ride, she'd felt her head swell. He'd approved finally. She'd used her own money, her own judgment, and there had been no criticism. She remembered the way he'd dragged her mother outside and pulled her into the backseat with him. Anna had tooled around Boston for nearly an hour with her parents as cozy as teenagers behind her.

She'd understood that they'd begun to think of her as something more than a little girl who needed guidance. Whether they'd realized it yet or not, they'd accepted her as an adult. Maybe, she thought, just maybe, there would be pride when she earned her diploma.

Giddy with success, Anna tossed her keys into the air and caught them again. She walked straight into Daniel.

"You weren't looking where you were going."

She'd been happy before, but was happier yet to have seen him. She could almost admit it. "No, I wasn't."

He'd already decided on the way to deal with her. His way. "You're having dinner with me tonight." When she opened her mouth, he took her by the shoulders. His voice was loud enough to turn heads, his eyes fierce enough to turn them forward again. "I won't have any arguments. I'm tired of them and don't have time at the moment, anyway. You're having dinner with me tonight. Be ready at seven."

There were a number of things she could do. In the space of seconds, Anna thought of them all. But she decided the best way was the least expected. "All right, Daniel," she said very demurely.

"I don't care what . . . What?"

"I said I'd be ready." She looked at him, her eyes calm, her smile serene. It threw him completely off balance, as she'd been certain it would.

"I— All right, then." He scowled and stuck his hands in his pockets. "See that you are." He'd gotten precisely what he'd wanted, but he stopped halfway to his car and looked back. Anna was standing just where she'd been, in a pool of sunlight. Her smile remained as quiet and sweet as an angel's kiss. "Damn women," Daniel mumbled as he yanked open the door of his car. You couldn't trust them.

Anna waited until he'd pulled off, then rocked with laughter. Seeing him stumble and stutter had been better than any argument. Still laughing, she went to her car. An evening with Daniel, she admitted, would certainly be more interesting than a book. Turning the key in the ignition, she felt the power. She had control. And she liked it.

He brought her flowers. Not the white roses he still insisted on sending her day after day, but some tiny, impudent violets from his own garden. It pleased him to watch her arrange them in a little glass vase as he spoke with her parents. He looked big and brash in her mother's dainty parlor. He felt as nervous as a scrawny boy on his first date. Edgy, he sat on a chair he felt was better suited to a dollhouse and shared a tepid cup of tea with Mrs. Whitfield.

"You must come to dinner soon," Mrs. Whitfield told him. The constant delivery of roses had made her quite hopeful. It had also given her something to brag about over bridge. The truth was she didn't understand her daughter and never had. Of course, she could tell herself that Anna had always been a sweet, lovely child, but she herself was simply out of her depth when doing something other than choosing material for a dress or a meal from a menu. Anna, with her calm stubbornness and unshakable ambitions, was completely beyond her mother's scope.

Still, Mrs. Whitfield wasn't a fool. She saw the way Daniel looked at her daughter and understood very well. With a strange mixture of relief and regret, she pictured Anna married and raising her own family. If Daniel's manners were a bit rough, she knew her Anna would smooth them out quickly enough. Perhaps she'd be a grandmother in a year or two. It was another thought that brought mixed feelings. Sipping her tea, Mrs. Whitfield studied Daniel.

"I realize you and John are business associates

now, but we'll have to keep that in the office. Of course, I know nothing about the business anyway." She reached over to pat Daniel's hand. "John won't tell me a thing, no matter how I badger him."

"And badger, she does," Mr. Whitfield put in.

"Now, John." With a light laugh, she aimed a killing look. If this man had serious intentions toward her daughter, and she was certain he did, she meant to find out everything there was to find out about him. "Everyone's curious about Mr. MacGregor's dealings. It's only natural. Why just the other day, Pat Donahue told me you'd bought some property of theirs in Hyannis Port. I hope you're not thinking of leaving Boston."

Daniel didn't have to scent the air to know which way the wind blew. "I'm fond of Boston."

Deciding she'd let him sweat long enough, Anna handed Daniel her wrap. Grateful, he was up like a shot and bundling her into it.

"You children have a lovely evening." Mrs. Whitfield would have risen to walk them to the door, but her husband put a hand on her shoulder.

"Good night, Mother." Anna kissed her mother's cheek, then smiled up at her father. She'd never realized he was so perceptive. With a smile, she kissed him as well.

"Enjoy yourself." In an old habit, he patted her head.

Daniel felt he could finally breathe again when they stepped outside. "Your house is very—"

"Crowded," Anna finished, then laughed as she tucked her arm through his. "My mother likes to fill it up with whatever catches her eye. I didn't realize until a few years ago how tolerant my father is." Pleased that he'd brought the blue convertible, she gathered her skirts and slid into her seat. "Where are we going for dinner?"

He took his own seat and let the engine roar. "We're having dinner at home. My home."

Anna felt a quiver of nerves come and go. Using her best weapon, will, she eliminated the fluttering in her stomach. She hadn't forgotten the feeling of control. She'd handle him. "I see."

"I'm tired of restaurants. I'm tired of crowds." His voice was tense and tight. Why, *he's* nervous, she realized, and felt a jolt of pleasure. He towered over her even when sitting. His voice had a timbre that could make the windowpanes rattle, but he was nervous about spending an evening with her. It wasn't easy, but she tried hard not to be smug.

"Oh? I had the impression you enjoyed being around a lot of people," she said very calmly.

"I don't want a bunch of them staring at us while we eat."

"Amazing how rude some people can be, isn't it?"

"And if I want to talk to you, I don't need half of Boston listening to me."

"Naturally not."

He fumed and turned into his driveway. "And if you're worried about propriety, I have servants."

She sent him a bland look. "I'm not worried in the least."

Not sure how to take that, he narrowed his eyes. She was playing games with him, of that he was sure. He just wasn't sure of what kind, or of the rules. "You're mighty sure of yourself all at once, Anna."

"Daniel." She reached for the door handle and let herself out. "I've always been sure of myself."

She decided with one sweeping look that she liked his house. It was separated from the road by a line of hedges that came to her shoulder. The privacy they provided wasn't as cold or impersonal as a wall, but it was just as sturdy. As she looked at the tall windows, some of which were already softly lit behind curtains, she could smell the mixture of scents from the side garden.

Sweet peas she recognized, and smiled. She had a weakness for them. He'd chosen an imposing house, large enough for a family of ten, but he hadn't forgotten to make it a home with something as simple as flowers. She waited until he'd joined her on the edge of the walkway.

"Why did you choose it?"

He looked at the house with her. He saw the brick, attractively faded with age, the windows, with their shutters freshly painted. There was no sense of kinship, only of ownership. After all, someone else had built it. As he drew in the evening air, he didn't smell the sweet peas, but her. "Because it was big."

She smiled at that and turned to watch a sparrow on a branch of a maple in the front yard. "I suppose that's reasonable. You looked uncomfortable in my mother's parlor, as if you thought if you turned around you might knock down a wall. This suits you better."

"For the moment," he murmured. He had other plans. "You can watch the sunset from those windows." He pointed, then took her arm to lead her up the walk. "You won't for very many more years."

"Why?"

"Progress. They're going to toss buildings up and block out the sky. Not everywhere, but enough. I'm breaking ground on one myself next month." Opening the door, he drew her into the hall and waited.

The swords crossed on the wall to her left drew her eyes first. They weren't the delicate, almost feminine foils used in duels by lace-cuffed swashbucklers. They were thick, heavy, deadly broadswords with underrated hilts and dull, well-used blades. It would take two hands and a strong man to lift one. It would take skill and brute strength to use one to attack or defend. Unable to resist, Anna walked closer. She had no trouble imagining what one of them could do to flesh and bone. Still, though she could term them lethal, she couldn't term them ugly.

"The swords are from my clan. My ancestors used them." There was pride in his voice, and simplicity. "The MacGregors were warriors, always."

Was it a challenge she heard from him? It might have been. Anna stepped closer to the swords. The edges of the blades weren't dulled, but as treacherous as ever. "Most of us are, aren't we?"

Her response surprised him, but perhaps it shouldn't have. He knew she wasn't a woman to shudder and faint over a weapon or spilled blood. "The English king"—he nearly spat it and had Anna's full attention—"he took our name, our land, but he couldn't take our pride. We hacked off heads when we had to." His eyes were deep, blue and brilliant when he looked at her. She had no doubt he would wield the sword with a ferocity equal to that of his ancestors if he felt justified. "Mostly the heads of Campbells." He grinned at that and took her arm. "They thought to wipe us out of Scotland, but they couldn't."

She found herself wondering how he'd look in the clothes of his country, the kilt, the plaid, the dirk. Not ridiculous, but dramatic. Anna looked back up at the swords. "No, I'm sure they couldn't. You've good reason to be proud."

His hand moved up to her cheek and lingered. "Anna..."

"Mr. MacGregor." McGee stood still as a stone as Daniel whirled on him. There was a look in Daniel's eyes that would have made a strong man shudder.

"Aye?" In the one word, Daniel conveyed a thousand pungent curses.

"A call from New York, sir. A Mr. Liebowitz says it's quite important."

"Show Miss Whitfield into the parlor, McGee. I'm sorry, Anna, I have to take this. I'll be as quick as I can."

"It's all right." Relieved she'd have a few moments alone, Anna watched Daniel stride down the hall.

"This way, miss."

She noticed the brogue, which was heavier than Daniel's, and smiled. He'd keep his own around him when he could. With a last glance at the swords, she followed McGee's ramrod-straight back into the parlor. It made her mother's look like a closet. If big was what Daniel wanted, big was what he had.

"Would you care for a drink, Miss Whitfield?"

Distracted, Anna turned blankly. "I'm sorry?"

"Would you care for a drink?"

"Oh, no, thank you, I'm fine."

He gave her the smallest and staunchest of bows. "Please ring if you require anything."

"Thank you," she said again, anxious to be rid of him. The minute she was alone, she turned a slow circle. Big, yes—much bigger than the average room. Unless she missed her guess, he'd had walls removed and combined two into one.

The unusual size was complemented by unusual furnishings. There was a Belker table twice the size of the wheel of a car, carved so ornately that the edges looked like lace. A high-backed chair done in rich red velvet sat beside it. He could hold court in it, she thought, and smiled at the idea. Why not?

Rather than sit, Anna simply wandered. The colors were flashy and bold, but somehow she felt perfectly comfortable with them. Maybe she'd lived with her mother's pastels long enough. A sofa took up nearly an entire wall and would have required four strong men to move it. With a laugh, she decided Daniel had chosen it for exactly that reason.

Along the west window was a collection of crystal, Waterford, Baccarat. A vase, two feet high, caught the beginnings of the sunset and danced with it. Anna picked up a bowl that fit into the palm of her hand and wondered what it was doing there among the giants.

He found her like that, standing in the western light, smiling at a small piece of glass. His mouth went dry. Though he said nothing, could say nothing, she turned toward him.

"What a wonderful room." Enthusiasm added color to her cheeks, deepened her eyes. "I imagine in the winter, with a fire, it would be spectacular." When he didn't speak, her smile faded. She took a step closer. "The telephone. Was it bad news?"

"What?"

"Your call. Has it upset you?"

He'd forgotten it, just as he'd forgotten everything. It didn't sit well with him that a look from her could tie his tongue and his stomach up in knots. "No. I'll have to go into New York for a couple of days and straighten out a few things." Including himself, he thought ruefully. "I have something for you."

"I hope it's dinner," she said, smiling again.

"We'll have that, too." It occurred to him that he'd never felt awkward around a woman until now. Drawing a box out of his pocket, he handed it to her.

There was a moment of panic. He had no business offering her a ring. Then as common sense took over, panic faded. The box wasn't the small velvet sort that held engagement rings, but an old cardboard one. Curious, Anna opened the lid.

The cameo was nearly as long as her thumb and perhaps twice as wide. Old and lovely, it sat in a little bed of tissue paper. The profile was gentle and serene, but the head was tilted up with just a touch of pride as well.

"It favors you," Daniel murmured. "I told you once."

"Your grandmother's," she remembered. Touched, she lifted a finger to trace the outline. "It's beautiful, really beautiful." It was more difficult than it should have been to close the lid again. "Daniel, you know I can't take this."

"No, I don't." Taking the box from her, he opened it again and drew out the cameo, which he'd attached to a velvet ribbon himself. "I'll put it on for you."

She could almost feel his fingers brush the nape of her neck. "I shouldn't take a gift from you."

He lifted a brow. "You can't tell me you worry about gossip, Anna. If you concerned yourself with what people said or thought, you wouldn't be going to your school in Connecticut."

He was right of course, but she tried to stand firm. "It's an heirloom, Daniel. It wouldn't be right."

"It's my heirloom, and I'm tired of having it shut in a box. My grandmother would want it to be worn by someone who'd appreciate it." In a surprisingly smooth manner, he slid the ribbon around her neck and fastened it. It fit into the subtle hollow of her throat as if it had been destined to rest there. "There now, that's where it belongs."

Unable to resist, she reached up to touch it. Common sense slipped away. "Thank you. We'll say I'm keeping it for you. If you want it back—"

"Don't spoil it," he interrupted, and took her chin in his hand. "I've wanted to see you wear it."

She couldn't stop the smile. "And you always get what you want?"

"Exactly." Pleased with himself he rubbed a thumb over her cheek before he dropped his hand. "Will you have a drink? There's some sherry."

"I'd rather not."

"Have a drink?"

"Drink sherry. Is there another choice?"

He felt his nervousness drop away. "I've some prime Scotch sent—smuggled if you want the truth—from a friend of mine in Edinburgh."

She wrinkled her nose. "It tastes like soap."

"Soap?" He looked so astonished that she laughed. "Don't take it personally."

"You'll try it," he told her as he went to the bar. "Soap." While he poured, his voice dropped to a mutter. "This isn't the swill you get at one of your stiff-necked Boston parties."

Damn it, the longer she knew him, the more endearing he became. Anna found her hand had wandered to the cameo again. She took a deep breath and reminded herself of the feeling of being at the wheel. Control. When he handed her a glass, she studied it. It was very dark and, she thought, very likely to be as lethal as the swords on the wall. "Ice?"

"Don't be silly." He tossed back his glass and challenged her. Anna took a deep breath and gulped some down.

Warm, potent and smooth. Frowning a bit, she sipped again. "I stand corrected," she told him, but handed back the glass. "And if I drink all of it, I won't stand at all."

"Then we'll get some food into you."

With a shake of her head, she offered her hand. "If that's your way of saying it's time for dinner, I accept."

He took her hand and held it. "You won't get too many pretty words out of me, Anna. I'm not polished. I don't have any plans to be."

His hair flowed around his face, untamed and magnificent. The beard gave him the look of the warrior they both knew was in his blood. "No, I don't think you should."

No, he wasn't polished, but he surrounded himself with beauty. It wasn't the quiet sort Anna had become used to, but a bold, bracing beauty that could grab you by the throat. He had a shield and a pike on the wall of the dining room and below them was a Chippendale breakfront any collector of fine antiques would have envied. The table itself was massive, but set on it was the loveliest china Anna had ever seen. She sat in a chair that would have suited a medieval castle and found herself completely relaxed.

The sun came in red-gold slants through the windows. As they ate, the light softened and dimmed. With silent efficiency, McGee came to light candles, then left them again.

"If I told my mother about this meal, she'd try to steal your cook." Anna took a bite of chocolate torte and understood the phrase *sinfully rich*.

It gave him a quiet sort of pleasure to watch her enjoy his food, eat from the plates he'd chosen himself. "You can see why I prefer this to a restaurant."

"Absolutely." She took another bite, because some things weren't meant to be resisted. "I'm going to miss home cooking when I move into my apartment."

"What about your own?"

"My own what?"

"Cooking."

"It doesn't exist." Studying him, she took another bite. "Your eyebrows come straight together when you frown, Daniel, but don't worry. I intend to learn my way around a kitchen. Self-preservation." Linking her fingers, she rested her chin on them. "I don't suppose you cook."

He started to laugh, then thought better of it. "No."

She discovered she liked catching him off guard that way. "But, naturally, you find it odd that I, as a woman, don't know how."

It was difficult not to admire her logic even when he was on the wrong end of it. "You've a habit of boxing a man into a corner, Anna."

"I enjoy the way you fight your way out. I know this may be a dangerous boon to your ego, but you're an interesting man."

"I've a very big ego. It takes a lot to fill it. Why don't you tell me how I'm interesting?"

She smiled and rose. "Another time perhaps."

He caught her hand as he stood. "There will be another time."

She didn't believe in lies, and in evasions only when the truth didn't suit. "It seems there will. Mrs. Higgs talked of nothing but you today," she said as they walked back toward the parlor.

"Lovely woman."

She had to grin. He said it with such self-satisfaction. "She expects you to come back."

"I said I would." He saw the question in her eyes and stopped. "I keep my word."

"Yes." She smiled again. "You would. It's very good of you, Daniel. She has no one."

Uncomfortable, he frowned. "Don't put a halo on me, Anna. I intend to win the bet, but I'd as soon do it without false pretenses."

"I've no intention of putting a halo on you." She flicked the hair from her shoulder. "And I've no intention of losing the bet."

At the doorway to the parlor, she stopped again. There were candles, dozens of them, glowing throughout the room. Moonlight spilled in through the window to compete. There was music, quiet, bluesy. It seemed to come from the shadows. Anna felt her pulse race but continued into the room.

"Lovely," she commented, noting the silver coffee urn had been set up near the sofa.

As Daniel went to pour brandy, she stood, looking completely at ease. She wondered if her muscles could knot any tighter. "I like the way you look in candlelight," he told her as he handed her a snifter. "It reminds me of the first night I met you, when you stood on the terrace near the gardens. There were moonbeams on your face, shadows in your eyes." When he took her hand, he thought for a moment that it trembled. But her eyes were so steady. "I knew then when I looked at you that I had to have you. I've thought of you every day and every night since."

It would have been easy, too easy, to give in to the thoughts bursting in her head. If she did, she could feel his mouth on hers again and would tingle for the touch of those big, wide-palmed hands on her skin. It would have been easy. But the life that she'd already chosen, or that had chosen her, wasn't.

"A man in your position must know how dangerous it is to make a decision on impulse."

"No." He lifted her hand and kissed her fingers, slowly, one by one. The breath backed up in her lungs.

Through sheer will she spoke calmly and, she hoped, carelessly. "Daniel, are you trying to seduce me?"

When would he ever, how would he ever, get used to that quiet voice and frank tongue? After a half laugh, he drank some brandy. "A man doesn't seduce the woman he intends to marry."

"Of course, he does," Anna corrected and patted his back when he choked. "Just the same as a man seduces women he doesn't intend to marry. But I'm not going to marry you, Daniel." She turned away to walk to the coffeepot then looked over her shoulder. "And I'm not going to be seduced. Coffee?"

He didn't just love her, he realized. He very nearly adored her. There were a great many things he found he wasn't certain of at that moment, but he knew without a doubt he couldn't live without her. "Aye." He walked to her and took the cup. Maybe he was better off with something in his hands. "You can't tell me you don't want me, Anna."

Her body was tingling. He had only to touch her to feel her need, her weakness. She made herself look at him. "No, I can't. That doesn't change anything."

He set the coffee down untasted. He'd have preferred throwing it. "The hell it doesn't. You came here tonight."

"For dinner," she reminded him calmly. "And because, for some odd reason, I enjoy your company. There are some things I have to accept. There are others I can't risk."

"I can." He reached out and cupped her neck gently, though it was difficult to be gentle when he wanted to drag her to him and plunder. He felt her quick move of resistance, ignored it and pulled her closer. "I will."

When his mouth was on hers, Anna accepted one

more thing. Inevitability. She'd known they couldn't be together without passion rising up. Yet, she'd come to him freely and on equal terms. Between them there was a fire raging that she could only bank for so long. There would come a time, she knew, when nothing would stop it from consuming both of them. She slid her arms up his back and stepped closer to the heat.

When he lowered her to the sofa, she didn't protest but drew him closer. Just for a moment, she promised herself hazily, just for a moment she'd have a taste of what it could be like. His body was so firm against her. She could sense the desperation, and despite all good judgment, she reveled in it.

His mouth raced over her face. Her name was murmured again and again against her lips, her throat. She could taste the fire of brandy as his tongue met hers. The scent of candlewax surrounded her. With the music came a low, pulsing beat that urged, teased, enticed.

He had to touch her. He thought he'd go mad if he couldn't have more. Then as he slid his hand over her, felt the softness, the race of her heart, he knew he'd never get enough. His hands, so wide, so large, passed over her with a tenderness that made her tremble. When he heard his name in her shaky whisper, he fought to keep himself from grabbing what he longed for. He brought his mouth back and found hers warm, willing and open.

Desperate, he fumbled with the buttons running down the front of her dress. His hands were so large, the buttons so small. The blood began to pound in his head. Then he discovered, to his delight, that his dignified Anna wore silk and lace next to her skin.

She arched when he found her, arched and shuddered, then strained for more. He was taking her beyond the expected, beyond the anticipated and into dreams. Large, wide-palmed hands continued to pass over her with incredible gentleness. They stroked, lingered, tested. Unable to resist, she let him guide her. Control no longer seemed essential. Ambitions became unimportant. Need. There was only one. For one mindless moment, she gave herself to it.

There was a desperation in him that grew sharper each time his heart beat. He knew what he wanted, what he would want until the grave. Anna. Only Anna. Her mouth was hot on his, her body cool and slim. The images that rushed through his mind were as dark and dangerous as any uncharted land. She clung to him and seemed to give everything. His head spun with it. Then she buried her face against his throat and went very still.

"Anna?" His voice was rough, his hands still gentle.

"I can't say this isn't what I want." The tug-of-war going on inside of her left her weak and frightened. "But I can't be sure it is." She shuddered once, then drew back. He could see her face in the candlelight, the skin pale, the eyes dark. Beneath his hand her heartbeat was fast and steady. "I never expected to feel this way, Daniel. I need to think."

Desire burned inside him. "I can think for both of us."

She lifted her hands to his face before he could kiss her again. "That's what I'm afraid of." Shifting, she sat up. Her dress was open nearly to her waist, with her soft white skin exposed for the first time to a man. But she felt no shame. Steadily she began to hook the buttons. "What is happening between us—what could happen between us—is the most important decision in my life. I have to make it myself."

He took her by the arms. "It's already been made."

Part of her thought he was right. Part of her was terrified he was. "You're sure of what you want. I'm not. Until I am, I can't promise you anything." The fingers that had been steady trembled before she could control them. "I may never be able to promise you anything."

"You know when I hold you that it's right. Can you tell me that when I touch you, you don't feel that?"

"No, I can't." The more agitated he became, the calmer she forced herself to be. "I can't, and that's why I need time. I need time because whatever decision I make has to be made with a clear head."

"Clear head." Furious, aching with need, he rose to stalk the room. "My head hasn't been clear since the first time I laid eyes on you."

She rose as well. "Then whether you like it or not, we both need time."

He picked up the brandy she'd left unfinished and downed it. "Time's what you need, Anna." He turned to her. She'd never seen him look fiercer, more formidable. A smart woman would guard her heart. Anna struggled to remember that. "I'll be in New York for three days. There's your time. When I come back, I'm coming for you. I want your decision then."

Her chin lifted, exposing a slender, elegant neck. Dignity covered her in a cool, silent wave. "Don't give me deadlines and ultimatums, Daniel."

"Three days," he repeated and set down the snifter before he snapped it in two. "I'll take you home."

CHAPTER 6

When three days turned into a week, Anna didn't know whether to be relieved or infuriated. Trying to be neither, to simply go about her life as she always had, wasn't possible. He'd given her a deadline, then didn't even bother to show up to hear her decision, which, she admitted, she hadn't made yet.

Invariably, whenever Anna set her mind to a problem, she solved it. It was a matter of thinking through all the levels and establishing priorities. There seemed to be too many levels in her relationship with Daniel for her to deal with each or any one of them rationally. On the one hand, he was a rude, boastful annoyance. On the other, he was fun. He could be unbearably arrogant—and unbearably sweet. His rough edges would never be completely smoothed off. His mind was admirably quick and clever. He schemed. He laughed at himself. He was overbearing. He was generous.

If she couldn't successfully analyze Daniel, how could she hope to analyze her feelings for him? Desire. She'd had very little experience with that feeling, aside from her ambitions, but she recognized it. How would she recognize love? And if she did, what would she do about it?

The only thing Anna became certain of during Daniel's absence was that she missed him. She was certain of it because she'd been so sure she wouldn't even give him a second thought. She thought of little else. But if she gave in, if she threw caution to the winds and agreed to marry him, what would happen to her dream?

She could marry him, have his children, dedicate her life to him—and resent everything they built together because she would have divorced herself from her vocation. That meant living half a life, and Anna didn't think she could do it. If she refused him and went on with her plans, would that mean half a life, as well?

Those were the questions that tormented her at night, that nagged at her throughout the day. Those were the questions she found, then rejected answers for. So she made no decision, knowing once it was made, it would be final.

She forced herself to continue her routine. To tone down speculation and questions, she went to the theater with friends and attended parties. During the day, she threw herself into her work at the hospital with energy born of frustration.

Habitually she visited Mrs. Higgs first. Anna didn't need a degree to see that the woman was fading. Before seeing to all her other duties, Anna could spend as much time in 521 as needed.

A week after she'd last seen Daniel, making certain her smile was in place, Anna opened the door to Mrs. Higgs's room. This time the shades were drawn and there were more shadows than light. They seemed to be waiting. Anna saw Mrs. Higgs was awake, staring listlessly at the faded flowers on her table. Her eyes brightened when she saw Anna.

"I'm so glad you came. I was just thinking of you."

"Of course I came." Anna set the magazines down. Instinct told her that pictures weren't what Mrs. Higgs needed today. "How else could I give you all the gossip about the party I went to last night?" On the pretext of tidying the sheets, Anna scanned the chart. Her heart sank. The deterioration of the past five days was increasing. But she was smiling as she took her seat beside the bed. "You know my friend, Myra?" Anna was aware how much Mrs. Higgs enjoyed stories about Myra's escapades. "Last night she wore a strapless black dress cut two inches past discretion. I thought some of the older ladies would faint"

"And the men?"

"Well, let's just say Myra didn't miss a dance."

Mrs. Higgs laughed, then caught her breath as pain sliced through. Anna was on her feet instantly.

"Lie still. I'll get the doctor."

"No." Surprisingly strong, the thin hand gripped hers. "No, he'll just give me another shot."

Trying to soothe, Anna rubbed the frail hand as she took her pulse. "Just for the pain, Mrs. Higgs. You don't have to be in pain."

Calmer, Mrs. Higgs settled back again. "I'd rather feel pain than nothing. I'm all right now." She managed a smile. "Talking to you is much better than medicine. Did your Daniel come back yet?"

Still monitoring her pulse, Anna sat again. "No."

"It was so kind of him to visit me before he left for New York. Imagine his coming by here before he went to the airport."

The fact that he had was just one of the things that

added to Anna's confusion. "He likes visiting you. He told me."

"He'd said he'd come again when he got back from New York." She looked at the week-old roses she refused to let the nurses take away. "It's so special to be young and in love."

Anna felt a stab of pain herself. Did he love her? He'd chosen her, he wanted her, but love was a different matter. She wished she had someone to talk to, but Myra had seemed so preoccupied lately and no one else would understand. She could hardly pour her problems out on Mrs. Higgs when she'd come to comfort. Instead, she grinned and patted her hand. "You must have been in love dozens of times."

"At least. Falling in love, that's the roller coaster, the ups and downs, the thrills. Being in love, that's the carousel—around and around with music playing. But staying in love . . ." She sighed, remembering. "That's the maze, Anna. There are all the twists and turns and dead ends. You have to keep going, keep trusting. I had such a short time with my husband, and never tried the maze again."

"What was he like, your husband?"

"Oh, he was young, and ambitious. Full of ideas. His father had a grocery store, and Thomas wanted to expand it. He was very clever. If he'd lived . . . But that wasn't meant. Do you believe some things are meant, Anna?"

She thought about her need to heal, her studies. She tried not to think of Daniel. "Yes. Yes, I do."

"Thomas was meant to die young, like a lovely flash fire. Still, he packed so much into the short years. I admire him more as I look back. Your Daniel reminds me of him."

"How?"

"That drive—the kind you can see on their faces. It tells you they're going to do amazing things." She smiled again, fighting back another surge of pain. "There's a ruthlessness that means they'll do whatever is necessary to accomplish it, and yet there's kindness, very basic kindness. The kind that made Thomas give a handful of candy to a child who didn't have the money. The kind that makes your Daniel visit an old woman he doesn't know. I've changed my will."

Alarmed, Anna straightened. "Mrs. Higgs—"

"Oh, don't fret." She closed her eyes a moment, willing her body to build back some strength. "I can see on your face you're worried I've tangled you up in it. Thomas left me a nest egg, and I invested. It's given me a comfortable life. I have no children, no grandchildren. It's too late for regrets. I need to give something back. I need to be remembered." She looked at Anna again. "I talked to Daniel about it."

"To Daniel?" Disturbed, Anna leaned closer.

"He's very smart, just like Thomas. I told him what I wanted to do, and he told me how it could be done. I've had my lawyer set up a scholarship. Daniel agreed to let me name him executor so he can handle the details."

Anna opened her mouth to brush the subject of death aside, then realized she would be doing so only for herself. "What kind of scholarship?"

"For young women going into medicine." Pleased with the stunned look on Anna's face, Mrs. Higgs smiled. "I knew you'd like it. I thought about what I could do, then I thought of you, and of all the nurses here who've been so kind to me."

"It's a wonderful thing, Mrs. Higgs."

"I could have died alone, without anyone to sit and talk to me. I was lucky." She reached out and curled her fingers around Anna's hand. Because it was difficult to feel, she tightened them. Anna felt barely any pressure. "Anna, don't make the same mistake I did by thinking you don't need anyone. Take love where it's offered. Let it live with you. Don't be afraid of the maze."

"No," Anna murmured. "I won't."

There was barely any pain now, barely anything at all. Mrs. Higgs stared at the outline of light around the shades. "Do you know what I'd do if I could start all over again, Anna?"

"What would you do?"

"I'd have it all." The light was blurring, but she managed to smile. "It's so foolish to think you have to settle for pieces. Thomas would have known better." Exhausted, she closed her eyes again. "Stay with me a little while."

"Of course I will."

So she sat in the shadowed room. Keeping the frail hand in hers, she listened to the sound of breathing. And waited. When it was over, she fought back the surge of anger, the wave of denial. Carefully, Anna rose and pressed a kiss to Mrs. Higgs's forehead. "I won't forget you."

Calm, controlled, she walked down the corridor to Mrs. Kellerman. Deluged by five new admissions, the nurse gave her a brief glance. "We're a bit rushed now, Miss Whitfield."

She stood very straight. When she spoke her voice held both authority and patience. "You'll need to call the doctor for Mrs. Higgs."

Instantly alert, Mrs. Kellerman rose. "She's having pain?"

"No." Anna folded her hands. "Not anymore."

Understanding flickered in her eyes, and, Anna

thought for a moment, regret. "Thank you, Miss Whitfield. Nurse Bates, call Doctor Liederman immediately. Five twenty-one." Without waiting for an answer, she went down the corridor herself. Anna followed her as far as the door and again waited. Moments later, Kellerman looked back. "Miss Whitfield, you don't need to stay here now."

Determined, Anna kept her hands folded and her eyes direct. "Mrs. Higgs had no one."

Compassion came through, and for the first time, respect. Stepping back from the bed, Kellerman put a hand on her arm. "Please wait outside. I'll tell the doctor you want to speak to him."

"Thank you." Anna walked down the corridor to the little L that was the waiting room and sat. As the minutes passed, she grew calmer. This was what she would face, she reminded herself, day after day for the rest of her life. This was the first time—her stomach knotted and unknotted—but not the last. Death would become an intimate part of her life, something to be fought, something to be faced. Starting now, this minute, she would have to learn to defend herself against it.

On a deep breath she closed her eyes. When she opened them again, she saw Daniel walking toward her.

For a moment, her mind went blank. Then she saw the roses in his hand. Tears welled up, brimmed and were controlled. When she rose her legs were steady.

"I thought I'd find you here." Everything about him was aggressive—his walk, his face, his voice. She thought only briefly of the luxury of throwing herself into his arms and weeping.

"I'm here every day." That wouldn't change. Now, more than ever she knew she couldn't let it.

"It took longer than I thought to work things out in New York." And he'd spent his nights restless and wakeful thinking of her. He started to speak again in the same tough, no-nonsense tone, but something in her eyes stopped him. "What's wrong?" He only had to see her glance at the roses to know. "Damn." With a whispered oath he let them fall to his side. "Was she alone?"

That he would ask that first, that he would think of that first, made her reach out her hand to him. "No, I was with her."

"That's good then." Her hand was icy in his. "Let me take you home."

"No." If he were too kind, her composure would never hold up. "I want to speak with her doctor."

He started to object, then slipped an arm around her shoulders. "I'll wait with you."

In silence, they sat together. The scent of the roses flowed over her. They were young buds, very fresh, still moist. Part of a cycle, she reminded herself. It wasn't possible to appreciate life unless you understood, accepted, the cycle.

Anna rose very slowly when the doctor joined them. "Miss Whitfield. Mrs. Higgs spoke of you to me many times. You're a medical student."

"That's right."

He nodded, reserving judgment. "You're aware that we removed a tumor—a malignant one some weeks ago. There was another. If we had operated again, it would have killed her. Our only choice was to make her as comfortable as possible."

"I understand." She understood, too, that one day she'd have to make such decisions herself. "Mrs. Higgs had no family. I want to make the funeral arrangements."

Her composure surprised him as much as her statement. Studying her face, he decided if she made it through medical school, he'd be interested in having her intern under him. "I'm sure that can be easily done. We'll have Mrs. Higgs's attorney contact you."

"Thank you." She offered her hand. Liederman found it cool, but firm. Yes, he'd like to watch her train.

"We're leaving," Daniel told her when they were alone.

"I haven't finished my shift."

"And you won't today." Taking her by the arm, he led her to the elevator. "You're allowed to let yourself breathe. Don't argue," he said, anticipating her. "Let's just say you're humoring me. There's something I want to show you."

She could have argued. Just knowing she had the strength to do so made her relent. She'd go with him because she knew she'd come back tomorrow and do whatever needed to be done.

"I'll have my driver take us to my house," he told her as they stepped outside. "We'll want my car."

"I have mine." Daniel only lifted a brow and nodded. "Wait a minute." Walking to the Rolls, he dismissed Steven. "We'll use yours. Do you feel like driving?"

"Yes. Yes, I do." She walked to the little white convertible.

"Very nice, Anna, but then I've always admired your taste."

"Where are we going?"

"North. I'll direct you."

Content to drive, to feel the wind and know no destination, she headed out of town. For a time, he left her to her own thoughts.

"Shedding tears doesn't make you weak."

"No." She sighed and watched the sun slant across the road. "I can't yet. Not yet. Tell me about New York."

"A mad place. I like it." He grinned and threw his arm over the seat. "It's not a place to live, not for me, but the excitement can get into your blood. You know Dunripple Publishing?"

"Yes, of course."

"Now it's Dunripple and MacGregor." He'd been satisfied with the way the deal had swung, or more accurately, the way he'd pushed it.

"Prestigious."

"Prestigious be damned," he told her. "They needed new blood and cold cash."

"What did you need?"

"To diversify. I don't like bundling all my interests together."

She frowned a bit, thinking. "How do you know what to buy?"

"Old companies losing ground, new companies breaking it. The first gives me something to fix, the second something to—" he hesitated, unsure of what word would suit "—explore," he said finally.

"But you can't be sure all the companies you buy will make it."

"All of them won't. That's the game."

"Sounds like a vicious one."

"Maybe; it's life." He studied her. Her face was still a bit too pale, her eyes a bit too calm. "A doctor knows all his patients won't make it. It doesn't stop him from taking a new one."

He understood. She should have expected it. "No, it doesn't."

"We all take risks, Anna, if we're really alive."

She drove mostly in silence, following Daniel's

directions. Thoughts rushed in and out of her head, feelings tossed freely inside of her. It was a long quiet drive and should have calmed her. By the time they drove along the coast, she was tight with nervous energy. Spotting a little store, Daniel gave a wave of his hand.

"Stop in here."

Agreeable, Anna pulled into the gravel lot beside it. "Is this what you wanted to show me?"

"No. But you're going to get hungry."

She pressed a hand on her stomach before she opened the door. "I think I already am." Thinking they'd hardly do better than a box of crackers, Anna followed him inside.

It was a crowded little hodgepodge of a store, with canned goods lined on shelves, dry goods packed in doorless cupboards. A freshly waxed floor shone back at her. A fan creaked in slow circles swirling the heat.

"Mr. MacGregor!" With obvious pleasure, a round woman eased herself from a stool behind the counter.

"Ah, Mrs. Lowe. Pretty as ever."

She had a face like a horse and knew it. She greeted the flattery with a loud guffaw. "What can I do for you today?" She gave Anna an unconcealed survey, grinned and showed a missing incisor.

"The lady and I need the makings of a picnic." He leaned over the counter. "Tell me you have some of that mouth-watering roast beef you gave me last time."

"Not an ounce." She winked at him. "But I have some ham that'll make you roll your eyes and thank your Maker."

All charm, he took her pudgy hand and kissed it. "I'll roll my eyes and thank you, Mrs. Lowe."

"I'll make a sandwich for the lady. And two for you." The look she gave him was as shrewd as it was friendly. "I'll throw in a thermos of lemonade—if you buy the thermos."

"Done."

With a cackle, she made her way into a back room.

"You've been here before," Anna said dryly.

"Now and again. Quite a little place." He knew the Lowes ran it themselves and kept it stocked and spotless. "I'm thinking if they added themselves another room, put in a counter and a grill, Mrs. Lowe could make herself famous with her sandwiches."

She saw the look in his eyes and smiled. "Lowe and MacGregor."

With a laugh, he leaned on the counter. "No, sometimes it's best to be a silent partner."

When Mrs. Lowe came back, she carried a huge wicker basket. "Have your picnic and bring the basket back—it's not new." She winked again. "But the thermos is."

Daniel took out his wallet and pulled out bills. Enough to make Anna's eyebrow lift. "My best to your husband, Mrs. Lowe."

The bills disappeared into some handy pocket. "You and the lady have a good time."

"We will." Toting the basket, Daniel swung through the door. "Do you trust me to drive?"

Anna already had the keys in her hands. She hadn't allowed anyone behind the wheel but herself, though her father had hinted and Myra had nagged. Hesitating only a moment, she handed them to him.

Moments later, they were driving straight up. She'd never seen a road so narrow, so winding. The view over the side took her breath away with its sheer cliffs. There was color among the endless gray: touches of red, hints of green. In places it seemed as though the rock had been hewn away with a broadax, in others hacked at with a pick. Waves crashed free against rock, then washed back only to crash again. There was violence here, she thought. An endless war that was also a cycle. With the smell of the sea around her, she leaned back.

Mile after mile they climbed. Trees that dotted the sides of the road grew slanted, leaning away from the constant wind. Anna wondered what Daniel would do if another car came down the road toward them. It didn't worry her. She watched a sea bird skim over the surface of the water below, then soar up toward the sun.

When the road leveled again, she was almost disappointed. Then she saw the stretch of land ahead. Overgrown, rocky, desolate, it spread out to the very edge of the cliff. Something shot into her, sharp as an arrow, sweet as a kiss. Recognition.

Daniel stopped the car and stood, absorbing everything. As it always did, the wildness of it drew him. He could feel the sea, feel the wind. He was home.

Saying nothing, Anna stepped from the car. She was buffeted by the turbulence there, but she could also sense the peace. Whether it was in the air or the land itself, she knew this sense of constant movement and inner stillness would always remain.

"This is your land," she murmured when he stood beside her.

"Aye."

The wind blew her hair into her face, but she pushed it back, impatient. She wanted to see clearly. "It's beautiful."

She said it so simply that he couldn't speak. Until that moment he hadn't realized just how desperately he wanted her to accept it, to understand it. More, he hadn't known how important it was to him that she love it as he had from the first moment he'd seen it. The sun beat down on his face as he brought her hand to his lips.

"The house will go there." He pointed, and began to walk with her. "Near the cliff, so you'll hear the sea, almost be part of it. It'll be made of stone, tons of it, so it'll rise up and hold its own. Some of the windows will come nearly to the ceiling and the front door will be as wide as three men. Here—" he stopped, gauging the position with his eyes "—there will be a tower."

"Towers?" Almost hypnotized, Anna looked up at him. "You make it sound like a castle."

"That's right. A castle. The MacGregor seal will stand above the door."

She tried to imagine it and shook her head. She found it both exciting and incomprehensible. "Why so much?"

"It'll last. My great-grandchildren will know it." Leaving her, he walked back to the car for the basket.

Unable to judge his mood or her own, Anna helped spread the blanket Mrs. Lowe had provided. Besides the sandwiches, there was a bowl of well-spiced potato salad and two thick slices of cake. With her skirt flowing over her knees, Anna sat cross-legged and ate while she watched the clouds.

So much was happening so fast, and yet it seemed her life was suspended in some kind of limbo. She no longer knew what she'd find if she turned right, if she turned left. The path that had once seemed so clear to her had taken on some odd curves. She couldn't see around them. Because Daniel was quiet, she kept her silence, aware he was no more comfortable than she.

"In Scotland," he began, as if talking to himself, "we lived in a little cottage no bigger than the garage on your house. I was five, maybe six, when my mother took sick. After she'd delivered my brother, she was never really well again. My grandmother would come every day to cook and help tend the baby. I'd sit with my mother, talk to her. I didn't realize then how young she was."

Anna sat with her hands in her lap and her eyes intense. A few weeks before, she would have listened politely if he had spoken of his past. Now, it seemed half her world hinged on what he would say. "Go on, please."

It wasn't easy for him, nor had he planned to speak of it. Now that he'd begun, he discovered he'd needed to tell her all along. "My father would come home from the mines, his skin black, his eyes red. God, how tired he must have been, but he sat with my mother, played with the baby, listened to me. She hung on, nearly five years, and when I was ten, she just slipped away. She was suffering the whole time, but she never complained."

Anna thought of Mrs. Higgs. This time she let the tears fall. Daniel said nothing for a moment but listened to the sea.

"My grandmother came to live with us. Tough old bird. She made me tow the line—study in books. When I was twelve I went to work in the mines, but I could read and write and work with figures better than the grown men. I was as big as some of them already." He laughed at that and flexed his hand into a fist. More than once he'd been grateful for it.

"The mines were hell. Dust in your lungs, in your eyes. Every time the earth shook, you waited to die and hoped it'd be quick. I was about fifteen when McBride, who owned the mine, took notice of me. He found out I was clever with numbers, so he used to have me come in and do a bit of figuring for him. In his way, he was a fair man, so I was paid for the extra work. Within a year, I was out of the mines and doing his books. My hands were clean. As soon as I'd started working, my father had me put half my earnings in a tin jar. We could have used the money day to day, but he wouldn't have it. Even when I was making more in the office, he made me put half the money aside in that jar. It was the same with my brother, Alan."

"He wanted you to get out," Anna murmured.

"Aye. He had a dream for me and Alan to get out of the mines, away from everything he'd had to live with." He turned to her, his eyes hot and angry. "I was twenty when the main shaft caved in. We dug for three days, three nights. Twenty men were gone, my father and my brother with them."

"Oh, Daniel." She reached out, resting her head against his shoulder. It was more than grief. She could feel the fury, the resentments, the guilt. "I'm sorry."

"When we buried them, I swore it wasn't the end. It was the beginning. I'd make enough to get out. By the time I did, it was too late to take my grandmother. She'd lived a long time and only asked me one thing before she died, that I see the line go on, that I not forget where we'd come from. I'm keeping that promise, Anna—" he turned her so she'd look at him "—for her, for me, with every stone that goes into this house."

She understood him now, perhaps too well for her own good. She understood that there on the windswept cliff in the middle of the barren land he'd chosen she'd finally, irreversibly fallen in love with him. But with understanding came only more questions.

Rising, she walked toward the plot of land where he envisioned his home. He'd build it, she knew. And it would be magnificent. "They'd be proud of you."

"I'll go back one day to see it all again, to remember it all. I'll want you with me."

She turned, and as she did, wondered if she'd been waiting to make that move all of her life. Perhaps it was the first step into the maze. "I'm afraid I'll never be able to give you everything you want, Daniel. I'm more afraid that I'll try."

He stood and walked toward her. There was still too much space between them when he stopped. "You told me you needed time. I asked you to make a decision. Now, I'm asking you what it is."

Anna stood, poised on the edge of everything.

CHAPTER 7

She wanted to give him everything he asked, to give him things he'd never even dreamed of. She wanted to take everything she could grab and hold on to. In that moment she understood what taking just one step forward could mean to both of them. She wondered if he did. One step forward would irrevocably change their lives even if a step back could somehow be taken later. One step and there would be no altering what was said, what was done or what was given. Anna believed in destiny, destiny met with eyes open and mind clear.

Though common sense fought to remain in charge, her heart slowly, willfully took command. What was love? In that moment she understood only that it was a force larger, stronger than the logic she had always lived by. Love had started wars, toppled empires, driven men mad and turned women into fools. She could reason for hours, but she would never diminish the power of that one all-encompassing force.

They stood on the cliffs, with the wind roaring against the rocks, moaning through the high grass, beating against the land he'd chosen to fulfill a dream and a promise. If Daniel was her destiny, she would meet him head on.

He looked fiercer than ever, almost frightening, with his eyes burning into hers and the sun fiery at his back. Zeus, Thor, he might have been either. But he was flesh and blood, a man who understood destiny and would break mountains to achieve the one he had chosen. He'd chosen her.

She took her time, determined to make her decision with a clear head. But the emotions boiling inside her weren't calm. How could she look at him, read the need in his eyes and be calm? He'd spoken of family, of promises, of a future she wasn't sure she could share with him. But there was something she could share now, something she could give, and give only once. Leading with her heart, Anna stepped forward and into his arms.

They came together like thunder, urgent, tempestuous, strong. Her mouth met his with all the chaotic longing she'd held down. She felt the power soar, the fire spread fast and out of control. There was only here; there was only now.

His hands were in her hair, his fingers raking desperately through it so that the combs she wore fell unheeded to the ground. His mouth was restless and urgent, rushing over her face, meeting her lips, then moving on, as if it were vital that he taste everything at once. She heard her name come low and vibrant, then tasted it herself as he murmured against her mouth. Even as she pressed strongly against him, she felt the give of her own body, the incredible fluid yielding only a woman can experience. Her mind leaped forward with the pleasure of discovering the magic of submission when mixed with demand. Then her thoughts scattered, leaving only one. She was where she wanted to be.

Together they lowered themselves to the grass, wrapped so tightly that even the wind couldn't come between them. Like lovers separated for years, they rushed together with no holding back, no hesitation. Eager to feel the delight of flesh against flesh, she tugged on his shirt. Muscles he'd earned while still a boy corded his arms, rippled over his back. Aroused by the sheer strength of him, she allowed her hands free play, and learned the spiraling joy of having a man—her man—groan at her touch.

He wanted her—here, now, exclusively. She could feel it with every beat of her own pulse. Until that moment she hadn't realized just how important it had been to her to be sure of it. Whatever else he wanted from her, whatever plans he'd scrupulously made were tossed to oblivion by one overpowering force. Desire. It was pure; it was desperate; it was theirs.

He'd wanted to be careful, to be gentle, but she was driving him beyond anything he'd experienced. Fantasies, dreams paled foolishly beside reality. She was much more than a goal to be won or a woman to be wooed. Her hands were slim and strong and curious, her mouth warm and insistent. The need that pounded through him concentrated at the base of his neck so that the sound of it roared through his brain, leaving him deaf to the crash of the waves far below. He could smell the wild grass as he buried his lips at her throat, but her scent, subtle, quiet, was more pervasive. She was so small, so heart-breakingly soft that he fought to keep his work-toughened hands easy as he undressed her, but she arched against each touch, wantonly demanding more.

He couldn't resist her, nor could he resist any longer the pressure building inside him. Racing against passion, he yanked the rest of her clothes aside and gave himself to need. Her skin was pale as milk under the hot summer sun, her body as trim and efficient as her mind. No other woman, no dream had ever aroused him more. With a sound that rumbled deep in his throat, he met her gasp of astonished pleasure.

There was more? She had thought it impossible, but everywhere his lips tarried brought her fresh bursts of unspeakable delight. Should she have known a man and a woman could share something so dark, so sultry under a full sun? Could she have known that she, always so self-disciplined, so rational, would give herself to passion in a field of grass on a cliff top? All she understood was that it didn't matter when, it didn't matter where, it was and would always be Daniel.

Her emotions seemed to race just ahead of reason. She wanted to savor each new experience, but before she could absorb one, another tumbled down on her, layering all into a mass of sensations impossible to separate. With a breathless laugh she realized it wasn't necessary to understand each one, but simply to feel. There was no fear in her as desire began to peak, but a wild anticipation.

The blood pounded in his veins, swam in his head until he thought he'd explode from it. Her body burned with the same fire as his, she moved to the same throbbing music. But she was innocent. He knew, even as he ached to take her with fury and speed, that control was vital. Her arms clutched him, her hips thrust up in uninhibited offering. And the fear of harming something so precious snaked through him. He struggled to catch his breath when she reached for him.

"Anna—"

"I want you." Her murmur was like thunder in his

ear. "I need you, Daniel." In hearing it, sweet pain spread through him. In saying it, she felt glorious.

"I won't hurt you." He lifted his head to see her lips curve, her eyes cloud.

"No, you won't hurt me."

He called on all his strength of will as he slipped into her. She was so warm, so moist that his head nearly burst with a new flood of emotion. He'd had women before. But not like this. He'd given himself to passion before. Never, never like this.

She felt him enter her, pierce her, fill her. Her innocence was gone in a heartbeat with a pleasure so vast that all pain was smothered. Power. It swept over her like the wind, like the thunder, eclipsing that first surge of wonder. Drunk with it, she gripped him tighter. She heard him call her name before his mouth fastened on hers. They hurled aside control and took each other.

He knew about the cat that swallowed the canary. As he lay on the wild grass with Anna at his side, Daniel felt like a cat who'd feasted on a baker's dozen. The contentment that had somehow always skidded just out of his reach settled through him with a sleepy sigh.

He'd chosen a lovely, intelligent woman to marry. It was a logical choice for a man who intended to build an empire that would last for generations. Wasn't it lucky he'd fallen in love and discovered she was also caring, sweet and passionate? His wife-to-be, the mother of his yet-to-be-born children fit him like a glove. He decided it paid to be lucky as well as shrewd.

She was quiet beside him but he knew from the easy way she breathed, the content way her hand rested in his that she was lost in thoughts, not in regrets. Her head was nestled in the crook of his shoulder so naturally that he could have sworn they'd lain just like this before, grass soft at their backs, the sky clear and blue above. Cloud watchers, he thought. Children would toss themselves on the ground to find images and dreams in the clouds. He'd never had much time for it as a boy. With Anna, he could make time, and he wouldn't have to look for dreams.

He could have lain there for hours, with the surf and the wind and the sun. He had his woman, his land, and it was only the beginning. But he knew, of course, that they had to leave for the city soon. What he wanted with her and for her couldn't be accomplished in an empty field. But he kept his arm around her and lingered while dozens of plans formed and shifted in his head.

"There's more than enough room for us in the house," he said, half to himself. With his eyes nearly closed and the quiet glow of loving still lingering, he could picture her there. She'd add the touches he too often forgot—bowls of flowers, music. "Of course, you might want to change some things. Flounce it up some."

She watched the way the sun played through leaves. She'd just taken the step forward. It was already time for the step back. "Your house is fine the way it is, Daniel."

"Aye, well it's only temporary." He stroked his fingers through her hair while he looked at the plot where he would build his dream. Their dream now. How much sweeter it was now that he had someone to share it with. "When this one's finished we'll sell the one in Boston. Or maybe we'll keep it for business. I'll be cutting down on my traveling once I have a wife."

Overhead clouds moved slowly, too lofty to be

persuaded by the wind that rustled the grass. "Traveling's important to your business."

"For now." She felt his shoulder move under her head in a careless shrug. "Before long, they'll come to me. And they'll come here. I don't intend to marry, then spend my time away from my wife."

Her hand rested lightly on his chest. She wondered if he knew how smugly he used the phrase *my wife*. A man might use the same tone to describe his shiny new car. "I'm not going to marry you, Daniel."

"I'll still have to fly into New York now and again, but you can go with me."

"I said I'm not going to marry you."

With a laugh, he pulled her up until she lay half across him. Her skin was warm from sun and loving. "What do you mean you're not going to marry me? Of course, you are."

"No." She laid a hand on his face. Her touch was as soft as her eyes. "I'm not."

"How can you say that now?" He had her by the shoulders. Panic was his first reaction as he recognized the calm, patient look. Part of his success was the ability to turn panic to anger, and anger to determination. "It's not the time for games."

"No, it's not." Calm, she shifted away and began to dress.

Torn between puzzlement and fury, he grabbed her wrists before she could slip into her blouse. "We've just made love. You came to me."

"I came to you freely," she returned. "We needed each other."

"And we're going to go on needing each other. That's why you're going to marry me."

She tried to let out her breath slowly, soundlessly. "I can't."

"Why in hell not?"

Her stomach muscles were beginning to quiver. Her skin was chilled under the bright summer sun. She wanted him to release her but knew he'd ignore any resistance. Suddenly she wanted to run, to run faster than she ever had. Instead, she remained still. "You want me to marry you, start a family, pick up and go whenever and wherever your business or whims take you." She had to swallow because she knew she spoke the truth. "To do that I'd have to give up something I've wanted almost as long as I can remember. I won't do it, Daniel, not even for you."

"This is nonsense." To prove it he gave her a brisk shake. "If the damn degree is so important, go on and get it then. You can study just as easily married to me."

"No." Easing away, she busied her hands with her clothes. She wouldn't be bullied, and she wouldn't be charmed, though he seemed to be an expert on both. "If I went back to school as Mrs. Daniel MacGregor, I'd never finish. You'd stop me even if you didn't mean to."

"Damn it, that's ridiculous." He stood naked and glorious with the sun at his back. For a moment Anna wanted to open her arms and invite him back to her, to agree with anything he said. Purposefully she stood.

"It's not. And I'm going to earn my degree, Daniel. I have to."

"So you're choosing your doctoring over me." Hurt, angry, he didn't care if his words were unfair. He saw the one thing that would make his life whole, make it real, slipping away.

"I want you both." She swallowed. How could she judge his reaction when she still wasn't sure of her own? "I won't marry you," she repeated. "But I'll live with you."

His eyes narrowed into slits. "You'll what?"

"I'll live with you in your house in Boston until September. After that we could get an apartment off campus. And then . . ."

"And then what?" His words shot out like sand from under a tire.

She lifted her hands then let them fall. "Then I don't know."

Her head was thrown back in pride so that the wind tossed her hair. But her face was very pale, her eyes unsure. He loved her to the point of madness and his anger was nearly as great. "Damn you, Anna, I want you for a wife, not for a mistress."

The doubts cleared from her eyes to be replaced by a fury to match his own. No longer pale, her skin glowed with indignation. "And I'm not offering to be one." Turning on her heel, she started back to the car. He grabbed her by the arm and whirled her around so quickly that her feet nearly slid out from under her.

"What the hell are you offering then?"

"To live with you." It wasn't often she shouted, but when she did, she gave it everything. If he hadn't been so angry, there would have been room for respect. "Not be kept by you. I don't want your money or your big house or your dozen roses a day. It's you I want. God knows why."

"Then marry me." Still naked, still raging, he dragged her against him.

"Do you think you can have anything you want just by yelling louder, just by being stronger?" She shoved him away and stood, small and slim and stunning. "I'll give you only so much and no more."

He dragged both hands through his hair. How was a man to deal with such a woman? "If you won't think of your reputation, I have to."

She lifted a brow. "You have to do nothing but think of your own." In the regal manner she could assume so effortlessly, she let her gaze drift over him. "You don't seem very concerned about it now."

In one furious move, he swept up his pants. Another man might have looked foolish. Daniel looked magnificent. "A few minutes ago I seduced you," he began.

"Don't delude yourself." Cool and confident she picked up his shirt. "A few minutes ago we made love. It had nothing to do with seduction."

He took the shirt from her and slipped it on. "You're tougher than you look, Anna Whitfield."

"That's right." Pleased with herself, she started to gather up the picnic things. "You told me once to take you as you are. Now I'm telling you the same. If you want me, Daniel, it has to be on my terms. Think about it." She left him half-dressed and walked to the car.

They barely spoke on the long drive back. Anna was no longer angry, but drained. So much had happened in a short span of time, and none of it had been in her carefully worked out plans. She needed time to think, to evaluate and to recharge. Daniel was electric. He didn't have to speak for her to read his temper.

The hell with his temper, she thought recklessly. Let him be angry. It was something he did well. Not everyone looked magnificent when he ranted and raged.

His mistress. Her own temper began to sizzle but she waited for it to subside. She'd be no man's mistress, Anna told herself as she settled back and folded her arms. And no man's wife until she was ready. She would, though the thought still made her pulse skittish, be one man's lover. In her own quiet fashion, she was as determined as Daniel to have her way.

Live with him. Daniel gripped the wheel tightly as he took a turn faster than a rational man would have dared. He was offering her half of everything he had, half of everything he was. Most importantly, he was offering her his name. And she was tossing it back in his face.

Did she think he would have taken her innocence if he hadn't believed they were committed to each other? What kind of woman would refuse an honest proposal and opt to run off like a renegade child thumbing her nose at what was proper? He wanted a wife, damn it, a family. She wanted a piece of paper that said she could poke needles into people.

He should have taken her advice from the beginning. Anna Whitfield was the last woman in Boston who would make him a suitable wife. So he would forget about her. He'd drop her at her door, say a cool goodbye and drive away. But he could still taste her, still feel the way her skin had slid under his fingers, still smell the scent of her hair as it had floated around her body—and his.

"I won't have it."

With a squeal of brakes he stopped at the curb in front of her house. A few yards away, Anna's mother clipped roses. At the explosion, she looked up and nervously gripped her shears. The fact that a quick glance showed her none of her neighbors were about relieved her only a little as Daniel gunned the convertible's engine.

"That," Anna said with perfect calm, "is your privilege."

"Now you listen to me." Turning slightly, Daniel gripped her by both shoulders. He didn't want to argue, he didn't want to fight; the moment those patient brown eyes met his he wanted to drag her against him and make love with her until they were both too exhausted to speak.

Anna lifted a brow. "I'm listening."

He groped for what needed to be said. "What happened between us doesn't happen with everyone. I know."

She smiled a little. "I'll have to take your word for that."

Frustration boiled. "That's part of the problem," he mumbled and ordered himself to be as calm as she. "I want to marry you, Anna." In the rose bushes, Mrs. Whitfield dropped her shears with a quiet thump. "I've wanted to marry you from the first minute I saw you."

"That's part of the problem." Because most of her heart was already his, Anna lifted both hands to his face. "You wanted what was suitable and decided I was it. You want me to fit a slot in your life. Perhaps I could, but I won't."

"It's more than that now—much more." As he dragged her closer, she saw the flare of desire in his eyes then tasted it on his lips. Without hesitation, without artifice, Anna met his greed with her own. Yes, it was more than that now—perhaps more than either of them could deal with. When they were together like this, everything else faded into insignificance. That's what frightened her. That's what exhilarated her.

Desperately, he pushed her away again. "You see what we have together. What we could have."

"Yes." Her voice wasn't as steady now, but her determination hadn't wavered. "And I want it. I want you—but not marriage."

"I want you to share my name."

"And I want to share your heart first."

"You're not thinking clearly." Neither was he. Cautious, he dropped his hands from her shoulders. "You need a little time."

"No, I don't." Before he could stop her she slipped from the car. "But it's obvious you do. Goodbye, Daniel."

Mrs. Whitfield watched her daughter stride easily toward the house. Moments later she watched Daniel drive recklessly down the street. Then remembering whose car he was driving, he ground the gears into reverse and backed up as recklessly as he'd gone forward. He slammed the door, shot a ferocious look at the house and stomped away in the opposite direction. Hand to her heart, she dashed up the walk and through the front door.

"Anna!" Fluttering her hands, she caught her daughter at the base of the staircase. "What's going on?"

Anna wanted to be alone. She wanted to go to her room, shut the door and lie on the bed. There was so much to absorb, so much to savor. She needed to weep and wasn't even sure why. Patient, she waited. "Going on?"

"I was clipping the roses." Flustered, Mrs. Whitfield shook her half-filled basket. "And I heard, well I couldn't help but hear . . ." She let her words trail off, unnerved by Anna's calm brown eyes, which suddenly seemed so mature. To give herself a minute, Mrs. Whitfield carefully pulled off her gardening gloves and laid them on a table.

"I understand you weren't eavesdropping, Mother."

"Of course not! I wouldn't dream—" She caught herself sliding away from the point and straightened her shoulders. "Anna, are you and Mr. MacGregor— Did you . . . ?" The sentence wandered away as she shifted her hands on the basket.

"Yes." With a private smile, Anna stepped from the landing. "We made love this afternoon."

"Oh." It was a feeble response, but the only one she could come up with.

"Mother—" Anna took the basket from her hands "—I'm not a child any longer."

"Obviously." With a deep breath, Mrs. Whitfield faced her duty. "However, if Mr. MacGregor has seduced you, then—"

"He didn't."

Having revved herself up, Mrs. Whitfield could only blink at the interruption. "But you said—"

"I said we made love. He didn't have to seduce me." Anna took her mother by the arm. "Maybe we should sit down."

"Yes." Shaky, she let herself be led. "Maybe we should."

In the parlor Anna sat beside her mother on the sofa. How should she begin? Never in her wildest dreams had she imagined sitting with her mother in this fussy parlor and discussing romance, love and sex. Taking a deep breath, she plunged. "Mother, I'd never been with a man before. I wanted to be with Daniel. It wasn't something I did impetuously, but something I gave a great deal of thought to."

"I've always said you think too much," Mrs. Whitfield responded automatically.

"I'm sorry." Used to parental criticism, Anna laid her hands quietly in her lap. "I know it's not something you want to hear, but I can't lie to you."

Love, propriety and confusion warred together. Love won. "Oh, Anna." In a rare gesture, Mrs. Whitfield gathered Anna close. "Are you all right?"

"Of course I am." Touched, Anna let her head rest

against her mother's shoulder. "I feel wonderful. It's like—I don't know—being unlocked."

"Yes." She blinked back tears. "That's how it should be. I know we've never really talked of such things. We should have, but then you went off to that school and those books. . . ." She remembered her shock when she had picked one up to give it a casual glance. "I suppose it all made me feel inadequate."

"It's nothing like books." Anna discovered she could savor it after all.

"No, it's not." She shifted to take both her daughter's hands. "Books can be closed. Anna, I don't want you to be hurt."

"Daniel won't hurt me." She was warmed even now, remembering how gentle he'd struggled to be. "In fact, he's much too concerned about not hurting me. He wants me to marry him."

Mrs. Whitfield breathed a sigh of relief. "I thought I heard him say so, but you sounded as though you were fighting."

"Not fighting, disagreeing. I'm not going to marry him."

"Anna." When her mother drew away, her face was stern. "What kind of nonsense is this? I admit I don't always understand you, but I know you well enough to be sure nothing would have happened between the two of you if you hadn't cared very deeply."

"I do." Losing some of her composure, Anna pressed her fingers to her eyes. "Maybe too much, it's frightening. He wants a wife, Mother, almost the way a man wants a shoe that fits well."

"That's just their way." On firmer ground, Mrs. Whitfield sat back. "Some men are poets, some are dreamers, but most are just men. I know girls think there should be pretty words and lovely music, but life is much more basic than that."

Curious, Anna studied her. Her mother, she knew from experience, had never been much of a philosopher. "Did you want pretty words?"

"Of course." With a smile, Mrs. Whitfield thought of her past. "Your father is a good man, a very good man, but most of his words come out of law books. I think Mr. MacGregor's a good man."

"He is. I don't want to lose him, but I can't marry him."

"Anna—"

"I'm going to live with him."

Mrs. Whitfield opened her mouth, shut it again and swallowed. "I think I'd like a drink."

Rising, Anna walked to the liquor cabinet. "Sherry?"

"Scotch. A double."

Tension dissolved in amusement as Anna poured. "Daniel had a very similar reaction." She handed her mother the glass and watched her gulp it down. "I've never hidden anything from you."

The Scotch burned through her system. "No, no, you've always been painfully honest."

"I care very much for Daniel." Honest, Anna reminded herself and let out a long breath. "I'm in love with him. That isn't something I chose, so now I feel as though I have to take back some control. If I marry him, I'll lose everything I've been working for."

Mrs. Whitfield set down the empty glass. "Your degree."

"I know you don't understand that, either. No one seems to." She ran her hands through her hair. It fell loose to her shoulders and made her remember that her combs still lay where they had fallen in the grass. The combs didn't matter, they could be replaced. Other things had been lost on that cliff top that couldn't. "What I know, in my heart, is that if I marry Daniel now I'll never finish. And if I don't, I'll never forgive myself or him. Mother, I've tried to explain to you before that being a doctor isn't simply what I want to do, it's what I have to do."

"Sometimes we have to weigh one important thing against another Anna, and choose."

"And sometimes we don't." Desperate for reassurance, she knelt at her mother's feet. "I know it's selfish to want it all, but I've thought it through over and over. I have to be a doctor, and I don't want to live without Daniel."

"And Daniel?"

"He wants marriage. He can't see beyond that, but he will."

"Always so sure of yourself, Anna." She recognized the look in her daughter's eyes: calm, clear and filled with ruthless determination. She nearly sighed. "You would never ask for anything, and I was fooled into thinking you were absolutely content. Then, all at once, you would demand everything."

"I didn't choose to be a doctor any more than I chose to fall in love with Daniel. Both things just are."

"Anna, a step like this can bring you a lot of pain, a lot of unhappiness. If you love Daniel, then marriage—"

"It isn't time, and I can't be sure it ever will be." Frustrated, she rose and paced the room. "I'm terrified to make that kind of mistake—for him, as well as for myself. All I know is that now, right now, I don't want to be without him. Maybe it's wrong, but would it be better, would it be right if we continued to be lovers in secret? Can you tell me it would be more acceptable if we stole a few hours here and there, a night, an afternoon?"

"I could never tell you anything," her mother murmured.

"Oh, please." More frightened than she wanted to admit, Anna went to her mother again. "Now more than ever I want your understanding. It's not just desire, though that's certainly part of it. It's a need to be with him, to share some of his dreams, because I'm not sure I'll be able to share them all. To love him in secret would be hypocrisy. He means too much for that. I won't hide what I feel. I won't hide what I am."

Mrs. Whitfield looked at her only child, at her dark, earnest eyes, her soft, sculpted mouth. She wished she had the answers. "You know what you'll be up against? What people will say?"

"That doesn't matter to me."

"It never has," her mother muttered. "I know how impossible it is to talk you out of anything once your mind's made up, and you're too old for me to forbid anything, but, Anna, you can't ask me to approve."

"I know." For a moment, she laid her head in her mother's lap. "But if somewhere inside you, if in some little part you could understand, it would be enough."

Sighing, she touched her daughter's hand. "I haven't forgotten what it is to be in love. Maybe I do understand, and maybe that's why I'm afraid for you. Anna, you've never been anything but a good daughter, but . . ."

She had to smile, just a little. "But?"

"You've also always been a puzzle. I know I've never actually told you I was proud of you, but I am."

Anna felt a little quiver of relief work through her. "I know I never actually told you I needed you to be proud, but I do."

"I have to admit that I always hoped that you'd forget about medicine and settle down into a marriage where I could see you happy, and yet another part of me has watched you and cheered."

Her fingers curled around her mother's. "I don't know how to tell you how much that means to me."

"I think I know. Now your father . . ." She closed her eyes, unable to even imagine his reaction.

"He'll be upset, I know. I'm sorry."

"I'll handle him." The words came out on impulse, but she discovered they were true. Mrs. Whitfield straightened her shoulders.

With a smile, Anna lifted her head. For a moment, for the first time, she and her mother looked at each other woman to woman. "I love you, Mother."

"And I love you." She drew her up on the sofa. "I don't have to understand you for that."

With a sigh, Anna laid her head on her mother's shoulder. "Is it too much to ask for you to wish me luck?"

"As a mother, yes." She found herself smiling. "But not as a woman."

CHAPTER 8

As the days passed, Anna began to fear that she'd lost. There were no phone calls, no irate visits. No white roses were delivered to the door. The ones still cluttering her room and her mother's parlor were a testimony to what might have been. And they were wilting.

More and more often she caught herself looking out the window at the sound of a car passing, dashing to the phone on the first ring. Each time she did so, she swore at herself and promised not to do it again. But, of course, she did.

She never left the hospital without scanning the lot for the blue convertible. Each time she stepped out of the wide white building she expected to see a big, broad-shouldered, red-bearded man waiting impatiently by the curb. He was never there, but she never stopped looking.

It was disconcerting to learn that she'd come to depend on him, but it was even more disconcerting to discover what she'd come to depend on him for. Happiness. She could be content without him. She could certainly be satisfied with her life and her career. But Anna was no longer sure she could be happy unless Daniel was a part of her day-to-day life.

One day, as she read aloud to a young patient with a broken leg, her mind wandered. To her annoyance she had caught herself daydreaming several times during working hours since Daniel had driven away from her house. Lecturing herself, she brought her attention back to the patient and the story. Like sand, her thoughts scattered again.

The happy-ever-after tale she spun to the sleepy little girl wasn't reality. Certainly the last thing Anna wanted was to sit quietly by and wait for a prince to fit her with a glass slipper. And of course she was too practical to believe in castles in the clouds or magic until midnight. It was nice perhaps, in a story, to dream about white chargers and heroes, but a woman wanted more in real life. In real life, a woman wanted—well, a partner, Anna supposed, not a knight or a prince who would always have to be looked up to and admired. A real woman wanted a real man, and a smart one wasn't going to sit around in a tower and wait for one to come along. She was going to live her own life and make her own choices.

Anna had always been a firm believer in the making of one's own destiny, of fighting—with logic and patience—for one's needs. So why was she waiting around? she asked herself abruptly. If she was as independent as she professed and as she intended to behave, then why was she mooning around and waiting for the phone to ring? Anyone who sat placidly by until someone else called the shots was a fool and a loser. She didn't intend to be either.

Her mind made up, Anna continued to read until the little girl's eyes closed. Shutting the book, she strode out into the hall. On the way down, she passed a frazzled, heavy-eyed intern and nearly smiled. At the moment she was certain he wouldn't understand her twinge of envy. Perhaps no one would but another med student. Still, in a few months she wouldn't be able to leave the hospital on her own whim. It wouldn't hurt to take advantage of the time she had left.

Outside, the weather was nasty. It was gray and stormy and so hot that the rain seemed to steam the moment it hit the concrete. By the time she made it to her car, she was humming and soaked to the skin. She drove across town with the radio turned up as high as her spirits.

The building that housed Old Line Savings and Loan was dignified, staid and trustworthy. As she raced across the little patch of lawn, Anna wondered if Daniel had made any changes. Inside, there was fresh paint and new carpeting but business was still transacted in hushed whispers. Anna ran a hand through her hair, scattering water, then headed for the nearest clerk. She crossed her fingers behind her back.

Upstairs, Daniel looked over the ads that would run in the paper the following week. His manager had cringed when he'd brought in the files, but the young assistant Daniel had hired had been enthusiastic. Some decisions were meant to be made on instinct. Instinct told Daniel that the ads would increase both his business and his reputation. And one was every bit as important as the other. He was not only going to put Old Line back on its feet, he would have a branch in Salem within two years.

Even as the idea germinated, his thoughts drifted away from business. He remembered a windy cliff top and a woman with sable hair and dark eyes. The thrill that rippled through him was as fresh as it had been when his arms had been around her. Her taste was a lingering sensation nothing else had been able to replace. Even here, in the privacy of his office he could smell her, quiet and sweet.

With an impatient mutter, he pushed the papers aside and strode to the window. He should be seeing other women. Hadn't he sworn he would when he'd driven away from Anna? He'd meant to, even started to. But each and every time he tried to so much as think of another woman, Anna was there. She was so firmly planted in his mind that there wasn't room for anyone else. He wasn't going to get over her.

Daniel stared out at the steadily driving rain. From the window, the Boston he looked at seemed gray and depressed. It suited his mood. After he was finished with his stacks of paperwork and meetings, he'd take a walk along the river, fair weather or foul. He needed to be alone, away from servants, employees. But not away from Anna. He could follow the Charles from end to end and never escape Anna. How could you escape what was in your blood, in your bone? And Anna was there. No matter how he tried to pretend he had a choice, Anna was there.

He wanted to marry her. Daniel whirled away from the window to pace the room with his hands thrust in his pockets and his brows lowered. He'd chosen anger over despair and fury over fear. Damn the woman, he thought yet again. He wanted to marry her. He wanted to wake up in the morning and know she was there. He wanted to come home at night and be able to reach for her. He wanted to see his child grow inside her. And he wanted these things with a desperation as foreign to him as failure.

Failure? The word alone had him clenching his teeth. He was far from ready to admit failure. The hell with other women, Daniel decided abruptly. There was only one. He was going after her.

When the phone on his desk rang he was halfway to the door. Cursing all the way he went back to yank it up. "MacGregor."

"Mr. MacGregor, this is Mary Miles, head cashier. I apologize for interrupting you but there's a young woman down in the lobby who insists on seeing you."

"Have her make an appointment with my secretary."

"Yes, sir, I suggested that, but she insists on seeing you now. She says she'll wait."

"I don't have time to see everyone who walks in off the street, Mrs. Miles." Daniel checked his watch. Anna would be out of the hospital. He'd have to catch her at home.

"Yes, sir." The cashier felt herself being squeezed between two ungiving forces. "I explained that to her, but she's very insistent. She's very polite, Mr. MacGregor, but I don't think she's going to budge."

Losing patience, Daniel swore again. "Tell her . . ." His voice trailed off as the cashier's words formed a picture in his mind. "What's her name?"

"Whitfield. Anna Whitfield."

"What have you got her waiting in the lobby for?" he demanded. "Send her up."

The cashier rolled her eyes and reminded herself of the raise Mr. MacGregor had given across the board when he'd bought the bank. "Yes, sir. Right away."

She'd changed her mind. Victory didn't settle over him. He soared with it. His patience, though it had cost him dearly, had paid off. She was ready to be sensible. True, he hadn't imagined discussing marriage in his office, but he was willing to make some concessions. The plain truth was he was willing to make a great many concessions. But she was coming to him. He would have everything he wanted, including his pride.

The knock on his door was brisk and businesslike before his secretary pushed it open. "Miss Whitfield to see you, sir."

He briefly nodded a dismissal before his gaze and every thought in his head focused on Anna. She stood on the thick gray carpet he'd recently had installed, dripping from head to foot. The rain had washed her face clean and left her hair dark and shiny and curling to her shoulders. She quite simply took his breath away.

"You're wet." His words came out sounding more like an accusation than a statement of concern. She met it with a smile.

"It's raining." Good God, it was good to see him. For a moment she could only smile foolishly and take him in. His tie was off, his collar open. His hair showed evidence of being combed impatiently with his fingers. She wanted to open her arms and take him to her, where she was beginning to understand he belonged. Instead, she continued to smile and drip quietly on his elegant carpet. While she smiled, he stared. For several humming seconds, neither of them spoke.

Catching himself, Daniel cleared his throat and scowled at her. "Seems to me anybody studying medicine should know better than to run around soaking wet." He pulled open the door to a cabinet and took out a bottle of brandy. "You'll find yourself spending more time in that hospital of yours than you'd like."

"I don't think a little summer shower should do me much harm." For the first time it occurred to her how she must look, with her hair dripping and tangled, her clothes splattered with rain and her shoes damp. She kept her chin up. Wet or not, she had her dignity.

"Drink this, anyway." He thrust a snifter into her hand. "Sit."

"No, I'll ruin—"

"Sit," he repeated in one terse bark.

Lifting a brow, she walked to a chair. "Very well."

She sat, but he didn't. The sweet taste of victory had already faded. He knew just by looking at her that she hadn't changed her mind. Not Anna. The truth was he never would have fallen so helplessly in love with a woman whose mind could be swayed. She hadn't come to accept his offer of marriage, and he was far from ready to accept her alternative.

His lips curved a bit. His eyes took on a light that those accustomed to doing business with him would have recognized—and been wary of. Stand off, Daniel told himself. But there was no way he would let Miss Anna Whitfield know she had him on edge. He let his gaze run down her once more as she sat ruining the upholstery of his chair.

"Interested in a loan, Anna?"

She sipped and let the brandy calm her sudden nervousness. The easy tone and slight smile didn't fool her for an instant. So, he was still angry. What else should she have expected? Would she have fallen in love with a man who could be too easily cajoled? No, she'd fallen in love with Daniel because he was precisely what he was.

"Not at the moment." To give herself time, she studied the room. "Your office is very nice, Daniel. Dignified but not stuffy." There was a bold abstract on the wall done in different tones and shades of blue. Though it seemed to be no more than random shapes and lines, the sense of sexuality was throbbingly clear. She shifted her gaze from it to his. "Definitely not stuffy."

He'd seen her study the abstract and knew she understood it. He'd paid a stiff price for the Picasso because it had appealed to him and because his instincts had told him the value would skyrocket within a generation. "You're a hard woman to shock, Anna."

"That's true." And because it was, she found herself relaxing. "I've always felt life was too important to go through it pretending to be offended by it. I've missed the roses."

He leaned a hip against the corner of his massive desk. "I thought you didn't like me sending them to you."

"I didn't. Until you stopped." She left it at that, deciding that even she was entitled to some quirks. "I hadn't heard from you in several days and I wondered if I'd shocked you."

"Shocked me?" A few moments before he'd wavered between tension and boredom. With Anna here, everything seemed settled into place again. "I'm not one to shock easily, either."

"Offended then," she suggested, "because I'd choose to live with you rather than marry you."

He nearly smiled. Had he once said he liked a woman to speak her mind—to a point? It didn't seem odd at all that his opinion on that had already changed radically. "Annoyed," he corrected. "We might even go to infuriated."

She remembered his reaction. "Yes, I think we might. You're still angry."

"Aye. You're still set in your mind?"

"Yes."

Thoughtfully he drew out a cigar, running his fingers over it once before lighting it. In business, he knew how to handle an opponent. Force him to make the pitch. It kept a man in the driver's seat when the other player had to do the explaining. Smoke wreathed over his head as he watched her and waited. "Why did you come here, Anna?"

So, he didn't intend to give an inch. She took another slow sip of brandy. All right then, neither would she. "Because I realized I didn't want to go another day without seeing you." She set the brandy aside as the haze of his smoke billowed then cleared. "Do you mind?"

He let out an impatient huff of breath. Business and personal matters didn't always have the same rules. Still, the aim was to win. "It's hard for a man to mind the woman he intends to marry wanting to be with him."

"Good." She rose then and made a vain attempt to tidy her damp skirts. "Then you'll have dinner with me tonight."

His eyes narrowed. "A man usually likes to do the asking."

She sighed and gave a little shake of her head as she walked to him. "You're forgetting what century you're in again. I'll pick you up at seven."

"You'll—"

"Pick you up at seven," she finished then rose to her toes. When she found his lips with hers, it was soft and easy and completely right. "Thanks for the brandy, Daniel. I won't keep you any longer."

He found his voice by the time she'd walked to the door. "Anna."

She turned, a half smile on her lips. "Yes?"

He saw in the smile that she expected, even anticipated an argument. Change tactics and confuse, Daniel thought, and easily drew on his cigar. "It'll have to be seven-thirty. I have a late meeting."

He had the satisfaction of seeing a quick flicker of doubt cross her face before she nodded. "Fine."

When she shut the door at her back, she let out a long pent-up breath.

By his desk, Daniel grinned, chuckled and ultimately roared with laughter. Though he wasn't sure who'd gotten the best of whom, he discovered it didn't matter. He'd always been one to try a new game, new rules. He'd give Anna the cards and the deal. But, by God, he'd still win.

The rain had slowed to a drizzle by the time Anna arrived home. She found the house empty, but the scent of her mother's perfume still lingered in the hallway. Pleased to find herself alone, she went upstairs to indulge in a long hot bath. It was a good feeling, she discovered, to have taken the initiative. Once again she was in control, though her foundation was a bit shakier than it could have been.

Daniel MacGregor was not a man who could be manipulated. She'd learned that right from the beginning. But she did believe he was a man who would respond to negotiation. Her main problem would be to keep him from seeing just how much she'd give.

Everything. She closed her eyes as she squeezed the sponge and dripped hot water over her throat and breasts. If he discovered that, if pressed into a corner, she'd give him anything he wanted, he'd press her there without hesitation. A man like Daniel hadn't made it to the top by being a pushover. But she intended to make it to the top in her own profession, as well. So she had to be equally strong, equally determined.

After she picked him up, they'd have a quiet dinner, easy conversation. Over coffee they'd discuss—rationally—their situation. Before it was over, he would understand her feelings and her position. Anna sank down in the waters with a sigh. Who was she trying to fool? That didn't sound like dinner with Daniel MacGregor for a minute.

They'd spar with each other, argue, disagree and probably laugh a great deal. He'd very likely shout. It was entirely possible she'd shout, as well. When it was over, she doubted he'd understand anything, except that he wanted her to marry him.

Something fluttered inside her at the thought. He did want her. She might have gone through her entire life without anyone looking at her in just the way Daniel did. She might have gone through her life without anyone opening those sturdy locks she'd kept on her passion. What would her life have been like then?

Bland. She smiled at the word that sprang to mind. She certainly wouldn't settle for that now. She wanted Daniel MacGregor. And she was going to have him.

Keeping her self-confidence at a peak was half the battle, she realized as she stepped from the tub. It was so easy for it to slip away degree by degree while he looked at her. She wouldn't allow it to happen tonight. With a towel wrapped around her hair, she bundled into a robe. *She was taking him* to dinner. Whatever slight edge that gave her, she wouldn't lose it.

Opening her closet, she frowned. Usually she knew precisely what best suited an evening she had planned. Tonight, everything she pulled out seemed too fussy, too plain or simply too ordinary. Calling herself a fool, she grabbed a sea-foam-green silk and laid it on her bed. Perhaps it was almost severely simple, but that was very possibly the best idea for the evening. If she wanted something dashing, she mused, she should have raided Myra's closet. As the thought came and went, she heard the doorbell chime.

She found herself grumbling at the interruption, something so out of character that she lectured herself all the way downstairs. As she opened the door, Myra dashed inside and grabbed both her hands.

"Oh, Anna, I'm so glad you're home."

"Myra, I was just thinking about you." By the time the words were out, she noticed the death grip on her fingers. "What's wrong?"

"I have to talk to you." For perhaps the first time in her life Myra found herself almost beyond words. "Alone. Are your parents in?"

"No."

"Good. I need a drink first. Offer me a brandy."

"All right." Amused, Anna began to lead her to the parlor. "Terrific hat."

"Is it?" Myra lifted a worried hand to the off-white cap and veil. "It's not too fussy?"

"Too fussy?" Anna poured her a double brandy. "Let me get this straight. You're asking me if something you're wearing is too fussy?"

"Don't be cute, Anna." Turning to a mirror, Myra toyed with the veil. "Maybe I should pull out the feather."

Anna glanced at the saucy little feather curling over Myra's ear. "Now I know something's wrong."

"How about the dress?" Myra slipped out of a vivid red raincoat to reveal a trim silk suit with lace at the collar and cuffs.

"It's exquisite. Is it new?"

"It's twenty minutes old."

Anna sat on the arm of a chair while her friend gulped down brandy. "You didn't have to dress up for me."

Myra let out a quick breath and straightened her shoulders before she set the empty snifter down. "This is no time for jokes."

"I can see that." But she smiled anyway. "What is it time for?"

"How soon can you toss on something wonderful and pack an overnight bag?"

"Pack?" She watched as Myra fingered the lace at her throat. "Myra, what's going on?"

"I'm getting married." She said it in a rush, then let out a small explosion of breath. Because her legs were unsteady she dropped onto the sofa.

"Getting married?" Stunned Anna sat exactly where she was. "Myra, I know you work fast and I haven't seen much of you in a couple of weeks, but *married*?"

"It wouldn't hurt to say it a few times so I'd stop losing my breath every time I hear the word. I've already babbled to the clerk in the dress shop and I don't want to do that again. If there's one thing I refuse to do, it's make a fool of myself."

"Married," Anna repeated for both of them. "To whom?" As Myra fastened and unfastened the top button of her jacket, Anna groped for a candidate. "Peter?"

"Who? No, no, of course not."

"Of course not," Anna murmured. "I know, Jack Holmes."

"Don't be ridiculous."

"Steven Marlowe."

Myra fiddled with the hem of her skirt. "Anna, really, I hardly know the man."

"Hardly know him? Why six months ago you—"

"That was six months ago," Myra interrupted, blushing for the first time since Anna had known her. "And I'd appreciate it if you'd forget anything I'd ever written you about him. Better yet, burn those letters."

"Darling, they self-destructed the moment I read them. You should have used fire-proof paper."

Despite herself, Myra grinned. "You're speaking to an engaged woman. I've put all that behind me. Look." Breathy with excitement, Myra held out her left hand.

"Oh." She was usually very casual about jewelry herself, but the simple square-cut diamond on Myra's finger seemed impossibly beautiful. "It's exquisite, really exquisite, Myra. I'm so happy for you." She was up and gathering Myra close for a hug before she laughed. "How do I know I'm happy for you? I don't know who you're going to marry."

"Herbert Ditmeyer." Myra waited for the look of astonishment and wasn't disappointed. "I know, I was pretty damn surprised myself."

"But I didn't think you even . . . that is you always said he was . . ." Catching herself, Anna cleared her throat.

"Stuffy," Myra finished and smiled beautifully. "And he is. He's stuffy and rather sober and frustratingly proper. He's also the sweetest man I've ever known. These past couple of weeks . . ." She sat back, a little dreamy, a little stunned. "I never knew what it could be like to have a man treat you as though you were special. Really special. I went out with him the first time, because he'd had such a hard time asking me and I felt sorry for him. And flattered," she admitted. "I went out with him the second time because I'd had such a good time. Herbert can be so funny. It kind of sneaks up on you."

Touched, Anna watched love bloom in Myra's eyes. "I know."

"You were always such a good friend to him. I'm lucky he didn't fall in love with you. The thing is, he's been in love with me for years." With a little shake of her head, she pulled a cigarette from her purse. "We'd been going out for a couple of weeks when he told me. I was so stunned I could hardly speak. Then I tried to ease myself out gently. After all, he was very sweet and I didn't want to hurt him."

Anna lifted the ringed hand again. "It doesn't appear you eased yourself out."

"No." Still dazed, Myra stared at the diamond winking up at her. "It occurred to me all at once that I didn't want to ease myself out, that I was crazy about him. Isn't that wild?"

"I think it's wonderful."

"Me, too." She stubbed out the cigarette without having taken the first puff. "And tonight. Tonight he put this ring on my finger, told me we were flying to Maryland at eight and getting married."

"Tonight." Anna took Myra's hand again. "Tonight. It's so quick, Myra."

"Why wait?"

Why wait, indeed? She could think of hundreds of reasons, but none of them would have gotten past that dreamy look in Myra's eyes. "Are you sure?"

"I'm more sure about this than I've ever been about anything in my life. Be happy for me, Anna."

"I am." Tears swam in her eyes as she held Myra again. "You know I am."

"Then get dressed." Half laughing, half crying, Myra pushed her away. "You're my maid of honor."

"You want me to fly to Maryland tonight?"

"We agreed to elope because it was simpler than dealing with his mother. She doesn't like me and probably never will."

"Oh, Myra—"

"It doesn't matter. Herbert and I love each other. Anyway, I don't want a big fancy wedding. It takes too long. But I don't want to be married without my best friend there. I really need you, Anna. I want this more than anything in the world, and I'm scared to death."

Any objections she might have had disappeared. "I can be dressed and packed in twenty minutes."

Grinning, Myra gave her a last hug. "Because it's you I believe it."

"Just let me leave a note for my parents." She already had the pen in her hand.

"Ah, Anna . . ." Myra ran her tongue over her teeth. "I know your sense of honesty won't let you lie—exactly. Could you just not mention what you're going away for? Herbert and I really want to keep this quiet until we tell his mother."

Anna thought a moment, then began to write. Taking a short trip with Myra. May do some antique shopping—which I may, she added half to herself. I'll be home in a day or two. She signed it and glanced up, showing it to Myra. "Vague enough?"

"Perfectly. Thanks."

"Come on, give me a hand." As she dashed into the hall, she remembered. "Oh, I have to call Daniel and cancel dinner."

"Daniel MacGregor?" Myra's brows arched as only they could.

"That's right." Ignoring the look, Anna headed for the phone. "I'll have to let him know I can't make it tonight."

"You can have dinner with him in Maryland." Myra took the receiver from her and replaced it. "Herbert's asking him to be best man."

"I see." Anna brushed a hand casually down her robe. "Well, that's handy, isn't it?"

"Very." With a grin, Myra pulled her upstairs.

CHAPTER 9

She'd never flown before. At twenty, Anna had sailed to Europe in luxury and comfort. She'd traveled hundreds of miles on trains, lulled by the swaying motion and watching the landscape whiz by. But she'd never been in the air. If anyone had told her she'd be climbing into a small private plane that looked as though it could land safely in her backyard, she'd have thought them mad.

Love, she thought as she set her teeth and took the last step inside. If she didn't love Myra, she'd turn around and run for her life. She was certain the tin can with propellers could get off the ground. She wished she felt as confident about how it would get down again.

"Quite a machine, isn't it?" Daniel watched Anna take her seat before he settled in his own.

"Quite," she muttered and wondered if it came with parachutes.

"First flight?"

She started to give him a stiff and dignified yes,

then saw he wasn't laughing at her. "Yeah." The word came out on a little breath.

"Try to think of it as an adventure," he suggested.

She glanced at the ground outside the window and wished she were still standing on it. "I'm trying not to think of it at all."

"You've more guts than that, Anna. I should know." Then he grinned at her. "It should be an adventure the first time. After a while flying becomes routine, and you really don't think much about it."

She told herself to relax and used the old trick of starting at her toes and working up. She never got past her knees. "I guess you're used to it. Is this the sort of plane you fly to New York in?"

With a chuckle he fastened her seat belt, then his own. "This is the plane I fly to New York in. I own it."

"Oh." As his words sank in she found that the fact that it was Daniel's plane somehow made flying in it all right. She glanced over to where Myra and Herbert were seated and strapped in, heads together. An adventure, she decided. She'd enjoy one. "So when do we start?"

"There's a lass," he murmured and signaled to the pilot. The engine started with a roar and they were off.

Though her anxiety had passed, there was an air of both celebration and tension all through the flight. Anna saw the tension in Myra as her friend twisted a lace handkerchief into knots as she laughed and talked. Herbert sat, a little pale, a little stiff, and spoke only when prodded. For herself, Anna heard the voices around her, watched the landscape beneath her with a sense of unreality. It was all happening so fast. If it hadn't been for Daniel's easy jokes and constant banter, the celebrational part of the flight might have dissolved into mild hysteria. He was, Anna noted as he flirted outrageously with Myra, enjoying himself. And while he was about it, he was keeping the bride-to-be from climbing the walls of the cabin. He wasn't just an interesting man, she realized. He was a good friend. Pulling herself out of her thoughts, Anna made an effort to be as good.

"You have excellent taste, Herbert."

"What?" He swallowed and straightened his tie. "Oh, yes. Thank you." Then he looked at Myra with his heart in his eyes. "She's wonderful, isn't she?"

"The best. I don't know what I'd have done without her. Life certainly would have been a great deal duller."

"We serious-minded people need someone with a little sparkle in our lives, don't we?" He gave Anna a nervous smile. "Otherwise, we'd just crawl into our careers and forget there was anything else out there."

Serious minded? She let the phrase play in her head. Yes, she supposed she was. In addition, she was coming to understand that Herbert was right. "And people with—sparkle," she murmured with a glance at Myra and Daniel, "need a serious-minded person in their lives to keep them from running off cliffs."

"I'm going to make her happy."

Because his words sounded more like a question than a statement, Anna took his hands. "Oh, yes. You're going to make her very happy."

The small private plane touched down in a rural airport in Maryland. The lingering drizzle had been left behind. Here, the late-evening sky was as clear as glass and crowded with stars. The sliver of moon was like a smile. It might have been a wedding night chosen on impulse, but it was perfect. Taking Myra by the arm, Herbert led the way to the little terminal.

"The justice of the peace who was recommended

to me is only about twenty miles from here. I'll check about getting a cab or a car."

"That won't be necessary." When they entered the terminal Daniel quickly scanned it then signaled to a tall uniformed chauffeur.

"Mr. MacGregor?"

"Aye. Give him the directions," he told Herbert. "I took the liberty of arranging for transportation."

Without fuss, the chauffeur gathered the suitcases and led the way outside. At the curb was a pearl-gray stretch limo.

"You didn't give a body much time to come up with a wedding present," Daniel explained. "This was the best I could do."

"It's perfect." With a laugh, Myra swung her arms around him. "Absolutely perfect."

Daniel winked at Herbert over her head. "The best man's supposed to handle the details."

Anna waited until Herbert had helped Myra inside. "This was very sweet of you."

"I'm a sweet man," he told her.

She laughed and accepted his hand. "Maybe. I wouldn't depend on it."

Inside, Myra already had her arm linked through Herbert's. "Two bottles of champagne?"

"One for before." Daniel lifted one from its bucket of ice. "One for after." He let out a cork with a hiss and a pop then poured four glasses. "To happiness."

Four glasses clinked solemnly together, but when Daniel drank, he looked at Anna. As the champagne exploded in her mouth, she realized the adventure was far from over.

By the time they arrived at the little white house, all the champagne and the lingering tension had been drained. With her usual aplomb, Myra tidied her hair and makeup in a powder room off the hall while Anna stood by and held her hat. She took her time, but Anna noted that her hands were steady.

"How do I look?" Myra demanded, and managed a quick turn in the cramped room.

"Beautiful."

"I've always been a couple of degrees away from beautiful, but tonight I think I've nearly managed stunning."

Hands firm, Anna turned her toward the mirror again. "Tonight you're beautiful. Take a good look."

Looking at their reflections together, Myra grinned. "He really loves me, Anna."

"I know." She slipped her arm around Myra's shoulder. "You're going to make quite a team."

"Yes, we are." As her chin tilted up, her grin softened into a smile. "I don't think he realizes just how much of a team yet, but he will." On a quick breath she turned and took Anna by the shoulders. "I don't like to get sentimental, but since I only intend to get married once, this seems to be the time. You're my best friend and I love you. I want you to be as happy as I am this minute."

"I'm working on it."

Satisfied, Myra nodded. "Okay then, let's go. And listen—" she put her hand on the knob and paused "—if I stutter, don't tell anyone—especially Catherine Donahue."

Solemn eyed, Anna put a hand over her heart. "I won't tell a soul."

In a parlor with a tiny marble fireplace and summer flowers in glass vases, Anna watched her closest friend promise to love, honor and cherish. When her eyes misted, she felt foolish and tried to blink them clear. It was silly to cry over two adults making a legal contract with each other. Marriage was, after all, a contract. That was why it had to be approached so cautiously, so practically. But the first tear escaped and ran slowly down her cheek. She felt Daniel press his handkerchief into her hand as he'd done once before. Even as she sniffed into it, the ceremony was over and she found herself hugging a dazed Myra.

"I did it," Myra murmured, then laughed and gave Anna a rib-crushing squeeze.

"And without one single stutter."

"I did it," she repeated and held out her hand. Snuggled next to the diamond was a slim gold band. "Engaged and married within five hours."

Daniel took the hand she was admiring and kissed it formally. "Mrs. Ditmeyer."

Chuckling, Myra curled her fingers around his. "Be sure to call me that several times this evening so I'll learn to answer to it. Oh, Anna, I'm going to cry and destroy my mascara."

"It's all right." Anna handed her Daniel's already crumpled handkerchief. "Herbert's stuck with you now." Anna wound her arms around him and held tight.

He laughed and gave Anna a long, hard squeeze. "And she's stuck with me."

"She'll complicate your life."

"I know."

"Isn't it wonderful?" Anna kissed him hard. "I don't know about you, but I'm starving. The wedding supper is on me."

Through the recommendation of the justice of the peace and the help of the chauffeur, they found a country inn at the peak of a wooded hill. It was, as they'd been told, small, quaint and possibly closed. With a little persuasion, and the exchange of a few bills, they persuaded the owner to open the restaurant and wake up the cook. While the others were led into the dining room, Anna made an excuse about freshening up and slipped aside. Moments later, she waylaid the owner again.

"Mr. Portersfield, I can't thank you enough for accommodating us."

Though he was always glad to receive paying guests, the lateness of the hour had put him a bit out of sorts. He found it difficult, however, to resist the smile Anna sent him. "My doors are always open," he told her. "Unfortunately the kitchen closes at nine, so the meal may not quite live up to our reputation."

"I'm sure everything will be wonderful. As a matter of fact, I can almost promise that my friends will tell you it's the best meal they've ever eaten. You see—" linking her arm through his, she strolled a little farther away from the others "—they were just married a half hour ago. That's why you and I have to arrange a few things."

"Newlyweds." Mr. Portersfield wasn't a man completely without romance. "We're always pleased to have newlyweds at the inn. If we'd had just a bit of notice—"

"Oh, I'm sure the few things we need won't be too much bother. Did I mention that Mr. Ditmeyer is the district attorney in Boston? I'm sure when he gets back from his honeymoon with his new bride, he's going to praise your inn to all his friends. And Mr. MacGregor—" she lowered her voice "—well, I don't have to tell you who he is."

He didn't have the vaguest idea, but implied importance was enough. "No, of course, not."

"A man in his position doesn't often find a quiet place like this to relax. Home cooking, country air. I can assure you he's very impressed by your establishment. Tell me, Mr. Portersfield, do you have a record player?"

"A record player? I have one in my room, but—"

"Perfect." Anna patted his hand and tried the smile again. "I knew you'd be able to help me."

Fifteen minutes later, she was back in the dining room. At the table was a loaf of crusty bread, a pot of butter and little else.

"Where'd you disappear to?" Daniel asked as she took her seat.

"Details. To the bride and groom," she said and lifted her water glass.

As they toasted, Myra laughed. "And I was just about to say to Herbert that he can look forward to many meals just like this—" she indicated the bread and water "—until we get a cook."

He took her hand and brought it to his lips. "I didn't marry you for your culinary prowess."

"A good thing," Anna said, then added, "she hasn't any."

A sleepy boy of about fifteen came into the room with a vase of wildflowers. A look at the dew on the petals told Anna they'd just been picked. It looked as if Mr. Portersfield was going to come through.

"Oh, how pretty." Myra reached to pluck one out as the boy wandered away and began to pull tables across the floor. Loudly. Mr. Portersfield shuffled into the room, lugging a phonograph. Within moments, there was music.

"The first dance for the Herbert Ditmeyers," Anna stated, and gestured to the space the boy had cleared on the floor. When they were alone at the table, Daniel buttered a chunk of bread and handed it to her. "You accomplished quite a lot in a short time."

Hungry, Anna bit into the bread. "Just the beginning, Mr. MacGregor."

"You know, when you asked me to dinner tonight, I had no idea we'd be having it in a country inn in Maryland."

Anna broke off another hunk of bread, buttered it and handed it to him. "I'd intended to keep things a bit closer to home myself."

"They look happy."

She glanced over to see Myra and Herbert smiling at each other as they moved around the tiny cleared space. "Yes, they do. Funny, I never pictured them together. Now that I see them, it seems so perfect."

"Contrasts." He took his palm and pressed it against hers. His was wide and hard, hers narrow and soft. "They make life more interesting."

"I've come to believe it." She linked fingers with him. "Lately."

With a smile that spread from ear to ear, Mr. Portersfield brought over a tray of salad. "You'll enjoy this," he told them as he served. "Everything straight from our own garden. The dressing is an old family recipe." After setting down the salad bowls, he fussed briefly with the flowers and then was off again.

"He certainly looks more cheerful," Daniel commented.

"And so he should," Anna murmured thinking just how much she'd paid to put a smile on his face. "Daniel . . ." Thoughtfully, she stabbed her fork into the salad. "About that loan you mentioned this afternoon." She took her first bite of the salad and found it as good as advertised. "I might want to take you up on it—just until we get back to Boston."

Daniel glanced over in time to see Portersfield heading into the kitchen, then looked back to see

Anna's eyes dark with humor. He'd never needed anyone to add two and two for him. On a roar of laughter, he took her face in his hands and kissed her. "Interest free for you, love."

There was champagne—the only two bottles to be had at the inn. There was pot roast that melted on the fork and a scratchy Billie Holiday record. When Daniel took Myra to the impromptu dance floor, she didn't waste time beating around the bush.

"You're in love with Anna."

Because he saw no reason to deny it, he ignored her bluntness. "Aye."

"What do you intend to do about it?"

He looked down. In the comfort of his beard, his lips twitched. "I could say that was none of your business."

"You could," Myra agreed. "But I intend to find out, anyway."

After a moment's thought he decided it was best to have her on his side. "I'd have married her tonight, but she's too damn stubborn."

"Or smart." Myra smiled when she saw the heat flash in his eyes. "Oh, I like you, Daniel. I did right away. But I know a steamroller when I see one."

"Like recognizes like."

"Exactly." Pleased rather than insulted, Myra matched her steps to his. "Anna's going to be a doctor, probably the best surgeon in the country."

He scowled down at her. "What would you know about doctors?"

"I know about Anna," she said easily. "And I think I know enough about men to guess that that doesn't suit you very well."

"I want a wife," he muttered, "not a knife wielder."

"I imagine you'd have more respect for a surgeon if you needed your appendix out."

"I wouldn't want my wife to do the cutting."

"If you want Anna, you'd better be prepared to take her career. Have you asked her to marry you?"

"You're nosy."

"Of course. Have you?"

American women, he thought. Would he ever acclimatize? "I did."

"And?"

"She says she won't marry me, but she'll live with me."

"That sounds sensible."

Daniel drew her hand down so they both could see the ring gleam on Myra's finger.

"Oh, that's entirely different. I love Herbert very much, but I wouldn't have married him unless I was certain he accepted me for what I am."

"Which is?"

"Nosy, meddling, flamboyant and ambitious." Her gaze drifted toward the table. "I'm going to make him a hell of a wife."

Daniel looked down at her. Her eyes might have been dewy with love, but her chin was set. "I believe you will."

Daniel had just pulled back Myra's chair when Portersfield wheeled up a cart with a small layer cake with frothy white icing and pink rosebuds. With considerable charm, he handed Myra a silver flat-edged knife.

"With the compliments of the inn," he told her, knowing he could afford to be generous. "Our best wishes to both of you for a long and happy marriage."

"Thank you." Finding herself near tears, Myra waited until Herbert wrapped his fingers around hers on the handle.

Anna waited until the champagne was empty and the cake little more than crumbs. "One more thing." She took a key from her purse and gave it to Herbert. "The bridal suite."

He slipped it into his pocket with a grin. "I didn't think a little place like this would have one."

"It didn't until a couple of hours ago." She accepted the hugs then watched the newlyweds walk away together.

"I like your style, Anna Whitfield."

"Do you?" Buoyed by success and champagne, she smiled at him. With her eyes on his she reached in her purse again. "I have another key."

Daniel glanced down to the single key in her palm. "You tend to take matters in your own hands."

Lifting a brow, she rose. "If it doesn't suit you, you can wake Portersfield up again. I'm sure he can find you another room."

He stood, took her wrist and plucked the key from her hand. "This'll do."

With her hand in his, they left the remains of the wedding supper behind.

They didn't speak as they climbed the stairs, which creaked slightly under their weight. There was a light at the top to guide them, shielded in beveled glass and dim. All the doors they passed were closed. The inn, so recently disturbed for a celebration, was quiet. When Daniel unlocked the door to their room, he smelled the spicy mix of potpourri. It made him think of his grandmother, of Scotland, of all he'd left behind. When Anna closed the door behind them, he thought of nothing but her. Still they didn't speak.

She turned the key on a little globed lamp by the door. Subtle light spilled into the room and pooled at their feet. The windows were open to let in the warm summer air. Thin curtains stirred with it. And just barely audible, from the woods beyond came the melancholy song of a night bird.

She waited. Once, on a cliff top, she'd gone to him. Now she needed him to turn to her. Her heart was already his, though she feared to tell him. Her body would never belong to another. But she waited, touched by lamplight, surrounded by summer air.

He thought she'd never looked more lovely, though he already had dozens of memories of her locked in his mind. Dozens of fantasies. Passion, needs, love, dreams—she was all of them. His heart took the first step, and he followed.

His hands cupped her face gently, so gently that she could barely feel the pressure of his fingers on her skin. Still, the touch rippled through her. His eyes never left hers as he lowered his mouth. The kiss was soft, a bare meeting of lips, a mingling of breath. Eyes open, bodies close, they explored the sensations evoked by the teasing and brushing of mouth against mouth, the tangling and retreating of tongues.

He touched only her face; she touched him not at all, and yet in seconds two hearts were pounding.

How long they stood like that she couldn't be sure. It might have been hours or only seconds while their needs built and twisted together into a desire that bordered on pain. With a moan of delight, she let her head fall back. Her arms came around him. For an instant, the kiss deepened toward delirium. She felt her bones liquefy from her toes up until her body was a fluid mass of sensation. Reveling in it, she went limp in his arms in unqualified surrender.

It nearly drove him mad. To have Anna, strong and eager, made his blood heat and his passion soar. But to have Anna, soft and pliant, was devastatingly arousing. It made him weak. It made him strong. She seemed to seep into him degree by degree until there was no room for anything but her.

He drew back, shaken by the intensity, wary of the merging. But she stood as she was, head thrown back, arms twined around him. It was more than need he saw in her eyes, more even than knowledge. It was acceptance. He waited, his body pulsing, until his mind was nearly clear again. Then he undressed her.

The thin, almost transparent jacket she wore over her dress slid away like an illusion. He let his hands roam up her arms, over her shoulders and back again so that he could feel the skin, the muscles, the texture. And as he lingered, bewitched by the thrill of his flesh against hers, she loosened his tie then tossed it aside. Slowly, while her own blood heated to his touch, she drew his jacket from his shoulders.

He was losing himself in her again but now it didn't seem to matter. While the summer breeze sighed through the windows behind them, he pulled down the zipper of her dress. Like the breeze, it drifted to the floor.

She heard him catch his breath and felt a wild, almost wanton pride in her own body. While she stood, he seemed to drink in the sight of her, inch by inch. Her skin hummed as though his hands had stroked it. The cameo he had given her nestled in the hollow of her throat. He could trace it with his finger and feel her profile come to life. The lacy fantasy she wore was caught snug at her breast and draped lazily at her thighs. The lamplight threw her silhouette into relief and made him hunger for what he already had.

Her fingers weren't steady as she unbuttoned his shirt, but her eyes never left his. More from desire than confidence, her palms stroked over him as his shirt joined her dress on the floor.

Somewhere in the inn a clock rang out the hour, but they'd long since forgotten such things as time and place. In unspoken agreement, they lowered themselves to the bed.

Under their weight, the old mattress creaked softly. Feather pillows yielded. He braced himself above her, needing to see her, all of her. He might have stayed like that for hours, but she reached for him.

Mouth against mouth, heated, impatient. Flesh to flesh, trembling, sensitive. The lamplight cast their shadows on the wall. The breeze carried off their sighs. The night bird still sang plaintively in the woods. They no longer heard. The world they both knew so much of, the world they both were so determined to discover had been whittled down to one room. Ambitions faded and died in the face of more desperate desires. To give, to take and to experience. To possess and to be possessed.

He buried his face against her skin and no longer noticed the scent of spices and dried flowers that wafted through the room. There was no fragrance but Anna, no taste but Anna, no voice but Anna's. Slowly, but not so gently, he took his mouth on a searing journey down her throat, over the lace and silk clinging to her breasts. Need thundered in his blood as she strained against him. With their hands caught tightly together, he let his tongue lap at the subtle curve just above the lace. With their legs tangled, he let his teeth scrape lightly over her flesh. When she called out his name, he vowed to bring her the thrill and the glory of madness.

Through the silk, his lips pulled and tugged on her nipple until it was hard and hot in his mouth and her body was as taut as a bowstring. He heard her breath tremble when he paused, then heard it catch in her throat as he turned all his skill to her other breast.

Just as slowly, just as ruthlessly, just as devastatingly, he worked his way over her body, touching off fires she hadn't known were there to be kindled. With his tongue and wide-palmed hands he took her again and again to the edge of release. She'd never known torture could be so glorious or pleasure so painful. Her skin was damp when he pulled the last barrier away from it.

She was caught in a haze of delights—dark, secret, desperate delights. The air was heavy and tasted of him as she drew in labored breaths. Everywhere he touched, flames burned. His beard brushed over the soft skin of her belly and set off an inferno of sensation. Her hands found his hair and stroked it as the lamplight turned even this to fire.

Her mind spinning, she locked her arms around his waist. Still riding a crest of sensation she rolled with him, her hands seeking, reaching, finding. She felt him quiver and pressed her mouth to his skin, tasting desire. Before he could anticipate, before he could prepare, she slid down and took him into her.

Sounds burst in her head. Perhaps it was her name on Daniel's lips. Chills coursed along her flesh. They might have been his strong fingers caressing her. As she threw her head back, abandoned, delighted, she saw his eyes on hers. The deep brilliant blue held its own fire, hotter, stronger than any other. Love. Clinging to it, she took them both beyond reason.

Sated and breathless, she still held tight, and her eyes closed, locked everything into her: the scent of him, the feel of his skin warmed from hers, the sound of his breathing, fast and harsh in her ear, the look of his hand closed tight around hers.

It was here she wanted to stay. And if the rest of the world and all other needs could be ignored, she would. If he were to ask now, if he were even to demand now, she was afraid she would give him all.

A hand moved down her back in one long stroke. Possession. She trembled a bit and knew she could do little to prevent it. Whatever else she wanted, whatever else she was, she belonged to him.

Her body was so small that it seemed almost weightless as she lay on him. He could feel the slight trembles, the aftershocks of passion. He couldn't live without her. He could wheel and deal and blithely slit the throat of a competitor, but he couldn't function any longer without the small serious woman whose hand was still locked in his.

Your way then, damn it. Even as he cursed her, he hooked an arm around her.

"You'll move in with me tomorrow." Grabbing a handful of hair he drew her head back. Her way, but he wasn't giving in. "You'll pack what you have when we get back to Boston. I won't spend another night without you."

Unable to speak, she stared at him. There were dregs of desire in his eyes mixed with the fury just breaking. How did she handle a man like Daniel? Anna had a feeling it would take more than a few weeks to learn. "Tomorrow?"

"That's right. You move into my house tomorrow. Do you have anything to say about it?"

She thought a moment, then smiled. "You'd better make room in your closet."

CHAPTER 10

Anna had her first tour of her new home under the guidance of a stiff-backed, tight-lipped McGee. She wondered which of them was more uncomfortable. Her bags had barely been carried upstairs when Daniel had been called to the bank on urgent business. He'd left, annoyed, with a quick kiss of reassurance for her and an absentminded order to McGee to show her around. So she was there alone with a politely indignant butler and a cook who had yet to poke her head out of the kitchen.

Her first reaction was to think of an excuse and go to the hospital where she belonged. Taking the afternoon off hadn't been anything she could afford to do any more than Daniel could. Now he was gone, and she was here. Something about the straight, unyielding back of the man who led her up the stairs had her holding her ground. For Anna, pride went hand in hand with dignity. She'd made her decision, and if a butler happened to be the first to disapprove, she'd accept it. More, she was going to learn to live with it. Starting now.

"We have several guest rooms on this floor," McGee told her in his low, rolling brogue. "Mr. MacGregor also keeps his office on this level, as he finds it convenient."

"I see."

McGee tested a small tilt-top table for dust as they went. Anna had a moment to reflect that it was fortunate for whoever was in charge of the dust department that McGee didn't find any. "Mr. MacGregor entertains out-of-town business associates from time to time. We keep two guest rooms prepared. This is the master bedroom." So saying he opened a thick, hand-tooled door.

The room was large, as Daniel seemed to prefer, but sparsely decorated, as though he spent little time there. She imagined his office would be cluttered with furniture and piled with papers, more revealing of the inner man than his bedroom, which should have been the more personal room. There were no photographs, no mementos. The paint was new and the curtains stiff with starch. She wondered if he'd ever pushed them aside to look at the view. The bed was big enough for four and of lovingly carved oak. Her bags sat neatly at the foot.

She'd expected to feel odd, walking into this intimate room for the first time. She felt little but a sense of vague curiosity. There was more of Daniel MacGregor on a cliff above the sea than there was in the room where he spent his nights. But this wasn't the time to try to dissect a puzzle where she hadn't expected to find one. Her chin was lifted just a tad higher than usual when she turned back to McGee.

"Mr. MacGregor wasn't clear on the housekeeping arrangements. Is that your responsibility?"

If McGee could have stiffened his already

ramrod-straight back, he would have. "A day maid comes in three times a week. Otherwise, I oversee the housekeeping. However, Mr. MacGregor informed both myself and the cook that you may wish changes."

If Daniel had walked in the door at that moment, Anna would cheerfully have strangled him. Instead, she took another deliberate study of the room. "I hardly think that will be necessary, McGee. You seem to be not only a man who knows his job, but his own worth."

Her coolly delivered compliment didn't soften him a whit, nor was it intended to. "Thank you, miss. Would you care to see the rest of the second floor?"

"Not at the moment. I think I'll unpack." And be alone, she thought desperately.

"Very well, miss." With a bow he walked to the door. "If you need anything you've only to ring."

"Thank you, McGee. I won't."

The moment he shut the door, she sank down on the enormous bed. What had she done? Every doubt she'd been able to hide, thrust aside or bury until that point came rushing out. She'd moved out of her childhood home, not into her own pretty little apartment, but into a big, rambling house where she was a stranger. A usurper. And to the stiff-lipped McGee, obviously a Jezebel. If she hadn't had her own nerves to deal with, that one point might have amused.

She'd left a nervous mother and a stunned father and had come to a huge half-empty room. She wasn't at the hospital, where the hurdles she had to navigate were at least familiar, if difficult. Nothing here belonged to her but what was in the bags at the foot of the bed.

Slowly she ran her hand over the thick white bed cover. Now, night after night, she thought, she'd be sharing this bed with Daniel. Sleeping with him, waking with him. There'd be no more simple good-nights and a retreat into privacy. He'd be there, within reach. And so would she.

What had she done? Panic rose. Gamely, Anna swallowed it. Her hand still stroked the cover. In a mirror on the far wall she saw herself—small, pale and wide-eyed on the too-big bed. She saw, too, the reflection of an oak chest of drawers, clean lined and masculine. Her legs were a little shaky as she rose to walk to it. Her fingers seemed a bit numb as she slipped the lid from a bottle of cologne. Then she smelled him—brash, vivid and very male. Her world seemed to steady. When she replaced the lid, her hands were firm and competent again.

What had she done? she asked herself for the last time. Exactly what she'd wanted to do. With a little laugh of relief, she began to unpack.

It didn't take long to distribute her things throughout the room. She'd taken little more than clothes and a few favorite pictures from her room. Still, after her things were tidied away, she felt more at ease, and somehow more at home. Of course, they would have to see about getting a dresser to match the nineteenth-century oak furniture Daniel had chosen for the room. The curtains would have to go in favor of something softer and more friendly.

Pleased, she glanced around again. It had never occurred to her that she would get such a charge out of making a few basic domestic decisions. Perhaps it wasn't anything like deciding whether to operate or treat internally, but it did bring a sense of satisfaction. Perhaps she could indeed have everything. At the moment, she thought, she was going to start by cornering McGee and going in search of a couple of comfortable chairs for the master bedroom. And a good reading lamp, she thought as she walked into the hall. If possible, she'd add a small desk for herself. The room was certainly big enough. Surely in a house this size they could find a few things that would suit. If they couldn't, she'd simply do a bit of shopping after her shift at the hospital the next day.

Once on the first floor, she was tempted to poke into the parlor or library and do some shifting herself. She held herself back for the simple reason that she understood pride. If she were to take on the project herself, it would surely damage McGee's. She would find a way to tactfully change what she wanted changed without damaging his butlerly ego. McGee was part of Daniel's life. If she were to make a success out of her decision, she would have to see that he was a part of hers.

Because she could think of no other logical place to find him, she headed for the kitchen. A few steps away from the door, she heard the voices and paused.

"If the lass is good enough for the MacGregor, she's good enough for me." It was a feminine voice but as musically Scottish as the butler's. "I see no reason for your griping, McGee."

"I don't gripe." Even through the wood, Anna detected the cool indignation. "The girl has no business here without a marriage license."

"Pish posh."

With that chuckled exclamation, Anna decided she could like the cook very well.

"Since when are you judge and confessor, I'd like to know. The MacGregor knows his mind, and so, I'd wager, does the lass, or he wouldn't give her the time of day. It's what she looks like that I want to know. Is she pretty?"

"Pretty enough," McGee muttered. "At least she has the good sense not to flaunt herself."

"Flaunt herself," the cook repeated even as Anna indignantly mouthed the phrase. "A woman makes herself up for a man, and she's flaunting herself. She doesn't, and she has good sense. I don't know which is more of the insult. Now, go on about your business and I'll be about mine, or I'll be too busy to have a look at her before dinner."

Anna was trying to decide whether to retreat or brazen it out when a cry of pain made her rush into the room. McGee was already bending over a plump white-haired woman. On the floor between them was a long-handled knife smeared with blood. Even as Anna dashed toward them, more blood was pooling at their feet.

"Let me see."

"Miss Whitfield—"

"Move!" Abandoning propriety, she shoved the butler aside. It only took a glance to show her that a slip of the knife had gashed the cook's wrist and knicked an artery. In an instant she pressed her fingers over it and stopped the pump of blood.

"It's nothing, miss." But tears were coursing down the woman's face. "I'll make a mess of you."

"Hush." Anna plucked up a dry dishcloth and tossed it at McGee. "Tear this into strips then go bring my car around."

Used to responding to authority, he began to rip. Still holding the cook's wrist, Anna led her to a chair. "Just be calm," she soothed.

"Blood," the cook managed, and went parchment white.

"We're going to take care of it." Anna continued to talk calmly, knowing how difficult it would be to manage the big woman if she keeled over. "McGee, tie a strip on her arm, just here." She indicated where he should fasten the tourniquet while she continued to close the artery with her fingers. "All right now, what's your name?"

"Sally, miss."

"All right, Sally, I want you just to close your eyes and relax. Not too tight," she cautioned McGee. "Bring the car around quickly. I'll want you to drive."

"Yes, miss." At twice his normal gait and none of his usual dignity, he scurried from the room.

"Now, Sally, can you walk?"

"I'll try. I feel light-headed."

"Of course you do," Anna murmured. "Lean on me. We're going right out the kitchen door to the car. We'll be at the hospital in five minutes."

"To the hospital." Beneath Anna's hand the woman's arm began to shake. "I don't like hospitals."

"There's nothing to worry about. I'll stay with you. I work there. Some of the doctors are very handsome." As she spoke, she eased the cook up and began to help her to the door. "So handsome you'll ask yourself why you didn't cut yourself before." By the time they got through the door, McGee was there to take most of the woman's weight.

A fine job of emergency first aid, Miss Whitfield." Dr. Liederman rinsed his hands in a basin as he spoke to Anna. "Without it, I'd wager that woman would have bled to death before she made it to the hospital."

Anna had gotten a good look at the wound and estimated the need for ten stitches once the artery had been sealed. "A bad place for the knife to slip."

"We get suicides that don't do that good a job. A lucky thing for her you didn't panic."

Anna lifted a brow, wondering if he considered that a compliment. "If blood made me panic, I'd make a poor surgeon."

"Surgery, is it?" She hadn't chosen an easy road. He glanced over his shoulder as he finished scrubbing the cook's blood from his hands. "It takes more than skill to use a scalpel, you know. It takes confidence."

"I thought it was arrogance," she said with a small smile.

It took him several seconds before he returned the smile. "A more accurate term. Now as to our patient, she'll be weak for a day or two and probably favor that hand for two or three weeks."

"You want the dressing changed every day?"

"Yes and kept dry. I'll want her back in a couple of weeks to take the stitches out." He turned then, drying his hands. "Though I don't imagine you'd have any trouble doing that for her."

She smiled again. "I wouldn't think of it—for another few months."

"You know, Miss Whitfield, you have a good reputation in this hospital."

That surprised her, but she reserved the pleasure. "Do I?"

"Yes, you do. And that's from the horse's mouth." He tossed the towel aside when she only stared. "The nurses."

The pleasure came now. "I appreciate that."

"You're going into your last year of medical school. I've seen enough to judge your . . . confidence. How are your grades?"

Pride lifted her chin. "Excellent."

With a little laugh, he studied her. "I appreciate that. Where do you want to intern?"

"Here."

He held out a hand. "Look me up."

Anna accepted it. "I'll do that."

So where in hell was everybody? Daniel had come home to find the house empty. Impatient to be with Anna, he'd taken the steps two at a time and burst into the master bedroom. He'd had to look at the closet to assure himself she'd actually been there. Though he'd found himself pleased to see her clothes hanging neatly beside his, it wasn't quite the welcome he'd had in mind. After a quick check of the second floor, he'd started down again.

"McGee!" Cursing all servants, he came to a halt on the landing and scowled. Bad enough his woman wasn't home, but now his butler had disappeared. "McGee!"

Opening and slamming doors as he went, he worked his way down the hall. He hadn't expected a brass band, but he'd thought someone might have found the time to be around when he got home. By the time he had entered the kitchen door, his temper was peaking.

"Where the devil is everyone?"

"Will you stop shouting?" Her voice pitched low, Anna stepped into the room. "I've just this minute gotten her into bed."

"A man ought to be able to shout in his own home," Daniel began, then his temper cleared enough for him to see the blood splattered over Anna's blouse and skirt. "Sweet God!" He closed the distance between them in two steps then swept her against him. "What have you done to yourself? Where are you hurt? I'll get you to the hospital."

"I've just been there." But she wasn't quick enough to stop him from taking her up in his arms. "Daniel, it's not my blood. I'm not hurt. Daniel!" He was nearly out the kitchen door before she could stop him. "Sally had an accident, not me."

"Sally?"

"Your cook," she began.

"I know who Sally is," he snapped at her, then gathered her close as relief shuddered through him. "You're not hurt?"

"No." Her tone softened. He was trembling. Who would have expected it? "I'm fine," she managed to tell him just before his mouth closed over hers. Passion soared, and through it she felt his relief, which was nearly as wild. Moved, she let him take whatever comfort he wanted. "Daniel, I didn't mean to frighten you."

"Well, you did." He kissed her again, hard, and was steadier. "What happened to Sally?"

"Apparently her hands were wet, and she wasn't paying as close attention to her chopping as she might have been. The knife slipped and slashed her at the wrist. She hit an artery. That's why there's so much blood. It's a serious cut, but McGee and I got her to the hospital. She's resting now. She'll need a couple of days off."

For the first time he noticed the chopping knife and the blood on the floor by the sink. With an oath, he tightened his grip on Anna. "I'll go in to her."

"No, please." From her position in his arms, she managed to stop him. "She's sleeping. It would really be better to wait until morning."

His cook, like his butler, like every one of his

employees was his responsibility. He glanced at the knife again and swore. "You're sure she's all right."

"I'm sure. She lost a good bit of blood, but I was right outside the door when it happened. Then once McGee realized I knew what I was doing, he couldn't have been more helpful."

"And where is he?"

"Parking my car. Here he is now," Anna corrected herself as the butler came through the kitchen door.

"Mr. MacGregor"—a bit pale, but as proper as ever, McGee stopped just inside the door—"I'll have this mess cleaned up right away. I'm afraid dinner will be delayed."

"So I'm told. Miss Whitfield said you were very helpful, McGee."

Something—it might have been an emotion—flickered across his face. "I'm afraid I did very little, sir. Miss Whitfield was very efficient, and if I may say so, sir, plucky."

Anna had to swallow a chuckle. "Thank you, McGee."

"Don't worry about dinner. We'll see to ourselves."

"Very good, sir. Good night, miss."

"Good night, McGee." The kitchen door swung shut behind them. "Daniel, you can put me down now."

"No." Easily he started up the stairs. "This isn't the welcome I'd wanted for you."

She hadn't realized how good it could feel to be carried as though you were something precious. "I hadn't planned it this way myself."

He paused on the stairs to nuzzle her neck. "I'm sorry."

"It wasn't anyone's fault."

God, she tasted so good. Every hunger he had could be sated with her alone. "You've ruined your blouse."

"Now you sound like Sally. She muttered about that all the way to the hospital."

"I'll buy you a new one."

"Thank goodness," she said and laughed at him. "Daniel, don't we have anything more important to do than worry about my blouse?"

"Do you know what I was thinking of the entire time I sat through that damned meeting?"

"No. What?"

"Making love to you. In my bed. Our bed."

"I see." As he pushed open the door, she linked her hands behind his head. Her pulse was already beginning to race. Anticipation. Imagination. "Do you know what I thought about as I was unpacking my things?"

"No. What?"

"Making love to you. In your bed. Our bed."

Hearing her say that made the room he rarely noticed seem special. "Then we should do something about it."

With her hands still linked behind his head, he tumbled with her onto the thick white cover.

It was easier to live with Daniel, to wake with him, to sleep with him than Anna could have imagined. It seemed to her that the part of her life she had lived without him had been no more than anticipation. Yet their first weeks together weren't without adjustments. Though she had lived most of her life with her parents and the rest in the regimentation of college, Anna had always managed to move at her own pace and protect her privacy.

It was an entirely different matter to wake up with someone beside her. Especially when that someone was a man who viewed the hours spent in sleep as a waste of vital time. Daniel MacGregor wasn't one to loiter in bed or to linger over coffee. Mornings were for business, and morning started the moment his eyes opened.

Because her system was on a different time clock, she usually found herself wandering down for her first cup of coffee when Daniel was finishing his second and last cup. Goodbyes were brief and hurried and anything but romantic. Daniel and his briefcase were out the door before her mind was completely ready to function. Not exactly a honeymoon, she'd thought more than once when she settled down to a solitary breakfast, but it was a routine she could live with.

By the time she drove to the hospital, Daniel was already wheeling and dealing. While she folded linens and read to patients, he played the stock market and planned mergers and takeovers. In living with him, Anna had a better view of just how powerful Daniel was and how potentially powerful he could become. She herself had taken a call from a senator and relayed a message from the governor of New York.

Politics, she began to realize, was an aspect of his career she had never considered. He also had contacts and interests in the entertainment field. A telegram from a well-known producer or a fledgling playwright wasn't uncommon. Though he rarely attended the ballet or the opera, she learned that he made enormous contributions to the arts. It would have pleased her more if she hadn't understood they were made for business purposes.

Culture, politics, stock-market ventures or housing projects—it was all business to Daniel. And though she learned that business consumed his time and his life, he passed off her inquiries into it with the equivalent of a pat on the head. Each time he did, she tried to ignore the futile twinge of frustration. In time, she told herself, he'd share. In time, he'd give her both his trust and respect.

Her life and her time were consumed by the hospital, her studies and her preparation for her final year of medical school. Daniel rarely asked her about her hours involving medicine. When and if he did, Anna took it as no more than polite interest and said little.

They spent their evenings lingering over a meal or over coffee in the parlor. Neither of them spoke of ambitions, of what drove them or of professional needs. While they were content just being with each other, it seemed to both as though a shade had been drawn over a part of their lives. Neither of them wanted to be the first to lift it.

They became misers with their social time, spending most of it alone at home. When they did socialize, it was with the newlywed Ditmeyers. Now and again there was a film, and they could sit in a darkened theater holding hands, forgetting about the pressures of the day or the uncertainty of the future. They learned of each other, of habits, whims and annoyances. Love, soothed and left to itself, deepened. But even as it did, they both fretted about what was missing from their relationship. Daniel wanted marriage. Anna wanted partnership. They hadn't yet discovered how to combine the two.

Summer heat soared in August. It boiled in the streets and hung mistily in the air. Those who could escaped to the shore. On the weekends Daniel and Anna took drives out of the city, with the top down. Twice they picnicked on Daniel's lot in Hyannis Port. They could make love there as freely and unrestrainedly as they had the first time. They could laugh or simply doze in the grass. And it was there, unexpectedly, that Daniel began to pressure her again.

"They'll be breaking ground here next week," Daniel told her one day as they shared the last of a bottle of Chablis.

"Next week?" Surprised, Anna glanced over to see him staring at the empty plot where his house would be. He could see it, she knew, as though there were already stone and mortar standing sturdy in the sun. "I didn't realize it would be so soon." He hadn't told her, she thought. He hadn't shown her, though she'd asked, any of the plans or blueprints for the house that was so important to him.

He merely moved his shoulders. "It would have been sooner, but I had some other things to tidy up first."

"I see." And he hadn't considered the other things worth mentioning, either. Anna bit back a sigh and tried to accept it. "I know the house is important to you, and it'll be beautiful, but I'll miss this." When he looked at her, she smiled and reached out to touch his face. "It's so peaceful here, so isolated—just water and rock and grass."

"It'll be all of those things after the house is up. After we're living in it." Because he felt her slight withdrawal, he took her hand. "It won't be quick—the best things aren't. It may be two years before the house is ready for us. But our children will grow up here."

"Daniel—"

"They will." His fingers tightened on hers as he cut her off. "And whenever we make love in that house, I'll remember our first time here. Fifty years from now I'll still remember our first time here."

It was all but impossible to resist him when he was like this. He was more dangerous when he spoke quietly, when his voice flowed over her. For a moment she almost believed him. Then she thought about how very far they had to go. "You're asking for promises, Daniel."

"Aye. I expect promises."

"Don't."

"And why not? You're the woman I want, the woman who wants me. It's time for promises between us." Keeping a firm hold on her hand, he reached into his pocket and drew out a small velvet box. "I want you to wear this, Anna." With a flick of his thumb, he opened the box to reveal a fiery pear-shaped diamond.

Something caught in her throat. Part of it was astonishment at the sheer beauty of the ring. The rest was fear of what the symbol meant: promises, vows, commitments. She wanted, she yearned, she feared.

"I can't."

"Of course, you can." When he started to pluck the ring from the box, she put both hands over his.

"No, I can't. I'm not ready for this, Daniel. I've tried to explain to you."

"And I've tried to understand." But his patience was wearing thin. Every day he lived with her he had to accept half of what he needed. "You don't want marriage—at least, not yet. But a ring's not marriage, just a promise."

"A promise I can't give you." But she wanted to. With each day that passed she wanted to more. "If I took the ring, I'd be giving you a promise that might be broken. I can't do that with you. You're too important."

"You don't make sense." He'd expected to feel frustration. Even when he'd bought the ring he'd known she wouldn't wear it. In some odd way, he'd even known she'd be right. But that knowledge didn't soothe the hurt. "I'm important to you, but you won't accept a ring from me."

"Oh, Daniel, I know you." Regrets washed over her as she took his face in her hands. "If I took this ring, you'd be pressuring me to accept a wedding ring in a month's time. Sometimes, I think you look at the two of us like a merger."

"Maybe I do." Anger flared in his eyes but he controlled it. He'd discovered he could when it was Anna he was angry with. "Maybe it's the only way I know."

"Maybe it is," she agreed quietly. "And maybe I'm trying to understand that."

"You look at it as a trial." He said it flatly. When she looked up, stunned, he continued in the same tone. "I'm not sure whether I'm on trial, Anna, or you are."

"It's not like that. You make it sound so cold and calculated."

"No more calculated than a merger."

"I'm not looking at what's between us as a business, Daniel."

Was he? He realized uncomfortably that he had been, but he wasn't so sure any longer. "Maybe it's time you told me just how you're looking at it."

"You frighten me." Her words came out so fast and strong that both of them sat in silence for several moments.

"Anna"—because her statement was the last response he'd expected from her, his voice was low and tentative—"I'd never do anything to hurt you."

"I know." She thought of the ring in the box, of the image of the house at their backs and rose with her nerves jumping. "If you could, I believe you'd treat me like glass, like something to be protected, cared for and admired. Somehow, it's easier for me when you lose sight of that and shout at me."

He couldn't pretend to understand her. But he rose and stood behind her. "Then I'll shout more often."

"I'm sure you will," she murmured, "when I frustrate you or disagree. But what happens when I give you everything you want?" She turned then, and her eyes were glowing with emotion. "What happens when I say all right, I give up?"

He grabbed her hands for fear she'd turn away again. "I don't know what you're talking about."

"I think you do, deep down. I think you know that part of me wants just what you want. But do either of us know if I want it for myself or just to please you? If I said yes and married you tomorrow, I'd have to toss away everything else."

"I'm not asking for that. I wouldn't."

"Wouldn't you?" She closed her eyes a moment and struggled for composure. "Can you tell me, can you be sure that you'll accept, care for, Dr. Anna Whitfield the same way you do for me now?"

He started to speak quickly, but her eyes were too dark, too vulnerable. There could be nothing with Anna but the truth. "I don't know."

She let out a quick, quiet sigh. Would he have lied if he'd known how much she'd wanted to hear it? And if he had lied, would she have taken the ring and given the promise? "Then give us both the time to be sure." Because he'd released her hands, her arms were free to go around him. "If I accept your ring, it'll be with my whole heart, with everything I am, and it'll be forever. Once it's there, Daniel, it's there to stay. That I can promise you. We both have to be sure it belongs there."

"It'll keep." The ring was back in his pocket. Anna was in his arms. They were alone, and the air was swirling with summer. When she lifted her face, he crushed his mouth to hers. "This won't," he murmured and drew her down with him.

CHAPTER 11

Anna took the news that they would be entertaining the governor calmly enough. Both her parents and her grandparents had entertained dignitaries from time to time. She'd been trained how to prepare a properly impressive menu, what wines to order and what brandy to serve. It really wasn't doing it that bothered her. It was the fact that Daniel had simply assumed she would.

She could have told him no. Anna lectured herself on this as she drove home from the hospital. She could have reminded him that she put in a full day between the hospital and her studies and didn't have the time or inclination to plan whether to serve oysters Rockefeller or coquilles St. Jacques as an appetizer. She could have and would have gained a brief moment of self-satisfaction. Then she would have spent the rest of her time feeling guilty for being petty and mean.

It would, after all, be their first dinner party as a couple. And it was so important to him. He wanted, she knew, to show her off as much as he wanted to give the governor a memorable meal. It should have infuriated her. Somehow she found it endearing. With a shake of her head, Anna admitted that loving Daniel could do strange things to common sense. So he could show her off; she wouldn't disappoint him. The time it took to plan the evening would be as much fun as work.

To be honest, she had to admit that preparing for a dinner party came as naturally to her as reciting the names of bones in the hand. Which reminded her, she wanted to look at Sally's the moment she got home.

Home. It made her smile. Only three weeks had passed since she'd unpacked in what had been Daniel's bedroom. It was their bedroom now. She might have her doubts about tomorrow, next week, next year, but she had none about today. She was happy. Living with Daniel had added a dimension to her life she had never expected. Because that was true, how could she explain that going on just as they were seemed the best way? The thought of marriage still sent a chill of unease down her back. And of distrust, she admitted. But whom did she distrust, Daniel or herself? She hadn't forgotten that he'd accused her of putting them both on trial. Perhaps she was, but only because she feared hurting him as much as she feared being hurt.

There were moments when it all seemed so clear to her. She'd marry him, bear his children, share his life. She'd be a doctor and develop her skill to the very height of its potential. He would be every bit as proud of her accomplishments as she was of his. She would have everything any woman could ever want, and so much more. It could happen. It would happen.

Then she would remember how carelessly uninterested he was in her work at the hospital. She would remember how he closeted himself in his office with business he never discussed with her. And how he never asked about the medical books that now littered the bedroom. Not once had he mentioned the fact that she was due back in Connecticut in a matter of weeks—or if he planned to be with her.

Could two people share a life, share a love and not share what was most vital to them? If she had the answer to that one question, she could stop asking herself any other.

With a shake of her head, Anna pulled into the driveway. She refused to be gloomy now. She was home, and that was enough.

As she walked in the kitchen door, Sally was bending over to pop something into the oven. "You're supposed to rest that hand."

"It's had all the rest it needs." Without turning around, Sally reached for a cup. "You're a bit late today."

"There was a car accident. Lots of bumps and scratches in Emergency. I stayed to hold some hands."

Sally poured coffee and set the cup on the table. "You'd rather have been cutting and sewing."

On a little sigh, Anna sat down with the coffee. "Yes. It's so hard not being allowed to do even the little things I could do. I'm not even allowed to take a blood pressure."

"It won't be long until you'll be doing a great deal more than that."

"I keep telling myself, one more year, just one more. But I'm so impatient, Sally."

"You and the MacGregor have that in common." Knowing she'd be welcome, Sally brought over a cup of her own. "He called to say he'd be late himself and for you to eat your supper if you didn't want to wait— but I could tell he was hoping you'd hold off till he got here."

"I can wait. Are you having any pain in that hand?"

"It's a bit stiff when I wake up, but there's barely a twinge even when I use it heavily." She held it out, admiring the scar that ran down the wrist. "There's a nice neat seam. Don't think I could do better myself." Then with a grin, she lowered her hand. "I don't suppose sewing up flesh is much like mending a tablecloth."

"The technique's pretty close." Anna gave the injured hand a pat. "Since Daniel's going to be late, this might be a good time for us to go over the guest list and menu for next week. I have some ideas, but if you've a specialty you'd rather—" She broke off and sniffed the air. "Sally, what have you got in the oven?"

"Peach pie." She preened. "My grandma's recipe."

"Oh." Anna closed her eyes and let the aroma flow through her. Warm peach pie on a summer's evening. "How late was Daniel going to be?"

"Eight, he said."

Anna glanced at her watch. "You know, I have a feeling that working on this menu is going to take a lot out of me." She smiled as she rose to fetch a pad and pencil. "I'll probably need a bit of something to tide me over."

"A piece of peach pie, perhaps?"

"That should do it."

When Daniel came in, Anna was still in the kitchen. Recipe cards, lists and scraps of paper littered the table where she and Sally sat. Between them was half of a peach pie and the remains of a bottle of white wine.

"I don't care how much we want to impress the governor," Anna said with her head close to Sally's.

"We're not serving haggis. I know for a fact I'd turn green if I had to eat anything with entrails."

"A fine surgeon you'll make if you're squeamish."

"I'm not squeamish about what I have to look at or what I have to get my hands in. What goes in my stomach is a different matter. I vote for the coq au vin."

"Good evening, ladies."

Anna's head came up, and the smile that was already on her face grew when she saw him. "Daniel." She was up and taking both his hands. "Sally and I have been planning the dinner party. I'm afraid I may have offended her about the haggis, but I think our guests might be more comfortable with coq au vin."

"I'll leave that to the two of you," he said, and leaned down for a kiss. "Things took longer than I'd thought. I'm glad you didn't wait supper for me."

"Supper?" She still held his hands, as much now for support as anything else. Until she'd stood, she hadn't realized how fuzzy her mind was. "Sally and I were just testing out her peach pie. Would you like some?"

"Later. Though I could use a glass of that wine if you've left any." His eyes were burning from reading pages of fine print.

"Oh." She looked blankly at the bottle, wondering how it had come to be nearly empty.

"I'll have a shower first."

"I'll go up with you." Anna rummaged through the piles of paper until she found the one she wanted. "I'd like to read you this guest list so you can add anyone I've forgotten before we send the invitations out."

"Fine. Go on to bed, Sally. I'll help myself to the pie when I'm ready."

"Yes, sir. Thank you."

"You look tired, Daniel. Was it a difficult day?"

"No more than most." He slipped his arm around her as they started up the stairs. "A few problems with the fine points of a deal I'm working on. I think we ironed them out."

"Can you talk about it?"

"I don't bring my troubles home." He gave her a little squeeze. "I spent the afternoon with your father."

"You did?" She felt a little skip of emotion but kept her voice level. "How is he?"

"Well, and keeping business and personal matters well apart."

"Yes." Her smile was a bit tight when they reached the top landing. "I suppose that's for the best."

"He asked about you." His voice was gentle now because he'd come to know her.

"He did?"

"Aye."

She entered first when Daniel pushed open the door to the bedroom. Because she felt so warm, she walked to the window to lean out. "Maybe if I hired him, he'd stop avoiding me."

"He's just worried about his daughter."

"There's nothing to worry about."

"He'll see that for himself at dinner next week."

Anna looked over, the guest list still clutched in her hand. "He'll come?"

"He'll come."

She let out a quick breath before she smiled again. "I suppose I have you to thank for that."

"Some, but I think your mother had more to do with it." He tossed his jacket and tie on one of the chairs Anna had arranged in front of the fireplace. As he unbuttoned his shirt, he could smell the summery scent of sweet peas that brimmed out of a bowl on a table by the window. Small things. Enormous things. Daniel stopped undressing to fold her tight in his arms.

She sensed the abrupt flurry of intense emotion that had taken hold of him. Anna circled his waist with her arms and let the feeling rush through her. Daniel kissed the top of her head before he drew her away.

"What was that for?"

"For being here," he told her. "For being you." He slid off his shoes with a little sigh of relief. "I won't be long. Why don't you just call out the names on that list to me." With economy of movement, Daniel stripped off the rest of his clothes, then walked into the bath.

With only a small frown, Anna looked at the pile of clothes on the floor. She wondered if she'd ever get used to his carelessness about such things. Ignoring the obvious alternative, she stepped over them. A woman who picked up after a grown man was asking for trouble.

"There's the governor and his wife, of course," she called out. "And Councilman and Mrs. Steers."

Daniel answered with a crude and accurate description of the councilman. Anna cleared her throat and made a note on the list to seat that particular couple at the opposite end of the table from their host.

"Myra and Herbert. The Maloneys and the Cooks." She lifted her voice over the sound of water. Still feeling warm, she unfastened the first three buttons of her blouse. "The Donahues, with John Fitzsimmons to balance out Cathleen." Anna peered at the list, blinking because her vision seemed blurred.

"John who?"

"Fitzspimmons—simmons. Fitzsimmons," she repeated when she managed to get her tongue around it. "And Carl Benson and Judith Mann. Myra told me they're about to be engaged."

"She's built like a—" Daniel caught himself. "Very attractive woman," he amended. "Who else?"

Anna walked into the bathroom with her eyes narrowed. "Built like what?"

Behind the curtain Daniel merely grinned. "I beg your pardon?" To his surprise, Anna drew the curtain back. "Woman, is nothing sacred?"

"Just what is Judith Mann built like?"

"Now how would I know?" For safety's sake, he stuck his head under the spray. "You'd better pull the curtain to. You'll get wet."

"And how *would* you know?" she demanded and stepped, fully dressed, into the shower.

"Anna!" Laughing, he watched the water plaster her blouse against her. "What in hell are you doing?"

"Trying to get a straight answer." She waved the now soaking list at him. "Just what do you know about Judith Mann's anatomy?"

"Only what a man with good eyesight can see." He caught her chin in his hand and took a good look. "Now that I think about it I see something else."

She put a hand to his soapy chest for balance. "And what's that?"

"You're drunk, Anna Whitfield."

Dignity streamed from her as thick as the water. "I beg your pardon?"

Her haughtily delivered reply delighted him. Daniel brushed wet hair out of her eyes. "You're drunk," he repeated.

"Don't be ridiculous."

"It's drunk you are. Drunk as an Irish roof thatcher and twice as pretty. I'll be damned."

"You may well be, but I've never been drunk a day in my life. You're just trying to avoid the question."

"What's the question?"

She opened her mouth, shut it again, then grinned. "I don't remember. Have I ever told you what a magnificent body you have, Daniel?"

"No." He drew her against it before he began the task of peeling off her clothes. "Why don't you?"

"Such well-developed pectoral muscles."

Her blouse fell with a muffled splash. "And where might they be?"

"Just here," she murmured and ran a hand over his chest. "The deltoids are very firm. And of course the biceps are impressive, not obviously bulging, just hard." Her fingers slid over his shoulders and down as he tugged off her skirt. "It shows not simply strength but discipline—like the abdomen—very flat and tight." His breath caught as she explored there.

"Tell me, Anna"—he lowered his mouth to her ear and began to trace it with his tongue—"just how many muscles are there?"

Her head fell back, and the water sluiced over her. Naked, wet, pliant, she smiled up at him. "There are over six hundred muscles in the body, all attached to the two hundred and six bones that make up the skeleton."

"Fascinating. I'm wondering how many of mine you might point out."

"We could start with the muscles of the lower limbs. I admire your walk."

"Do you?"

"Yes, it's very firm and arrogant, but not quite a swagger. This, naturally, has something to do with your personality, but you also need your antigravity muscles, such as the soleus. . . ." She bent down just enough to run a finger up his calf. Water poured over her hair. "The vasti," she continued, running a finger up his thigh, "and . . ." With a sound of approval, she slid her hands around to his bottom.

He grinned and let himself enjoy. He'd never had a woman give him quite so interesting a lesson. "I thought that muscle had more to do with sitting. The things you learn in anatomy class."

He switched off the water then reached for a towel to cover both of them.

"The gluteus maximus"—with an approving murmur, she ran her hands over him again—"has to stretch sufficiently or else you'd have a tendency to jackknife forward as you walk."

"Can't have that," he murmured as he gathered her up in his arms. "Especially when you're carrying precious cargo."

"And this is one of your most attractive muscles."

"Thank you." Flinging the towel aside, he lay with her on the bed. Warm night air played over damp skin.

"Now the adductors, the muscles on the inside of the thighs . . ."

"Show me."

"Just here." Her fingers reached down and skimmed over him just as his mouth closed over hers.

With her eyes half shut, she sighed and nuzzled into him. "I don't think you're paying attention."

"Oh, but I am. The adductors. Just here." Strong fingers pressed into firm thighs. "Just here," he repeated, "where your skin's like silk and already warm for me. And here." His hand journeyed up to tease the sensitive area where hip and thigh joined. "What are these muscles here?"

"They're—" But she could only moan and arch against him.

He caught the lobe of her ear in his teeth. "Have you forgotten?"

"Just touch me," she whispered. "It doesn't matter where."

With a sound of triumph, he took his hands over her, skimming, caressing, kneading, arousing. Like putty, she seemed willing to be molded. Like fire, she tempted and dared. Like a woman, she softened and tensed and gave. Her hands were as eager as his, her lips as hungry. Their skin dried in the warm summer air, then became damp again with excitement.

Each time, she thought hazily, each time they made love, it was more thrilling, more beautiful. The first time, the hundredth time, the edge of desire was never dulled. In a field of grass, on feather pillows it was just as volatile. In the bright light of day, in the dark secret night it was just as frenzied. She'd never stop wanting him. Of all the questions she'd asked herself, she was sure of that answer. Need for him would never fade.

They rolled over the big bed, frantic for each other, lost in each other. Trapped in pleasure, she rose up, back arched, eyes closed, her hair a wild, wet tangle. The sliver of light from the next room shot a nimbus around her that seemed to shiver with her ecstasy. Half-mad he came to her, so that kneeling on the bed they could pour pleasures over each other. Weak, vibrating, they tumbled down again and took the last step into passion.

Her limbs were wrapped around him. Her face was buried against his throat as her breath heaved in and out. Her fingers dug into his back and felt hard flesh and sweat. And as he moved into her, moved with her, she rode on the carousel, flew on the roller coaster and lost herself in the maze.

"You're stunning." Daniel stared at her as she studied herself in the mirror. "Absolutely stunning."

It pleased her to hear it, though she'd never thought

much of compliments. The dress left her shoulders bare and fell in a loose sweeping line to just above her ankles. Pearls crusted the bodice and danced along the skirt. Myra had talked her into it, though she'd needed little persuasion. True, it had taken a healthy chunk out of the money she'd put aside for board during the fall, but she was confident she'd find a way to balance her books. The look on Daniel's face, and the satisfaction she felt seeing her own reflection made it worthwhile.

"You like it?"

How could he explain that, though he knew every intimate inch of her, just looking at her could still take his breath away? She'd been right when she'd thought he wanted to show her off. When a man had something exquisite, he needed to share it. No, he couldn't explain. "I like it so well I'm wishing the evening was already over."

She gave a last swirl, as much for herself as for him. "You look wonderful in a dinner jacket. Elegantly barbarian."

His brow lifted. "Barbarian?"

"Never change that." She held out both hands and took his. "No matter what else has to change, don't change that."

He brought her hands to his lips, kissed one, then the other. "I doubt I could, any more than you could change being a lady—even after too much wine and peach pie."

She tried to look stern but laughed. "You'll never let me forget that."

"God, no. It was one of the most fascinating evenings of my life. I'm crazy about you, Anna."

"So you've said." She lifted their joined hands to

her cheek. "That's something else I don't want you to change."

"I won't. I like seeing you wear the cameo." He brushed a finger over it as was his habit.

"It means a great deal to me."

"You wouldn't take my ring."

"Daniel—"

"You wouldn't take my ring," he continued, "but you took the cameo. I'd like you to take this." Drawing a box out of his pocket, he waited.

Anna folded her hands together. "Daniel, you don't have to buy me presents."

"I think I've figured that out." But he'd yet to figure out how to accept that fact. "It might be why I want to. Humor me," he said, and made her smile.

"You've said that before." Because he smiled back, she accepted the box. "Thank you." Then she opened the box and found she could say nothing.

"Is something wrong with them?"

She managed to shake her head. Pearls and diamonds, pure in simplicity, arrogant in beauty, the earrings lay against black velvet and nearly breathed with life. From the simple orbs of milky white pearls dripped the tear-shaped glamour of diamonds. One gleamed, the other flashed and together they made a stunning unit.

"Daniel, they're . . ." She shook her head and looked back up at him. "They're absolutely beautiful. I don't know what to say."

"You just said it." Relieved, he took the box and removed the earrings. "I suppose you'll have to thank Myra. I asked her advice. She said something about class and flash making the best team."

"Did she?" Anna murmured as Daniel fastened the earrings on her himself.

"There now." Pleased, he stepped back to inspect. "Yes, they'll do nicely. Now maybe they'll draw the attention and keep men's eyes off all that beautiful skin you've exposed."

Laughing again, Anna lifted a hand to her ear. "Ah, an ulterior motive."

"It's hard not to worry that you'll take a good look around and see someone who appeals to you more."

"Don't be silly." Taking it as a joke, she linked arms with him. "I suppose we'd better go down or the guests will be arriving. Then McGee will scowl at us for being late and unpardonably rude."

"Hah." As they walked through the door, Daniel found her hand with his. "As if you hadn't twisted him around your finger already."

Anna gave him an innocent look as they started downstairs. "I don't know what you mean."

"Fixes scones for you in the middle of the week. Never did that for me."

"Ah, there's the door now." She paused on the bottom landing. "Promise not to glare—even at Councilman Steers."

"I never glare," he lied easily, and led her down the hall to greet the first guests.

In less than twenty minutes the big parlor was crowded with bodies and buzzing with conversation. Though Anna was perfectly aware that she and Daniel were often the topic of the moment, she made her way calmly from group to group. She hadn't needed her mother's warning to know that her decision would alienate her from some. But her choices were never made with other people's opinions in mind.

Louise Ditmeyer's greeting was a bit stiff, but Anna ignored it and chatting, steered her to a group of friends. More than once she caught someone aiming a speculative look in her direction. It was easy enough to meet this calmly. That was her way. Anna had no idea that her cool confidence and natural graciousness did more to squelch gossip than Daniel's power or her own family name.

If there was a shadow on the evening, it came from the governor's careless request for her opinion on Daniel's projected textile factory. How could she have an opinion or even an intelligent comment? Daniel had never mentioned it to her, and she was faced with the governor's glowing praise of a project that would bring employment to hundreds and fat revenues to the state. Training kept her smile in place and brought easy answers. There was no time for anger as she introduced the governor and his wife to another couple. There was time for only a moment's envy that the governor's wife appeared to be deeply involved in his work. Pressed by her duties as hostess, Anna pushed personal disappointment to the back of her mind.

Not until her parents arrived did she feel any real tension. Holding her breath, she approached her father.

"I'm so glad you came." She rose on her toes to kiss his cheek, though she was far from sure of her reception.

"You look well." He didn't speak coldly, but she felt his reserve.

"So do you. Hello, Mother." She pressed her cheek against her mother's and smiled at the encouraging squeeze.

"You look beautiful, Anna." She shot her husband a quick look. "Happy."

"I am happy. Let me get you both a drink."

"Now don't fuss with us," her mother told her.

"You have all these guests. There's Pat Donahue, I see. Just run along. We'll be fine."

"All right, then." As she started to turn away, her father caught her hand.

"Anna . . ." As he hesitated, he felt her hand tighten on his. "It's good to see you."

It was enough. She wrapped her arms around his neck and held for just a moment. "If I came by your office one day, would you play hooky and go for a ride with me?"

"You going to let me drive your car?"

She smiled brilliantly. "Maybe."

He winked and patted her head as he'd always done. "See to your guests."

When she turned, it was to see Daniel a few feet away, smiling at her. She walked to him with her heart in her eyes. "Now you look even more beautiful," he murmured to her.

"What's all this?" Myra came up to stand between them. "The host and hostess aren't even supposed to have time to speak to each other at an affair like this. Daniel, I really believe you should go rescue the governor from our esteemed councilman before he loses his appetite. The governor, that is." When Daniel muttered something rude, she merely nodded. "Just so. Now, Anna, why don't we walk over to where Cathleen is boring the daylights out of the Maloneys. I'm dying to see her gag over your earrings."

"Subtle, Myra," Anna warned as they maneuvered through the groups. "Remember the beauty of subtlety."

"Darling, of course. But I'd really appreciate it if you'd be sure to toss your head just a little now and then. Why, Cathleen, what a nice dress."

Cathleen stopped her dissertation on her summer

schedule to study Myra. Anna wasn't sure, but she thought the Maloneys sighed in unison. "Thank you, Myra. I suppose congratulations and best wishes are in order. I haven't seen you since you and Herbert ran away."

"No, you haven't." Myra sipped her drink and ignored the less than complimentary description of her marriage. Envy was the simplest of things to ignore when you were happy.

"I suppose there's something to be said for elopements, though for myself, I'd find it a rather cut-and-dried way of marrying."

"To each his own," Myra returned, and tried to remember it was Anna's dinner party.

"Oh, indeed." Cathleen gave a little nod. "But what a shame you and Herbert have decided to be hermits even after cheating us all out of a big wedding."

"I'm afraid Herbert and I haven't entertained on a grand scale yet. We want to finish our redecorating before we have more than our most intimate friends over. You understand."

Seeing the need to intervene, Anna stepped a bit closer. "I'm sure you've had a busy summer, Cathleen."

"Oh, quite busy." She gave Anna a cool smile. "Though others seem to get more accomplished in a shorter time. I took a little trip to the shore, and when I got back to Boston, I learned Myra and Herbert had run off and you'd changed addresses. Are congratulations of a different sort in order?"

Anna laid a hand on Myra's arm to silence her. "Not at all. You've brought back a beautiful tan. I'm sorry I missed getting to the beach. I didn't seem to find the time."

"I'm sure you didn't." Lifting her drink, Cathleen

took a long, slow sip. It wasn't easy to accept that two of the women she'd debuted with had snagged two of the most influential men in the city—particularly when she'd all but decided to set her sights on Daniel. "Tell me, Anna, just how do I introduce you and Daniel if the occasion comes up? I'm afraid I'm naive about these things."

Even Anna's patience only lasted so long. "Why should it matter?"

"Oh, it does. As a matter of fact, I'm thinking of giving a little dinner party myself. I haven't a clue how to write your invitation."

"I wouldn't worry about it."

"Oh, but I do." Her eyes widened and rounded. "I'd hate to make a faux pas."

"What a pity."

If Cathleen couldn't get a rise one way, she'd get one another. "Well, after all, one doesn't know how to politely address a man's mistress." Then she let out a gasp and squeal as Myra's drink ran down her bodice.

"Oh, how dreadfully clumsy of me." Rocking back on her heels, Myra surveyed the damage to Cathleen's pink crepe de chine. It was almost enough to satisfy Myra. "I feel like such a mule," she said lightly. "Come, I'll go up with you, Cathleen. I'll be more than happy to sponge you off."

"I can take care of myself," she said between gritted teeth. "Just keep away from me."

Myra lit a cigarette and blew smoke at the ceiling. "Whatever you say."

Feeling obligated, Anna started to take her arm. "Here, let me take you up."

"Keep your hands off me," she hissed. "You and your imbecile friend." Skirts swirling, she was pushing herself through the crowd.

"Subtlety," Anna sighed. "Didn't we speak of subtlety?"

"I didn't toss it in her face," Myra said. "And to tell the truth, I've been wanting to do that for so long. This was the first time I could and feel absolutely justified." She gave Anna a wide grin. "Do I have time for another drink before dinner?"

CHAPTER 12

Perhaps if Daniel hadn't overheard the incident with Cathleen Donahue, he would have handled things differently. But he had. Perhaps if his anger at the insult hadn't eaten away at him, their relationship could have continued smoothly enough. But it didn't. Throughout the rest of the evening, he managed to remain the congenial host. Guests left his home well fed and content. He could barely wait to close the door behind the last of them.

"We need to talk," he told Anna before she could take her first sigh of relief.

Though she was wilting a bit around the edges, she nodded. Others might have been fooled by Daniel's easy conversation and careless generosity through the evening, but she had sensed both strain and anger. In tacit agreement, they walked upstairs to the privacy of the bedroom.

"Something has upset you," she began, and sat on the arm of a chair, though she longed to take off her clothes and fall mindlessly into bed. "I know you had business with the governor. Did something go wrong?"

"My business is fine." He paced to the window and pulled out a cigar. "It's my personal life that's the problem."

She folded her hands in her lap, a sure sign of annoyance or nerves. "I see."

"No, you don't." He turned to her then, ready to snipe or charge. "If you understood, there'd be no argument about marriage. It would simply be a fact."

"Simply a fact," she repeated, and struggled to remember how unproductive anger was. "Daniel, our biggest problem seems to stem from our diverse outlooks on marriage. I don't see it as simply a fact, but as the biggest step one person can take with another. I can't take that step with you until I'm ready."

"If you ever are," he shot back.

She moistened her lips. Behind her growing temper were regrets. "If I ever am."

The anger he'd held in all evening gnawed at him. "So, you'll give me no promises, Anna. Nothing."

"I told you before I wouldn't give a promise I may have to break. I'll give you everything I can, Daniel."

"It's not enough." He drew on the cigar then watched her through a haze of smoke.

"I'm sorry. If I could, I'd give you more."

"If you could?" Fury whipped through him, blinding him to reason. "If you could? Nothing's stopping you but your own stubbornness."

"If that were true, I'd be a fool." She rose because it was time to face him. Time, in fact, to face herself. "And perhaps I am, because I expect you to give my needs and ambitions as much respect as you give your own."

"What in hell does that have to do with marriage?"

"Everything. In nine months I'll have my degree."

"A piece of paper," he shot back.

Everything about her turned cold: her skin, her voice, her eyes. "A piece of paper? I wonder if you would call your deeds and stocks and contracts pieces of paper—pieces of paper too lofty, too important to ever be discussed with me. Or perhaps, as with the textile factory the governor asked me about tonight, you don't consider me intelligent enough to understand your work."

"I've never doubted your intelligence," he shot back. "What do deeds and stock have to do with us?"

"They're part of you, just as my degree will be part of me. I've devoted years of my life to earning it. I would think you could understand that."

"I'll tell you what I understand." Rigid with anger, he crushed out his cigar. "I understand I'm tired of coming in second place to this precious degree."

"Damn you, Daniel, no one can tell you anything." Fighting for control, she leaned both hands on her dresser. "It isn't a matter of places; it isn't a competition."

"What is it then? Just what in hell is it?"

"A matter of respect," she said more calmly, and turned to him again. "It's a matter of respect."

"And what about love?"

He spoke of love so seldom that his question nearly broke her. Tears swam in her eyes and smothered her voice. "Love is an empty word without respect. I'd rather not have it from a man who can't accept me for what I am. I'd rather not give it to a man who won't share his problems with me as well as his successes."

His pride was as strong as hers. Even as he felt her slip away from him, he gripped his pride as though it were all he had left. "Then perhaps you'd prefer it if I stopped loving you. I'll do my best." With that, he turned on his heel. Moments later, Anna heard the front door slam.

She could have fallen on the bed and given in to tears. She wanted to—maybe too much. Because she couldn't, there seemed to be only one thing left to do. Mechanically she began to pack.

The drive to Connecticut was a long and lonely one. Weeks later, Anna could remember it vividly. She drove through the night until her eyes were gritty and the sun was up. Exhausted, she checked into a motel and slept until dusk. When she woke, she tried to forget what she'd left behind. The first few days were spent finding a small apartment near the campus. She needed privacy and indulged herself by having her own place. Her days were full with planning, preparing. Anna thought it a pity that her nights couldn't be full as well.

Anna could block Daniel out of her mind for long stretches during the day, but at night she would lie in her bed and remember what it had been like to curl up against him. She would eat alone at her little table in her little kitchen and remember how she and Daniel had lingered over coffee in the dining room simply because it was so comfortable just to talk.

She deliberately refused to install a phone. It would have made it too easy to call him. When classes began, she fell into them with an almost desperate relief.

Her fellow students noticed a change in her. The usually friendly, if slightly reserved Miss Whitfield was now completely withdrawn. She rarely spoke unless it was to ask or answer a question in class. Those who happened to drive by her apartment in the evening or late on a Saturday night invariably saw a light burning in her window. Incessant study brought shadows to eyes that even her professors began to note. She blocked any comment or question with polite but firm withdrawal.

The days blurred together as she wanted them to. If she studied hard enough, long enough, she could fall into oblivion for six hours a night and not think at all.

Connecticut in mid-September was brisk and beautiful, but Anna had taken little time to notice the foliage. The strong colors and rich scents of fall were bypassed in favor of medical journals and anatomy classes. In previous years, she'd managed to enjoy her surroundings while devoting herself to her studies. Now, if she stopped for a moment to admire the wild riot of leaves, she would think only of a cliff top and the roar of water on rock. And she would wonder, in that moment before she pulled herself away, if Daniel was building his house.

In defense, she had even avoided contacting Myra, though her friend sent her long, annoyed letters. When the telegram arrived, Anna realized she couldn't hide forever. It read simply: IF YOU DON'T WANT ME ON YOUR DOORSTEP IN TWENTY-FOUR HOURS CALL STOP MYRA STOP.

With the telegram mixed in with her notes on the circulatory system, Anna stopped between classes at a pay phone in the student lounge. Armed with change, she put the call through and waited.

"Hello."

"Myra, if you arrived on my doorstep, you'd have to sleep there. I don't have an extra bed."

"Anna! Good God, I was beginning to think you'd slid into the Atlantic." Anna heard the quick snap of a lighter and an indrawn breath. "That was easier to believe than that you'd been too rude to answer my letters."

"I'm sorry. I've been busy."

"You've been hiding," Myra corrected. "And I'll tolerate that as long as it's not from me. I've been worried about you."

"Don't be. I'm fine."

"Of course."

"No, I'm not fine," she admitted because it was Myra. "But I am busy, up to my ears in books and notes."

"You haven't called Daniel?"

"No, I can't." She closed her eyes and rested her forehead against the cool metal of the phone. "How is he? Have you seen him?"

"Seen him?" Anna could almost see Myra roll her eyes. "He went crazy the night you left. Woke Herbert and I up after two a.m., demanding if you were here. Herbert calmed him down. The man's positively amazing—Herbert that is. We haven't seen a great deal of Daniel since, but I hear he's spending a lot of time in Hyannis Port supervising the building of his house."

"Yes, he would." And she could see him there, watching the machines dig and the men laying stone.

"Anna, did you know that Daniel overheard that little incident with Cathleen the night of the dinner party?"

She caught herself wallowing in self-pity and shook her head. "No. No, he didn't tell me. Oh . . ." She remembered the underlying fury she'd sensed in him—the same fury he'd turned on her. It explained a great deal.

"I heard him tell Herbert he'd like to wring her skinny neck. Though I approved, Herbert talked him out of it. It did seem though that the entire business had thrown him off. The man has the idea that you should be protected from any kind of insult. It's sweet really, though we can certainly take care of ourselves."

"I can't marry Daniel in order not to be insulted," she murmured.

"No. And though I'm sure he deserves a kick in the behind, darling, I'd swear his heart's in the right place. He loves you, Anna."

"Only part of me." She closed her eyes and willed herself to be strong. "I'm sorry we involved you."

"Oh, please, you know I thrive on being involved. Anna, do you want to talk about it? Would you like me to come?"

"No, really. At least not yet." Though she rubbed at her temple, Anna laughed. "I'm glad I didn't answer your letters. Talking to you has done me more good than anything else."

"Then give me your number. There's no reason why we can't talk instead of writing."

"I don't have a phone."

"No phone?" There was a shocked and pregnant pause. "Anna, darling, how do you survive?"

She stopped rubbing at her temple and really laughed. "I'm very primitive here. You'd be shocked if you saw my apartment." And she wondered if even Myra would understand the enthusiasm she'd felt while spending the best part of the afternoon with a dozen other students and a cadaver. Some things were best left unsaid. "Look, I promise, I'll sit down and write you a long letter tonight. I'll even call again next week."

"All right, then. But one word of advice before you go. Daniel's a man, so he starts with one strike against him. Just try to remember that."

"Thanks. Give my love to Herbert."

"I will. I'm counting on that letter."

"Tonight," she promised again. "Bye, Myra."

When Anna hung up, she felt truly steady for the first time in weeks. True, she'd taken charge of her own life when she'd left Boston. She'd leased her own apartment, registered for classes. She set her own study time and was responsible for her own success, her own failure. But she hadn't been happy. She was responsible for that, as well, she reminded herself as she walked back down the hall. It was time to face the fact that she'd made her choice. If she had to live as it seemed she did—alone—then she had to make the best of it.

A glance at her watch showed her she had ten minutes before her next class. This time she'd step outside and enjoy the autumn weather instead of hurrying to the next building and burying her face in a book.

Outside, she saw the symphony of color she had almost deliberately ignored for weeks. She saw other students hurrying to class or stretched on the grass reading by sunlight. She saw the slight slope and the old red brick of the hospital. And she saw the blue convertible at the curb.

For an instant, she couldn't move. Weeks peeled away, and she was coming out of the hospital in Boston to find Daniel waiting for her. Her fingers tightened on the books she carried. But it wasn't Boston, she thought more calmly. And Daniel's wasn't the only blue convertible on the East Coast. It was simply a mean twist of fate that had made her walk out and see it. Pulling herself together, she started to walk away. Seconds later, she was going back to the car for a closer look.

"Want a ride?"

At the sound of his voice, she felt her heart roll over in her chest. When she turned, her face was touched with both wariness and pleasure. "Daniel, what are you doing here?" And what did she care? It was enough just to look at him.

"It appears I'm waiting for you." He wanted to touch her, but if he touched, he'd grab. Deliberately he kept his hands in his pockets. "What time is your last class over?"

"Last class?" She'd forgotten what day it was. "Ah, an hour or so. I only have one more today."

"All right, then, I'll be back."

Be back? Dazed, she watched him walk around the hood and open the driver's door. Before she realized she intended to do it, Anna pulled open the passenger's.

"What are you doing?"

"I'm going with you," she blurted out.

He gave her a long, cool stare. "What about your class?"

She gave a desperate look around the campus before she climbed in the car. "I'll borrow someone's notes. I can make it up." But she couldn't make up another hour away from him.

"You're not the type to skip classes."

"No, I'm not." Giddy, she set her books in her lap. "My apartment isn't far. We can have some coffee. Just turn left past the hospital then—"

"I know where it is," he interrupted, but didn't add he'd known almost before the ink had dried on the lease.

The five-minute drive went quickly as dozens of thoughts ran through her head. How should she treat him? Politely? Was he still angry? For the first time since she'd known him, Anna couldn't gauge his mood. Her nerves were jumping by the time he stopped the car again. He seemed perfectly calm.

"I wasn't expecting anyone," she began as they walked up the steps to her apartment on the second floor.

"A person might be able to call if you had a phone."

"I hadn't given it much thought," she told him, then unlocked the door. "Come in," she invited.

The moment he stepped inside she realized how impossibly small the apartment was. In the living area, Daniel could all but touch the walls if he were to spread out his arms. She had a divan, a coffee table and a lamp, and hadn't seen the necessity for anything else.

"Sit down," she offered, discovering she desperately needed a moment to herself. "I'll make coffee."

Without waiting for his answer, she fled to the kitchen. When he was alone, Daniel unclenched his hands. He didn't see simply a small room, but the touches of charm. She had colorful pillows tossed on the couch and a bowl of shells on the coffee table. More than that, the tiny sun-washed room carried her scent—the same scent that had faded from their bedroom. He couldn't sit, and he couldn't stand alone. Clenching his hands again, he followed her into the kitchen.

He couldn't tell how much cooking she did in the cramped space, but she obviously worked here. On the table by the window was a portable typewriter and stacks of notes and books. Pencils worn down to nubs and freshly sharpened ones were held in a china cup. He was out of his element. He felt it. He fought it.

"Coffee will just be a minute," she said to fill the silence. He was there again, and she hadn't had enough time. She couldn't know that he was feeling precisely the same. "I don't have anything else to offer you. I haven't shopped this week."

She was nervous, he realized, hearing the jumps in her usually smooth voice. Curious, he watched and saw her hands tremble lightly as she reached for cups. He felt the knots in his stomach loosen just a little. How did he approach her? Daniel pulled up a chair and sat.

"You're looking pale, Anna."

"I haven't been getting much sun. The schedule's always frantic the first few weeks."

"And weekends?"

"There's the hospital."

"Mmm. If you were a doctor, you might diagnose overwork."

"I'm not a doctor yet." She set the coffee down, then hesitated. After a moment, she sat across from him. It was so much like their time together before. Yet it was nothing like it at all. "I happened to talk to Myra today. She said that you've started the house in Hyannis Port."

"That's right." He'd watched them break the ground, seen the foundation rise. And it had meant nothing. Nothing at all. "If we stay on schedule, the main part will be livable by next summer."

"You must be pleased." Her coffee tasted like mud, and she pushed it aside.

"I have the blueprints in the car. You might like to see them."

Her chest was tight as she lifted her head. He saw the surprise in her eyes and cursed himself for a fool. "Of course, I would."

For a moment he scowled down at his own hands. He was a gambler, wasn't he? It was time to take another chance. "I'm thinking of buying an office building downtown. Small businesses and low rent, but I think the property value should double in five to seven years."

He added a lump of sugar to his coffee but didn't stir it. "I've run into some problems with the textile factory. Your father's working on the kinks so we can be in production by spring."

She kept her gaze steady on his. "Why are you telling me?"

He took a minute. Confessions didn't come easily to him. But her eyes were so dark, so patient. Hard as it was, he'd realized he needed her as much as his own pride. "A man doesn't like to admit he was wrong, Anna. But more than that, he doesn't like to face that his woman turned away from him because he couldn't admit it."

He could have said nothing that could have made her love him more. "I didn't turn away from you, Daniel."

"Ran away."

She swallowed. "All right, I ran away. From both of us. Do you realize you've offered me more of yourself in the last five minutes than you did the entire time we lived together?"

"It never occurred to me that you'd want to know about factories and interest rates." He started to rise, then changed his mind when he saw the impatience in her eyes. "You'd better say what's on your mind."

"The first time I walked into the bedroom, I saw how little of yourself was there. After a while, I figured out why. You were so determined to go forward. Daniel, as much as you spoke of the home and family you wanted, you've had it in your head to do it yourself. I was to be swept along."

"There'd be no family without you, Anna."

"But you wanted to give, not to share. You never offered to show me the blueprints of the home you said you wanted for both of us. You never asked for an opinion or a suggestion."

"No. And as I watched them build the foundation, I realized I was going to have the house I wanted, but not the home I needed." He set down his spoon with a snap. "I never thought it really mattered to you."

"I didn't know how to show you." She smiled a little. "Stupid." Because she needed just a bit of distance, she rose to stand at the window. Strange, she realized, she worked here every evening and hadn't noticed the big red maple that spread in the yard. It was beautiful. How much beauty was she cutting out of her life? "Part of me wanted to share that home with you. More than anything."

"But only part."

"I guess it's the part you can't accept that held me back. That held us both back. Do you know, you never asked about my work at the hospital, about the books or about why I want to be a surgeon."

He rose, too. He'd already faced himself. Now he had to face her. "A man doesn't ask the woman he loves about her other lover."

Torn between anger and confusion, she turned. "Daniel—"

"Don't ask me to be reasonable," he interrupted. "I'm damn near ready to crawl if I have to, but don't ask me to be reasonable."

On a huff of breath, she shook her head. "All right, I won't. Let's just say then that some women can have two lovers and be happy spending their lives trying to give each what they need."

"It's a hard life."

"Not if the woman has two lovers that are willing to give her back what she needs."

There was no room to pace in the little kitchen. Instead, Daniel rocked back on his heels, his hands still clenched in his pockets. "You know, I did a lot of thinking about your doctoring these last few weeks. More, I guess, than I've wanted to do since I first saw you. There were times, Anna, when I could see you were meant for something more, but I managed to block it out. When you left and I spent my nights alone, I didn't have any choice but to think. I remembered the way you'd been with Mrs. Higgs. And the way you'd look when you'd walk out of the hospital in the evening. I remembered how you'd stood in the kitchen with blood on your blouse and explained, very calmly, how you'd dealt with Sally's wrist. She told me the doctor said you'd saved her life. Something you'd learned in one of these," he said, indicating the stack of books. "Not so hard to learn, maybe, but I wouldn't think so easy to do." He picked up a book and held it as he faced her. "No, I haven't asked you before why you want to be a surgeon. I'm asking now."

She hesitated, afraid he might make some cutting, or worse, patronizing remark. He'd come to her—a gamble. She could gamble as well. "I have a dream," she told him quietly. "I want to make a difference."

He studied her in silence, his eyes narrowed, the irises a deep, intense blue. "I have a dream," he said at length then set the book down again. For the first time, he stepped toward her. "It's a small apartment, Anna. But I think there's room enough for two."

He heard her long broken breath before she wrapped her arms around him. "We'll need a bigger bed."

"There's a lass." On a laugh, he picked her up off the floor and gave himself the pleasure of her mouth. Relief poured through him like wine until he was drunk with it. "I've missed you, Anna. I can't do without you again."

"No." With her face buried against his throat, she drew in his scent and filled herself with it. "Not again. Daniel, I've only been half alive here without you. I tried to crowd the day with studies, to work harder, longer at the hospital, but it just didn't mean anything. I want you with me, need you with me."

"You'll have me. A bigger bed and three phones should do it."

With a laugh, she found his lips with hers. He could have his phones as long as she had him. "I love you."

"You never told me that." Unsteady, he drew her away. "You never once told me that before."

"I was afraid to. I thought if you knew how much I loved you, you might use it to make me give up the rest."

He started to deny it, then swore at himself because it was true. "And now?"

"The rest doesn't mean much if you're not with me."

He drew farther away. "Once I told you I'd thought of you looking around and seeing someone who appealed to you more. I wasn't joking."

She gave him a little shake. "You should have been."

Didn't she realize how lovely she was, how regal? Didn't she know how clumsy she could make a man feel with just a smile? "Don't believe I've taken you for granted or ever will. I may act like it, but it won't be true. You're my answer, Anna, and I want to be yours."

She rested her cheek on his shoulder a moment. It had never occurred to her that his confidence would ever waver. She loved him more knowing it could. "You are, Daniel. I haven't been sure I could give you what you seemed to want."

"I wanted a wife, a woman who'd be there at night when I came home. One who'd keep flowers in the vases and lace at the windows. One who'd be content with whatever I could give her."

She looked at the books stacked on the table, then at the man standing in front of her. "And now?"

"I'm beginning to think a woman like that would bore me within a week."

She pressed her fingers to her eyes to hold back the tears. "I'd like to think so."

"I'm not backing down." His voice was suddenly rough as he dragged her back against him. "You're going to marry me, Anna, the day after you have that degree. You'll be Dr. Whitfield for less than twenty-four hours."

Her fingers curled into his shirt. "Daniel, I—"

"Then it's Dr. MacGregor."

Her fingers froze. She took three quiet breaths before she dared to speak. "Do you mean that?"

"Aye. I always mean what I say. And you'll have to put up with me introducing my wife as the best surgeon in the country. I want to share your dream, Anna, as much as I want you to share mine."

"It won't be easy for you. While I'm an intern, the hours will be hateful."

"And in twenty years, we'll look back and wonder how we got through them. I like the long view, Anna. I wanted you to marry me because I thought you fit a slot. You didn't fit it." He took her hands in his. "Now I'm asking you to marry me because I love you exactly as you are."

She took a long time to study him. This time there would be no stepping back. "Do you still have the ring?"

"Aye." He reached in his pocket. "I got into the habit of carrying it with me."

Laughing, she lifted both hands to his face. "I'll take it now." As he started to slip it on, she closed her hand over his. "Here's a promise for you, Daniel. I'll do my best."

The ring slid on. "That's good enough."

EPILOGUE

Anna had slept in snatches through the night, rejecting the cot an orderly had brought her, preferring the chair beside Daniel's bed. From time to time during the night, he'd murmured in his sleep. Whenever she'd heard her name, she tried to soothe him, talking to him, reminiscing until he was restful again.

Only once did she leave him to go down and check on Shelby. The rest of the time she sat watching him sleep and listening to the all-too-familiar beeps and clicks of machines.

The nurses changed shifts. Someone brought her coffee before going off duty. The moon began to set. She thought of the man she loved, of the life they'd built and sat in silence to wait.

Just before dawn, she leaned over to rest her head on the bed beside his hand. When Daniel woke, he saw her first. She was sleeping lightly.

He was disoriented for only a moment. Even though the drugs were still swimming in his system, he remembered the accident with perfect clarity. He thought briefly of his car. He was very fond of that particular toy. Then he felt the pressure in his chest, saw the tubes running from his arm.

He remembered more than the accident now. He remembered Anna leaning over him, talking, reassuring him as he was being wheeled on a gurney down the hospital corridor. He remembered the fear he'd read in her eyes, and before he slipped into unconsciousness, his one moment of blind, naked terror that he was being taken away from her.

Oddly, he thought he remembered looking down at himself from somewhere while doctors and nurses scrambled around. Then it seemed he'd been sucked back into his body, but the sensation was too vague to pinpoint. He remembered one more thing. Anna again, leaning over him, cursing at him, kissing his hand. Then he had simply dreamed.

She looked so tired, he realized. Then it came home to him how old and battered his own body felt. Furious at his weakness, he struggled to sit up and couldn't. Because the effort it cost him embarrassed him, he reached out to touch Anna's cheek. She was awake in an instant.

"Daniel." Her fingers curled around his. In a matter of seconds, he saw it all on her face: terror, relief, grief, weariness and strength. Through sheer will she controlled the need to simply drop her head to his chest and weep. "Daniel"—her voice was as cool and calm as the first time he'd ever heard it—"do you know me?"

Though it cost him, he lifted a brow. "Why in hell wouldn't I know the woman I've lived with for almost forty years?"

"Why in hell not," she agreed and gave herself the pleasure of pressing her lips to his.

"You might be more comfortable if you climbed in here with me."

"Maybe later," she promised, and lifted one of his eyelids to study his pupil.

"Don't start poking and prodding at me. I want a real doctor." He managed to grin at her.

She pressed a button beside the bed. "Is your vision blurred?"

"I can see you well enough. You're as pretty as you were the first night we waltzed."

"Hallucinating," she said dryly, then looked up as a nurse came in. "Please call Dr. Feinstein. Mr. MacGregor is awake and requesting a real doctor."

"Yes, Dr. MacGregor."

"I love it when they call you that," he murmured, and shut his eyes for just a minute. "How much damage did I do, Anna?"

"You were concussed. You've broken three ribs, and—"

"Not to me," he said impatiently, "to the car."

Setting her teeth, she folded her arms. "You never change. I don't know why I bothered to worry. I'm terribly sorry I disturbed the children."

"The children." The light in his eyes wasn't as fierce as it might have been, but it was there. "You called the children?"

He'd given her precisely the reaction she'd needed for her own reassurance. Anna pretended indifference. "Yes, I must apologize to them."

"They came?"

She knew his tactics too well. "Of course."

"What were you going to do, have a wake?"

She tidied his top sheet. "We wanted to be prepared."

He scowled at her and nearly managed to gesture toward the door. "Well, send them in."

"I wouldn't have them spend the night here. They're at home."

His mouth dropped open. "Home? You mean they didn't stay here? They left their father on his deathbed and went to drink his Scotch?"

"Yes, I'm afraid they're very feckless children, Daniel. Take after their father. Here's Dr. Feinstein now." She gave his hand a quick pat before she walked to the door. "I'll leave you two alone."

"Anna."

She paused at the door and smiled back at him. "Yes, Daniel?"

"Don't stay away long."

She saw him then as he'd been so many years before: indomitable, arrogant and strong enough to need. "Do I ever?"

She walked straight out of Intensive Care to her own office. Locking the door, she gave herself the luxury of a twenty-minute weeping spell. She'd cried there before, after losing a patient. This time she wept from a relief too great to measure and a love too strong to soothe. After rinsing her face several times in cold water, she went to the phone.

"Hello."

"Caine."

"Mom, we were just about to call. Is he—"

"Your father wants to see you," she said easily. "He's afraid you've been drinking his Scotch."

He swore, and she heard his momentary struggle for control. "Tell him we didn't put much of a dent in it. Are you okay?"

"I'm terrific. Ask Rena to bring me a change of clothes when you come."

"We'll be there in a half hour."

* * *

"It's a shame when a man has to all but die to get his children to visit him." Propped on pillows, swathed in bandages, Daniel held court.

"A couple of broken ribs," Serena said lightly and tweaked his toe from her position at the foot of the bed. She'd lain wakeful through the night in Justin's arms.

"Hah! Tell that to the doctor who put this tube in my chest. And you didn't even bring my grandson." He glared briefly at Serena before turning to Caine. "Or my granddaughter. They'll be in college before I see them again. Won't even know who I am."

"We show Laura your picture once a week," Caine offered. He continued to hold Diana's hand, wondering if he would have made it through the past twenty-four hours without her quiet, unflagging strength. "Don't we, love?"

"Every Sunday," Diana agreed.

With a grumpy mutter he turned to Grant and Gennie. "I suppose your sister has an excuse for not coming up," he said to Grant. "And it's only right Alan's with her, though he's my firstborn. After all, she's due to give me another grandchild in a couple of weeks."

"Any excuse," Grant said smoothly as Caine grinned and examined his nails.

"You're looking well, lass," he told Gennie. "A woman just blooms when she's carrying a child."

"And spreads," Gennie returned, touching a hand to her rounded stomach. "Another couple of months and I won't be able to reach my easel."

"See that you use a stool," he ordered. "A pregnant woman shouldn't be on her feet all day."

"And see that you're out of this place and on your own feet by spring," Grant told him as he slipped an arm around his wife. "You'll have to come to Maine to be the baby's godfather."

"Godfather." He preened. "It's a sad thing for a MacGregor to be godfather to a Campbell." He ignored Grant's grin, though it made his lips twitch, and looked at Gennie. "But I'll do it for you. Are you getting enough rest?"

Anna slipped a hand to his wrist to unobtrusively monitor his pulse. "He forgets that I was pregnant with Alan the last three months I interned. Never felt better in my life."

"I felt wonderful during pregnancy myself," Serena commented. "I suppose that's why I'm doing it again."

It only took Daniel a minute. "Again?"

Serena rose on her toes to kiss Justin before she smiled at her father. "Again. Seven months to go."

"Well now—"

"No Scotch, Daniel," Anna said, anticipating him. "At least not until you're out of Intensive Care."

He scowled, muttered, then opened his arms as best he could. "Come here then, little girl."

Serena leaned over the bed and held him as hard as she dared. "Don't you ever scare me like this again," she whispered fiercely.

"Now, now, don't scold," he murmured and stroked her hair. "Bad as your mother. You take good care of her," he ordered Justin. "I don't want my next grandchild born in front of a slot machine."

"Eight to five this one's a girl," Justin answered.

"You're on." Grinning, he turned to Diana. "You have to catch up."

"Don't be greedy," she told him and took his hand.

"A man's entitled to greed when he reaches a certain age, isn't that right, Anna?"

"A woman's entitled to make her own decisions—at any age."

"Hah!" Enormously pleased with himself, he surveyed the room. "I never mentioned that your mother picketed for equal rights before it was stylish, did I? Living with her's been nothing but a trial. And stop taking my pulse, woman. No better medicine for a man than family."

"Then maybe we should give you a bit more." Anna nodded to the nurse outside the door. With a sigh, she leaned against the bed. They were breaking all manner of hospital rules already. What was one more? She felt Daniel's fingers tighten on hers as Alan wheeled Shelby into the room.

"What's this?" he demanded and would have attempted to sit up if Anna hadn't eased him back.

"This," Shelby began, uncovering the bundle in her arms, "is Daniel Campbell MacGregor. He's eight hours and twenty minutes old and wanted to see his grandpa."

Alan took his son to set him in his father's arms. He'd spent the night praying he'd be able to do just that.

"What a sight," Daniel murmured, not bothering to blink the tears from his eyes. "A grandson, Anna. He has my nose. Look, he smiled at me." As Anna leaned down, he laughed. "And don't give me that hogwash about gas. Doctors. I know a smile when I see one." Looking up, he grinned at his son. "Fine job, Alan."

"Thanks." Still awed by his son, Alan sat on the edge of the bed. With one hand he covered his father's over the baby's. For a moment, three generations of MacGregor males were content.

"Campbell," Daniel said abruptly. "Did you say, Campbell?" His gaze locked on Shelby.

"I most certainly did." Her hand slipped into Alan's as she rose. She might be less than nine hours out of the delivery room, but she felt as strong as a bull. Certainly as strong as a MacGregor. "You'd better accept the fact that he's half Campbell, MacGregor." At her brother's chuckle, her chin lifted higher. "Very possibly the best half."

His eyes flashed. Anna took note of his color and approved. He opened his mouth then laughed until he was weak from it. "What a tongue the girl has. At least you had the good sense to name him Daniel."

"I named him after someone I love and admire."

"Flattery." He signaled, reluctantly, for Alan to take the baby. Taking Shelby's hand he held it between both of his. "You look beautiful."

She smiled, a bit stunned by the tears that swam in her eyes. "I feel beautiful."

"You should have heard her swear at the doctor." Delighted with her, Alan pressed a kiss to her temple. "She threatened to get up and go home to have the baby without his interference. She would have, too, if young Daniel hadn't had different ideas."

"Good for you," Daniel decided, and thought his name suited his grandson very well. "Nothing worse than having a doctor fussing around when you just want to get on with your business." After sending Anna a bland smile, he turned back to Shelby. "Now, I want you to get back in bed where you belong. I don't want to worry about you. You've given us all a gift."

She leaned down to kiss his cheek. "You gave me one. Alan. I love you, you old badger."

"Just like a Campbell. Go to bed."

"I'm afraid you're all going to have to run along before the hospital board calls me on the carpet."

"Now, Anna."

"If your father gets enough rest"—she turned to give him a telling look—"he'll be moved out of ICU in the morning."

It wasn't quick, and it wasn't quiet, but Anna finally managed to clear the room. She pretended not to hear Daniel's muttered request to Justin for a game of poker later or his demand to Caine for the cigars Daniel had hidden in his office. If he hadn't made the demands, she'd have worried. No matter how Daniel had protested, she knew visits were as much a strain as a blessing. Until she was satisfied with his condition, she'd keep the future ones short. The trick would be making him think it was his idea. She'd had years of practice.

"Now"—she walked back to the bed and smoothed the hair from his brow—"I've a dozen things to see to that I let go while I was fussing unnecessarily over you. I want you to sleep."

He could be weaker now, now that it was only her. "I don't want you to go yet, Anna. I know you're tired, but I need you to stay just a little longer."

"All right." Dropping the bed guard again, she sat beside him. "Just rest."

"We did a good job, didn't we?"

She smiled, knowing he spoke of the children. "Yes, we did a very good job."

"No regrets?"

Puzzled, she shook her head. "What a foolish question."

"No." He took her hand in his. "Last night I dreamed. I dreamed of you. It started on the night we met, that first waltz."

"The summer ball," she murmured. She had only to smile to see the moonlight, smell the flowers. Odd, it had been in her dreams as well. "It was a beautiful night."

"You were beautiful," he corrected. "And I wanted you more than I'd ever wanted anything in my life."

"You were arrogant," she remembered, smiling. "And desperately attractive." Leaning over, she kissed him softly, lingeringly. The same passion that they'd felt in the beginning hovered over them. "You still are, Daniel."

"I'm old, Anna."

"We're both old."

He pressed her hand to his lips. The ring he'd given her so many years before was cool against his skin. "And I still want you more than I've ever wanted anything in my life."

Ignoring rules and procedure, Anna lay next to him and rested her head on his shoulder. "I'll lose my reputation for this." She closed her eyes. "It's worth it."

"A fine one you are to talk of reputations." He brushed his lips over her hair. The scent was the same after all the years. "It's a funny thing, Anna. I keep having this fierce craving for peach pie."

She lay still a minute, drifting, then her eyes opened on a laugh. They were young and wicked as she tilted her head toward his. "The minute you have a private room."

The Welcoming

For my friend Catherine Coulter,
because she's always good for a laugh.

CHAPTER 1

Everything he needed was in the backpack slung over his shoulders. Including his .38. If things went well he would have no use for it.

Roman drew a cigarette out of the crumpled pack in his breast pocket and turned away from the wind to light it. A boy of about eight raced along the rail of the ferry, cheerfully ignoring his mother's calls. Roman felt a tug of empathy for the kid. It was cold, certainly. The biting wind off Puget Sound was anything but springlike. But it was one hell of a view. Sitting in the glass-walled lounge would be cozier, but it was bound to take something away from the experience.

The kid was snatched by a blond woman with pink cheeks and a rapidly reddening nose. Roman listened to them grumble at each other as she dragged the boy back inside. Families, he thought, rarely agreed on anything. Turning away, he leaned over the rail, lazily smoking as the ferry steamed by clumpy islands.

They had left the Seattle skyline behind, though the mountains of mainland Washington still rose up to amaze and impress the viewer. There was an aloneness here, despite the smattering of hardy passengers walking the slanting deck or bundling up in the patches of sunlight along wooden benches. He preferred the city, with its pace, its crowds, its energy. Its anonymity. He always had. For the life of him, he couldn't understand where this restless discontent he felt had come from, or why it was weighing so heavily on him.

The job. For the past year he'd been blaming it on the job. The pressure was something he'd always accepted, even courted. He'd always thought life without it would be bland and pointless. But just lately it hadn't been enough. He moved from place to place, taking little away, leaving less behind.

Time to get out, he thought as he watched a fishing boat chug by. Time to move on. And do what? he wondered in disgust, blowing out a stream of smoke. He could go into business for himself. He'd toyed with that notion a time or two. He could travel. He'd already been around the world, but it might be different to do it as a tourist.

Some brave soul came out on deck with a video camera. Roman turned, shifted, eased out of range. It was in all likelihood an unnecessary precaution; the move was instinctive. So was the watchfulness, and so was the casual stance, which hid a wiry readiness.

No one paid much attention to him, though a few of the women looked twice.

He was just over average height, with the taut, solid build of a lightweight boxer. The slouchy jacket and worn jeans hid well-toned muscles. He wore no hat and his thick black hair flew freely away from his tanned, hollow-cheeked face. It was unshaven, tough-featured. The eyes, a pale, clear green, might have softened the go-to-hell appearance, but they were intense, direct and, at the moment, bored.

It promised to be a slow, routine assignment.

Roman heard the docking call and shifted his pack. Routine or not, the job was his. He would get it done, file his report, then take a few weeks to figure out what he wanted to do with the rest of his life.

He disembarked with the smattering of other walking passengers. There was a wild, sweet scent of flowers now that competed with the darker scent of the water. The flowers grew in free, romantic splendor, many with blossoms as big as his fist. Some part of him appreciated their color and their charm, but he rarely took the time to stop and smell the roses.

Cars rolled off the ramp and cruised toward home or a day of sightseeing. Once the car decks were unloaded, the new passengers would board and set off for one of the other islands or for the longer, colder trip to British Columbia.

Roman pulled out another cigarette, lit it and took a casual look around—at the pretty, colorful gardens, the charming white hotel and restaurant, the signs that gave information on ferries and parking. It was all a matter of timing now. He ignored the patio café, though he would have dearly loved a cup of coffee, and wound his way to the parking area.

He spotted the van easily enough, the white-and-blue American model with Whale Watch Inn painted on the side. It was his job to talk himself onto the van and into the inn. If the details had been taken care of on this end, it would be routine. If not, he would find another way.

Stalling, he bent down to tie his shoe. The waiting cars were being loaded, and the foot passengers were already on deck. There were no more than a dozen vehicles in the parking area now, including the van. He was taking another moment to unbutton his jacket when he saw the woman.

Her hair was pulled back in a braid, not loose as it had been in the file picture. It seemed to be a deeper, richer blond in the sunlight. She wore tinted glasses, big-framed amber lenses that obscured half of her face, but he knew he wasn't mistaken. He could see the delicate line of her jaw, the small, straight nose, the full, shapely mouth.

His information was accurate. She was five-five, a hundred and ten pounds, with a small, athletic build. Her dress was casual—jeans, a chunky cream-colored cable-knit sweater over a blue shirt. The shirt would match her eyes. The jeans were tucked into suede ankle boots, and a pair of slim crystal earrings dangled at her ears.

She walked with a sense of purpose, keys jingling in one hand, a big canvas bag slung over her other shoulder. There was nothing flirtatious about the walk, but a man would notice it. Long, limber strides, a subtle swing at the hips, head up, eyes ahead.

Yeah, a man would notice, Roman thought as he flicked the cigarette away. He figured she knew it.

He waited until she reached the van before he started toward her.

Charity stopped humming the finale of Beethoven's *Ninth*, looked down at her right front tire and swore. Because she didn't think anyone was watching, she kicked it, then moved around to the back of the van to get the jack.

"Got a problem?"

She jolted, nearly dropped the jack on her foot, then whirled around.

A tough customer. That was Charity's first thought

as she stared at Roman. His eyes were narrowed against the sun. He had one hand hooked around the strap of his backpack and the other tucked in his pocket. She put her own hand on her heart, made certain it was still beating, then smiled.

"Yes. I have a flat. I just dropped a family of four off for the ferry, two of whom were under six and candidates for reform school. My nerves are shot, the plumbing's on the fritz in unit 6, and my handyman just won the lottery. How are you?"

The file hadn't mentioned that she had a voice like café au lait, the rich, dark kind you drink in New Orleans. He noted that, filed it away, then nodded toward the flat. "Want me to change it?"

Charity could have done it herself, but she wasn't one to refuse help when it was offered. Besides, he could probably do it faster, and he looked as though he could use the five dollars she would give him.

"Thanks." She handed him the jack, then dug a lemon drop out of her bag. The flat was bound to eat up the time she'd scheduled for lunch. "Did you just come in on the ferry?"

"Yeah." He didn't care for small talk, but he used it, and her friendliness, as handily as he used the jack. "I've been doing some traveling. Thought I'd spend some time on Orcas, see if I can spot some whales."

"You've come to the right place. I saw a pod yesterday from my window." She leaned against the van, enjoying the sunlight. As he worked, she watched his hands. Strong, competent, quick. She appreciated someone who could do a simple job well. "Are you on vacation?"

"Just traveling. I pick up odd jobs here and there. Know anyone looking for help?"

"Maybe." Lips pursed, she studied him as he pulled

off the flat. He straightened, keeping one hand on the tire. "What kind of work?"

"This and that. Where's the spare?"

"Spare?" Looking into his eyes for more than ten seconds was like being hypnotized.

"Tire." The corner of his mouth quirked slightly in a reluctant smile. "You need one that isn't flat."

"Right. The spare." Shaking her head at her own foolishness, she went to get it. "It's in the back." She turned and bumped into him. "Sorry."

He put one hand on her arm to steady her. They stood for a moment in the sunlight, frowning at each other. "It's all right. I'll get it."

When he climbed into the van, Charity blew out a long, steadying breath. Her nerves were more ragged than she'd have believed possible. "Oh, watch out for the—" She grimaced as Roman sat back on his heels and peeled the remains of a cherry lollipop from his knee. Her laugh was spontaneous and as rich as her voice. "Sorry. A souvenir of Orcas Island from Jimmy 'The Destroyer' MacCarthy, a five-year-old delinquent."

"I'd rather have a T-shirt."

"Yes, well, who wouldn't?" Charity took the sticky mess from him, wrapped it in a tattered tissue and dropped it into her bag. "We're a family establishment," she explained as he climbed out with the spare. "Mostly everyone enjoys having children around, but once in a while you get a pair like Jimmy and Judy, the twin ghouls from Walla Walla, and you think about turning the place into a service station. Do you like children?"

He glanced up as he slipped the tire into place. "From a safe distance."

She laughed appreciatively at his answer. "Where are you from?"

"St. Louis." He could have chosen a dozen places. He couldn't have said why he'd chosen to tell the truth. "But I don't get back much."

"Family?"

"No."

The way he said it made her stifle her innate curiosity. She wouldn't invade anyone's privacy any more than she would drop the lint-covered lollipop on the ground. "I was born right here on Orcas. Every year I tell myself I'm going to take six months and travel. Anywhere." She shrugged as he tightened the last of the lug nuts. "I never seem to manage it. Anyway, it's beautiful here. If you don't have a deadline, you may find yourself staying longer than you planned."

"Maybe." He stood up to replace the jack. "If I can find some work, and a place to stay."

Charity didn't consider it an impulse. She had studied, measured and considered him for nearly fifteen minutes. Most job interviews took little more. He had a strong back and intelligent—if disconcerting—eyes, and if the state of his pack and his shoes was any indication, he was down on his luck. As her name implied, she had been taught to offer people a helping hand. And if she could solve one of her more immediate and pressing problems at the same time . . .

"You any good with your hands?" she asked him.

He looked at her, unable to prevent his mind from taking a slight detour. "Yeah. Pretty good."

Her brow—and her blood pressure—rose a little when she saw his quick survey. "I mean with tools. Hammer, saw, screwdriver. Can you do any carpentry, household repairs?"

"Sure." It was going to be easy, almost too easy. He wondered why he felt the small, unaccustomed tug of guilt.

"Like I said, my handyman won the lottery, a big one. He's gone to Hawaii to study bikinis and eat poi. I'd wish him well, except we were in the middle of renovating the west wing. Of the inn," she added, pointing to the logo on the van. "If you know your way around two-by-fours and drywall, I can give you room and board and five an hour."

"Sounds like we've solved both our problems."

"Great." She offered a hand. "I'm Charity Ford."

"DeWinter." He clasped her hand. "Roman DeWinter."

"Okay, Roman." She swung her door open. "Climb aboard."

She didn't look gullible, Roman thought as he settled into the seat beside her. But then, he knew—better than most—that looks were deceiving. He was exactly where he wanted to be, and he hadn't had to resort to a song and dance. He lit a cigarette as she pulled out of the parking lot.

"My grandfather built the inn in 1938," she said, rolling down her window. "He added on to it a couple of times over the years, but it's still really an inn. We can't bring ourselves to call it a resort, even in the brochures. I hope you're looking for remote."

"That suits me."

"Me too. Most of the time." Talkative guy, she mused with a half smile. But that was all right. She could talk enough for both of them. "It's early in the season yet, so we're a long way from full." She cocked her elbow on the opened window and cheerfully took over the bulk of the conversation. The sunlight played on her earrings and refracted into brilliant colors. "You should have plenty of free time to knock around. The view from Mount Constitution's really spectacular. Or, if you're into it, the hiking trails are great."

"I thought I might spend some time in B.C."

"That's easy enough. Take the ferry to Sidney. We do pretty well with tour groups going back and forth."

"We?"

"The inn. Pop—my grandfather—built a half dozen cabins in the sixties. We give a special package rate to tour groups. They can rent the cabins and have breakfast and dinner included. They're a little rustic, but the tourists really go for them. We get a group about once a week. During the season we can triple that."

She turned onto a narrow, winding road and kept the speed at fifty.

Roman already knew the answers, but he knew it might seem odd if he didn't ask the questions. "Do you run the inn?"

"Yeah. I've worked there on and off for as long as I can remember. When my grandfather died a couple of years ago I took over." She paused a moment. It still hurt; she supposed it always would. "He loved it. Not just the place, but the whole idea of meeting new people every day, making them comfortable, finding out about them."

"I guess it does pretty well."

She shrugged. "We get by." They rounded a bend where the forest gave way to a wide expanse of blue water. The curve of the island was clear, jutting out and tucking back in contrasting shades of deep green and brown. A few houses were tucked high in the cliffs beyond. A boat with billowing white sails ran with the wind, rippling the glassy water. "There are views like this all around the island. Even when you live here they dazzle you."

"And scenery's good for business."

She frowned a little. "It doesn't hurt," she said, and

glanced back at him. "Are you really interested in seeing whales?"

"It seemed like a good idea since I was here."

She stopped the van and pointed to the cliffs. "If you've got patience and a good set of binoculars, up there's a good bet. We've spotted them from the inn, as I said. Still, if you want a close look, your best bet's out on a boat." When he didn't comment, she started the van again. He was making her jittery, she realized. He seemed to be looking not at the water or the forest but at her.

Roman glanced at her hands. Strong, competent, nononsense hands, he decided, though the fingers were beginning to tap a bit nervously on the wheel. She continued to drive fast, steering the van easily through the switchbacks. Another car approached. Without slackening speed, Charity lifted a hand in a salute.

"That was Lori, one of our waitresses. She works an early shift so she can be home when her kids get back from school. We usually run with a staff of ten, then add on five or six part-time during the summer."

They rounded the next curve, and the inn came into view. It was exactly what he'd expected, and yet it was more charming than the pictures he'd been shown. It was white clapboard, with weathered blue trim around arched and oval windows. There were fanciful turrets, narrow walkways and a wide skirting porch. A sweep of lawn led directly to the water, where a narrow, rickety dock jutted out. Tied to it was a small motorboat that swung lazily in the current.

A mill wheel turned in a shallow pond at the side of the inn, slapping the water musically. To the west, where the trees began to thicken, he could make out one of the cabins she had spoken of. Flowers were everywhere.

"There's a bigger pond out back." Charity drove around the side and pulled into a small graveled lot that was already half full. "We keep the trout there. The trail takes you to cabins 1, 2 and 3. Then it forks off to 4, 5 and 6." She stepped out and waited for him to join her. "Most everyone uses the back entrance. I can show you around the grounds later, if you like, but we'll get you settled in first."

"It's a nice place." He said it almost without thinking, and he meant it. There were two rockers on the square back porch, and an Adirondack chair that needed its white paint freshened. Roman turned to study the view a guest would overlook from the empty seat. Part forest, part water, and very appealing. Restful. Welcoming. He thought of the pistol in his backpack. Appearances, he thought again, were deceiving.

With a slight frown, Charity watched him. He didn't seem to be looking so much as absorbing. It was an odd thought, but she would have sworn if anyone were to ask him to describe the inn six months later he would be able to, right down to the last pinecone.

Then he turned to her, and the feeling remained, more personal now, more intense. The breeze picked up, jingling the wind chimes that hung from the eaves.

"Are you an artist?" she asked abruptly.

"No." He smiled, and the change in his face was quick and charming. "Why?"

"Just wondering." You'd have to be careful of that smile, Charity decided. It made you relax, and she doubted he was a man it was wise to relax around.

The double glass doors opened up into a large, airy room that smelled of lavender and woodsmoke. There were two long, cushiony sofas and a pair of overstuffed chairs near a huge stone fireplace where logs crackled. Antiques were scattered throughout the room—a desk and chair with a trio of old inkwells, an oak hat rack, a buffet with glossy carved doors. Tucked into a corner was a spinet with yellowing keys, and the pair of wide arched windows that dominated the far wall made the water seem part of the room's decor. At a table near them, two women were playing a leisurely game of Scrabble.

"Who's winning today?" Charity asked.

Both looked up. And beamed. "It's neck and neck." The woman on the right fluffed her hair when she spotted Roman. She was old enough to be his grandmother, but she slipped her glasses off and straightened her thin shoulders. "I didn't realize you were bringing back another guest, dear."

"Neither did I." Charity moved over to add another log to the fire. "Roman DeWinter, Miss Lucy and Miss Millie."

His smile came again, smoothly. "Ladies."

"DeWinter." Miss Lucy put on her glasses to get a better look. "Didn't we know a DeWinter once, Millie?"

"Not that I recall." Millie, always ready to flirt, continued to beam at Roman, though he was hardly more than a myopic blur. "Have you been to the inn before, Mr. DeWinter?"

"No, ma'am. This is my first time in the San Juans."

"You're in for a treat." Millie let out a little sigh. It was really too bad what the years did. It seemed only yesterday that handsome young men had kissed her hand and asked her to go for a walk. Today they called her ma'am. She went wistfully back to her game.

"The ladies have been coming to the inn longer than I can remember," Charity told Roman as she led the way down a hall. "They're lovely, but I should warn you about Miss Millie. I'm told she had quite a reputation in her day, and she still has an eye for an attractive man."

"I'll watch my step."

"I get the impression you usually do." She took out a set of keys and unlocked the door. "This leads to the west wing." She started down another hall, brisk, businesslike. "As you can see, renovations were well under way before George hit the jackpot. The trim's been stripped." She gestured to the neat piles of wood along the freshly painted wall. "The doors need to be refinished yet, and the original hardware's in that box."

After taking off her sunglasses, she dropped them into her bag. He'd been right. The collar of her shirt matched her eyes almost exactly. He looked into them as she examined George's handiwork.

"How many rooms?"

"There are two singles, a double and a family suite in this wing, all in varying stages of disorder." She skirted a door that was propped against a wall, then walked into a room. "You can take this one. It's as close to being finished as I have in this section."

It was a small, bright room. Its window was bordered with stained glass and looked out over the mill wheel. The bed was stripped, and the floors were bare and in need of sanding. Wallpaper that was obviously new covered the walls from the ceiling down to a white chair rail. Below that was bare drywall.

"It doesn't look like much now," Charity commented.

"It's fine." He'd spent time in places that made the little room look like a suite at the Waldorf.

Automatically she checked the closet and the adjoining bath, making a mental list of what was needed. "You can start in here, if it'll make you more comfortable. I'm not particular. George had his own system.

I never understood it, but he usually managed to get things done."

He hooked his thumbs in the front pockets of his jeans. "You got a game plan?"

"Absolutely."

Charity spent the next thirty minutes taking him through the wing and explaining exactly what she wanted. Roman listened, commenting little, and studied the setup. He knew from the blueprints he'd studied that the floor plan of this section mirrored that of the east wing. His position in it would give him easy access to the main floor and the rest of the inn.

He'd have to work, he mused as he looked at the half-finished walls and the paint tarps. He considered it a small bonus. Working with his hands was something he enjoyed and something he'd had little time for in the past.

She was very precise in her instructions. A woman who knew what she wanted and intended to have it. He appreciated that. He had no doubt that she was very good at what she did, whether it was running an inn . . . or something else.

"What's up there?" He pointed to a set of stairs at the end of the hallway.

"My rooms. We'll worry about them after the guest quarters are done." She jingled the keys as her thoughts went off in a dozen directions. "So, what do you think?"

"About what?"

"About the work."

"Do you have tools?"

"In the shed, the other side of the parking area."

"I can handle it."

"Yes." Charity tossed the keys to him. She was certain he could. They were standing in the octagonal parlor of the family suite. It was empty but for stacks of material and tarps. And it was quiet. She noticed all at once that they were standing quite close together and that she couldn't hear a sound. Feeling foolish, she took a key off her ring.

"You'll need this."

"Thanks." He tucked it in his pocket.

She drew a deep breath, wondering why she felt as though she'd just taken a long step with her eyes closed. "Have you had lunch?"

"No."

"I'll show you down to the kitchen. Mae'll fix you up." She started out, a little too quickly. She wanted to escape from the sensation that she was completely alone with him. And helpless. Charity moved her shoulders restlessly. A stupid thought, she told herself. She'd never been helpless. Still, she felt a breath of relief when she closed the door behind them.

She took him downstairs, through the empty lobby and into a large dining room decorated in pastels. There were small milk-glass vases on each table, with a handful of fresh flowers in each. Big windows opened onto a view of the water, and as if carrying through the theme, an aquarium was built into the south wall.

She stopped there for a moment, hardly breaking stride, scanning the room until she was satisfied that the tables were properly set for dinner. Then she pushed through a swinging door into the kitchen.

"And I say it needs more basil."

"I say it don't."

"Whatever you do," Charity murmured under her breath, "don't agree with either of them. Ladies," she said, using her best smile. "I brought you a hungry man."

The woman guarding the pot held up a dripping

spoon. The best way to describe her was wide—face, hips, hands. She gave Roman a quick, squint-eyed survey. "Sit down, then," she told him, jerking a thumb in the direction of a long wooden table.

"Mae Jenkins, Roman DeWinter."

"Ma'am."

"And Dolores Rumsey." The other woman was holding a jar of herbs. She was as narrow as Mae was wide. After giving Roman a nod, she began to ease her way toward the pot.

"Keep away from that," Mae ordered, "and get the man some fried chicken."

Muttering, Dolores stalked off to find a plate.

"Roman's going to pick up where George left off," Charity explained. "He'll be staying in the west wing."

"Not from around here." Mae looked at him again, the way he imagined a nanny would look at a small, grubby child.

"No."

With a sniff, she poured him some coffee. "Looks like you could use a couple of decent meals."

"You'll get them here," Charity put in, playing peacemaker. She winced only a little when Dolores slapped a plate of cold chicken and potato salad in front of Roman.

"Needed more dill." Dolores glared at him, as if she were daring him to disagree. "She wouldn't listen."

Roman figured the best option was to grin at her and keep his mouth full. Before Mae could respond, the door swung open again.

"Can a guy get a cup of coffee in here?" The man stopped and sent Roman a curious look.

"Bob Mullins, Roman DeWinter. I hired him to finish the west wing. Bob's one of my many right hands."

"Welcome aboard." He moved to the stove to pour

himself a cup of coffee, adding three lumps of sugar as Mae clucked her tongue at him. The sweet tooth didn't seem to have an effect on him. He was tall, perhaps six-two, and he couldn't weigh more than 160. His light brown hair was cut short around his ears and swept back from his high forehead.

"You from back east?" Bob asked between sips of coffee.

"East of here."

"Easy to do." He grinned when Mae flapped a hand to move him away from her stove.

"Did you get that invoice business straightened out with the greengrocer?" Charity asked.

"All taken care of. You got a couple of calls while you were out. And there's some papers you need to sign."

"I'll get to it." She checked her watch. "Now." She glanced over at Roman. "I'll be in the office off the lobby if there's anything you need to know."

"I'll be fine."

"Okay." She studied him for another moment. She couldn't quite figure out how he could be in a room with four other people and seem so alone. "See you later."

Roman took a long, casual tour of the inn before he began to haul tools into the west wing. He saw a young couple who had to be newlyweds locked in an embrace near the pond. A man and a young boy played one-on-one on a small concrete basketball court. The ladies, as he had come to think of them, had left their game to sit on the porch and discuss the garden. Looking exhausted, a family of four pulled up in a station wagon, then trooped toward the cabins. A man in a fielder's cap walked down the pier with a video camera on his shoulder.

There were birds trilling in the trees, and there was the distant sound of a motorboat. He heard a baby crying halfheartedly, and the strains of a Mozart piano sonata.

If he hadn't pored over the data himself he would have sworn he was in the wrong place.

He chose the family suite and went to work, wondering how long it would take him to get into Charity's rooms.

There was something soothing about working with his hands. Two hours passed, and he relaxed a little. A check of his watch had him deciding to take another, unnecessary trip to the shed. Charity had mentioned that wine was served in what she called the gathering room every evening at five. It wouldn't hurt for him to get another, closer look at the inn's guests.

He started out, then stopped by the doorway to his room. He'd heard something, a movement. Cautious, he eased inside the door and scanned the empty room.

Humming under her breath, Charity came out of the bath, where she'd just placed fresh towels. She unfolded linens and began to make the bed.

"What are you doing?"

Muffling a scream, she stumbled backward, then eased down on the bed to catch her breath. "My God, Roman, don't do that."

He stepped into the room, watching her with narrowed eyes. "I asked what you were doing."

"That should be obvious." She patted the pile of linens with her hand.

"You do the housekeeping, too?"

"From time to time." Recovered, she stood up and smoothed the bottom sheet on the bed. "There's soap and towels in the bath," she told him, then tilted her head. "Looks like you can use them." She unfolded the top sheet with an expert flick. "Been busy?"

"That was the deal."

With a murmur of agreement, she tucked up the corners at the foot of the bed the way he remembered his grandmother doing. "I put an extra pillow and blanket in the closet." She moved from one side of the bed to the other in a way that had him watching her with simple male appreciation. He couldn't remember the last time he'd seen anyone make a bed. It stirred thoughts in him that he couldn't afford. Thoughts of what it might be like to mess it up again—with her.

"Do you ever stop?"

"I've been known to." She spread a white wedding-ring quilt on the bed. "We're expecting a tour tomorrow, so everyone's a bit busy."

"Tomorrow?"

"Mmm. On the first ferry from Sidney." She fluffed his pillows, satisfied. "Did you—"

She broke off when she turned and all but fell against him. His hands went to her hips instinctively as hers braced against his shoulders. An embrace—unplanned, unwanted and shockingly intimate.

She was slender beneath the long, chunky sweater, he realized, even more slender than a man might expect. And her eyes were bluer than they had any right to be, bigger, softer. She smelled like the inn, smelled of that welcoming combination of lavender and woodsmoke. Drawn to it, he continued to hold her, though he knew he shouldn't.

"Did I what?" His fingers spread over her hips, drawing her just a fraction closer. He saw the dazed confusion in her eyes; her reaction tugged at him.

She'd forgotten everything. She could only stare,

almost stupefied by the sensations that spiked through her. Involuntarily her fingers curled into his shirt. She got an impression of strength, a ruthless strength with the potential for violence. The fact that it excited her left her speechless.

"Do you want something?" he murmured.

"What?"

He thought about kissing her, about pressing his mouth hard on hers and plunging into her. He would enjoy the taste, the momentary passion. "I asked if you wanted something." Slowly he ran his hands up under her sweater to her waist.

The shock of heat, the press of fingers, brought her back. "No." She started to back away, found herself held still, and fought her rising panic. Before she could speak again, he had released her. Disappointment. That was an odd reaction, she thought, when you'd just missed getting burned.

"I was—" She took a deep breath and waited for her scattered nerves to settle. "I was going to ask if you'd found everything you needed."

His eyes never left hers. "It looks like it."

She pressed her lips together to moisten them. "Good. I've got a lot to do, so I'll let you get back."

He took her arm before she could step away. Maybe it wasn't smart, but he wanted to touch her again. "Thanks for the towels."

"Sure."

He watched her hurry out, knowing her nerves were as jangled as his own. Thoughtfully he pulled out a cigarette. He couldn't remember ever having been thrown off balance so easily. Certainly not by a woman who'd done nothing more than look at him. Still, he made a habit of landing on his feet.

It might be to his advantage to get close to her,

to play on the response he'd felt from her. Ignoring a wave of self-disgust, he struck a match.

He had a job to do. He couldn't afford to think about Charity Ford as anything more than a means to an end.

He drew smoke in, cursing the dull ache in his belly.

CHAPTER 2

It was barely dawn, and the sky to the east was fantastic. Roman stood near the edge of the narrow road, his hands tucked in his back pockets. Though he rarely had time for them, he enjoyed mornings such as this, when the air was cool and sparkling clear. A man could breathe here, and if he could afford the luxury he could empty his mind and simply experience.

He'd promised himself thirty minutes, thirty solitary, soothing minutes. The blooming sunlight pushed through the cloud formations, turning them into wild, vivid colors and shapes. Dream shapes. He considered lighting a cigarette, then rejected it. For the moment he wanted only the taste of morning air flavored by the sea.

There was a dog barking in the distance, a faint yap, yap, yap that only added to the ambience. Gulls, out for an early feeding, swooped low over the water, slicing the silence with their lonely cries. The fragrance of flowers, a celebration of spring, carried delicately on the quiet breeze.

He wondered why he'd been so certain he preferred the rush and noise of cities.

As he stood there he saw a deer come out of the trees and raise her head to scent the air. That was freedom, he thought abruptly. To know your place and to be content with it. The doe cleared the trees, picking her way delicately toward the high grass. Behind her came a gangly fawn. Staying upwind, Roman watched them graze.

He was restless. Even as he tried to absorb and accept the peace around him he felt the impatience struggling through. This wasn't his place. He had no place. That was one of the things that made him so perfect for his job. No roots, no family, no woman waiting for his return. That was the way he wanted it.

But he'd felt enormous satisfaction in doing the carpentry the day before, in leaving his mark on something that would last. All the better for his cover, he told himself. If he showed some skill and some care in the work he would be accepted more easily.

He was already accepted.

She trusted him. She'd given him a roof and a meal and a job, thinking he needed all three. She seemed to have no guile in her. Something had simmered between them the evening before, yet she had done nothing to provoke or prolong it. She hadn't—though he knew all females were capable of it from birth—issued a silent invitation that she might or might not have intended to keep.

She'd simply looked at him, and everything she felt had been almost ridiculously clear in her eyes.

He couldn't think of her as a woman. He couldn't think of her as ever being *his* woman.

He felt the urge for a cigarette again, and this time he deliberately suppressed it. If there was something you wanted that badly, it was best to pass it by. Once you gave in, you surrendered control.

He'd wanted Charity. For one brief, blinding instant the day before, he had craved her. A very serious error. He'd blocked the need, but it had continued to surface—when he'd heard her come into the wing for the night, when he'd listened to the sound of Chopin drifting softly down the stairway from her rooms. And again in the middle of the night, when he'd awakened to the deep country silence, thinking of her, imagining her.

He didn't have time for desires. In another place, at another time, they might have met and enjoyed each other for as long as enjoyments lasted. But now she was part of an assignment—nothing less, nothing more.

He heard the sound of running footsteps and tensed instinctively. The deer, as alert as he, lifted her head, then sprinted back into the trees with her young. His weapon was strapped just above his ankle, more out of habit than necessity, but he didn't reach for it. If he needed it it could be in his hand in under a second. Instead he waited, braced, to see who was running down the deserted road at dawn.

Charity was breathing fast, more from the effort of keeping pace with her dog than from the three-mile run. Ludwig bounded ahead, tugged to the right, jerked to the left, tangled and untangled in the leash. It was a daily routine, one that both of them were accustomed to. She could have controlled the little golden cocker, but she didn't want to spoil his fun. Instead, she swerved with him, adjusting her pace from a flat-out run to an easy jog and back again.

She hesitated briefly when she saw Roman. Then, because Ludwig sprinted ahead, she tightened her grip on the leash and kept pace.

"Good morning," she called out, then skidded to a halt when Ludwig decided to jump on Roman's shins and bark at him. "He doesn't bite."

"That's what they all say." But he grinned and crouched down to scratch between the dog's ears. Ludwig immediately collapsed, rolled over and exposed his belly for rubbing. "Nice dog."

"A nice spoiled dog," Charity added. "I have to keep him fenced because of the guests, but he eats like a king. You're up early."

"So are you."

"I figure Ludwig deserves a good run every morning, since he's so understanding about being fenced."

To show his appreciation, Ludwig raced once around Roman, tangling his lead around his legs.

"Now if I could only get him to understand the concept of a leash." She stooped to untangle Roman and to control the now-prancing dog.

Her light jacket was unzipped, exposing a snug T-shirt darkened with sweat between her breasts. Her hair, pulled straight, almost severely, back from her face, accented her bone structure. Her skin seemed almost translucent as it glowed from her run. He had an urge to touch it, to see how it felt under his fingertips. And to see if that instant reaction would rush out again.

"Ludwig, be still a minute." She laughed and tugged at his collar.

In response, the dog jumped up and lapped at her face. "He listens well," Roman commented.

"You can see why I need the fence. He thinks he can play with everyone." Her hand brushed Roman's leg as she struggled with the leash.

When he took her wrist, both of them froze.

He could feel her pulse skip, then sprint. It was a

quick, vulnerable response that was unbearably arousing. Though it cost him, he kept his fingers loose. He had only meant to stop her before she inadvertently found his weapon. Now they crouched, knee to knee, in the center of the deserted road, with the dog trying to nuzzle between them.

"You're trembling." He said it warily, but he didn't release her. "Do you always react that way when a man touches you?"

"No." Because it baffled her, she kept still and waited to see what would happen next. "I'm pretty sure this is a first."

It pleased him to hear it, and it annoyed him, because he wanted to believe it. "Then we'll have to be careful, won't we?" He released her, then stood up.

More slowly, because she wasn't sure of her balance, she rose. He was angry. Though he was holding on to his temper, it was clear enough to see in his eyes. "I'm not very good at being careful."

His gaze whipped back to hers. There was a fire in it, a fire that raged and then was quickly and completely suppressed. "I am."

"Yes." The brief, heated glance had alarmed her, but Charity had always held her own. She tilted her head to study him. "I think you'd have to be, with that streak of violence you have to contend with. Who are you mad at, Roman?"

He didn't like to be read that easily. Watching her, he lowered a hand to pet Ludwig, who was resting his front paws on his knees. "Nobody at the moment," he told her, but it was a lie. He was furious—with himself.

She only shook her head. "You're entitled to your secrets, but I can't help wondering why you'd be angry with yourself for responding to me."

He took a lazy scan of the road, up, then down.

They might have been alone on the island. "Would you like me to do something about it, here and now?"

He could, she realized. And he would. If he was pushed too far he would do exactly what he wanted, when he wanted. The frisson of excitement that passed through her annoyed her. Macho types were for other women, different women—not Charity Ford. Deliberately she looked at her watch.

"Thanks. I'm sure that's a delightful offer, but I have to get back and set up for breakfast." Struggling with the dog, she started off at what she hoped was a dignified walk. "I'll let you know if I can squeeze in, say, fifteen minutes later."

"Charity?"

She turned her head and aimed a cool look. "Yes?"

"Your shoe's untied."

She just lifted her chin and continued on.

Roman grinned at her back and tucked his thumbs in his pockets. Yes, indeed, the woman had one hell of a walk. It was too damn bad all around that he was beginning to like her.

He was interested in the tour group. It was a simple matter for Roman to loiter on the first floor, lingering over a second cup of coffee in the kitchen, passing idle conversation with the thick-armed Mae and the skinny Dolores. He hadn't expected to be put to work, but when he'd found himself with an armful of table linens he had made the best of it.

Charity, wearing a bright red sweatshirt with the inn's logo across the chest, meticulously arranged a folded napkin in a water glass. Roman waited a moment, watching her busy fingers smoothing and tapering the cloth.

"Where do you want these?"

She glanced over, wondering if she should still be annoyed with him, then decided against it. At the moment she needed every extra hand she could get. "On the tables would be a good start. White on the bottom, apricot on top, slanted. Okay?" She indicated a table that was already set.

"Sure." He began to spread the cloths. "How many are you expecting?"

"Fifteen on the tour." She held a glass up to the light and placed it on the table only after a critical inspection. "Their breakfast is included. Plus the guests already registered. We serve between seven-thirty and ten." She checked her watch, satisfied, then moved to another table. "We get some drop-ins, as well." After setting a chipped bread plate aside, she reached for another. "But it's lunch and dinner that really get hectic."

Dolores swooped in with a stack of china, then dashed out again when Mae squawked at her. Before the door had swung closed, the waitress they had passed on the road the day before rushed out with a tray of clanging silverware.

"Right," Roman murmured.

Charity rattled off instructions to the waitress, finished setting yet another table, then rushed over to a blackboard near the doorway and began to copy out the morning menu in a flowing, elegant hand.

Dolores, whose spiky red hair and pursed lips made Roman think of a scrawny chicken, shoved through the swinging door and set her fists on her skinny hips. "I don't have to take this, Charity."

Charity calmly continued to write. "Take what?"

"I'm doing the best that I can, and you know I told you I was feeling poorly."

Dolores was always feeling poorly, Charity thought

as she added a ham-and-cheese omelet to the list. Especially when she didn't get her way. "Yes, Dolores."

"My chest's so tight that I can hardly take a breath."

"Um-hmm."

"Was up half the night, but I come in, just like always."

"And I appreciate it, Dolores. You know how much I depend on you."

"Well." Slightly mollified, Dolores tugged at her apron. "I guess I can be counted on to do my job, but you can just tell that woman in there—" She jerked a thumb toward the kitchen. "Just tell her to get off my back."

"I'll speak to her, Dolores. Just try to be patient. We're all a little frazzled this morning, with Mary Alice out sick again."

"Sick." Dolores sniffed. "Is that what they're calling it these days?"

Listening with only half an ear, Charity continued to write. "What do you mean?"

"Don't know why her car was in Bill Perkin's driveway all night again if she's sick. Now, with my condition—"

Charity stopped writing. Roman's brow lifted when he heard the sudden thread of steel in her voice. "We'll talk about this later, Dolores."

Deflated, Dolores poked out her lower lip and stalked back into the kitchen.

Storing her anger away, Charity turned to the waitress. "Lori?"

"Almost ready."

"Good. If you can handle the registered guests, I'll be back to give you a hand after I check the tour group in."

"No problem."

"I'll be at the front desk with Bob." Absently she pushed her braid behind her back. "If it gets too busy, send for me. Roman—"

"Want me to bus tables?"

She gave him a quick, grateful smile. "Do you know how?"

"I can figure it out."

"Thanks." She checked her watch, then rushed out.

He hadn't expected to enjoy himself, but it was hard not to, with Miss Millie flirting with him over her raspberry preserves. The scent of baking—something rich, with apples and cinnamon—the quiet strains of classical music and the murmur of conversation made it almost impossible not to relax. He carried trays to and from the kitchen. The muttered exchanges between Mae and Dolores were more amusing than annoying.

So he enjoyed himself. And took advantage of his position by doing his job.

As he cleared the tables by the windows, he watched a tour van pull up to the front entrance. He counted heads and studied the faces of the group. The guide was a big man in a white shirt that strained across his shoulders. He had a round, ruddy, cheerful face that smiled continually as he piloted his passengers inside. Roman moved across the room to watch them mill around in the lobby.

They were a mix of couples and families with small children. The guide—Roman already knew his name was Block—greeted Charity with a hearty smile and then handed her a list of names.

Did she know that Block had done a stretch in Leavenworth for fraud? he wondered. Was she aware that the man she was joking with had escaped a second term only because of some fancy legal footwork?

Roman's jaw tensed as Block reached over and flicked a finger at Charity's dangling gold earring.

As she assigned cabins and dealt out keys, two of the group approached the desk to exchange money. Fifty for one, sixty for the other, Roman noted as Canadian bills were passed to Charity's assistant and American currency passed back.

Within ten minutes the entire group was seated in the dining room, contemplating breakfast. Charity breezed in behind them, putting on an apron. She flipped open a pad and began to take orders.

She didn't look as if she were in a hurry, Roman noted. The way she chatted and smiled and answered questions, it was as though she had all the time in the world. But she moved like lightning. She carried three plates on her right arm, served coffee with her left hand and cooed over a baby, all at the same time.

Something was eating at her, Roman mused. It hardly showed . . . just a faint frown between her eyes. Had something gone wrong that morning that he'd missed? If there was a glitch in the system, it was up to him to find it and exploit it. That was the reason he was here on the inside.

Charity poured another round of coffee for a table of four, joked with a bald man wearing a paisley tie, then made her way over to Roman.

"I think the crisis has passed." She smiled at him, but again he caught something. . . . Anger? Disappointment?

"Is there anything you don't do around here?"

"I try to stay out of the kitchen. The restaurant has a three-star rating." She glanced longingly at the coffeepot. There would be time for that later. "I want to thank you for pitching in this morning."

"That's okay." He discovered he wanted to see her

smile. Really smile. "The tips were good. Miss Millie slipped me a five."

She obliged him. Her lips curved quickly, and whatever had clouded her eyes cleared for a moment. "She likes the way you look in a tool belt. Why don't you take a break before you start on the west wing?"

"All right."

She grimaced at the sound of glass breaking. "I didn't think the Snyder kid wanted that orange juice." She hurried off to clean up the mess and listen to the parents' apologies.

The front desk was deserted. Roman decided that Charity's assistant was either shut up in the side office or out hauling luggage to the cabins. He considered slipping behind the desk and taking a quick look at the books but decided it could wait. Some work was better done in the dark.

An hour later Charity let herself into the west wing. She'd managed to hold on to her temper as she'd passed the guests on the first floor. She'd smiled and chatted with an elderly couple playing Parcheesi in the gathering room. But when the door closed behind her she let loose with a series of furious, pent-up oaths. She wanted to kick something.

Roman stepped into a doorway and watched her stride down the hall. Anger had made her eyes dark and brilliant.

"Problem?"

"Yes," she snapped. She stalked half a dozen steps past him, then whirled around. "I can take incompetence, and even some degree of stupidity. I can even tolerate an occasional bout of laziness. But I won't be lied to."

Roman waited a beat. Her anger was ripe and rich,

but it wasn't directed at him. "All right," he said, and waited.

"She could have told me she wanted time off, or a different shift. I might have been able to work it out. Instead she lies, calling in sick at the last minute five days out of the last two weeks. I was worried about her." She turned again, then gave in and kicked a door. "I hate being made a fool of. And I *hate* being lied to."

It was a simple matter to put two and two together. "You're talking about the waitress . . . Mary Alice?"

"Of course." She spun around. "She came begging me for a job three months ago. That's our slowest time, but I felt sorry for her. Now she's sleeping with Bill Perkin—or I guess it's more accurate to say she's not getting any sleep, so she calls in sick. I had to fire her." She let out a breath with a sound like an engine letting off steam. "I get a headache whenever I have to fire anybody."

"Is that what was bothering you all morning?"

"As soon as Dolores mentioned Bill, I knew." Calmer now, she rubbed at the insistent ache between her eyes. "Then I had to get through the check-in and the breakfast shift before I could call and deal with her. She cried." She gave Roman a long, miserable look. "I knew she was going to cry."

"Listen, baby, the best thing for you to do is take some aspirin and forget about it."

"I've already taken some."

"Give it a chance to kick in." Before he realized what he was doing, he lifted his hands and framed her face. Moving his thumbs in slow circles, he massaged her temples. "You've got too much going on in there."

"Where?"

"In your head."

She felt her eyes getting heavy and her blood growing warm. "Not at the moment." She tilted her head back and let her eyes close. Moving on instinct, she stepped forward. "Roman . . ." She sighed a little as the ache melted out of her head and stirred in the very center of her. "I like the way you look in a tool belt, too."

"Do you know what you're asking for?"

She studied his mouth. It was full and firm, and it would certainly be ruthless on a woman's. "Not exactly." Perhaps that was the appeal, she thought as she stared up at him. She didn't know. But she felt, and what she felt was new and thrilling. "Maybe it's better that way."

"No." Though he knew it was a mistake, he couldn't resist skimming his fingers down to trace her jaw, then her lips. "It's always better to know the consequences before you take the action."

"So we're being careful again."

He dropped his hands. "Yeah."

She should have been grateful. Instead of taking advantage of her confused emotions he was backing off, giving her room. She wanted to be grateful, but she felt only the sting of rejection. He had started it, she thought. Again. And he had stopped it. Again. She was sick and tired of being jolted along according to his whims.

"You miss a lot that way, don't you, Roman? A lot of warmth, a lot of joy."

"A lot of disappointment."

"Maybe. I guess it's harder for some of us to live our lives aloof from others. But if that's your choice, fine." She drew in a deep breath. Her headache was coming back, doubled. "Don't touch me again. I make it a habit to finish whatever I start." She glanced into the room behind them. "You're doing a nice job here," she said briskly. "I'll let you get back to it."

He cursed her as he sanded the wood for the window trim. She had no right to make him feel guilty just because he wanted to keep his distance. Noninvolvement wasn't just a habit with him; it was a matter of survival. It was self-indulgent and dangerous to move forward every time you were attracted to a woman.

But it was more than attraction, and it was certainly different from anything he'd felt before. Whenever he was near her, his purpose became clouded with fantasies of what it would be like to be with her, to hold her, to make love with her.

And fantasies were all they were, he reminded himself. If things went well he would be gone in a matter of days. Before he was done he might very well destroy her life.

It was his job, he reminded himself.

He saw her, walking out to the van with those long, purposeful strides of hers, the keys jingling in her hand. Behind her were the newlyweds, holding hands, even though each was carrying a suitcase.

She would be taking them to the ferry, he thought. That would give him an hour to search her rooms.

He knew how to go through every inch of a room without leaving a trace. He concentrated first on the obvious—the desk in the small parlor. It was common for people to be careless in the privacy of their own homes. A slip of paper, a scribbled note, a name in an address book, were often left behind for the trained eye to spot.

It was an old desk, solid mahogany with a few rings and scratches. Two of the brass pulls were loose. Like the rest of the room, it was neat and well organized. Her personal papers—insurance documents, bills, correspondence—were filed on the left. Inn business took up the three drawers on the right.

He could see from a quick scan that the inn made a reasonable profit, most of which she funneled directly back into it. New linens, bathroom fixtures, paint. The stove Mae was so territorial about had been purchased only six months earlier.

She took a salary for herself, a surprisingly modest one. He didn't find, even after a more critical study, any evidence of her using any of the inn's finances to ease her own way.

An honest woman, Roman mused. At least on the surface.

There was a bowl of potpourri on the desk, as there was in every room in the inn. Beside it was a framed picture of Charity standing in front of the mill wheel with a fragile-looking man with white hair.

The grandfather, Roman decided, but it was Charity's image he studied. Her hair was pulled back in a ponytail, and her baggy overalls were stained at the knees. From gardening, Roman guessed. She was holding an armful of summer flowers. She looked as if she didn't have a care in the world, but he noted that her free arm was around the old man, supporting him.

He wondered what she had been thinking at that moment, what she had done the moment after the picture had been snapped. He swore at himself and looked away from the picture.

She left notes to herself: Return wallpaper samples. New blocks for toy chest. Call piano tuner. Get flat repaired.

He found nothing that touched on his reason for

coming to the inn. Leaving the desk, he meticulously searched the rest of the parlor.

Then he went into the adjoining bedroom. The bed, a four-poster, was covered with a lacy white spread and plumped with petit-point pillows. Beside it was a beautiful old rocker, its arms worn smooth as glass. In it sat a big purple teddy bear wearing yellow suspenders.

The curtains were romantic priscillas. She'd left the windows open, and the breeze came through, billowing them. A woman's room, Roman thought, unrelentingly feminine with its lace and pillows, its fragile scents and pale colors. Yet somehow it welcomed a man, made him wish, made him want. It made him want one hour, one night, in that softness, that comfort.

He crossed the faded handhooked rug and, burying his self-disgust, went through her dresser.

He found a few pieces of jewelry he took to be heirlooms. They belonged in a safe, he thought, annoyed with her. There was a bottle of perfume. He knew exactly how it would smell. It would smell the way her skin did. He nearly reached for it before he caught himself. Perfume wasn't of any interest to him. Evidence was.

A packet of letters caught his eye. From a lover? he wondered, dismissing the sudden pang of jealousy he felt as ridiculous.

The room was making him crazy, he thought as he carefully untied the slender satin ribbon. It was impossible not to imagine her there, curled on the bed, wearing something white and thin, her hair loose and the candles lit.

He shook himself as he unfolded the first letter. A room with a purple teddy bear wasn't seductive, he told himself.

The date showed him that they had been written when she had attended college in Seattle. From her grandfather, Roman realized as he scanned them. Every one. They were written with affection and humor, and they contained dozens of little stories about daily life at the inn. Roman put them back the way he'd found them.

Her clothes were casual, except for a few dresses hanging in the closet. There were sturdy boots, sneakers spotted with what looked like grass stains, and two pairs of elegant heels on either side of fuzzy slippers in the shape of elephants. Like the rest of her rooms, they were meticulously arranged. Even in the closet he didn't find a trace of dust.

Besides an alarm clock and a pot of hand cream she had two books on her nightstand. One was a collection of poetry, the other a murder mystery with a gruesome cover. She had a cache of chocolate in the drawer and Chopin on her small portable stereo. There were candles, dozens of them, burned down to various heights. On one wall hung a seascape in deep, stormy blues and grays. On another was a collection of photos, most taken at the inn, many of her grandfather. Roman searched behind each one. He discovered that her paint was fading, nothing more.

Her rooms were clean. Roman stood in the center of the bedroom, taking in the scents of candle wax, potpourri and perfume. They couldn't have been cleaner if she'd known they were going to be searched. All he knew after an hour was that she was an organized woman who liked comfortable clothes and Chopin and had a weakness for chocolate and lurid paperback novels.

Why did that make her fascinating?

He scowled and shoved his hands in his pockets,

struggling for objectivity as he had never had to struggle before. All the evidence pointed to her being involved in some very shady business. Everything he'd discovered in the last twenty-four hours indicated that she was an open, honest and hardworking woman.

Which did he believe?

He walked toward the door at the far end of the room. It opened onto a postage-stamp-size porch with a long set of stairs that led down to the pond. He wanted to open the door, to step out and breathe in the air, but he turned his back on it and went out the way he had come in.

The scent of her bedroom stayed with him for hours.

CHAPTER 3

"I told you that girl was no good."

"I know, Mae."

"I told you you were making a mistake taking her on like you did."

"Yes, Mae." Charity bit back a sigh. "You told me."

"You keep taking in strays, you're bound to get bit."

Charity resisted—just barely—the urge to scream. "So you've told me."

With a satisfied grunt, Mae finished wiping off her pride and joy, the eight-burner gas range. Charity might run the inn, but Mae had her own ideas about who was in charge. "You're too softhearted, Charity."

"I thought you said it was hardheaded."

"That too." Because she had a warm spot for her young employer, Mae poured a glass of milk and cut a generous slab from the remains of her double chocolate cake. Keeping her voice brisk, she set both on the table. "You eat this now. My baking always made you feel better as a girl."

Charity took a seat and poked a finger into the icing. "I would have given her some time off."

"I know." Mae rubbed her wide-palmed hand on Charity's shoulder. "That's the trouble with you. You take your name too seriously."

"I hate being made a fool of." Scowling, Charity took a huge bite of cake. Chocolate, she was sure, would be a better cure for her headache than an entire bottle of aspirin. Her guilt was a different matter. "Do you think she'll get another job? I know she's got rent to pay."

"Types like Mary Alice always land on their feet. Wouldn't surprise me if she moved in lock, stock and barrel with that Perkin boy, so don't you be worrying about the likes of her. Didn't I tell you she wouldn't last six months?"

Charity pushed more cake into her mouth. "You told me," she mumbled around it.

"Now then, what about this man you brought home?"

Charity took a gulp of her milk. "Roman DeWinter."

"Screwy name." Mae glanced around the kitchen, surprised and a little disappointed that there was nothing left to do. "What do you know about him?"

"He needed a job."

Mae wiped her reddened hands on the skirt of her apron. "I expect there's a whole slew of pickpockets, cat burglars and mass murderers who need jobs."

"He's not a mass murderer," Charity stated. She thought she had better reserve judgment on the other occupations.

"Maybe, maybe not."

"He's a drifter." She shrugged and took another bite of the cake. "But I wouldn't say aimless. He knows where he's going. In any case, with George off doing the hula, I needed someone. He does good work, Mae."

Mae had determined that for herself with a quick trip into the west wing. But she had other things on her mind. "He looks at you."

Stalling, Charity ran a fingertip up and down the side of her glass. "Everyone looks at me. I'm always here."

"Don't play stupid with me, young lady. I powdered your bottom."

"Whatever that has to do with anything," Charity answered with a grin. "So he looks?" She moved her shoulders again. "I look back." When Mae arched her brows, Charity just smiled. "Aren't you always telling me I need a man in my life?"

"There's men and there's men," Mae said sagely. "This one's not bad on the eyes, and he ain't afraid of working. But he's got a hard streak in him. That one's been around, my girl, and no mistake."

"I guess you'd rather I spent time with Jimmy Loggerman."

"Spineless worm."

After a burst of laughter, Charity cupped her chin in her hands. "You were right, Mae. I do feel better."

Pleased, Mae untied the apron from around her ample girth. She didn't doubt that Charity was a sensible girl, but she intended to keep an eye on Roman herself. "Good. Don't cut any more of that cake or you'll be up all night with a bellyache."

"Yes'm."

"And don't leave a mess in my kitchen," she added as she tugged on a practical brown coat.

"No, ma'am. Good night, Mae."

Charity sighed as the door rattled shut. Mae's leaving usually signaled the end of the day. The guests would be tucked into their beds or finishing up a late card game. Barring an emergency, there was nothing left for Charity to do until sunrise.

Nothing to do but think.

Lately she'd been toying with the idea of putting in a whirlpool. That might lure a small percentage of the resort-goers. She'd priced a few solarium kits, and in her mind she could already see the sunroom on the inn's south side. In the winter guests could come back from hiking to a hot, bubbling tub and top off the day with rum punch by the fire.

She would enjoy it herself, especially on those rare winter days when the inn was empty and there was nothing for her to do but rattle around alone.

Then there was her long-range plan to add on a gift shop supplied by local artists and craftsmen. Nothing too elaborate, she thought. She wanted to keep things simple, in keeping with the spirit of the inn.

She wondered if Roman would stay around long enough to work on it.

It wasn't wise to think of him in connection with any of her plans. It probably wasn't wise to think of him at all. He was, as she had said herself, a drifter. Men like Roman didn't light in one spot for long.

She couldn't seem to stop thinking about him. Almost from the first moment, she'd felt something. Attraction was one thing. He was, after all, an attractive man, in a tough, dangerous kind of way. But there was more. Something in his eyes? she wondered. In his voice? In the way he moved? She toyed with the rest of her cake, wishing she could pin it down. It might simply be that he was so different from herself. Taciturn, suspicious, solitary.

And yet . . . was it her imagination, or was part of him waiting, to reach out, to grab hold? He needed someone, she thought, though he was probably unaware of it.

Mae was right, she mused. She had always had a weakness for strays and a hard-luck story. But this was different. She closed her eyes for a moment, wishing she could explain, even to herself, why it was so very different.

She'd never experienced anything like the sensations that had rammed into her because of Roman. It was more than physical. She could admit that now. Still it made no sense. Then again, Charity had always thought that feelings weren't required to make sense.

For a moment out on the deserted road this morning she'd felt emotions pour out of him. They had been almost frightening in their speed and power. Emotions like that could hurt . . . the one who felt them, the one who received them. They had left her dazed and aching—and wishing, she admitted.

She thought she knew what his mouth would taste like. Not soft, not sweet, but pungent and powerful. When he was ready, he wouldn't ask, he'd take. It worried her that she didn't resent that. She had grown up knowing her own mind, making her own choices. A man like Roman would have little respect for a woman's wishes.

It would be better, much better, for them to keep their relationship—their short-term relationship, she added—on a purely business level. Friendly but careful. She let her chin sink into her hands again. It was a pity she had such a difficult time combining the two.

He watched her toy with the crumbs on her plate. Her hair was loose now and tousled, as if she had pulled it out of the braid and ran impatient fingers through it. Her bare feet were crossed at the ankles, resting on the chair across from her.

Relaxed. Roman wasn't sure he'd ever seen anyone so fully relaxed except in sleep. It was a sharp contrast to the churning energy that drove her during the day.

He wished she were in her room, tucked into bed and sleeping deeply. He'd wanted to avoid coming across her at all. That was personal. He needed her out of his way so that he could go through the office off the lobby. That was business.

He knew he should step back and keep out of sight until she retired for the night.

What was it about this quiet scene that was so appealing, so irresistible? The kitchen was warm and the scents of cooking were lingering, pleasantly overlaying those of pine and lemon from Mae's cleaning. There was a hanging basket over the sink that was almost choked with some leafy green plant. Every surface was scrubbed, clean and shiny. The huge refrigerator hummed.

She looked so comfortable, as if she were waiting for him to come in and sit with her, to talk of small, inconsequential things.

That was crazy. He didn't want any woman waiting for him, and especially not her.

But he didn't step back into the shadows of the dining room, though he could easily have done so. He stepped toward her, into the light.

"I thought people kept early hours in the country."

She jumped but recovered quickly. She was almost used to the silent way he moved. "Mostly. Mae was giving me chocolate and a pep talk. Want some cake?"

"No."

"Just as well. If you had I'd have taken another

piece and made myself sick. No willpower. How about a beer?"

"Yeah. Thanks."

She got up lazily and moved to the refrigerator to rattle off a list of brands. He chose one and watched her pour it into a pilsner glass. She wasn't angry, he noted, though she had certainly been the last time they were together. So Charity didn't hold grudges. She wouldn't, Roman decided as he took the glass from her. She would forgive almost anything, would trust everyone and would give more than was asked.

"Why do you look at me that way?" she murmured.

He caught himself, then took a long, thirsty pull on the beer. "You have a beautiful face."

She lifted a brow when he sat down and pulled out a cigarette. After taking an ashtray from a drawer, she sat beside him. "I like to accept compliments whenever I get them, but I don't think that's the reason."

"It's reason enough for a man to look at a woman." He sipped his beer. "You had a busy night."

Let it go, Charity told herself. "Busy enough that I need to hire another waitress fast. I didn't get a chance to thank you for helping out with the dinner crowd."

"No problem. Lose the headache?"

She glanced up sharply. But, no, he wasn't making fun of her. It seemed, though she couldn't be sure why the impression was so strong, that his question was a kind of apology. She decided to accept it.

"Yes, thanks. Getting mad at you took my mind off Mary Alice, and Mae's chocolate cake did the rest." She thought about brewing some tea, then decided she was too lazy to bother. "So, how was your day?"

She smiled at him in an easy offer of friendship that he found difficult to resist and impossible to accept. "Okay. Miss Millie said the door to her room was sticking, so I pretended to sand it."

"And made her day."

He couldn't prevent the smile. "I don't think I've ever been ogled quite so completely before."

"Oh, I imagine you have." She tilted her head to study him from a new angle. "But, with apologies to your ego, in Miss Millie's case it's more a matter of nearsightedness than lust. She's too vain to wear her glasses in front of any male over twenty."

"I'd rather go on thinking she's leering at me," he said. "She said she's been coming here twice a year since '52." He thought that over for a moment, amazed that anyone could return time after time to the same spot.

"She and Miss Lucy are fixtures here. When I was young I thought we were related."

"You been running this place long?"

"Off and on for all of my twenty-seven years." Smiling, she tipped back in her chair. She was a woman who relaxed easily and enjoyed seeing others relaxed. He seemed so now, she thought, with his legs stretched out under the table and a glass in his hand. "You don't really want to hear the story of my life, do you, Roman?"

He blew out a stream of smoke. "I've got nothing to do." And he wanted to hear her version of what he'd read in her file.

"Okay. I was born here. My mother had fallen in love a bit later in life than most. She was nearly forty when she had me, and fragile. There were complications. After she died, my grandfather raised me, so I grew up here at the inn, except for the periods of time when he sent me away to school. I loved this place." She glanced around the kitchen. "In school I pined for it, and for Pop. Even in college I missed it so much I'd ferry home every weekend. But he wanted me to see something else before I settled down here. I was going to travel some, get new ideas for the inn. See New York, New Orleans, Venice. I don't know...." Her words trailed off wistfully.

"Why didn't you?"

"My grandfather was ill. I was in my last year of college when I found out *how* ill. I wanted to quit, come home, but the idea upset him so much I thought it was better to graduate. He hung on for another three years, but it was . . . difficult." She didn't want to talk about the tears and the terror, or about the exhaustion of running the inn while caring for a near-invalid. "He was the bravest, kindest man I've ever known. He was so much a part of this place that there are still times when I expect to walk into a room and see him checking for dust on the furniture."

He was silent for a moment, thinking as much about what she'd left out as about what she'd told him. He knew her father was listed as unknown—a difficult obstacle anywhere, but especially in a small town. In the last six months of her grandfather's life his medical expenses had nearly driven the inn under. But she didn't speak of those things; nor did he detect any sign of bitterness.

"Do you ever think about selling the place, moving on?"

"No. Oh, I still think about Venice occasionally. There are dozens of places I'd like to go, as long as I had the inn to come back to." She rose to get him another beer. "When you run a place like this, you get to meet people from all over. There's always a story about a new place."

"Vicarious traveling?"

It stung, perhaps because it was too close to her own thoughts. "Maybe." She set the bottle at his elbow, then took her dishes to the sink. Even knowing that she was overly sensitive on this point didn't stop her from bristling. "Some of us are meant to be boring."

"I didn't say you were boring."

"No? Well, I suppose I am to someone who picks up and goes whenever and wherever he chooses. Simple, settled and naive."

"You're putting words in my mouth, baby."

"It's easy to do, *baby*, since you rarely put any there yourself. Turn off the lights when you leave."

He took her arm as she started by in a reflexive movement that he regretted almost before it was done. But it was done, and the sulky, defiant look she sent him began a chain reaction that raced through his system. There were things he could do with her, things he burned to do, that neither of them would ever forget.

"Why are you angry?"

"I don't know. I can't seem to talk to you for more than ten minutes without getting edgy. Since I normally get along with everyone, I figure it's you."

"You're probably right."

She calmed a little. It was hardly his fault that she had never been anywhere. "You've been around a little less than forty-eight hours and I've nearly fought with you three times. That's a record for me."

"I don't keep score."

"Oh, I think you do. I doubt you forget anything. Were you a cop?"

He had to make a deliberate effort to keep his face bland and fingers from tensing. "Why?"

"You said you weren't an artist. That was my first guess." She relaxed, though he hadn't removed his hand from her arm. Anger was something she enjoyed only in fast, brief spurts. "It's the way you look at people, as if you were filing away descriptions and any distinguishing marks. And sometimes when I'm with you I feel as though I should get ready for an interrogation. A writer, then? When you're in the hotel business you get pretty good at matching people with professions."

"You're off this time."

"Well, what are you, then?"

"Right now I'm a handyman."

She shrugged, making herself let it go. "Another trait of hotel people is respecting privacy, but if you turn out to be a mass murderer Mae's never going to let me hear the end of it."

"Generally I only kill one person at a time."

"That's good news." She ignored the suddenly very real anxiety that he was speaking the simple truth. "You're still holding my arm."

"I know."

So this was it, she thought, and struggled to keep her voice. "Should I ask you to let go?"

"I wouldn't bother."

She drew a deep, steadying breath. "All right. What do you want, Roman?"

"To get this out of the way, for both of us."

He rose. Her step backward was instinctive, and much more surprising to her than to him. "I don't think that's a good idea."

"Neither do I." With his free hand, he gathered up her hair. It was soft, as he'd known it would be. Thick and full and so soft that his fingers dived in and were lost. "But I'd rather regret something I did than something I didn't do."

"I'd rather not regret at all."

"Too late." He heard her suck in her breath as he

yanked her against him. "One way or the other, we'll both have plenty to regret."

He was deliberately rough. He knew how to be gentle, though he rarely put the knowledge into practice. With her, he could have been. Perhaps because he knew that, he shoved aside any desire for tenderness. He wanted to frighten her, to make certain that when he let her go she would run, run away from him, because he wanted so badly for her to run to him.

Buried deep in his mind was the hope that he could make her afraid enough, repelled enough, to send him packing. If she did, she would be safe from him, and he from her. He thought he could accomplish it quickly. Then, suddenly, it was impossible to think at all.

She tasted like heaven. He'd never believed in heaven, but the flavor was on her lips, pure and sweet and promising. Her hand had gone to his chest in an automatic defensive movement. Yet she wasn't fighting him, as he'd been certain she would. She met his hard, almost brutal kiss with passion laced with trust.

His mind emptied. It was a terrifying experience for a man who kept his thoughts under such stringent control. Then it filled with her, her scent, her touch, her taste.

He broke away—for his sake now, not for hers. He was and had always been a survivor. His breath came fast and raw. One hand was still tangled in her hair, and his other was clamped tight on her arm. He couldn't let go. No matter how he chided himself to release her, to step back and walk away, he couldn't move. Staring at her, he saw his own reflection in her eyes.

He cursed her—it was a last quick denial—before he crushed his mouth to hers again. It wasn't heaven he was heading for, he told himself. It was hell.

She wanted to soothe him, but he never gave her

the chance. As before, he sent her rushing into some hot, airless place where there was room only for sensation.

She'd been right. His mouth wasn't soft, it was hard and ruthless and irresistible. Without hesitation, without thought of self-preservation, she opened for him, greedily taking what was offered, selflessly giving what was demanded.

Her back was pressed against the smooth, cool surface of the refrigerator, trapped there by the firm, taut lines of his body. If it had been possible, she would have brought him closer.

His face was rough as it scraped against hers, and she trembled at the thrill of pleasure even that brought her. Desperate now, she nipped at his lower lip, and felt a new rush of excitement as he groaned and deepened an already bottomless kiss.

She wanted to be touched. She tried to murmur this new, compelling need against his mouth, but she managed only a moan. Her body ached. Just the anticipation of his hands running over her was making her shudder.

For a moment their hearts beat against each other in the same wild rhythm.

He tore away, aware that he had come perilously close to a line he didn't dare cross. He could hardly breathe, much less think. Until he was certain he could do both, he was silent.

"Go to bed, Charity."

She stayed where she was, certain that if she took a step her legs would give way. He was still close enough for her to feel the heat radiating from his body. But she looked into his eyes and knew he was already out of reach.

"Just like that?"

Hurt. He could hear it in her voice, and he wished he could make himself believe she had brought it on herself. He reached for his beer but changed his mind when he saw that his hand was unsteady. Only one thing was clear. He had to get rid of her, quickly, before he touched her again.

"You're not the type for quick sex on the kitchen floor."

The color that passion had brought to her cheeks faded. "No. At least I never have been." After taking a deep breath, she stepped forward. She believed in facing facts, even unpleasant ones. "Is that all this would have been, Roman?"

His hand curled into a fist. "Yes," he said. "What else?"

"I see." She kept her eyes on his, wishing she could hate him. "I'm sorry for you."

"Don't be."

"You're in charge of your feelings, Roman, not mine. And I am sorry for you. Some people lose a leg or a hand or an eye. They either deal with that loss or become bitter. I can't see what piece of you is missing, Roman, but it's just as tragic." He didn't answer; she hadn't expected him to. "Don't forget the lights."

He waited until she was gone before he fumbled for a match. He needed time to gain control of his head—and his hands—before he searched the office. What worried him was that it was going to take a great deal longer to gain control of his heart.

Nearly two hours later he hiked a mile and a half to use the pay phone at the nearest gas station. The road was quiet, the tiny village dark. The wind had come up, and it tasted of rain. Roman hoped dispassionately that it would hold off until he was back at the inn.

He placed the call, waited for the connection.

"Conby."

"DeWinter."

"You're late."

Roman didn't bother to check his watch. He knew it was just shy of 3:00 a.m. on the East Coast. "Get you up?"

"Am I to assume that you've established yourself?"

"Yeah, I'm in. Rigging the handyman's lottery ticket cleared the way. Arranging the flat gave me the opening. Miss Ford is . . . trusting."

"So we were led to believe. Trusting doesn't mean she's not ambitious. What have you got?"

A bad case of guilt, Roman thought as he lit a match. A very bad case. "Her rooms are clean." He paused and held the flame to the tip of his cigarette. "There's a tour group in now, mostly Canadians. A few exchanged money. Nothing over a hundred."

The pause was very brief. "That's hardly enough to make the business worthwhile."

"I got a list out of the office. The names and addresses of the registered guests."

There was another, longer pause, and a rustling sound that told Roman that his contact was searching for writing materials. "Let me have it."

He read them off from the copy he'd made. "Block's the tour guide. He's the regular, comes in once a week for a one- or two-night stay, depending on the package."

"Vision Tours."

"Right."

"We've got a man on that end. You concentrate on Ford and her staff." Roman heard the faint *tap-tap-*

tap of Conby's pencil against his pad. "There's no way they can be pulling this off without someone on the inside. She's the obvious answer."

"It doesn't fit."

"I beg your pardon?"

Roman crushed the cigarette under his boot heel. "I said it doesn't fit. I've watched her. I've gone through her personal accounts, damn it. She's got under three thousand in fluid cash. Everything else goes into the place for new sheets and soap."

"I see." The pause again. It was maddening. "I suppose our Miss Ford hasn't heard of Swiss bank accounts."

"I said she's not the type, Conby. It's the wrong angle."

"I'll worry about the angles, DeWinter. You worry about doing your job. I shouldn't have to remind you that it's taken us nearly a year to come close to pinning this thing down. The Bureau wants this wrapped quickly, and that's what I expect from you. If you have a personal problem with this, you'd better let me know now."

"No." He knew personal problems weren't permitted. "You want to waste time, and the taxpayers' money, it's all the same to me. I'll get back to you."

"Do that."

Roman hung up. It made him feel a little better to scowl at the phone and imagine Conby losing a good night's sleep. Then again, his kind rarely did. He'd wake some hapless clerk up at six and have the list run through the computer. Conby would drink his coffee, watch the *Today* show and wait in his comfortable house in the D.C. suburbs for the results.

Grunt work and dirty work were left to others.

That was the way the game was played, Roman reminded himself as he started the long walk back to the inn. But lately, just lately, he was getting very tired of the rules.

Charity heard him come in. Curious, she glanced at the clock after she heard the door close below. It was after one, and the rain had started nearly thirty minutes before with a gentle hissing that promised to gain strength through the night.

She wondered where he had been.

His business, she reminded herself as she rolled over and tried to let the rain lull her to sleep. As long as he did his job, Roman DeWinter was free to come and go as he pleased. If he wanted to walk in the rain, that was fine by her.

How could he have kissed her like that and felt nothing?

Charity squeezed her eyes shut and swore at herself. It was her feelings she had to worry about, not Roman's. The trouble was, she always felt too much. This was one time she couldn't afford that luxury.

Something had happened to her when he'd kissed her. Something thrilling, something that had reached deep inside her and opened up endless possibilities. No, not possibilities, fantasies, she thought, shaking her head. If she were wise she would take that one moment of excitement and stop wanting more. Drifters made poor risks emotionally. She had the perfect example before her.

Her mother had turned to a drifter and had given him her heart, her trust, her body. She had ended up pregnant and alone. She had, Charity knew, pined for him for months. She'd died in the same hospital where her baby had been born, only days later. Betrayed, rejected and ashamed.

Charity had only discovered the extent of the shame after her grandfather's death. He'd kept the diary her mother had written. Charity had burned it, not out of shame but out of pity. She would always think of her mother as a tragic woman who had looked for love and had never found it.

But she wasn't her mother, Charity reminded herself as she lay awake listening to the rain. She was far, far less fragile. Love was what she had been named for, and she had felt its warmth all her life.

Now a drifter had come into her life.

He had spoken of regrets, she remembered. She was afraid that whatever happened—or didn't happen—between them, she would have them.

CHAPTER 4

The rain continued all morning, soft, slow, steady. It brought a chill, and a gloom that was no less appealing than the sunshine. Clouds hung over the water, turning everything to different shades of gray. Raindrops hissed on the roof and at the windows, making the inn seem all the more remote. Occasionally the wind gusted, rattling the panes.

At dawn Roman had watched Charity, bundled in a hooded windbreaker, take Ludwig out for his morning run. And he had watched her come back, dripping, forty minutes later. He'd heard the music begin to play in her room after she had come in the back entrance. She had chosen something quiet and floating with lots of violins this time. He'd been sorry when it had stopped and she had hurried down the hallway on her way to the dining room.

From his position on the second floor he couldn't hear the bustle in the kitchen below, but he could imagine it. Mae and Dolores would be bickering as waffle or muffin batter was whipped up. Charity would have grabbed a quick cup of coffee before rushing out to help the waitress set up tables and write the morning's menu.

Her hair would be damp, her voice calm as she smoothed over Dolores's daily complaints. She'd smell of the rain. When the early risers wandered down she would smile, greet them by name and make them feel as though they were sharing a meal at an old friend's house.

That was her greatest skill, Roman mused. Making a stranger feel at home.

Could she be as uncomplicated as she seemed? A part of him wanted badly to believe that. Another part of him found it impossible. Everyone had an angle, from the mailroom clerk dreaming of a desk job to the CEO wheeling another deal. She couldn't be any different.

He wouldn't have called the kiss they'd shared uncomplicated. There had been layers to it he couldn't have begun to peel away. It seemed contradictory that such a calm-eyed, smooth-voiced woman could explode with such towering passion. Yet she had. Perhaps her passion was as much a part of the act as her serenity.

It annoyed him. Just remembering his helpless response to her infuriated him. So he made himself dissect it further. If he was attracted to what she seemed to be, that was reasonable enough. He'd lived a solitary and often turbulent life. Though he had chosen to live that way, and certainly preferred it, it wasn't unusual that at some point he would find himself pulled toward a woman who represented everything he had never had. And had never wanted, Roman reminded himself as he tacked up a strip of molding.

He wasn't going to pretend he'd found any answers

in Charity. The only answers he was looking for pertained to the job.

For now he would wait until the morning rush was over. When Charity was busy in her office, he would go down and charm some breakfast out of Mae. There was a woman who didn't trust him, Roman thought with a grin. There wasn't a naive bone in her sturdy body. And except for Charity there was no one, he was sure, who knew the workings of the inn better.

Yes, he'd put some effort into charming Mae. And he'd keep some distance between himself and Charity. For the time being.

"You're looking peaked this morning."

"Thank you very much." Charity swallowed a yawn as she poured her second cup of coffee. *Peaked* wasn't the word, she thought. She was exhausted right down to the bone. Her body wasn't used to functioning on three hours' sleep. She had Roman to thank for that, she thought, and shoved the just-filled cup aside.

"Sit." Mae pointed to the table. "I'll fix you some eggs."

"I haven't got time. I—"

"Sit," Mae repeated, waving a wooden spoon. "You need fuel."

"Mae's right," Dolores put in. "A body can't run on coffee. You need protein and carbohydrates." She set a blueberry muffin on the table. "Why, if I don't watch my protein intake I get weak as a lamb. 'Course, the doctor don't say, but I think I'm hydroglycemic."

"Hypoglycemic," Charity murmured.

"That's what I said." Dolores decided she liked the sound of it. At the moment, however, it was just as much fun to worry about Charity as it was to worry about herself. "She could use some nice crisp bacon with those eggs, Mae. That's what I think."

"I'm putting it on."

Outnumbered, Charity sat down. The two women could scrap for days, but when they had a common cause they stuck together like glue.

"I'm not peaked," she said in her own defense. "I just didn't sleep well last night."

"A warm bath before bed," Mae told her as the bacon sizzled. "Not hot, mind you. Lukewarm."

"With bath salts. Not bubbles or oils," Dolores added as she plunked down a glass of juice. "Good old-fashioned bath salts. Ain't that right, Mae?"

"Couldn't hurt," Mae mumbled, too concerned about Charity to think of an argument. "You've been working too hard, girl."

"I agree," Charity said, because it was easiest that way. "The reason I don't have time for a long, leisurely breakfast is that I have to see about hiring a new waitress so I don't have to work so hard. I put an ad in this morning's paper, so the calls should be coming in."

"Told Bob to cancel the ad," Mae announced, cracking an egg into the pan.

"What? Why?" Charity started to rise. "Damn it, Mae, if you think I'm going to take Mary Alice back after she—"

"No such thing, and don't you swear at me, young lady."

"Testy." Dolores clucked her tongue. "Happens when you work too hard."

"I'm sorry," Charity mumbled, managing not to grind her teeth. "But, Mae, I was counting on setting up interviews over the next couple of days. I want someone in by the end of the week."

"My brother's girl left that worthless husband of

hers in Toledo and came home." Keeping her back to Charity, Mae set the bacon to drain, then poked at the eggs. "She's a good girl, Bonnie is. Worked here a couple of summers while she was in school."

"Yes, I remember. She married a musician who was playing at one of the resorts in Eastsound."

Mae scowled and began to scoop up the eggs. "Saxophone player," she said, as if that explained it all. "She got tired of living out of a van and came home a couple weeks back. Been looking for work."

With a sigh, Charity pushed a hand through her bangs. "Why didn't you tell me before?"

"You didn't need anyone before." Mae set the eggs in front of her. "You need someone now."

Charity glanced over as Mae began wiping off the stove. The cook's heart was as big as the rest of her. "When can she start?"

Mae's lips curved, and she cleared her throat and wiped at a spill with more energy. "Told her to come in this afternoon so's you could have a look at her. Don't expect you to hire her unless she measures up."

"Well, then." Charity picked up her fork. Pleased at the thought of having one job settled, she stretched out her legs and rested her feet on an empty chair. "I guess I've got time for breakfast after all."

Roman pushed through the door and almost swore out loud. The dining room was all but empty. He'd been certain Charity would be off doing one of the dozens of chores she took on. Instead, she was sitting in the warm, fragrant kitchen, much as she had been the night before. With one telling difference, Roman reflected. She wasn't relaxed now.

Her easy smile faded the moment he walked in. Slowly she slipped her feet off the chair and straightened her back. He could see her body tense, almost muscle by muscle. Her fork stopped halfway to her lips. Then she turned slightly away from him and continued to eat. It was, he supposed, as close to a slap in the face as she could manage.

He rearranged his idea about breakfast and gossip in the kitchen. For now he'd make do with coffee.

"Wondered where you'd got to," Mae said as she pulled bacon out of the refrigerator again.

"I didn't want to get in your way." He nodded toward the coffeepot. "I thought I'd take a cup up with me."

"You need fuel." Dolores busied herself arranging a place setting across from Charity. "Isn't that right, Mae? Man can't work unless he has a proper breakfast."

Mae poured a cup. "He looks like he could run on empty well enough."

It was quite true, Charity thought. She knew what time he'd come in the night before, and he'd been up and working when she'd left the wing to oversee the breakfast shift. He couldn't have gotten much more sleep than she had herself, but he didn't look any the worse for wear.

"Meals are part of your pay, Roman." Though her appetite had fled, Charity nipped off a bite of bacon. "I believe Mae has some pancake batter left over, if you'd prefer that to eggs."

It was a cool invitation, so cool that Dolores opened her mouth to comment. Mae gave her a quick poke and a scowl. He accepted the coffee Mae shoved at him and drank it black.

"Eggs are fine." But he didn't sit down. The welcoming feel that was usually so much a part of the kitchen was not evident. Roman leaned against the counter and sipped while Mae cooked beside him.

She wasn't going to feel guilty, Charity told herself, ignoring a chastising look from Dolores. After all, she was the boss, and her business with Roman was . . . well, just business. But she couldn't bear the long, strained silence.

"Mae, I'd like some petits fours and tea sandwiches this afternoon. The rain's supposed to last all day, so we'll have music and dancing in the gathering room." Because breakfast seemed less and less appealing, Charity pulled a notepad out of her shirt pocket. "Fifty sandwiches should do if we have a cheese tray. We'll set up an urn of tea, and one of hot chocolate."

"What time?"

"At three, I think. Then we can bring out the wine at five for anyone who wants to linger. You can have your niece help out."

She began making notes on the pad.

She looked tired, Roman thought. Pale and heavy-eyed and surprisingly fragile. She'd apparently pulled her hair back in a hasty ponytail when it had still been damp. Little tendrils had escaped as they'd dried. They seemed lighter than the rest, their color more delicate than rich. He wanted to brush them away from her temples and watch the color come back into her cheeks.

"Finish your eggs," Mae told her. Then she nodded at Roman. "Yours are ready."

"Thanks." He sat down, wishing no more fervently than Charity that he was ten miles away.

Dolores began to complain that the rain was making her sinuses swell.

"Pass the salt," Roman murmured.

Charity pushed it in his direction. Their fingers brushed briefly, and she snatched hers away.

"Thanks."

"You're welcome." Charity poked her fork into her

eggs. She knew from experience that it would be difficult to escape from the kitchen without cleaning her plate, and she intended to do it quickly.

"Nice day," he said, because he wanted her to look at him again. She did, and pent-up anger was simmering in her eyes. He preferred it, he discovered, to the cool politeness that had been there.

"I like the rain."

"Like I said"—he broke open his muffin—"it's a nice day."

Dolores blew her nose heartily. Amusement curved the corners of Charity's mouth before she managed to suppress it. "You'll find the paint you need—wall, ceiling, trim—in the storage cellar. It's marked for the proper rooms."

"All right."

"The brushes and pans and rollers are down there, too. Everything's on the workbench on the right as you come down the stairs."

"I'll find them."

"Good. Cabin 4 has a dripping faucet."

"I'll look at it."

She didn't want him to be so damn agreeable, Charity thought. She wanted him to be as tense and out of sorts as she was. "The window sticks in unit 2 in the east wing."

He sent her an even look. "I'll unstick it."

"Fine." Suddenly she noticed that Dolores had stopped complaining and was gawking at her. Even Mae was frowning over her mixing bowl. The hell with it, Charity thought as she shoved her plate away. So she was issuing orders like Captain Bligh. She damn well felt like Captain Bligh.

She took a ring of keys out of her pocket. She'd just put them on that morning, having intended to see to the minor chores herself. "Make sure to bring these back to the office when you've finished. They're tagged for the proper doors."

"Yes, ma'am." Keeping his eyes on hers, he dropped the ring into his breast pocket. "Anything else?"

"I'll let you know." She rose, took her plate to the sink and stalked out.

"What got into her?" Dolores wanted to know. "She looked like she wanted to chew somebody's head off."

"She just didn't sleep well." More concerned than she wanted to let on, Mae set down the mixing bowl in which she'd been creaming butter and sugar. Because she felt like the mother of an ill-mannered child, she picked up the coffeepot and carried it over to Roman. "Charity's not feeling quite herself this morning," she told him as she poured him a second cup. "She's been overworked lately."

"I've got thick skin." But he'd felt the sting. "Maybe she should delegate more."

"Ha! That girl?" Pleased that he hadn't complained, she became more expansive. "It ain't in her. Feels responsible if a guest stubs his toe. Just like her grandpa." Mae added a stream of vanilla to the bowl and went back to her mixing. "Not a thing goes on around here she don't have a finger—more likely her whole hand—in. Except my cooking." Mae's wide face creased in a smile. "I shooed her out of here when she was a girl, and I can shoo her out of here today if need be."

"Girl can't boil water without scorching the pan," Dolores put in.

"She could if she wanted to," Mae said defensively, turning back to Roman with a sniff. "There's no need for her to cook when she's got me, and she's smart enough to know it. Everything else, though, from painting the porch to keeping the books, has to have her stamp on it. She's one who takes her responsibilities to heart."

Roman played out the lead she had offered him. "That's an admirable quality. You've worked for her a long time."

"Between Charity and her grandfather, I've worked at the inn for twenty-eight years come June." She jerked her head in Dolores's direction. "She's been here eight."

"Nine," Dolores said. "Nine years this month."

"It sounds like when people come to work here they stay."

"You got that right," Mae told him.

"It seems the inn has a loyal, hardworking staff."

"Charity makes it easy." Competently Mae measured out baking powder. "She was just feeling moody this morning."

"She did look a little tired," Roman said slowly, ignoring a pang of guilt. "Maybe she'll rest for a while today."

"Not likely."

"The housekeeping staff seems tight."

"She'll still find a bed to make."

"Bob handles the accounts."

"She'll poke her nose in the books and check every column." There was simple pride in her voice as she sifted flour into the bowl. "Not that she don't trust those who work for her," Mae added. "It would just make her heart stop dead to have a bill paid late or an order mixed up. Thing is, she'd rather blame herself than somebody else if a mistake's made."

"I guess nothing much gets by her."

"By Charity?" With a snicker, Mae plugged in her

electric mixer. "She'd know if a napkin came back from the laundry with a stain on it. Watch where you sneeze," she added as Dolores covered her face with a tissue. "Drink some hot water with a squeeze of lemon."

"Hot tea with honey," Dolores said.

"Lemon. Honey'll clog your throat."

"My mother always gave me hot tea with honey," Dolores told her.

They were still arguing about it when Roman slipped out of the kitchen.

He spent most of his time closed off in the west wing. Working helped him think. Though he heard Charity pass in and out a few times, neither of them sought the other's company. He could be more objective, Roman realized, when he wasn't around her.

Mae's comments had cemented his observations and the information that had been made available to him. Charity Ford ran the inn from top to bottom. Whatever went on in it or passed through it was directly under her eye. Logically that meant that she was fully involved with, perhaps in charge of, the operation he had come to destroy.

And yet . . . what he had said to Conby the night before still held true. It didn't fit.

The woman worked almost around the clock to make the inn a success. He'd seen her do everything from potting geraniums to hauling firewood. And, unless she was an astounding actress, she enjoyed it all.

She didn't seem the type who would want to make money the easy way. Nor did she seem the type who craved all the things easy money could buy. But that was instinct, not fact.

The problem was, Conby ran on facts. Roman had always relied heavily on instinct. His job was to prove her guilt, not her innocence. Yet, in less than two days, his priorities had changed.

It wasn't just a matter of finding her attractive. He had found other women attractive and had brought them down without a qualm. That was justice. One of the few things he believed in without reservation was justice.

With Charity he needed to be certain that his conclusions about her were based on more than the emotions she dragged out of him. Feelings and instincts were different. If a man in his position allowed himself to be swayed by feelings, he was useless.

Then what was it? No matter how long or how hard he thought it through, he couldn't pinpoint one specific reason why he was certain of her innocence. Because it was the whole of it, Roman realized. Her, the inn, the atmosphere that surrounded her. It made him want to believe that such people, such places, existed. And existed untainted.

He was getting soft. A pretty woman, big blue eyes, and he started to think in fairy tales. In disgust, he took the brushes and the paint pans to the sink to clean them. He was going to take a break, from work and from his own rambling thoughts.

In the gathering room, Charity was thinking just as reluctantly of him as she set a stack of records on the table between Miss Millie and Miss Lucy.

"What a lovely idea." Miss Lucy adjusted her glasses and peered at the labels. "A nice old-fashioned tea dance." From one of the units in the east wing came the unrelenting whine of a toddler. Miss Lucy sent a sympathetic glance in the direction of the noise, "I'm sure this will keep everyone entertained."

"It's hard for young people to know what to do with themselves on a rainy day. It makes them cross. Oh, look." Miss Millie held up a 45. "Rosemary Clooney. Isn't this delightful?"

"Pick out your favorites." Charity gave the room a distracted glance. How could she prepare for a party when all she could think of was the way Roman had looked at her across the breakfast table? "I'm depending on you."

The long buffet and a small server had been cleared off to hold the refreshments. If she could count on Mae—and she always had—they should be coming up from the kitchen shortly.

Would Roman come in? she wondered. Would he hear the music and slip silently into the room? Would he look at her until her heart started to hammer and she forgot there was anything or anyone but him?

She was going crazy, Charity decided. She glanced at her watch. It was a quarter to three. Word had been passed to all the guests, and with luck she would be ready for them when they began to arrive. The ladies were deep in a discussion of Perry Como. Leaving them to it, Charity began to tug on the sofa.

"What are you doing?"

A squeal escaped her, and she cursed Roman in the next breath. "If you keep sneaking around I'm going to take Mae's idea of you being a cat burglar more seriously."

"I wasn't sneaking around. You were so busy huffing and puffing you didn't hear me."

"I wasn't huffing or puffing." She tossed her hair over her shoulder and glared at him. "But I am busy, so if you'd get out of my way—"

She waved a hand at him, and he caught it and held it. "I asked what you were doing."

She tugged, then tugged harder, struggling to control her temper. If he wanted to fight, she thought, she'd be happy to oblige him. "I'm knitting an afghan," she snapped. "What does it look like I'm doing? I'm moving the sofa."

"No, you're not."

She could, when the occasion called for, succeed in being haughty. "I beg your pardon?"

"I said you're not moving the sofa. It's too heavy."

"Thank you for your opinion, but I've moved it before." She lowered her voice when she noticed the interested glances the ladies were giving her. "And if you'd get the hell out of my way I'd move it again."

He stood where he was, blocking her. "You really do have to do everything yourself, don't you?"

"Meaning?"

"Where's your assistant?"

"The computer sprang a leak. Since Bob's better equipped to deal with that, he's playing with components and I'm moving furniture. Now—"

"Where do you want it?"

"I didn't ask you to—" But he'd already moved to the other end of the sofa.

"I said, where do you want it?"

"Against the side wall." Charity hefted her end and tried not to be grateful.

"What else?"

She smoothed down the skirt of her dress. "I've already given you a list of chores."

He hooked a thumb in his pocket as they stood on either side of the sofa. He had an urge to put his hand over her angry face and give it a nice hard shove. "I've finished them."

"The faucet in cabin 4?"

"It needed a new washer."

"The window in unit 2?"

"A little sanding."

She was running out of steam. "The painting?"

"The first coat's drying." He angled his head. "Want to check it out?"

She blew out a breath. It was difficult to be annoyed when he'd done everything she'd asked. "Efficient, aren't you, DeWinter?"

"That's right. Got your second wind?"

"What do you mean?"

"You looked a little tired this morning." He skimmed a glance over her. The dark plum-colored dress swirled down her legs. Little silver buttons ranged down from the high neck to the hem, making him wonder how long it would take him to unfasten them. There was silver at her ears, as well, a fanciful trio of columns he remembered having seen in her drawer. "You don't now," he added, bringing his eyes back to hers.

She started to breathe again, suddenly aware that she'd been holding her breath since he'd started his survey. Charity reminded herself that she didn't have time to let him—or her feelings for him—distract her.

"I'm too busy to be tired." Relieved, she signaled to a waitress who was climbing the steps with a laden tray. "Just set it on the buffet, Lori."

"Second load's right behind me."

"Great. I just need to—" She broke off when the first damp guests came through the back door. Giving up, she turned to Roman. If he was going to be in the way anyway, he might as well make himself useful. "I'd appreciate it if you'd roll up the rug and store it in the west wing. Then you're welcome to stay and enjoy yourself."

"Thanks. Maybe I will."

Charity greeted the guests, hung up their jackets, offered them refreshments and switched on the music almost before Roman could store the rug out of sight. Within fifteen minutes she had the group mixing and mingling.

She was made for this, he thought as he watched her. She was made for being in the center of things, for making people feel good. His place had always been on the fringe.

"Oh, Mr. DeWinter." Smelling of lilacs, Miss Millie offered him a cup and saucer. "You must have some tea. Nothing like tea to chase the blues away on a rainy day."

He smiled into her blurred eyes. If even she could see that he was brooding, he'd better watch his step. "Thanks."

"I love a party," she said wistfully as she watched a few couples dance to a bluesy Clooney ballad. "Why, when I was a girl, I hardly thought of anything else. I met my husband at a tea like this. That was almost fifty years ago. We danced for hours."

He would never have considered himself gallant, but she was hard to resist. "Would you like to dance now?"

The faintest of blushes tinted her cheeks. "I'd love to, Mr. DeWinter."

Charity watched Roman lead Miss Millie onto the floor. Her heart softened. She tried to harden it again but found it was a lost cause. It was a sweet thing to do, she thought, particularly since he was anything but a sweet man. She doubted that teas and dreamy little old ladies were Roman's style, but Miss Millie would remember this day for a long time.

What woman wouldn't? Charity mused. To dance with a strong, mysterious man on a rainy afternoon was a memory to be pressed in a book like a red rose. It was undoubtedly fortunate he hadn't asked her. She had already stored away too many memories of Roman. With a sigh, she herded a group of children into the television room and pushed a Disney movie into the VCR.

Roman saw her leave. And he saw her come back.

"That was lovely," Miss Millie told him when the music had stopped.

"What?" Quickly he brought himself back. "My pleasure." Then he made her pleasure complete by kissing her hand. By the time she had walked over to sigh with her sister he had forgotten her and was thinking of Charity.

She was laughing as an older man led her onto the floor. The music had changed. It was up-tempo now, something brisk and Latin. A mambo, he thought. Or a merengue. He wouldn't know the difference. Apparently Charity knew well enough. She moved through the complicated, flashy number as if she'd been dancing all her life.

Her skirt flared, wrapped around her legs, then flared again as she turned. She laughed, her face level and close to her partner's as they matched steps. The first prick of jealousy infuriated Roman and made him feel like a fool. The man Charity was matching steps with was easily old enough to be her father.

By the time the music ended he had managed to suppress the uncomfortable emotion but another had sprung up to take its place. Desire. He wanted her, wanted to take her by the hand and pull her out of that crowded room into someplace dim and quiet where all they would hear was the rain. He wanted to see her eyes go big and unfocused the way they had when he'd kissed her. He wanted to feel the incredible sensation of her mouth softening and heating under his.

"It's an education to watch her, isn't it?"

Roman jerked himself back as Bob eased over to pluck a sandwich from the tray. "What?"

"Charity. Watching her dance is an education." He popped the tiny sandwich into his mouth. "She tried to teach me once, hoping I'd be able to entertain some of the ladies on occasions like this. Trouble is, I not only have two left feet, I have two left legs." He gave a cheerful shrug and reached for another sandwich.

"Did you get the computer fixed?"

"Yeah. Just a couple of minor glitches." The little triangle of bread disappeared. Roman caught a hint of nerves in the way Bob's knuckle tapped against the server. "I can't teach Charity about circuit boards and software any more than she can teach me the samba. How's the work going?"

"Well enough." He watched as Bob poured a cup of tea and added three sugars to it. "I should be done in two or three weeks."

"She'll find something else for you to do." He glanced over to where Charity and a new partner were dancing a fox-trot. "She's always got a new idea for this place. Lately she's been making noises about adding on a sunroom and putting in one of those whirlpool tubs."

Roman lit a cigarette. He was watching the guests now, making mental notes to pass on to Conby. There were two men who seemed to be alone, though they were chatting with other members of the tour group. Block stood by the doors, holding a plate full of sandwiches that he was dispatching with amazing ease and grinning at no one in particular.

"The inn must be doing well."

"Oh, it's stable." Bob turned his attention to the petits fours. "A couple of years ago things were a little rocky, but Charity would always find a way to keep the ship afloat. Nothing's more important to her."

Roman was silent for a moment. "I don't know much about the hotel business, but she seems to know what she's doing."

"Inside and out." Bob chose a cake with pink frosting. "Charity *is* the inn."

"Have you worked for her long?"

"About two and a half years. She couldn't really afford me, but she wanted to turn things around, modernize the bookkeeping. Pump new life into the place, was what she said." Someone put on a jitterbug, and he grinned. "She did just that."

"Apparently."

"So you're from back east." Bob paused for a moment, then continued when Roman made no comment. "How long are you planning to stay?"

"As long as it takes."

He took a long sip of tea. "As long as what takes?"

"The job." Roman glanced idly toward the west wing. "I like to finish what I start."

"Yeah. Well . . ." He arranged several petits fours on a plate. "I'm going to go offer these to the ladies and hope they let me eat them."

Roman watched him pass Block and exchange a quick word with him before he crossed the room. Wanting time to think, Roman slipped back into the west wing.

It was still raining when he came back hours later. Music was playing, some slow, melodic ballad from the fifties. The room was dimmer now, lit only by the fire and a glass-globed lamp. It was empty, too, except for Charity, who was busy tidying up, humming along with the music.

"Party over?"

She glanced around, then went hurriedly back to stacking cups and plates. "Yes. You didn't stay long."

"I had work to do."

Because she wanted to keep moving, she switched to emptying ashtrays. She'd held on to her guilt long enough. "I was tired this morning, but that's no excuse for being rude to you. I'm sorry if I gave you the impression that you couldn't enjoy yourself for a few hours."

He didn't want to accept an apology that he knew he didn't deserve. "I enjoy the work."

That only made her feel worse. "Be that as it may, I don't usually go around barking orders. I was angry with you."

"Was?"

She looked up, and her eyes were clear and direct. "Am. But that's my problem. If it helps, I'm every bit as angry with myself for acting like a child because you didn't let things get out of hand last night."

Uncomfortable, he picked up the wine decanter and poured a glass. "You didn't act like a child."

"A woman scorned, then, or something equally dramatic. Try not to contradict me when I'm apologizing."

Despite his best efforts, his lips curved against the rim of his glass. If he didn't watch himself he could find he was crazy about her. "All right. Is there more?"

"Just a little." She picked up one of the few petits fours that were left over, debated with herself, then popped it into her mouth. "I shouldn't let my personal feelings interfere with my running of the inn. The problem is, almost everything I think or feel connects with the inn."

"Neither of us were thinking of the inn last night. Maybe that's the problem."

"Maybe."

"Do you want the couch moved back?"

"Yes." Business as usual, Charity told herself as she walked over to lift her end. The moment it was in place she scooted around to plump the pillows. "I saw you dancing with Miss Millie. It thrilled her."

"I like her."

"I think you do," Charity said slowly, straightening and studying him. "You're not the kind of man who likes easily."

"No."

She wanted to go to him, to lift a hand to his cheek. That was ridiculous, she told herself. Apology notwithstanding, she was still angry with him for last night. "Has life been so hard?" she murmured.

"No."

With a little laugh, she shook her head. "Then again, you wouldn't tell me if it had been. I have to learn not to ask you questions. Why don't we call a truce, Roman? Life's too short for bad feelings."

"I don't have any bad feelings toward you, Charity."

She smiled a little. "It's tempting, but I'm not going to ask what kind of feelings you do have."

"I wouldn't be able to tell you, because I haven't figured it out." He was amazed that the words had come out. After draining the wine, he set the empty glass aside.

"Well." Nonplussed, she pushed her hair back with both hands. "That's the first thing you've told me I can really understand. Looks like we're in the same boat. Do I take it we have a truce?"

"Sure."

She glanced back as another record dropped onto the turntable. "This is one of my favorites. 'Smoke Gets in Your Eyes.' " She was smiling again when she looked back at him. "You never asked me to dance."

"No, I didn't."

"Miss Millie claims you're very smooth." She held out a hand in a gesture that was as much a peace offering as an invitation. Unable to resist, he took it in his. Their eyes stayed locked as he drew her slowly toward him.

CHAPTER 5

A fire simmered in the grate. Rain pattered against the windows. The record was old and scratchy, the tune hauntingly sad. Whether they wanted it or not, their bodies fitted. Her hand slid gently over his shoulder, his around her waist. With their faces close, they began to dance.

The added height from her heels brought her eyes level with his. He could smell the light fragrance that seemed so much a part of her. Seduced by it, he brought her closer, slowly. Their thighs brushed. Still closer. Her body melted against his.

It was so quiet. There was only the music, the rain, the hissing of the fire. Gloomy light swirled into the room. He could feel her heart beating against his, quick now, and not too steady.

His wasn't any too steady now, either.

Was that all it took? he wondered. Did he only have to touch her to think that she was the beginning and the end of everything? And to wish . . . His hand slid up her back, fingers spreading until they tangled in her hair. To wish she could belong to him.

He wasn't sure when that thought had sunk its roots in him. Perhaps it had begun the first moment he had seen her. She was—should have been—unattainable for him. But when she was in his arms, warm, just bordering on pliant, dozens of possibilities flashed through his head.

She wanted to smile, to make some light, easy comment. But she couldn't push the words out. Her throat was locked. The way he was looking at her now, as if she were the only woman he had ever seen or ever wanted to see, made her forget that the dance was supposed to be a gesture of friendship.

She might never be his friend, she knew, no matter how hard she tried. But with his eyes on hers she understood how easily she could be his lover.

Maybe it was wrong, but it didn't seem to matter as they glided across the floor. The song spoke of love betrayed, but she heard only poetry. She felt her will ebb away even as the music swelled inside her head. No, it didn't seem to matter. Nothing seemed to matter as long as she went on swaying in his arms.

She didn't even try to think, never attempted to reason. Following her heart, she pressed her lips to his.

Instant. Irresistible. Irrevocable. Emotions funneled from one to the other, then merged in a torrent of need. She didn't expect him to be gentle, though her kiss had offered comfort, as well as passion. He dived into it, into her, with a speed and force that left her reeling, then fretting for more.

So this was what drove people to do mad, desperate acts, she thought as their tongues tangled. This wild, painful pleasure, once tasted, would never be forgotten, would always be craved. She wrapped her arms around his neck as she gave herself to it.

With quick, rough kisses he drove them both to

the edge. It was more than desire, he knew. Desire had never hurt, not deeply. It was like a scratch, soon forgotten, easily healed. This was a raw, deep wound.

Lust had never erased every coherent thought from his mind. Still, he could only think of her. Those thoughts were jumbled, and all of them were forbidden. Desperate, he ran his lips over her face, while wild fantasies of touching, of tasting every inch of her whirled in his head. It wouldn't be enough. It would never be enough. No matter how much he took from her, she would draw him back. And she could make him beg. The certainty of it terrified him.

She was trembling again, even as she strained against him. Her soft gasps and sighs pushed him toward the brink of reason. He found her mouth again and feasted on it.

He hardly recognized the change, could find no reason for it. All at once she was like glass in his arms, something precious, something fragile, something he needed to protect and defend. He lifted his hands to her face, his fingers light and cautiously caressing. His mouth, ravenous only a moment before, gentled.

Stunned, she swayed. New, vibrant emotions poured into her. Weak from the onslaught, she let her head fall back. Her arms slipped, boneless, to her sides. There was beauty here, a soft, shimmering beauty she had never known existed. Tenderness did what passion had not yet accomplished. As freely as a bird taking wing, her heart flew out to him.

Love, first experienced, was devastating. She felt tears burn the back of her eyes, heard her own quiet moan of surrender. And she tasted the glory of it as his lips played gently with hers.

She would always remember that one instant when the world changed—the music, the rain, the scent of fresh flowers. Nothing would ever be quite the same again. Nor would she ever want it to be.

Shaken, she drew back to lift a hand to her spinning head. "Roman—"

"Come with me." Unwilling to think, he pulled her against him again. "I want to know what it's like to be with you, to undress you, to touch you."

With a moan, she surrendered to his mouth again.

"Charity, Mae wants to—" Lori stopped on a dime at the top of the stairs. After clearing her throat, she stared at the painting on the opposite wall as if it fascinated her. "Excuse me. I didn't mean to . . ."

Charity had jerked back like a spring and was searching for composure. "It's all right. What is it, Lori?"

"It's, well . . . Mae and Dolores . . . Maybe you could come down to the kitchen when you get a minute." She rushed down the stairs, grinning to herself.

"I should . . ." Charity paused to draw in a steadying breath but managed only a shaky one. "I should go down." She retreated a step. "Once they get started, they need—" She broke off when Roman took her arm. He waited until she lifted her head and looked at him again.

"Things have changed."

It sounded so simple when he said it. "Yes. Yes, they have."

"Right or wrong, Charity, we'll finish this."

"No." She was far from calm, but she was very determined. "If it's right, we'll finish it. I'm not going to pretend I don't want you, but you're right when you say things have changed, Roman. You see, I know what I'm feeling now, and I have to get used to it."

He tightened his grip when she turned to go. "What are you feeling?"

She couldn't have lied if she'd wanted to. Dishonesty was abhorrent to her. When it came to feelings, she had neither the ability nor the desire to suppress them. "I'm in love with you."

His fingers uncurled from her arm. Very slowly, very carefully, as if he were retreating from some dangerous beast, he released her.

She read the shock on his face. That was understandable. And she read the distrust. That was painful. She gave him a last unsmiling look before she turned away.

"Apparently we both have to get used to it."

She was lying. Roman told himself that over and over as he paced the floor in his room. If not to him, then certainly to herself. People seemed to find love easy to lie about.

He stopped by the window and stared out into the dark. The rain had stopped, and the moon was cruising in and out of the clouds. He jerked the window open and breathed in the damp, cool air. He needed something to clear his head.

She was working on him. Annoyed, he turned away from the view of trees and flowers and started pacing again. The easy smiles, the openhanded welcome, the casual friendliness . . . then the passion, the uninhibited response, the seduction. He wanted to believe it was a trap, even though his well-trained mind found the idea absurd.

She had no reason to suspect him. His cover was solid. Charity thought of him as a drifter, passing through long enough to take in some sights and pick up a little loose change. It was he who was setting the trap.

He dropped down on the bed and lit a cigarette, more out of habit than because he wanted one. Lies were part of his job, a part he was very good at. She hadn't lied to him, he reflected as he inhaled. But she was mistaken. He had made her want, and she had justified her desire for a relative stranger by telling herself she was in love.

But if it was true . . .

He couldn't allow himself to think that way. Leaning back against the headboard, he stared at the blank wall. He couldn't allow himself the luxury of wondering what it would be like to be loved, and especially not what it would be like to be loved by a woman to whom love would mean a lifetime. He couldn't afford any daydreams about belonging, about having someone belong to him. Even if she hadn't been part of his assignment he would have to sidestep Charity Ford.

She would think of love, then of white picket fences, Sunday dinners and evenings by the fire. He was no good for her. He would never be any good for her. Roman DeWinter, he thought with a mirthless smile. Always on the wrong side of the tracks. A questionable past, an uncertain future. There was nothing he could offer a woman like Charity.

But God, he wanted her. The need was eating away at his insides. He knew she was upstairs now. He imagined her curled up in the big four-poster, under white blankets, perhaps with a white candle burning low on the table.

He had only to climb the stairs and walk through the door. She wouldn't send him away. If she tried, it would take him only moments to break down her resistance. Believing herself in love, she would yield, then open her arms to him. He ached to be in them, to sink into that bed, into her, and let oblivion take them both.

But she had asked for time. He wasn't going to deny her what he needed himself. In the time he gave her he would use all his skill to do the one thing he knew how to do for her. He would prove her innocence.

Roman watched the tour group check out the following morning. Perched on a stepladder in the center of the lobby, he took his time changing bulbs in the ceiling fixture. The sun was out now, full and bright, bathing the lobby in light as a few members of the tour loitered after breakfast.

At the front desk, Charity was chatting with Block. He was wearing a fresh white shirt and his perpetual smile. Taking a calculator from his briefcase, he checked to see if Charity's tallies matched his own.

Bob poked his head out of the office and handed her a computer printout. Roman didn't miss the quick, uncertain look Bob sent in his direction before he shut himself away again.

Charity and Block compared lists. Still smiling, he took a stack of bills out of his briefcase. He paid in Canadian, cash. Having already adjusted the bill to take the exchange rate into account, Charity locked the cash away in a drawer, then handed Block his receipt.

"Always a pleasure, Roger."

"Your little party saved the day," he told her. "My people consider this the highlight of the tour."

Pleased, she smiled at him. "They haven't seen Mount Rainier yet."

"You're going to get some repeaters out of this." He patted her hand, then checked his watch. "Time to move them out. See you next week."

"Safe trip, Roger." She turned to make change for

a departing guest, then sold a few postcards and a few souvenir key chains with miniature whales on them.

Roman replaced the globe on the ceiling fixture, taking his time until the lobby was clear again. "Isn't it strange for a company like that to pay cash?"

Distracted from her reservations list, Charity glanced up at him. "We never turn down cash." She smiled at him as she had promised herself she would. Her feelings, her problem, she reminded herself as he climbed down from the ladder. She only wished the hours she'd spent soul-searching the night before had resulted in a solution.

"It seems like they'd charge, or pay by check."

"It's their company policy. Believe me, with a small, independent hotel, a cash-paying customer like Vision can make all the difference."

"I'll bet. You've been dealing with them for a while?"

"A couple of years. Why?"

"Just curious. Block doesn't look much like a tour guide."

"Roger? No, I guess he looks more like a wrestler." She went back to her papers. It was difficult to make small talk when her feelings were so close to the surface. "He does a good job."

"Yeah. I'll be upstairs."

"Roman." There was so much she wanted to say, but she could feel, though they were standing only a few feet apart, that he had distanced himself from her. "We never discussed a day off," she began. "You're welcome to take Sunday, if you like."

"Maybe I will."

"And if you'd give Bob your hours at the end of the week, he generally takes care of payroll."

"All right. Thanks."

A young couple with a toddler walked out of the dining room. Roman left her to answer their questions on renting a boat.

It wasn't going to be easy to talk to him, Charity decided later. But she had to do it. She'd spent all morning on business, she'd double-checked the housekeeping in the cabins, she'd made every phone call on her list, and if Mae's comments were anything to go on she'd made a nuisance of herself in the kitchen.

She was stalling.

That wasn't like her. All her life she'd made a habit of facing her problems head-on and plowing through them. Not only with business, she thought now. Personal problems had always been given the same kind of direct approach. She had handled being parentless. Even as a child she had never evaded the sometimes painful questions about her background.

But then, she'd had her grandfather. He'd been so solid, so loving. He'd helped her understand that she was her own person. Just as he'd helped her through her first high-school crush, Charity remembered.

He wasn't here now, and she wasn't a fifteen-year-old mooning over the captain of the debating team. But if he had taught her anything, it was that honest feelings were nothing to be ashamed of.

Armed with a thermos full of coffee, she walked into the west wing. She wished it didn't feel so much like bearding the lion in his den.

He'd finished the parlor. The scent of fresh paint was strong, though he'd left a window open to air it out. The doors still had to be hung and the floors varnished, but she could already imagine the room with sheer, billowy curtains and the faded floral-print rug she'd stored in the attic.

From the bedroom beyond, she could hear the buzz

of an electric saw. A good, constructive sound, she thought as she pushed the door open to peek inside.

His eyes were narrowed in concentration as he bent over the wood he had laid across a pair of sawhorses. Wood dust flew, dancing gold in the sunlight. His hands, and his arms where he'd rolled his sleeves up past the elbow, were covered with it. He'd used a bandanna to keep the hair out of his eyes. He didn't hum while he worked, as she did. Or talk to himself, she mused, as George had. But, watching him, she thought she detected a simple pleasure in doing a job and doing it well.

He could do things, she thought as she watched him measure the wood for the next cut. Good things, even important things. She was sure of it. Not just because she loved him, she realized. Because it was in him. When a woman spent all her life entertaining strangers in her home, she learned to judge, and to see.

She waited until he put the saw down before she pushed the door open. Before she could speak he whirled around. Her step backward was instinctive, defensive. It was ridiculous, she told herself, but she thought that if he'd had a weapon he'd have drawn it.

"I'm sorry." The nerves she had managed to get under control were shot to hell. "I should have realized I'd startle you."

"It's all right." He settled quickly, though it annoyed him to have been caught off guard. Perhaps if he hadn't been thinking of her he would have sensed her.

"I needed to do some things upstairs, so I thought I'd bring you some coffee on my way." She set the thermos on the stepladder, then wished she'd kept it, as her empty hands made her feel foolish. "And I wanted to check how things were going. The parlor looks great."

"It's coming along. Did you label the paint?"

"Yes. Why?"

"Because it was all done in this tidy printing on the lid of each can in the color of the paint. That seemed like something you'd do."

"Obsessively organized?" She made a face. "I can't seem to help it."

"I liked the way you had the paintbrushes arranged according to size."

She lifted a brow. "Are you making fun of me?"

"Yeah."

"Well, as long as I know." Her nerves were calmer now. "Want some of this coffee?"

"Yeah. I'll get it."

"You've got sawdust all over your hands." Waving him aside, she unscrewed the top. "I take it our truce is back on."

"I didn't realize it had been off."

She glanced back over her shoulder, then looked around and poured the coffee into the plastic cup. "I made you uncomfortable yesterday. I'm sorry."

He accepted the cup and sat down on a sawhorse. "You're putting words in my mouth again, Charity."

"I don't have to this time. You looked as if I'd hit you with a brick." Restless, she moved her shoulders. "I suppose I might have reacted the same way if someone had said they loved me out of the blue like that. It must have been pretty startling, seeing as we haven't known each other for long."

Finding he had no taste for it, he set the coffee aside. "You were reacting to the moment."

"No." She turned back to him, knowing it was important to talk face-to-face. "I thought you might think that. In fact, I even considered playing it safe and letting you. I'm lousy at deception. It seemed more fair to tell you that I'm not in the habit of . . . What I mean is, I don't throw myself at men as a rule. The truth is, you're the first."

"Charity." He dragged a hand through his hair, pulling out the bandanna and sending more wood dust scattering. "I don't know what to say to you."

"You don't have to say anything. The fact is, I came in here with my little speech all worked out. It was a pretty good one, too . . . calm, understanding, a couple of dashes of humor to keep it light. I'm screwing it up."

She kicked a scrap of wood into the corner before she paced to the window. Columbine and bluebells grew just below in a bed where poppies were waiting to burst into color. On impulse, she pushed up the window to breathe in their faint, fragile scents.

"The point is," she began, hating herself for keeping her back to him, "we can't pretend I didn't say it. I can't pretend I don't feel it. That doesn't mean I expect you to feel the same way, because I don't."

"What do you expect?"

He was right behind her. She jumped when his hand gripped her shoulder. Gathering her courage, she turned around. "For you to be honest with me." She was speaking quickly now, and she didn't notice his slight, automatic retreat. "I appreciate the fact that you don't pretend to love me. I may be simple, Roman, but I'm not stupid. I know it might be easier to lie, to say what you think I want to hear."

"You're not simple," he murmured, lifting a hand and brushing it against her cheek. "I've never met a more confusing, complicated woman."

Shock came first, then pleasure. "That's the nicest thing you've ever said to me. No one's ever accused me of being complicated."

He'd meant to lower his hand, but she had already lifted hers and clasped it. "I didn't mean it as a compliment."

That made her grin. Relaxed again, she sat back on the windowsill. "Even better. I hope this means we're finished feeling awkward around each other."

"I don't know what I feel around you." He ran his hands up her arms to her shoulders, then down to the elbows again. "But awkward isn't the word for it."

Touched—much too deeply—she rose. "I have to go."

"Why?"

"Because it's the middle of the day, and if you kiss me I might forget that."

Already aroused, he eased her forward. "Always organized."

"Yes." She put a hand to his chest to keep some distance between them. "I have some invoices I have to go over upstairs." Holding her breath, she backed toward the door. "I do want you, Roman. I'm just not sure I can handle that part of it."

Neither was he, he thought after she shut the door. With another woman he would have been certain that physical release would end the tension. With Charity he knew that making love with her would only add another layer to the hold she had on him.

And she did have a hold on him. It was time to admit that, and to deal with it.

Perhaps he'd reacted so strongly to her declaration of love because he was afraid, as he'd never been afraid of anything in his life, that he was falling in love with her.

"Roman!" He heard the delight in Charity's voice when she called to him. He swung open the door and saw her standing on the landing at the top of the stairs. "Come up. Hurry. I want you to see them."

She disappeared, leaving him wishing she'd called him anyplace but that innocently seductive bedroom.

When he walked into her sitting room, she called again, impatience in her tone now. "Hurry. I don't know how long they'll stay."

She was sitting on the windowsill, her upper body out the opening, her long legs hooked just above the ankles. There was music playing, something vibrant, passionate. How was it he had never thought of classical music as passionate?

"Damn it, Roman, you're going to miss them. Don't just stand in the doorway. I didn't call you up to tie you to the bedposts."

Because he felt like a fool, he crossed to her. "There goes my night."

"Very funny. Look." She was holding a brass spyglass, and she pointed with it now, out to sea. "Orcas."

He leaned out the window and followed her guiding hand. He could see a pair of shapes in the distance, rippling the water as they swam. Fascinated, he took the spyglass from Charity's hand.

"There are three of them," he said. Delighted, he joined her on the windowsill. Their legs were aligned now, and he rested his hand absently on her knee. This time, instead of fire, there was simple warmth.

"Yes, there's a calf. I think it might be the same pod I spotted a few days ago." She closed a hand over his as they both stared out to sea. "Great, aren't they?"

"Yeah, they are." He focused on the calf, which was just visible between the two larger whales. "I never really expected to see any."

"Why? The island's named after them." She narrowed her eyes, trying to follow their path. She didn't have the heart to ask Roman for the glass. "My first clear memory of seeing one was when I was about four.

Pop had me out on this little excuse for a fishing boat. One shot up out of the water no more than eight or ten yards away. I screamed my lungs out." Laughing, she leaned back against the windowframe. "I thought it was going to swallow us whole, like Jonah or maybe Pinocchio."

Roman lowered the glass for a moment. "Pinocchio?"

"Yes, you know the puppet who wanted to be a real boy. Jiminy Cricket, the Blue Fairy. Anyway, Pop finally calmed me down. It followed us for ten or fifteen minutes. After that, I nagged him mercilessly to take me out again."

"Did he?"

"Every Monday afternoon that summer. We didn't always see something, but they were great days, the best days. I guess we were a pod, too, Pop and I." She turned her face into the breeze. "I was lucky to have him as long as I did, but there are times—like this—when I can't help wishing he were here."

"Like this?"

"He loved to watch them," she said quietly. "Even when he was ill, really ill, he would sit for hours at the window. One afternoon I found him sitting there with the spyglass on his lap. I thought he'd fallen asleep, but he was gone." There was a catch in her breath when she slowly let it out. "He would have wanted that, to just slip away while watching for his whales. I haven't been able to take the boat out since he died." She shook her head. "Stupid."

"No." He reached for her hand for the first time and linked his fingers with hers. "It's not."

She turned her face to his again. "You can be a nice man." The phone rang, and she groaned but slipped dutifully from the windowsill to answer it.

"Hello. Yes, Bob. What does he mean he won't deliver them? New management be damned, we've been dealing with that company for ten years. Yes, all right. I'll be right there. Oh, wait." She glanced up from the phone. "Roman, are they still there?"

"Yes. Heading south. I don't know if they're feeding or just taking an afternoon stroll."

She laughed and put the receiver at her ear again. "Bob— What? Yes, that was Roman." Her brow lifted. "That's right. We're in my room. I called Roman up here because I spotted a pod out my bedroom window. You might want to tell any of the guests you see around. No, there's no reason for you to be concerned. Why should there be? I'll be right down."

She hung up, shaking her head. "It's like having a houseful of chaperones," she muttered.

"Problem?"

"No. Bob realized that you were in my bedroom—or rather that we were alone in my bedroom—and got very big-brotherly. Typical." She opened a drawer and pulled out a fabric-covered band. In a few quick movements she had her hair caught back from her face. "Last year Mae threatened to poison a guest who made a pass at me. You'd think I was fifteen."

He turned to study her. She was wearing jeans and a sweatshirt with a silk-screened map of the island. "Yes, you would."

"I don't take that as a compliment." But she didn't have time to argue. "I have to deal with a small crisis downstairs. You're welcome to stay and watch the whales." She started toward the door, but then she stopped. "Oh, I nearly forgot. Can you build shelves?"

"Probably."

"Great. I think the parlor in the family suite could use them. We'll talk about it."

He heard her jog down the stairs. Whatever crisis there might be at the other end of the inn, he was sure she would handle it. In the meantime, she had left him alone in her room. It would be a simple matter to go through her desk again, to see if she'd left anything that would help him move his investigation forward.

It should be simple, anyway. Roman looked out to sea again. It should be something he could do without hesitation. But he couldn't. She trusted him. Sometime during the past twenty-four hours he reached the point where he couldn't violate that trust.

That made him useless. Swearing, Roman leaned back against the windowframe. She had, without even being aware of it, totally undermined his ability to do his job. It would be best for him to call Conby and have himself taken off the case. It would simply be a matter of him turning in his resignation now, rather than at the end of the assignment. It was a question of duty.

He wasn't going to do that, either.

He needed to stay. It had nothing to do with being loved, with feeling at home. He needed to believe that. He also needed to finish his job and prove, beyond a shadow of a doubt, Charity's innocence. That was a question of loyalty.

Conby would have said that his loyalty belonged to the Bureau, not to a woman he had known for less than a week. And Conby would have been wrong, Roman thought as he set aside the spyglass. There were times, rare times, when you had a chance to do something good, something right. Something that proved you gave a damn. That had never mattered to him before, but it mattered now.

If the only thing he could give Charity was a clear

name, he intended to give it to her. And then get out of her life.

Rising, he looked around the room. He wished he were nothing more than the out-of-work drifter Charity had taken into her home. If he were, maybe he would have the right to love her. As it was, all he could do was save her.

CHAPTER 6

The weather was warming. Spring was busting loose, full of glory and color and scent. The island was a treasure trove of wildflowers, leafy trees and birdsong. At dawn, with thin fingers of fog over the water, it was a mystical, timeless place.

Roman stood at the side of the road and watched the sun come up as he had only days before. He didn't know the names of the flowers that grew in tangles on the roadside. He didn't know the song of a jay from that of a sparrow. But he knew Charity was out running with her dog and that she would pass the place he stood on her return.

He needed to see her, to talk to her, to be with her.

The night before, he had broken into her cash drawer and examined the bills she had neatly stacked and marked for today's deposit. There had been over two thousand dollars in counterfeit Canadian currency. His first impulse had been to tell her, to lay everything he knew and needed to know out in front of her. But he had quashed that. Telling her wouldn't prove her innocence to men like Conby.

He had enough to get Block. And nearly enough, he thought, to hang Bob along with him. But he couldn't get them without casting shadows on Charity. By her own admission, and according to the statements of her loyal staff, a pin couldn't drop in the inn without her knowing it.

If that was so, how could he prove that there had been a counterfeiting and smuggling ring going on under her nose for nearly two years?

He believed it, as firmly as he had ever believed anything. Conby and the others at the Bureau wanted facts. Roman drew on his cigarette and watched the fog melt away with the rising of the sun. He had to give them facts. Until he could, he would give them nothing.

He could wait and make sure Conby dropped the ax on Block on the guide's next trip to the inn. That would give Roman time. Time enough, he promised himself, to make certain Charity wasn't caught in the middle. When it went down, she would be stunned and hurt. She'd get over it. When it was over, and she knew his part in it, she would hate him. He would get over that. He would have to.

He heard a car and glanced over, then returned his gaze to the water. He wondered if he could come back someday and stand in this same spot and wait for Charity to run down the road toward him.

Fantasies, he told himself, pitching his half-finished cigarette into the dirt. He was wasting too much time on fantasies.

The car was coming fast, its engine protesting, its muffler rattling. He looked over again, annoyed at having his morning and his thoughts disturbed.

His annoyance saved his life.

It took him only an instant to realize what was

happening, and a heartbeat more to evade it. As the car barreled toward him, he leaped aside, tucking and rolling into the brush. A wave of displaced air flattened the grass before the car's rear tires gripped the roadbed again. Roman's gun was in his hand even as he scrambled to his feet. He caught a glimpse of the car's rear end as it sped around a curve. There wasn't even time to swear before he heard Charity's scream.

He ran, unaware of the fire in his thigh where the car had grazed him and the blood on his arm where he had rolled into a rock. He had faced death. He had killed. But he had never understood terror until this moment, with her scream still echoing in his head. He hadn't understood agony until he'd seen Charity sprawled beside the road.

The dog was curled beside her, whimpering, nuzzling her face with her nose. He turned at Roman's approach and began to growl, then stood, barking.

"Charity." Roman crouched beside her, and felt for a pulse, his hand shaking. "Okay, baby. You're going to be okay," he murmured to her as he checked for broken bones.

Had she been hit? A sickening vision of her being tossed into the air as the car slammed into her pulsed through his head. Using every ounce of control he possessed, he blocked it out. She was breathing. He held on to that. The dog whined as he turned her head and examined the gash on her temple. It was the only spot of color on her face. He stanched the blood with his bandanna, cursing when he felt its warmth on his fingers.

Grimly he replaced his weapon, then lifted her into his arms. Her body seemed boneless. Roman tightened his grip, half afraid she might melt through his arms. He talked to her throughout the half-mile walk back to the inn, though she remained pale and still.

Bob raced out the front door of the inn. "My God! What happened? What the hell did you do to her?"

Roman paused just long enough to aim a dark, furious look at him. "I think you know better. Get me the keys to the van. She needs a hospital."

"What's all this?" Mae came through the door, wiping her hands on her apron. "Lori said she saw—" She went pale, but then she began to move with surprising speed, elbowing Bob aside to reach Charity. "Get her upstairs."

"I'm taking her to the hospital."

"Upstairs," Mae repeated, moving back to open the door for him. "We'll call Dr. Mertens. It'll be faster. Come on, boy. Call the doctor, Bob. Tell him to hurry."

Roman passed through the door, the dog at his heels. "And call the police," he added. "Tell them they've got a hit-and-run."

Wasting no time on words, Mae led the way upstairs. She was puffing a bit by the time she reached the second floor, but she never slowed down. When they moved into Charity's room, her color had returned.

"Set her on the bed, and be careful about it." She yanked the lacy coverlet aside and then just as efficiently, brushed Roman aside. "There, little girl, you'll be just fine. Go in the bathroom," she told Roman. "Get me a fresh towel." Easing a hip onto the bed, she cupped Charity's face with a broad hand and examined her head wound. "Looks worse than it is." She let out a long breath. After taking the towel Roman offered, she pressed it against Charity's temple. "Head wounds bleed heavy, make a mess. But it's not too deep."

He only knew that her blood was still on his hands. "She should be coming around."

"Give her time. I want you to tell me what happened later, but I'm going to undress her now, see if she's hurt anywhere else. You go on and wait downstairs."

"I'm not leaving her."

Mae glanced up. Her lips were pursed, and lines of worry fanned out from her eyes. After a moment, she simply nodded, "All right, then, but you'll be of some use. Get me the scissors out of her desk. I want to cut this shirt off."

So that was the way of it, Mae mused as she untied Charity's shoes. She knew a man who was scared to death and fighting his heart when she saw one. Well, she'd just have to get her girl back on her feet. She didn't doubt for a moment that Charity could deal with the likes of Roman DeWinter.

"You can stay," she told him when he handed her the scissors. "But whatever's been going on between the two of you, you'll turn your back till I make her decent."

He balled his hands into impotent fists and shoved them into his pockets as he spun around. "I want to know where she's hurt."

"Just hold your horses." Mae peeled the shirt away and put her emotions on hold as she examined the scrapes and bruises. "Look in that top right-hand drawer and get me a nightshirt. One with buttons. And keep your eyes to yourself," she added, "or I'll throw you out of here."

In answer, he tossed a thin white nightshirt onto the bed. "I don't care what she's wearing. I want to know how badly she's hurt."

"I know, boy." Mae's voice softened as she slipped Charity's limp arm into a sleeve. "She's got some bruises and scrapes, that's all. Nothing broken. The cut on her head's going to need some tending, but cuts heal. Why, she hurt herself worse when she fell out of a tree some time back. There's my girl. She's coming around."

He turned to look then, shirt or no shirt. But Mae had already done up the buttons. He controlled the urge to go to her—barely—and, keeping his distance, watched Charity's lashes flutter. The sinking in his stomach was pure relief. When she moaned, he wiped his clammy hands on his thighs.

"Mae?" As she struggled to focus her eyes, Charity reached out a hand. She could see the solid bulk of her cook, but little else. "What— Oh, God, my head."

"Thumping pretty good, is it?" Mae's voice was brisk, but she cradled Charity's hand in hers. She would have kissed it if she'd thought no one would notice. "The doc'll fix that up."

"Doctor?" Baffled, Charity tried to sit up, but the pain exploded in her head. "I don't want the doctor."

"Never did, but you're having him just the same."

"I'm not going to . . ." Arguing took too much effort. Instead, she closed her eyes and concentrated on clearing her mind. It was fairly obvious that she was in bed—but how the devil had she gotten there?

She'd been walking the dog, she remembered, and Ludwig had found a tree beside the road irresistible. Then . . .

"There was a car," she said, opening her eyes again. "They must have been drunk or crazy. It seemed like they came right at me. If Ludwig hadn't already been pulling me off the road, I—" She wasn't quite ready to consider that. "I stumbled, I think. I don't know."

"It doesn't matter now," Mae assured her. "We'll figure it all out later."

After a brisk knock, the outside door opened. A

short, spry little man with a shock of white hair hustled in. He carried a black bag and was wearing grubby overalls and muddy boots. Charity took one look, then closed her eyes again.

"Go away, Dr. Mertens. I'm not feeling well."

"She never changes." Mertens nodded to Roman, then walked over to examine his patient.

Roman slipped quietly out into the sitting room. He needed a moment to pull himself together, to quiet the rage that was building now that he knew she would be all right. He had lost his parents, he had buried his best friend, but he had never, never felt the kind of panic he had experienced when he had seen Charity bleeding and unconscious beside the road.

Taking out a cigarette, he went to the open window. He thought about the driver of the old, rusted Chevy that had run her down. Even as his rage cooled, Roman understood one thing with perfect clarity. It would be his pleasure to kill whoever had hurt her.

"Excuse me." Lori was standing in the hall doorway, wringing her hands. "The sheriff's here. He wants to talk to you, so I brought him up." She tugged at her apron and stared at the closed door on the other side of the room. "Charity?"

"The doctor's with her," Roman said. "She'll be fine."

Lori closed her eyes and took a deep breath. "I'll tell the others. Go on in, Sheriff."

Roman studied the paunchy man, who had obviously been called out of bed. His shirttail was only partially tucked into his pants, and he was sipping a cup of coffee as he came into the room.

"You Roman DeWinter?"

"That's right."

"Sheriff Royce." He sat, with a sigh, on the arm of Charity's rose-colored Queen Anne chair. "What's this about a hit-and-run?"

"About twenty minutes ago somebody tried to run down Miss Ford."

Royce turned to stare at the closed door just the way Lori had done. "How is she?"

"Banged up. She's got a gash on her head and some bruises."

"Were you with her?" He pulled out a pad and a stubby pencil.

"No. I was about a quarter mile away. The car swerved at me, then kept going. I heard Charity scream. When I got to her, she was unconscious."

"Don't suppose you got a good look at the car?"

"Dark blue Chevy. Sedan, '67, '68. Muffler was bad. Right front fender was rusted through. Washington plates Alpha Foxtrot Juliet 847."

Royce lifted both brows as he took down the description. "You got a good eye."

"That's right."

"Good enough for you to guess if he ran you down on purpose?"

"I don't have to guess. He was aiming."

Without a flicker of an eye, Royce continued taking notes. He added a reminder to himself to do a routine check on Roman DeWinter. "He? Did you see the driver?"

"No," Roman said shortly. He was still cursing himself for that.

"How long have you been on the island, Mr. DeWinter?"

"Almost a week."

"A short time to make enemies."

"I don't have any—here—that I know of."

"That makes your theory pretty strange." Still scribbling, Royce glanced up. "There's nobody on the island who knows Charity and has a thing against her. If what you're saying's true, we'd be talking attempted murder."

Roman pitched his cigarette out the window. "That's just what we're talking about. I want to know who owns that car."

"I'll check it out."

"You already know."

Royce tapped his pad on his knee. "Yes, sir, you do have a good eye. I'll say this. Maybe I do know somebody who owns a car that fits your description. If I do, I know that that person wouldn't run over a rabbit on purpose, much less a woman. Then again, there's no saying you have to own a car to drive it."

Mae opened the connecting door, and he glanced up. "Well, now, Maeflower."

Mae's lips twitched slightly before she thinned them. "If you can't sit in a chair proper you can stand on your feet, Jack Royce."

Royce rose, grinning. "Mae and I went to school together," he explained. "She liked to bully me then, too. I don't suppose you've got any waffles on the menu today, Maeflower."

"Maybe I do. You find out who hurt my girl and I'll see you get some."

"I'm working on it." His face sobered again as he nodded toward the door. "Is she up to talking to me?"

"Done nothing but talk since she came around." Mae blinked back a flood of relieved tears. "Go ahead in."

Royce turned to Roman. "I'll be in touch."

"Doc said she could have some tea and toast." Mae sniffled, then made a production out of blowing her nose. "Hay fever," she said roughly. "I'm grateful you were close by when she was hurt."

"If I'd been closer she wouldn't have been hurt."

"And if she hadn't been walking that dog she'd have been in bed." She paused and gave Roman a level look. "I guess we could shoot him."

She surprised a little laugh out of him. "Charity might object to that."

"She wouldn't care to know you're out here brooding, either. Your arm's bleeding, boy."

He looked down dispassionately at the torn, bloodstained sleeve of his shirt. "Some."

"Can't have you bleeding all over the floor." She walked to the door, waving a hand. "Well, come on downstairs. I'll clean you up. Then you can bring the girl up some breakfast. I haven't got time to run up and down these steps all morning."

After the doctor had finished his poking and the sheriff had finished his questioning, Charity stared at the ceiling. She hurt everywhere there was to hurt. Her head especially, but the rest of her was throbbing right along in time.

The medication would take the edge off, but she wanted to keep her mind clear until she'd worked everything out. That was why she had tucked the pill Dr. Mertens had given her under her tongue until she'd been alone. As soon as she'd organized her thoughts she would swallow it and check into oblivion for a few hours.

She'd only caught a flash of the car, but it had

seemed familiar. While she'd spoken with the sheriff she'd remembered. The car that had nearly run her over belonged to Mrs. Norton, a sweet, flighty lady who crocheted doilies and doll clothes for the local craft shops. Charity didn't think Mrs. Norton had ever driven over twenty-five miles an hour. That was a great deal less than the car had been doing when it had swerved at her that morning.

She hadn't seen the driver, not really, but she had the definite impression it had been a man. Mrs. Norton had been widowed for six years.

Then it was simple, Charity decided. Someone had gotten drunk, stolen Mrs. Norton's car, and taken it for a wild joyride around the island. They probably hadn't even seen her at the side of the road.

Satisfied, she eased herself up in the bed. The rest was for the sheriff to worry about. She had problems of her own.

The breakfast shift was probably in chaos. She thought she could rely on Lori to keep everyone calm. Then there was the butcher. She still had her list to complete for tomorrow's order. And she had yet to choose the photographs she wanted to use for the ad in the travel brochure. The deposit hadn't been paid, and the fireplace in cabin 3 was smoking.

What she needed was a pad, a pencil and a telephone. That was simple enough. She'd find all three at the desk in the sitting room. Carefully she eased her legs over the side of the bed. Not too bad, she decided, but she gave herself a moment to adjust before she tried to stand.

Annoyed with herself, she braced a hand on one of the bedposts. Her legs felt as though they were filled with Mae's whipped cream rather than muscle and bone.

"What the hell are you doing?"

She winced at the sound of Roman's voice, then gingerly turned her head toward the doorway. "Nothing," she said, and tried to smile.

"Get back in bed."

"I just have a few things to do."

She was swaying on her feet, as pale as the nightshirt that buttoned modestly high at the neck and skimmed seductively high on her thighs. Without a word, he set down the tray he was carrying, crossed to her and scooped her up in his arms.

"Roman, don't. I—"

"Shut up."

"I was going to lie back down in a minute," she began. "Right after—"

"Shut up," he repeated. He laid her on the bed, then gave up. Keeping his arms around her, he buried his face against her throat. "Oh, God, baby."

"It's all right." She stroked a hand through his hair. "Don't worry."

"I thought you were dead. When I found you I thought you were dead."

"Oh, I'm sorry." She rubbed at the tension at the back of his neck, trying to imagine how he must have felt. "It must have been awful, Roman. But it's only some bumps and bruises. In a couple of days they'll be gone and we'll forget all about it."

"I won't forget." He pulled himself away from her. "Ever."

The violence she saw in his eyes had her heart fluttering. "Roman, it was an accident. Sheriff Royce will take care of it."

He bit back the words he wanted to say. It was best that she believe it had been an accident. For now. He got up to get her tray. "Mae said you could eat."

She thought of the lists she had to make and decided she had a better chance getting around him if she cooperated. "I'll try. How's Ludwig?"

"Okay. Mae put him out and gave him a ham bone."

"Ah, his favorite." She bit into the toast and pretended she had an appetite.

"How's your head?"

"Not too bad." It wasn't really a lie, she thought. She was sure a blow with a sledgehammer would have been worse. "No stitches." She pulled back her hair to show him a pair of butterfly bandages. A bruise was darkening around them. "You want to hold up some fingers and ask me how many I see?"

"No." He turned away, afraid he would explode. The last thing she needed was another outburst from him, he reminded himself. He wasn't the kind to fall apart—at least he hadn't been until he'd met her.

He began fiddling with bottles and bowls set around the room. She loved useless little things, he thought as he picked up a wand-shaped amethyst crystal. Feeling clumsy, he set it down again.

"The sheriff said the car swerved at you." She drank the soothing chamomile tea, feeling almost human again. "I'm glad you weren't hurt."

"Damn it, Charity." He whirled, then made an effort to get a handle on his temper. "No, I wasn't hurt." And he was going to see to it that *she* wasn't hurt again. "I'm sorry. This whole business has made me edgy."

"I know what you mean. Want some tea? Mae sent up two cups."

He glanced at the pretty flowered pot. "Not unless you've got some whiskey to go in it."

"Sorry, fresh out." Smiling again, she patted the bed. "Why don't you come sit down?"

"Because I'm trying to keep my hands off you."

"Oh." Her smile curved wider. It pleased her that she was resilient enough to feel a quick curl of desire. "I like your hands on me, Roman."

"Bad timing." Because he couldn't resist, he crossed to the bed to take her hand in his. "I care about you, Charity. I want you to believe that."

"I do."

"No." His fingers tightened insistently on hers. He knew he wasn't clever with words, but he needed her to understand. "It's different with you than it's ever been with anyone." Fighting a fresh wave of frustration, he relaxed his grip. "I can't give you anything else."

She felt her heart rise up in her throat. "If I had known I could get that much out of you I might have bashed my head on a rock before."

"You deserve more." He sat down and ran a gentle finger under the bruise on her temple.

"I agree." She brought his hand to her lips and watched his eyes darken. "I'm patient."

Something was moving inside him, and he was helpless to prevent it. "You don't know enough about me. You don't know anything about me."

"I know I love you. I figured you'd tell me the rest eventually."

"Don't trust me, Charity. Not so much."

There was trouble here. She wanted to smooth it from his face, but she didn't know how. "Have you done something so unforgivable, Roman?"

"I hope not. You should rest." Knowing he'd already said too much, he set her tray aside.

"I was going to, really. Right after I take care of a few things."

"The only thing you have to take care of today is yourself."

"That's very sweet of you, and as soon as I—"

"You're not getting out of bed for at least twenty-four hours."

"That's the most ridiculous thing I've ever heard. What possible difference does it make whether I'm lying down or sitting down?"

"According to the doctor, quite a bit." He picked up a tablet from the nightstand. "Is this the medication he gave you?"

"Yes."

"The same medication that you were supposed to take before he left?"

She struggled to keep from pouting. "I'm going to take it after I make a few phone calls."

"No phone calls today."

"Now listen, Roman, I appreciate your concern, but I don't take orders from you."

"I know. You give them to me."

Before she could respond, he lowered his lips to hers. Here was gentleness again, whisper-soft, achingly warm. With a little sound of pleasure, she sank into it.

He'd thought it would be easy to take one, only one, fleeting taste. But his hand curled into a fist as he fought the need to demand more. She was so fragile now. He wanted to soothe, not arouse . . . to comfort, not seduce. But in seconds he was both aroused and seduced.

When he started to pull back, she gave a murmur of protest and pressed him close again. She needed this sweetness from him, needed it more than any medication.

"Easy," he told her, clawing for his self-control. "I'm a little low on willpower, and you need rest."

"I'd rather have you."

She smiled at him, and his stomach twisted into knots. "Do you drive all men crazy?"

"I don't think so." Feeling on top of the world, she brushed his hair back from his brow. "Anyway, you're the first to ask."

"We'll talk about it later." Determined to do his best for her, he held out the pill. "Take this."

"Later."

"Uh-uh. Now."

With a sound of disgust, she popped the pill into her mouth, then picked up her cooling tea and sipped it. "There. Satisfied?"

He had to grin. "I've been a long way from satisfied since I first laid eyes on you, baby. Lift up your tongue."

"I beg your pardon?"

"You heard me. You're pretty good." He put a hand under her chin. "But I'm better. Let's have the pill."

She knew she was beaten. She took the pill out of her mouth, then made a production out of swallowing it. She touched the tip of her tongue to her lips. "It might still be in there. Want to search me for it?"

"What I want"—he kissed her lightly—"is for you to stay in bed." He shifted his lips to her throat. "No calls, no paperwork, no sneaking downstairs." He caught her earlobe between his teeth and felt her shudder, and his own. "Promise."

"Yes." Her lips parted as his brushed over them. "I promise."

"Good." He sat back and picked up the tray. "I'll see you later."

"But—" She set her teeth as he walked to the door. "You play dirty, DeWinter."

"Yeah." He glanced back at her. "And to win."

He left her, knowing she would no more break her word than she would fly out the window. He had business of his own to attend to.

CHAPTER 7

An important part of Roman's training had been learning how to pursue an assignment in a thorough and objective manner. He had always found it second nature to do both. Until now. Still, for very personal reasons, he fully intended to be thorough.

When he left Charity, Roman expected to find Bob in the office, and he hoped to find him alone. He wasn't disappointed. Bob had the phone receiver at his ear and the computer monitor blinking above his fingers. After waving a distracted hand in Roman's direction, he went on with his conversation.

"I'll be happy to set that up for you and your wife, Mr. Partington. That's a double room for the nights of the fifteenth and sixteenth of July."

"Hang up," Roman told him. Bob merely held up a finger, signaling a short wait.

"Yes, that's available with a private bath and includes breakfast. We'd be happy to help you arrange the rentals of kayaks during your stay. Your confirmation number is—"

Roman slammed a hand down on the phone, breaking the connection.

"What the hell are you doing?"

"Wondering if I should bother to talk to you or just kill you."

Bob sprang out of his chair and managed to put the desk between him and Roman. "Look, I know you've had an upsetting morning—"

"Do you?" Roman didn't bother to try to outmaneuver. He simply stood where he was and watched Bob sweat. "Upsetting. That's a nice, polite word for it. But you're a nice, polite man, aren't you, Bob?"

Bob glanced at the door and wondered if he had a chance of getting that far. "We're all a bit edgy because of Charity's accident. You could probably use a drink."

Roman moved over to a stack of computer manuals and unearthed a small silver flask. "Yours?" he said. Bob stared at him. "I imagine you keep this in here for those long nights when you're working late—and alone. Wondering how I knew where to find it?" He set it aside. "I came across it when I broke in here a couple of nights ago and went through the books."

"You broke in?" Bob wiped the back of his hand over suddenly dry lips. "That's a hell of a way to pay Charity back for giving you a job."

"Yeah, you're right about that. Almost as bad as using her inn to pass counterfeit bills and slip undesirables in and out of the country."

"I don't know what you're talking about." Bob took one cautious sideways step toward the door. "I want you out of here, DeWinter. When I tell Charity what you've done—"

"But you're not going to tell her. You're not going to tell her a damn thing—yet. But you're going to tell me." One look stopped Bob's careful movement cold. "Try for the door and I'll break your leg." Roman tapped a cigarette out of his pack. "Sit down."

"I don't have to take this." But he took a step back, away from the door, and away from Roman. "I'll call the police."

"Go ahead." Roman lit the cigarette and watched him through a veil of smoke. It was a pity Bob was so easily cowed. He'd have liked an excuse to damage him. "I was tempted to tell Royce everything I knew this morning. The problem with that was that it would have spoiled the satisfaction of dealing with you and the people you're with personally. But go ahead and call him." Roman shoved the phone across the desk in Bob's direction. "I can find a way of finishing my business with you once you're inside."

Bob didn't ask him to explain. He had heard the cell door slam the moment Roman had walked into the room. "Listen, I know you're upset. . . ."

"Do I look upset?" Roman murmured.

No, Bob thought, his stomach clenched. He looked cold—cold enough to kill. Or worse. But there had to be a way out. There always was. "You said something about counterfeiting. Why don't you tell me what this is all about, and we'll try to settle this calm—?" Before he got the last word out he was choking as Roman hauled him out of the chair by the collar.

"Do you want to die?"

"No." Bob's fingers slid helplessly off Roman's wrists.

"Then cut the crap." Disgusted, Roman tossed him back into the chair. "There are two things Charity doesn't do around here. Only two. She doesn't cook, and she doesn't work the computer. *Can't* would be a better word. She can't cook because Mae didn't teach her. Pretty easy to figure why. Mae wanted to rule in the kitchen, and Charity wanted to let her."

He moved to the window and casually lowered the shades so that the room was dim and private. "It's just as simple to figure why she can't work a basic office computer. You didn't teach her, or you made the lessons so complicated and contradictory she never caught on. You want me to tell you why you did that?"

"She was never really interested." Bob swallowed, his throat raw. "She can do the basics when she has to, but you know Charity—she's more interested in people than machines. I show her all the printouts."

"All? You and I know you haven't shown her all of them. Should I tell you what I think is on those disks you've got hidden in the file drawer?"

Bob pulled out a handkerchief with fumbling fingers and mopped at his brow. "I don't know what you're talking about."

"You keep the books for the inn, and for the little business you and your friends have on the side. I figure a man like you would keep backups, a little insurance in case the people you work for decided to cut you out." He opened a file drawer and dug out a disk. "We'll take a look at this later," he said, and tossed it onto the desk. "Two to three thousand a week washes through this place. Fifty-two weeks a year makes that a pretty good haul. Add that to the fee you charge to get someone back and forth across the border mixed with the tour group and you've got a nice, tidy sum."

"That's crazy." Barely breathing, Bob tugged at his collar. "You've got to know that's crazy."

"Did you know your references were still on file here?" Roman asked conversationally. "The problem is, they don't check out. You never worked for a hotel back in Fort Worth, or in San Francisco."

"So I padded my chances a bit. That doesn't prove anything."

"I think we'll turn up something more interesting when we run your prints."

Bob stared down at the disk. Sometimes you could bluff, and sometimes you had to fold. "Can I have a drink?"

Roman picked up the flask, tossed it to him and waited while he twisted off the cap. "You made me for a cop, didn't you? Or you were worried enough to keep your ear to the ground. You heard me asking the wrong questions, were afraid I'd told Charity about the operation and passed it along to your friends."

"It didn't feel right." Bob wiped the vodka from his lips, then drank again. "I know a scam when I see one, and you made me nervous the minute I saw you."

"Why?"

"When you're in my business you get so you can spot cops. In the supermarket, on the street, buying underwear at a department store. It doesn't matter where, you get so you can make them."

Roman thought of himself and of the years he'd spent on the other side of the street. He'd made his share of cops, and he still could. "Okay. So what did you do?"

"I told Block I thought you were a plant, but he figured I was going loopy. I wanted to back off until you'd gone, but he wouldn't listen. Last night, when you went down for dinner, I looked through your room. I found a box of shells. No gun, just the shells. That meant you were wearing it. I called Block and told him I was sure you were a cop. You'd been spending a lot of time with Charity, so I figured she was working with you on it."

"So you tried to kill her."

"No, not me." Panicked, Bob pressed back in his chair. "I swear. I'm not a violent man, DeWinter. Hell, I like Charity. I wanted to pull out, take a breather. We'd already set up another place, in the Olympic Mountains. I figured we could take a few weeks, run legit, then move on it. Block just said he'd take care of it, and I thought he meant we'd handle next week's tour on the level. That would give me time to fix everything here and get out. If I'd known what he was planning . . ."

"What? Would you have warned her?"

"I don't know." Bob drained the flask, but the liquor did little to calm his nerves. "Look, I do scams, I do cons. I don't kill people."

"Who was driving the car?"

"I don't know. I swear it," he said. Roman took a step toward him, and he gripped the arms of his chair. "Listen, I got in touch with Block the minute this happened. He said he'd hired somebody. He couldn't have done it himself, because he was on the mainland. He said the guy wasn't trying to kill her. Block just wanted her out of the way for a few days. We've got a big shipment coming in and—" He broke off, knowing he was digging himself in deeper.

Roman merely nodded. "You're going to find out who was driving the car."

"Okay, sure." He made the promise without knowing if he could keep it. "I'll find out."

"You and I are going to work together for the next few days, Bob."

"But . . . aren't you going to call Royce?"

"Let me worry about Royce. You're going to go on doing what you do best. Lying. Only now you're going to lie to Block. You do exactly what you're told and you'll stay alive. If you do a good job I'll put in a word for you with my superior. Maybe you can make a deal, turn state's evidence."

After resting a hip on the desk, Roman leaned closer. "If you try to check out, I'll hunt you down. I'll find you wherever you hide, and when I'm finished you'll wish I'd killed you."

Bob looked into Roman's eyes. He believed him. "What do you want me to do?"

"Tell me about the next shipment."

Charity was sick of it. It was bad enough that she'd given her word to Roman and had to stay in bed all day. She couldn't even use the phone to call the office and see what was going on in the world.

She'd tried to be good-humored about it, poking through the books and magazines that Lori had brought up to her. She'd even admitted—to herself— that there had been times, when things had gotten crazy at the inn, that she'd imagined having the luxury of an idle day in bed.

Now she had it, and she hated it.

The pill Roman had insisted she swallow had made her groggy. She drifted off periodically, only to wake later, annoyed that she didn't have enough control to stay awake and be bored. Because reading made her headache worse, she tried to work up some interest in the small portable television perched on the shelf across the room.

When she'd found *The Maltese Falcon* flickering in black and white she'd felt both pleasure and relief. If she had to be trapped in bed, it might as well be with Bogart. Even as Sam Spade succumbed to the Fat

Man's drug, Charity's own medication sent her under. She awoke in a very poor temper to a rerun of a sitcom.

He'd made her promise to stay in bed, she thought, jabbing an elbow at her pillow. And he didn't even have the decency to spend five minutes keeping her company. Apparently he was too busy to fit a sickroom call into his schedule. That was fine for him, she decided, running around doing something useful while she was moldering between the sheets. It wasn't in her nature to do nothing, and if she had to do it for five minutes longer she was going to scream.

Charity smiled a bit as she considered that. Just what would he do if she let out one long bloodcurdling scream? It might be interesting to find out. Certainly more interesting, she decided, than watching a blond airhead jiggle around a set to the beat of a laugh track. Nodding, she sucked in her breath.

"What are you doing?"

She let it out again in a long huff as Roman pushed open the door. Pleasure came first, but she quickly buried it in resentment. "You're always asking me that."

"Am I?" He was carrying another tray. Charity distinctly caught the scent of Mae's prize chicken soup and her biscuits. "Well, what were you doing?"

"Dying of boredom. I think I'd rather be shot." After eyeing the tray, she decided to be marginally friendly. But not because she was glad to see him, she thought. It was dusk, and she hadn't eaten for hours. "Is that for me?"

"Possibly." He set the tray over her lap, then stayed close and took a long, hard look at her. There was no way for him to describe the fury he felt when he saw the bruises and the bandages. Just as there was no way for him to describe the sense of pleasure and relief he experienced when he saw the annoyance in her eyes and the color in her cheeks.

"I think you're wrong, Charity. You're going to live."

"No thanks to you." She dived into the soup. "First you trick a promise out of me, then you leave me to rot for the next twelve hours. You might have come up for a minute to see if I had lapsed into a coma."

He *had* come up, about the time Sam Spade had been unwrapping the mysterious bird, but she'd been sleeping. Nonetheless, he'd stayed for nearly half an hour, just watching her.

"I've been a little busy," he told her, and broke off half of her biscuit for himself.

"I'll bet." Feeling far from generous, she snatched it back. "Well, since you're here, you might tell me how things are going downstairs."

"They're under control," he murmured, thinking of Bob and the phone calls that had already been made.

"It's only Bonnie's second day. She hasn't—"

"She's doing fine," he said, interrupting her. "Mae's watching her like a hawk. Where'd all these come from?" He gestured toward half a dozen vases of fresh flowers.

"Oh, Lori brought up the daisies with the magazines. Then the ladies came up. They really shouldn't have climbed all those stairs. They brought the wood violets." She rattled off more names of people who had brought or sent flowers.

He should have brought her some, Roman thought, rising and thrusting his hands into his pockets. It had never crossed his mind. Things like that didn't, he admitted. Not the small, romantic things a woman like Charity was entitled to.

"Roman?"

"What?"

"Did you come all the way up here to scowl at my peonies?"

"No." He hadn't even known the name for them. He turned away from the fat pink blossoms. "Do you want any more to eat?"

"No." She tapped the spoon against the side of her empty bowl. "I don't want any more to eat, I don't want any more magazines, and I don't want anyone else to come in here, pat my hand and tell me to get plenty of rest. So if that's what you've got in mind you can leave."

"You're a charming patient, Charity." Checking his own temper, he removed the tray.

"No, I'm a miserable patient." Furiously, she tossed aside her self-control, and just as furiously tossed a paperback at his head. Fortunately for them both, her aim was off. "And I'm tired of being stuck in here as though I had some communicable disease. I have a bump on the head, damn it, not a brain tumor."

"I don't think a brain tumor's contagious."

"Don't be clever with me." Glaring at him, she folded her arms and dropped them over her chest. "I'm sick of being here, and sicker yet of being told what to do."

"You don't take that well, do you? No matter how good it is for you?"

When she was being unreasonable there was nothing she wanted to hear less than the truth. "I have an inn to run, and I can't do it from bed."

"Not tonight you don't."

"It's my inn, just like it's my body and my head." She tossed the covers aside. Even as she started to scramble out of bed her promise weighed on her like a chain. Swinging her legs up again, she fell back against the pillows.

Thumbs hooked in his pockets, he measured her. "Why don't you get up?"

"Because I promised. Now get out, damn it. Just get out and leave me alone."

"Fine. I'll tell Mae and the rest that you're feeling more like yourself. They've been worried about you."

She threw another book—harder—but had only the small satisfaction of hearing it slap against the closing door.

The hell with him, she thought as she dropped her chin on her knees. The hell with everything.

The hell with her, He hadn't gone up there to pick a fight, and he didn't have to tolerate a bad-tempered woman throwing things at him, especially when he couldn't throw them back. Roman got halfway down the stairs, turned around and stalked back up again.

Charity was moping when he pushed open the door. She knew it, she hated it, and she wished everyone would leave her in peace to get on with it.

"What now?"

"Get up."

Charity straightened her spine against the headboard. "Why?"

"Get up," Roman repeated. "Get dressed. There must be a floor to mop or a trash can to empty around here."

"I said I wouldn't get up"—she set her chin—"and I won't."

"You can get out of bed on your own, or I can drag you out."

Temper had her eyes darkening and her chin thrusting out even farther. "You wouldn't dare." She regretted the words even as she spoke them. She'd already decided he was a man who would dare anything.

She was right. Roman crossed to the bed and grabbed her arm. Charity gripped one of the posts. Despite her hold, he managed to pull her up on her knees before she dug in. Before the tug-of-war could get much further she began to giggle.

"This is stupid." She felt her grip slipping and hooked her arm around the bedpost. "Really stupid. Roman, stop. I'm going to end up falling on my face and putting another hole in my head."

"You wanted to get up. So get up."

"No, I wanted to feel sorry for myself. And I was doing a pretty good job of it, too. Roman, you're about to dislocate my shoulder."

"You're the most stubborn, hardheaded, unreasonable woman I've ever met," he said. But he released her.

"I have to go along with the first two, but I'm not usually unreasonable." Offering him a smile, she folded her legs lotus style. The storm was over. At least hers was, she thought. She recognized the anger that was still darkening his eyes. She let out a long sigh. "I guess you could say I was having a really terrific pity party for myself when you came in. I'm sorry I took it out on you."

"I don't need an apology."

"Yes, you do." She would have offered him a hand, but he didn't look ready to sign any peace treaties. "I'm not used to being cut off from what's going on. I'm hardly ever sick, so I haven't had much practice in taking it like a good little soldier." She idly pleated the sheet between her fingers as she slanted a look at him. "I really am sorry, Roman. Are you going to stay mad at me?"

"That might be the best solution." Anger had nothing to do with what he was feeling at the moment. She looked so appealing with that half smile on her face, her hair tousled, the nightshirt buttoned to her chin and skimming her thighs.

"Want to slug me?"

"Maybe." It was hopeless. He smiled and sat down beside her. He balled his hand into a fist and skimmed it lightly over her chin. "When you're back on your feet again I'll take another shot."

"It was nice of you to bring me dinner. I didn't even thank you."

"No, you didn't."

She leaned forward to kiss his cheek. "Thanks."

"You're welcome."

After blowing the hair out of her eyes, she decided to start over. "Did we have a good crowd tonight?"

"I bused thirty tables."

"I'm going to have to give you a raise. I guess Mae made her chocolate mousse torte."

"Yeah." Roman found his lips twitching again.

"I don't suppose there was any left over."

"Not a crumb. It was great."

"You had some?"

"Meals are part of my pay."

Feeling deprived, Charity leaned back against the pillows. "Right."

"Are you going to sulk again?"

"Just for a minute. I wanted to ask you if the sheriff had any news about the car."

"Not much. He found it about ten miles from here, abandoned." He reached over to smooth away a line between her brows. "Don't worry about it."

"I'm not. Not really. I'm just glad the driver didn't hurt anyone else. Lori said you'd cut your arm."

"A little." Their hands were linked. He didn't know whether he had taken hers or she had taken his.

"Were you taking a walk?"

"I was waiting for you."

"Oh." She smiled again.

"You'd better get some rest." He was feeling awkward again, awkward and clumsy. No other woman had ever drawn either reaction from him.

Reluctantly she released his hand. "Are we friends again?"

"I guess you could say that. Good night, Charity."

"Good night."

He crossed to the door and opened it. But he couldn't step across the threshold. He stood there, struggling with himself. Though it was only a matter of seconds, it seemed like hours to both of them.

"I can't." He turned back, shutting the door quietly behind him.

"Can't what?"

"I can't leave."

Her smile bloomed, in her eyes, on her lips. She opened her arms to him, as he had known she would. Walking back to her was nearly as difficult as walking away. He took her hands and held them hard in his.

"I'm no good for you, Charity."

"I think you're very good for me." She brought their joined hands to her cheek. "That means one of us is wrong."

"If I could, I'd walk out the door and keep going."

She felt the sting and accepted it. She'd never expected loving Roman to be painless. "Why?"

"For reasons I can't begin to explain to you." He stared down at their linked hands. "But I can't walk away. Sooner or later you're going to wish I had."

"No." She drew him down onto the bed. "Whatever happens, I'll always be glad you stayed." This time she smoothed the lines from his brow. "I told you before that this wouldn't happen unless it was right. I meant that." Lifting her hands, she linked them behind his neck. "I love you, Roman. Tonight is something I want, something I've chosen."

Kissing her was like sinking into a dream. Soft, drugging, and too impossibly beautiful to be real. He wanted to take care, such complete, such tender care, not to hurt her now, knowing that he would have no choice but to hurt her eventually.

But tonight, for a few precious hours, there would be no future. With her he could be what he had never tried to be before. Gentle, loving, kind. With her he could believe it was possible for love to be enough.

He loved her. Though he'd never known he was capable of that strong and fragile emotion, he felt it with her. It streamed through him, painless and sweet, healing wounds he'd forgotten he had, soothing aches he'd lived with forever. How could he have known when he'd walked into her life that she would be his salvation? In the short time he had left he would show her. And in showing her he would give himself something he had never expected to have.

He made her feel beautiful. And delicate, Charity thought as his mouth whispered over hers. It was as though he knew that this first time together was to be savored and remembered. She heard her own sigh, then his, as her hands slid up his back. Whatever she had wished they could have together was nothing compared to this.

He laid her back gently, barely touching her as the kiss lengthened. Even loving him as she did, she hadn't known he'd possessed such tenderness. Nor could she know that he had just discovered it in himself.

The lamplight glowed amber. He hadn't thought to light the candles. But he could see her in the brilliance of it, her eyes dark and on his, her lips curved as he brought his to meet them. He hadn't thought to set the music. But her nightshirt whispered as she brought her arms around him. It was a sound he would remember always. Air drifted in through the open window, stirring the scent of the flowers others had brought to her. But it was the fragrance of her skin that filled his head. It was the taste of it that he yearned for.

Lightly, almost afraid he might bruise her with a touch, he cupped her breasts in his hands. Her breath caught, then released on a moan against the side of his neck. He knew that nothing had ever excited him more.

Then her hands were on his shirt, her fingers undoing his buttons as her eyes remained on his. They were as dark, as deep, as vibrant, as the water that surrounded her home. He could read everything she felt in them.

"I want to touch you," she said as she drew the shirt from his shoulders. Her heart began to sprint as she looked at him, the taut muscles, the taut skin.

There was a strength in him that excited, perhaps because she understood that he could be ruthless. There was a toughness to his body, a toughness that made her realize he was a man who had fought, a man who would fight. But his hands were gentle on her now, almost hesitant. Her excitement leaped higher, and there was no fear in it.

"It seems I've wanted to touch you like this all my life." She ran her fingertips lightly over the bandage on his arm. "Does it hurt?"

"No." Every muscle in his body tensed when she trailed her hands from his waist to his chest. It was impossible for him to understand how anyone could bring him peace and torment at the same time. "Charity..."

"Just kiss me again, Roman," she murmured.

He was helpless to refuse. He wondered what she would ask him for if she knew that he was powerless to deny her anything at this moment. Fighting back a flood of desperation, he kept his hands easy, sliding and stroking them over her until he felt the tremors begin.

He knew he could give her pleasure. The need to do so pulsed heavily inside him. He could ignite her passions. The drive to fan them roared through him like a brushfire. As he touched her he knew he could make her weak or strong, wild or limp. But it wasn't power that filled him at the knowledge. It was awe.

She would give him whatever he asked, without questions, without restrictions. This strong, beautiful, exciting woman was his. This wasn't a dream that would awaken him to frustration in the middle of the night. This wasn't a wish that he'd have to pretend he'd never made. It was real. She was real, and she was waiting for him.

He could have torn the nightshirt from her with one pull of his hand. Instead he released button after tiny button, hearing her breath quicken, following the narrow path with soft, lingering kisses. Her fingers dug into his back, then went limp as her system churned. She could only groan as his tongue moistened her flesh, teasing and heating it. The night air whispered over her as he undressed her. Then he was lifting her, cradling her in his arms.

She was twined around him, her heart thudding frantically against his lips. He needed a moment to drag himself back, to find the control he wanted so that he could take her up, take her over. Murmuring to her, he used what skills he had to drive her past the edge of reason.

Her body was rigid against his. He watched her dazed eyes fly open. She gasped his name, and then he covered her mouth with his to capture her long, low moan as her body went limp.

She seemed to slide like water through his hands when he laid her down again. To his delight, her arousal burst free again at his lightest touch.

It was impossible. It was impossible to feel so much and still need more. Blindly she reached for him. Fresh pleasure poured into her until her arms felt too heavy to move. She was a prisoner, a gloriously willing prisoner, of the frantic sensations he sent tearing through her. She wanted to lock herself around him, to keep him there, always there. He was taking her on a long, slow journey to places she had never seen, places she never wanted to leave.

When he slid inside her she heard his low, breathless moan. So he was as much a captive as she.

With his face pressed against her neck, he fought the need to sprint toward release. He was trapped between heaven and hell, and he gloried in it. In her. In them. He heard her sob out his name, felt the strength pour into her. She was with him as no one had ever been.

Charity wrapped her arms around Roman to keep him from shifting away. "Don't move."

"I'm hurting you."

"No." She let out a long, long sigh. "No, you're not."

"I'm too heavy," he insisted, and compromised by gathering her close and rolling so that their positions were reversed.

"Okay." Satisfied, she rested her head on his shoulder. "You are," she said, "the most incredible lover."

He didn't even try to prevent the smile. "Thanks." He stroked a possessive hand down to her hip. "Have you had many?"

It was her turn to smile. The little trace of jealousy in his voice was a tremendous addition to an already glorious night. "Define *many*."

Ignoring the quick tug of annoyance he felt, he played the game. "More than three. Three is a few. Anything more than three is many."

"Ah. Well, in that case." She almost wished she could lie and invent a horde. "I guess I've had less than a few. That doesn't mean I don't know an incredible one when I find him."

He lifted her head to stare at her. "I've done nothing in my life to deserve you."

"Don't be stupid." She inched up to kiss him briefly. "And don't change the subject."

"What subject?"

"You're clever, DeWinter, but not that clever." She lifted a brow and studied him in the lamplight. "It's my turn to ask you if you've had many lovers."

He didn't smile this time. "Too many. But only one who's meant anything."

The amusement faded from her eyes before she closed them. "You'll make me cry," she murmured, lowering her head to his chest again.

Not yet, he thought, stroking her hair. Soon enough, but not yet. "Why haven't you ever gotten married?" he wondered aloud, "Had babies?"

"What a strange question. I haven't loved anyone enough before." She winced at her own words, then made herself smile as she lifted her head. "That wasn't a hint."

But it was exactly what he'd wanted to hear. He knew he was crazy to let himself think that way, even for a few hours, but he wanted to imagine her loving him enough to forgive, to accept and to promise.

"How about the traveling you said you wanted to do? Shouldn't that come first?"

She shrugged and settled against him again. "Maybe I haven't traveled because I know deep down I'd hate to go all those places alone. What good is Venice if you don't have someone to ride in a gondola with? Or Paris if there's no one to hold hands with?"

"You could go with me."

Already half asleep, she laughed. She imagined Roman had little more than the price of a ferry ticket to his name. "Okay. Let me know when to pack."

"Would you?" He lifted her chin to look into her drowsy eyes.

"Of course." She kissed him, snuggled her head against his shoulder and went to sleep.

Roman switched off the lamp beside the bed. For a long time he held her and stared into the dark.

CHAPTER 8

Charity opened her eyes slowly, wondering why she couldn't move. Groggy, she stared into Roman's face. It was only inches from hers. He had pulled her close in his sleep, effectively pinning her arms and legs with his. Though his grip on her was somewhat guardlike, she found it unbearably sweet.

Ignoring the discomfort, she lay still and took advantage of the moment by looking her fill.

She'd always thought that people looked softer, more vulnerable, in sleep. Not Roman. He had the body of a fighter and the eyes of a man accustomed to facing trouble head-on. His eyes were closed now, and his body was relaxed. Almost.

Still, studying him, she decided that, asleep or awake, he looked tough as nails. Had he always been? she wondered. Had he had to be? It was true that smiling lent a certain charm to his face. It lightened the wariness in his eyes. In Charity's opinion, Roman smiled much too seldom.

She would fix that. Her own lips curved as she

watched him. In time she would, gently, teach him to relax, to enjoy, to trust. She would make him happy. It wasn't possible to love as she had loved and not have it returned. And it wasn't possible to share what they had shared during the night without his heart being as lost as hers.

Sooner or later—sooner, if she had her way—he would come to accept how good they were together. And how much better they would become in all the years to follow. Then there would be time for promises and families and futures.

I'm not letting you go, she told him silently. You don't realize it yet, but I've got a hold on you, and it's going to be mighty hard to break it.

He had such a capacity for giving, she thought. Not just physically, though she wasn't ashamed to admit that his skill there had dazed and delighted her. He was a man full of emotions, too many of them strapped down. What had happened to him, she wondered, that had made him so wary of love, and so afraid to give it?

She loved him too much to demand an answer. It was a question he had to answer on his own ... a question she knew he would answer as soon as he trusted her enough. When he did, all she had to do was show him that none of it mattered. All that counted, from this moment on, was what they felt for each other.

Inching over, she brushed a light kiss on his mouth. His eyes opened instantly. It took only a heartbeat longer for them to clear. Fascinated, Charity watched their expression change from one of suspicion to one of desire.

"You're a light sleeper," she began. "I just—"

Before she could complete the thought, his mouth,

hungry and insistent, was on hers. She managed a quiet moan as she melted into his kiss.

It was the only way he knew to tell her what it meant to him to wake and find her close and warm and willing. Too many mornings he had woken alone in strange beds in empty rooms.

That was what he expected. For years he had deliberately separated himself from anyone who had tried to get close. The job. He'd told himself it was because of the job. But that was a lie, one of many. He'd chosen to remain alone because he hadn't wanted to risk losing again. Grieving again. Now, overnight, everything had changed.

He would remember it all, the pale fingers of light creeping into the room, the high echoing sound of the first birds calling to the rising sun, the scent of her skin as it heated against his. And her mouth . . . he would remember the taste of her mouth as it opened eagerly under his.

There were such deep, dark needs in him. She felt them, understood them, and met them unquestioningly. As dawn swept the night aside, he stirred her own until their needs mirrored each other's.

Slowly, easily, while his lips cruised over her face, he slipped inside her. With a sigh and a murmur, she welcomed him.

She felt as strong as an ox and as content as a cat with cream on its whiskers. With her eyes closed, Charity stretched her arms to the ceiling.

"And to think I used to consider jogging the best way to start the day." Laughing, she curled over against him again. "I have to thank you for showing me how very wrong I was."

"My pleasure." He could still feel his own heart thudding like a jackhammer against his ribs. "Give me a minute and I'll show you the best reason for staying in bed in the morning."

Lord, it was tempting. Before her blood could begin to heat she shook her head. She took a quick nip at his chin before she sat up. "Maybe if you've got some time when I get back."

He took her wrist but kept his fingers light. "From where?"

"From taking Ludwig for his run."

"No."

The hand that had lifted to push back her hair paused. Deliberately she continued to lift it to finger-comb the hair away from her face. "No, what?"

He recognized that tone. She was the boss again, despite the fact that her face was still glowing from love-making and she was naked to where the sheets pooled at her waist. This was the woman who didn't take orders. Roman decided he would have to show her again that she was wrong.

"No, you're not taking the dog out for a run."

Because she wanted to be reasonable, she added a smile. "Of course I am. I kept my promise and stayed in bed all day yesterday. And all night, for that matter. Now I'm going to get back to work."

Around the inn, that was fine. In fact, the sooner everything got back to normal the better it would be. But there was no way he was having her walking down a deserted road by herself. "You're in no shape to go for a mile hike."

"Three miles, and yes, I am."

"Three?" Lifting a brow, he stroked a hand over her thigh. "No wonder you've got such great muscle tone."

"That's not the point." She shifted away before his touch could weaken her.

"You have the most incredible body."

She shoved at his seeking hands. "Roman . . . I do?"

His lips curved. This was the way she liked them best. "Absolutely. Let me show you."

"No, I . . ." She caught his hands as they stroked her thighs. "We'll probably kill each other if we try this again."

"I'll risk it."

"Roman, I mean it." Her head fell back and she gasped when he scraped his teeth over her skin. It was impossible, she thought, impossible, for this deep, dark craving to take over again. "Roman—"

"Fabulous legs," he murmured, skimming his tongue behind her knee. "I didn't pay nearly enough attention to them last night."

"Yes, you—" She braced a hand against the mattress as she swayed. "You're trying to distract me."

"Yeah."

"You can't." She closed her eyes. He could, and he was. "Ludwig needs the run," she managed. "He enjoys it."

"Fine." He sat up and circled her waist with his hands. "I'll take him."

"You?" Wanting to catch her breath, she turned her head to avoid his kiss, then shuddered as his lips trailed down her throat. "It's not necessary. I'm perfectly . . . Roman." She said his name weakly as his thumbs circled her breasts.

"Yes, a truly incredible body," he murmured. "Long and lean and incredibly responsive. I can't seem to touch you and not want you."

She came up on her knees as he dragged another gasp out of her. "You're trying to seduce me."

"Nothing gets by you, does it?"

She was losing, weakening shamelessly. She knew it would infuriate her later, but for now all she could do was cling to him and let him have his way. "Is this your answer for everything?"

"No." He lifted her hips and brought her to him. "But it'll do."

Unable to resist, she wrapped her limbs around him and let passion take them both. When it was spent, she slid bonelessly down in the bed. She didn't argue when he drew the sheets over her shoulders.

"Stay here," he told her, kissing her hair. "I'll be back."

"His leash is on a hook under the steps," Charity murmured. "He gets two scoops of dog food when he gets back. And fresh water."

"I think I can handle a dog, Charity."

She yawned and tugged the blankets higher. "He likes to chase the Fitzsimmonses' cat. But don't worry, he can't catch her."

"That makes me breathe easier." He laced up his shoes. "Anything else I should know?"

"Mmm." She snuggled into the pillow. "I love you."

As always, it knocked him backward to hear her say it, to know she meant it. In silence, he stepped outside.

She wasn't tired, Charity thought as she stretched under the sheets. But Roman was right. Sleep wasn't the best reason for staying in bed in the morning. Despite her bumps and bruises, she knew she'd never felt better in her life.

Still, she indulged herself, lingering in bed, half dreaming, until guilt finally prodded her out.

Moving automatically, she turned on the stereo, then tidied the bed. In the parlor she glanced over the notes she'd left for herself, made a few more. Then she headed for the shower. She was humming along to Tchaikovsky's violin concerto when the curtain swished open.

"Roman!" She pressed both hands to her heart and leaned back against the tile. "You might as well shoot me as scare me to death. Didn't you ever hear of the Bates Motel?"

"I left my butcher knife in my other pants." She had her hair piled on top of her head and a cake of some feminine scented soap in her hand. Her skin was gleaming wet and already soapy. He pulled off his shirt and tossed it aside. "Did you ever consider teaching that dog to heel?"

"No." She grinned as she watched Roman unfasten his jeans. "I guess you could use a shower." Saying nothing, he tossed his jeans on top of his shirt. Charity took a moment to make a long, thorough survey. "Well, apparently that run didn't . . . tire you out." She was laughing when he stepped in with her.

It was nearly an hour later when Charity made it down to the lobby. "I could eat one of everything." She pressed a hand to her stomach. "Good morning, Bob." She paused at the front desk to smile at him.

"Charity." Bob felt the sweat spring onto his palms when he spotted Roman behind her. "How are you feeling? It's awfully soon for you to be up and around."

"I'm fine." Idly she glanced at the papers on the desk. "Sorry I left you in the lurch yesterday."

"Don't be silly." Fear ground in his stomach as he eyed the wound on her temple. "We were worried about you."

"I appreciate that, but there's no need to worry anymore." She slanted a smile at Roman. "I've never felt better in my life."

Bob caught the look, and his stomach sank. If the cop was in love with her, he thought, things were going to be even stickier. "Glad to hear it. But—"

She stopped his protest by raising a hand. "Is there anything urgent?"

"No." He glanced at Roman again. "No, nothing."

"Good." After setting the papers aside again, Charity studied his face. "What's wrong, Bob?"

"Nothing. What could be wrong?"

"You look a little pale. You're not coming down with anything, are you?"

"No, everything's fine. Just fine. We got some new reservations. July's almost booked solid."

"Great. I'll look things over after breakfast. Get yourself some coffee." She patted his hand and walked into the dining room.

Three tables were already occupied, the patrons enjoying Mae's coffee cake before their meal was served. Bonnie was busy taking orders. The breakfast menu was neatly listed on the board, and music was playing in the background, soft and soothing. The flowers were fresh, and the coffee was hot.

"Something wrong?" Roman asked her.

"No." Charity smoothed down the collar of her shirt. "What could be wrong? It looks like everything's just dandy." Feeling useless, she walked into the kitchen.

There was no bickering to referee. Mae and Dolores were working side by side, and Lori loaded up a tray with her first order.

"We need more butter for the French toast," Mae called out.

"Coming right up." Cheerful as a bird, Dolores began to scoop up neat balls of butter. As she offered the newly filled bowl to Lori, she spotted Charity standing inside the door. "Well, good morning." Her thin face creased with a smile. "Didn't expect to see you up."

"I'm fine."

"Sit down, girl." Hardly glancing around, Mae continued to sprinkle shredded cheese into an omelet. "Dolores will get you some tea."

Charity smiled with clenched teeth. "I don't want any tea."

"Want and need's two different things."

"Glad to see you're feeling better," Lori said as she rushed out with her tray.

Bonnie came in, pad in hand. "Oh, hi, Charity, we thought you'd rest another day. Feeling better?"

"I'm fine," Charity said tightly. "Just fine."

"Great. Two omelets with bacon, Mae. And an order of French toast with sausage. Two herb teas, an English muffin—crisp. And we're running low on coffee." After punching her order sheet on a hook by the stove, she took the fresh pot Dolores handed her and hurried out.

Charity walked over to get an apron, only to have Mae smack her hand away. "I told you to sit."

"And I told you I'm fine. That's *f-i-n-e*. I'm going to help take orders."

"The only orders you're taking today are from me. Now sit." She ran a hand up and down Charity's arm. Nobody recognized or knew how to deal with that stubborn look better than Mae. "Be a good girl, now. I won't worry so much if I know you've had a good breakfast. You don't want me to worry, do you?"

"No, of course not, but—"

"That's right. Now take a seat. I'll fix you some French toast. It's your favorite."

She sat down. Dolores set a cup of tea in front of

her and patted her head. "You sure did give us all a fright yesterday. Have a seat, Roman. I'll get your coffee."

"Thanks. You're sulking," he murmured to Charity.

"I am not."

"Doc's coming by this morning to take another look at you."

"Oh, for heaven's sake, Mae—"

"You're not doing nothing till he gives the okay." With a nod, she began preparing Bonnie's order. "Fat lot of good you'll do if you're not a hundred percent. Things were hard enough yesterday."

Charity stopped staring into her tea and looked up. "Were they?"

"Everybody asking questions nobody had the answer to. Whole stacks of linens lost."

"Lost? But—"

"Found them." Mae made room at the stove for Dolores. "But it sure was confusing for a while. Then the dinner shift . . . Could have used an extra pair of hands for sure." Mae winked at Roman over Charity's head. "We'll all be mighty glad when the doc gives you his okay. Let that bacon crisp, Dolores."

"It is crisp."

"Not enough."

"Want me to burn it?"

Charity smiled and sipped her tea. It was good to be back.

It was midafternoon before she saw Roman again. She had a pencil behind her ear, a pad in one pocket and a dustcloth in another, and she was dashing down the hallway toward her rooms.

"In a hurry?"

"Oh." She stopped long enough to smile at him.

"Yes. I have some papers up in my room that should be in the office."

"What's this?" He tugged at the dustcloth.

"One of the housekeepers came down with a virus. I sent her home." She looked at her watch and frowned. She thought she could spare about two minutes for conversation. "I really hope that's not what's wrong with Bob."

"What's wrong with Bob?"

"I don't know. He just doesn't look well." She tossed her hair back, causing the slender gold spirals in her ears to dance. "Anyway, we're short a housekeeper, and we've got guests checking into units 3 and 5 today. The Garsons checked out of 5 this morning. They won't win any awards for neatness."

"The doctor said you were supposed to rest an hour this afternoon."

"Yes, but— How did you know?"

"I asked him." Roman pulled the dustcloth out of her pocket. "I'll clean 5."

"Don't be ridiculous. It's not your job."

"My job's to fix things. I'll fix 5." He took her chin in his hand before she could protest. "When I'm finished I'm going to go upstairs. If you aren't in bed I'm coming after you."

"Sounds like a threat."

He bent down and kissed her, hard. "It is."

"I'm terrified," she said, and dashed up the stairs.

It wasn't that she meant to ignore the doctor's orders. Not really. It was only that a nap came far down on her list of things to be done. Every phone call she made had to include a five-minute explanation of her injuries.

No, she was really quite well. Yes, it was terrible that someone had stolen poor Mrs. Norton's car and driven it so recklessly. Yes, she was sure the sheriff would get to the bottom of it. No, she had not broken her legs . . . her arm . . . her shoulder. . . . Yes, she intended to take good care of herself, thank you very much.

The goodwill and concern would have warmed her if she hadn't been so far behind in her work. To make it worse, Bob was distracted and disorganized. Worried that he was ill or dealing with a personal problem, Charity took on the brunt of his work.

Twice she'd fully intended to take a break and go up to her rooms, and twice she'd been delayed by guests checking in. Taking it on faith that Roman had spruced up unit 5, she showed a young pair of newlyweds inside.

"You have a lovely view of the garden from here," Charity said as a cover while she made sure there were fresh towels. Roman had hung them on the rack, exactly where they belonged. The bed, with its heart-shaped white wicker headboard, was made up with a military precision she couldn't have faulted. It cost her, but she resisted the temptation to turn up the coverlet and check sheets.

"We serve complimentary wine in the gathering room every evening at five. We recommend that you make a reservation for dinner if you plan to join us, particularly since it's Saturday night. Breakfast is served between seven-thirty and ten. If you'd like to—" She broke off when Roman stepped into the room. "I'll be with you in a minute," she told him, and started to turn back to the newlyweds.

"Excuse me." Roman gave them both a friendly nod before he scooped Charity up in his arms. "Miss Ford is needed elsewhere. Enjoy your stay."

As the first shock wore off she began to struggle. "Are you out of your mind? Put me down."

"I intend to—when I get you to bed."

"You can't just . . ." The words trailed off into a groan as he carried her through the gathering room.

Two men sitting on the sofa stopped telling fish stories. A family coming in from a hike gawked from the doorway. Miss Millie and Miss Lucy halted their daily game of Scrabble by the window.

"Isn't that the most romantic thing?" Miss Millie said when they disappeared into the west wing.

"You have totally embarrassed me."

Roman shifted her weight in his arms and carried her upstairs. "You're lucky that's all I did."

"You had no right interrupting me when I was welcoming guests. Then, to make matters worse, you decide to play Rhett Butler."

"As I recall, he had something entirely different in mind when he carried another stubborn woman up to bed." He dropped her, none too gently, on the mattress. "You're going to rest."

"I'm tempted to tell you to go to hell."

He leaned down to cage her head between his hands. "Be my guest."

She'd be damned if she'd smile. "My manners are too ingrained to permit it."

"Aren't I the lucky one?" He leaned a little closer. There was amusement in his eyes now, enough of it so she had to bite her lip to keep from laughing. "I don't want you to get out of this bed for sixty minutes."

"Or?"

"Or . . . I'll sic Mae on you."

"A low blow, DeWinter."

He brushed a kiss just below the fresh bandage on

her temple. "Tune out for an hour, baby. It won't kill you."

She reached up to toy with the top button of his shirt. "I'd like it better if you got in with me."

"I said tuned out, not turned on." When the phone in the parlor rang, he held her down with one hand. "Not a chance. Stay here and I'll get it."

She rolled her eyes behind his back as he walked into the adjoining room.

"Yes? She's resting. Tell him she'll get back to him in an hour. Hold her calls until four. That's right." He glanced down idly at a catalog she'd left open on her desk. She had circled a carved gold bracelet with a square-cut purple stone. "You handle whatever needs to be handled for the next hour. That's right."

"What was it?" Charity called from the next room.

"I'll tell you in an hour."

"Damn it, Roman."

He stopped in the doorway. "You want the message, I'll give it to you in an hour."

"But if it's important—"

"It's not."

She sent him a smoldering look. "How do you know?"

"I know it's not more important than you. Nothing is." He closed the door on her astonished expression.

He needed to keep Bob on a tight leash, he thought as he headed downstairs. As long as he was more afraid of him than of Block, things would be fine. He only had to keep the pressure on for a few more days. Block and Vision Tours would be checking in on Tuesday. When they checked out on Thursday morning he would lock the cage.

Roman pushed open the door of the office to find

Bob staring at the computer screen and gulping coffee. "For somebody who's made his living from scams you're a mess."

Bob gulped more coffee. "I never worked with a cop looking over my shoulder before."

"Just think of me as your new partner," Roman advised him. He took the mug out of his hand and sniffed at it. "And lay off the booze."

"Give me a break."

"I'm giving you more of one than you deserve. Charity's worried that you're coming down with something—something other than a stretch in federal prison. I don't want her worrying."

"Look, you want me to carry on like it's business as usual. I'm lying to Block, setting him up." His hand shook as he passed it over his hair. "You don't know what he's capable of. *I* don't know what he's capable of." He looked at the mug, which Roman had set out of reach. "I need a little something to help me through the next few days."

"Let this get you through." Roman calmly lit a cigarette. "You pull this off and I'll go to bat for you. Screw up and I'll see to it that you're in a cage for a long time. Now take a break."

"What?"

"I said, take a break, go for a walk, get some real coffee." Roman tapped the ash from his cigarette into a little mosaic bowl.

"Sure." As he rose, Bob rubbed his palms on his thighs. "Look, DeWinter, I'm playing it straight with you. When this goes down, I expect you to keep Block off me."

"I'll take care of Block." That was a promise he intended to keep. When the door closed behind Bob, he picked up the phone. "DeWinter," he said when the connection was made.

"Make it quick," Conby told him. "I'm entertaining friends."

"I'll try not to let your martini get warm. I want to know if you've located the driver."

"DeWinter, an underling is hardly important at this point."

"It's important to me. Have you found him?"

"A man answering the description your informant gave you was detained in Tacoma this morning. He's being held for questioning by the local police." Conby put his hand over the receiver. Roman heard him murmur something that was answered by light laughter.

"We're using our influence to lengthen the procedure," Conby continued. "I'll be flying out there on Monday. By Tuesday afternoon I should be checked into the inn. I'm told I'll have a room overlooking a fish pond. It sounds very quaint."

"I want your word that Charity will be left out of this."

"As I explained before, if she's innocent she has nothing to worry about."

"It's not a matter of *if*." Struggling to hold his temper, Roman crushed out his cigarette. "She is innocent. We've got it on record."

"On the word of a whimpering little bookkeeper."

"She was damn near killed, and she doesn't even know why."

"Then keep a closer eye on her. We have no desire to see Miss Ford harmed, or to involve her any more deeply than necessary. There's a police officer out there who shares the same passionate opinion of Miss Ford as you do. Sheriff Royce managed to trace you to us."

"How?"

"He's a smart cop with connections. He has a cousin or brother-in-law or some such thing with the Bureau. He wasn't at all pleased at being left in the dark."

"I'll bet."

"I imagine he'll be paying you a visit before long. Handle him carefully, DeWinter, but handle him."

Just as Roman heard the phone click in his ear the office door opened. For once, Roman thought, Conby was right on target. He replaced the receiver before settling back in his chair.

"Sheriff."

"I want to know what the hell's going on around here, Agent DeWinter."

"Close the door." Roman pushed back in the chair and considered half a dozen different ways of handling Royce. "I'd appreciate it if you'd drop the 'Agent' for now."

Royce just laid both palms on the surface of the desk. "I want to know what a federal agent is doing undercover in my territory."

"Following orders. Sit down?" He indicated a chair.

"I want to know what case you're working on."

"What did they tell you?"

Royce snorted disgustedly. "It got to the point where even my cousin started giving me the run-around, DeWinter, but I've got to figure that your being here had something to do with Charity being damn near run down yesterday."

"I'm here because I was assigned here." Roman waited a moment, sending Royce a long, direct look. "But my first priority is keeping Charity safe."

Royce hadn't been in law enforcement for nearly twenty years without being able to take the measure of a man. He took Roman's now, and was satisfied. "I got a load of bull from Washington about her being under investigation."

"She was. Now she's not. But she could be in trouble. Are you willing to help?"

"I've known that girl all her life." Royce took off his hat and ran his fingers through his hair. "Why don't you stop asking fool questions and tell me what's going on?"

Roman briefed him, pausing only once or twice to allow Royce to ask questions. "I don't have time to get into any more specifics. I want to know how many of your men you can spare Thursday morning."

"All of them," Royce said immediately.

"I only want your most experienced. I have information that Block will not only be bringing the counterfeit money, but also a man who'll register as Jack Marshall. His real name is Vincent Dupont. A week ago he robbed two banks in Ontario, killed a guard and wounded a civilian. Block will smuggle him out of Canada in the tour group, keep him here for a couple of days, then send him by short routes to South America. For his travel service to men like Dupont he takes a nice stiff fee. Both Dupont and Block are dangerous men. We'll have agents here at the inn, but we also have civilians. There's no way we can clear the place without tipping them off."

"It's a chancy game you're playing."

"I know." He thought of Charity dozing upstairs. "It's the only way I know how to play it."

CHAPTER 9

Charity drove back to the inn after dropping a trio of guests at the ferry. She was certain it was the most beautiful morning she'd ever seen. After the most wonderful night of her life, she thought. No, two of the most wonderful nights of her life.

Though she'd never considered herself terribly romantic, she'd always imagined what it would be like to really be in love. Her daydreams hadn't come close to what she was feeling now. This was solid and bewildering. It was simple and staggering. He filled her thoughts just as completely as he filled her heart. She couldn't wait to walk back into the inn, just knowing Roman would be there.

It seemed that every hour they spent together brought them closer. Gradually, step by step, she could feel the barriers he had placed around him lowering. She wanted to be there when they finally dropped completely.

He was in love with her. She was sure he was, whether he knew it or not. She could tell by the way he looked at her, by the way he touched her hair when he thought she was sleeping. By the way he held her so tightly all through the night, as if he were afraid she might somehow slip away from him. In time she would show him that she wasn't going anywhere—and that he wasn't going anywhere, either.

Something was troubling him. That was another thing she was sure of. Her eyes clouded as she drove along the water. There were times when she could feel the tension pulsing in him even when he was across the room. He seemed to be watching, waiting. But for what?

Since the accident he'd barely let her out of his sight. It was sweet, she mused. But it had to stop. She might love him, but she wouldn't be pampered. She was certain that if he had known she planned to drive to the ferry that morning he would have found a way to stop her.

She was right again. It had taken Roman some time to calm down after he had learned Charity wasn't in the office or the kitchen or anywhere else in the inn.

"She's driven up to drop some guests at the ferry," Mae told him, then watched in fascination as he let his temper loose.

"My, my," she said when the air was clear again. "You've got it bad, boy."

"Why did you let her go?"

"Let her go?" Mae let out a rich, appreciative laugh. "I haven't *let* that girl do anything since she could walk. She just does it." She stopped stirring custard to study him. "Any reason she shouldn't drive to the ferry?"

"No."

"All right, then. Just cool your britches. She'll be back in half an hour."

He sweated and paced, nearly the whole time she

was away. Mae and Dolores exchanged glances across the room. There would be plenty of gossip to pass around once they had the kitchen to themselves.

Mae thought of the way Charity had been smiling that morning. Why, the girl had practically danced into the kitchen. She kept her eye on Roman as he brooded over a cup of coffee and watched the clock. Yes, indeed, she thought, the boy had it bad.

"You got today off, don't you?" Mae asked him.

"What?"

"It's Sunday," she said patiently. "You got the day off?"

"Yeah, I guess."

"Nice day, too. Good weather for a picnic." She began slicing roast beef for sandwiches. "Got any plans?"

"No."

"Charity loves picnics. Yes, sir, she's mighty partial to them. You know, I don't think that girl's had a day away from this place in better than a month."

"Got any dynamite?"

Dolores piped up. "What's that?"

"I figure it would take dynamite to blast Charity out of the inn for a day."

It took her a minute, but Dolores finally got the joke. She chuckled. "Hear that, Mae? He wants dynamite."

"Pair of fools," Mae muttered as she cut generous pieces of chocolate cheesecake. "You don't move that girl with dynamite or threats or orders. Might as well bash your head against a brick wall all day." She tried not to sound pleased about it, and failed. "You want her to do something, you make her think she's doing you a favor. Make her think it's important to you. Dolores, you go on in that back room and get me the big wicker hamper. Boy, if you keep walking back and forth you're going to wear out my floor."

"She should have been back by now."

"She'll be back when she's back. You know how to run a boat?"

"Yes, why?"

"Charity always loved to picnic on the water. She hasn't been out in a boat in a long time. Too long."

"I know. She told me."

Mae turned around. Her face was set. "Do you want to make my girl happy?"

He tried to shrug it off, but he couldn't. "Yes. Yes, I do."

"Then you take her out on the boat for the day. Don't let her say no."

"All right."

Satisfied, she turned around again. "Go down in the cellar and get a bottle of wine. French. She likes the French stuff."

"She's lucky to have you."

Her wide face colored a bit, but she kept her voice brisk. "Around here, we got each other. You're all right," she added. "I wasn't sure of it when you first came around, but you're all right."

He was ready for her when she came back. Even as she stepped out of the van he was walking across the gravel lot, the wicker hamper in his hand.

"Hi."

"Hi." She greeted him with a smile and a quick kiss. Despite the two teenagers shooting hoops on the nearby court, Roman wrapped an arm around her and brought her hard against him for a longer, more satisfying embrace. "Well . . ." She had to take a deep breath and steady herself against the van. "Hello again." She noted then that he had pulled a loose black sweater over his jeans and was carrying a hamper. "What's this?"

"It's a basket," he told her. "Mae put a few things in it for me. It's my day off."

"Oh." She tossed her braid behind her back. "That's right. Where are you off to?"

"Out on the water, if I can use the boat."

"Sure." She glanced up at the sky, a bit wistfully. "It's a great day for it. Light wind, hardly a cloud."

"Then let's go."

"Let's?" He was already pulling her toward the pier. "Oh, Roman, I can't. I have dozens of things to do this afternoon. And I . . ." She didn't want to admit she wasn't ready to go out on the water again. "I can't."

"I'll have you back before the dinner shift." He laid a hand on her cheek. "I need you with me, Charity. I need to spend some time with you, alone."

"Maybe we could go for a drive. You haven't seen the mountains."

"Please." He set the hamper down to take both of her arms. "Do this for me."

Had he ever said "Please" before? she wondered. She didn't think so. With a sigh, she looked out at the boat rocking gently against the pier. "All right. Maybe for an hour. I'll go in and change."

The red sweater and jeans would keep her warm enough on the water, he decided. She would know that, too. She was stalling. "You look fine." He kept her hand in his as they walked down the pier. "This could use a little maintenance."

"I know. I keep meaning to." She waited until Roman stepped down into the boat. When he held up a hand, she hesitated, then forced herself to join him. "I have a key on my ring."

"Mae already gave me one."

"Oh." Charity sat down in the stern. "I see. A conspiracy."

It took him only two pulls to start the engine. Mae had told him Charity kept the boat for the staff to use. "From what you said to me the other day, I don't think he'd want you to grieve forever."

"No." As her eyes filled, she looked back toward the inn. "No, he wouldn't. But I loved him so much." She took a deep breath. "I'll cast off."

Before he sent the boat forward, Roman took her hand and drew her down beside him. After a moment she rested her head on his shoulder.

"Have you done much boating?"

"From time to time. When I was a kid we used to rent a boat a couple times each summer and take it on the river."

"Who's we?" She watched the shutters come down over his face. "What river?" she asked instead.

"The Mississippi." He smiled and slipped an arm over her shoulders. "I come from St. Louis, remember?"

"The Mississippi." Her mind was immediately filled with visions of steamboats and boys on wooden rafts. "I'd love to see it. You know what would be great? Taking a cruise all the way down, from St. Louis to New Orleans. I'll have to put that in my file."

"Your file?"

"The file I'm going to make on things I want to do." With a laugh, she waved to a passing sailboat before leaning over to kiss Roman's cheek. "Thanks."

"For what?"

"For talking me into this. I've always loved spending an afternoon out here, watching the other boats, looking at the houses. I've missed it."

"Have you ever considered that you give too much to the inn?"

"No. You can't give too much to something you love." She turned. If she shielded her eyes with her hand she could just see it in the distance. "If I didn't have such strong feelings for it, I would have sold it, taken a job in some modern hotel in Seattle or Miami or . . . or anywhere. Eight hours a day, sick leave, two weeks' paid vacation." Just the idea made her laugh. "I'd wear a nice neat business suit and sensible shoes, have my own office and quietly go out of my mind." She dug into her bag for her sunglasses. "You should understand that. You have good hands and a sharp mind. Why aren't you head carpenter for some big construction firm?"

"Maybe when the time came I made the wrong choices."

With her head tilted, she studied him, her eyes narrowed and thoughtful behind the tinted lenses. "No, I don't think so. Not for you."

"You don't know enough about me, Charity."

"Of course I do. I've lived with you for a week. That probably compares with knowing someone on a casual basis for six months. I know you're very intense and internal. You have a wicked temper that you seldom lose. You're an excellent carpenter who likes to finish the job he starts. You can be gallant with little old ladies." She laughed a little and turned her face into the wind. "You like your coffee black, you're not afraid of hard work . . . and you're a wonderful lover."

"And that's enough for you?"

She lifted her shoulders. "I don't imagine you

know too much more about me. I'm starving," she said abruptly. "Do you want to eat?"

"Pick a spot."

"Head over that way," she told him. "See that little jut of land? We can anchor the boat there."

The land she'd indicated was hardly more than a jumble of big, smooth rocks that fell into the water. As they neared it he could see a narrow stretch of sand crowded by trees. Cutting back the engine, he maneuvered toward the beach, Charity guiding him in with hand signals. As the current lapped at the sides of the boat, she pulled off her shoes and began to roll up her jeans.

"You'll have to give me a hand." As she said it she plunged into the knee-high water. "God, it's cold!" Then she was laughing and securing the line. "Come on."

The water was icy on his bare calves. Together they pulled the boat up onto a narrow spit of sand.

"I don't suppose you brought a blanket."

He reached into the boat and took out the faded red blanket Mae had given him. "This do?"

"Great. Grab the basket." She splashed through the shallows and onto the shore. After spreading the blanket at the base of the sheltering rocks she rolled down the damp legs of her jeans. "Lori and I used to come here when we were kids. To eat peanut butter sandwiches and talk about boys." Kneeling on the blanket, she looked around.

There were pines at her back, deep and green and thick all the way up the slope. A few feet away the water frothed at the rock, which had been worn smooth by wind and time. A single boat cruised in the distance, its sails full and white.

"It hasn't changed much." Smiling, she reached

for the basket. "I guess the best things don't." She threw back the top and spotted a bottle of champagne. "Well." With a brow arched, she pulled it out. "Apparently we're going to have some picnic."

"Mae said you liked the French stuff."

"I do. I've never had champagne on a picnic."

"Then it's time you did." He took the bottle and walked back to dunk it in the water, screwing it down in the wet sand. "We'll let it chill a little more." He came back to her, taking her hand before she could explore deeper in the basket. He knelt. When they were thigh to thigh, he gathered her close and closed his mouth over hers.

Her quiet sound of pleasure came first, followed by a gasp as he took the kiss deeper. Her arms came around him, then slid up until her hands gripped his shoulders. Desire was like a flood, rising fast to drag her under.

He needed . . . needed to hold her close like this, to taste the heat of passion on his lips, to feel her heart thud against him. He dragged his hands through her hair, impatiently tugging it free of the braid. All the while his mouth ravaged hers, gentleness forgotten.

There was a restlessness in him, and an anger that she couldn't understand. Responding to both, she pressed against him, unhesitatingly offering whatever he needed. Perhaps it would be enough. Slowly his mouth gentled. Then he was only holding her.

"That's a very nice way to start a picnic," Charity managed when she found her voice again.

"I can't seem to get enough of you."

"That's okay. I don't mind."

He drew away to frame her face in his hands. The crystal drops at her ears swung and shot out light. But her eyes were calm and deep and full of understanding.

It would be better, he thought, and certainly safer, if he simply let her pull out the sandwiches. They could talk about the weather, the water, the people at the inn. There was so much he couldn't tell her. But when he looked into her eyes he knew he had to tell her enough about Roman DeWinter that she would be able to make a choice.

"Sit down."

Something in his tone sent a frisson of alarm down her spine. He was going to tell her he was leaving, she thought. "All right." She clasped her hands together, promising herself she'd find a way to make him stay.

"I haven't been fair with you." He leaned back against a rock. "Fairness hasn't been one of my priorities. There are things about me you should know, that you should have known before things got this far."

"Roman—"

"It won't take long. I did come from St. Louis. I lived in a kind of neighborhood you wouldn't even understand. Drugs, whores, Saturday night specials." He looked out at the water. The spiffy little sailboat had caught the wind. "A long way from here, baby."

So the trust had come, she thought. She wouldn't let him regret it. "It doesn't matter where you came from, Roman. It's where you are now."

"That's not always true. Part of where you come from stays with you." He closed a hand over hers briefly, then released it. It would be better, he thought, to break the contact now. "When he was sober enough, my father drove a cab. When he wasn't sober enough, he sat around the apartment with his head in his hands. One of my first memories is waking up at night hearing my mother screaming at him. Every couple of months she'd threaten to leave. Then he'd straighten up. We'd live in the eye of the hurricane until he'd stop off at the bar to have a drink. So she finally stopped threatening and did it."

"Where did you go?"

"I said she left."

"But . . . didn't she take you with her?"

"I guess she figured she was going to have it rough enough without dealing with a ten-year-old."

Charity shook her head and struggled with a deep, churning anger. It was hard for her to understand how a mother could desert her child. "She must have been very confused and frightened. Once she—"

"I never saw her again," Roman said. "You have to understand that not everyone loves unconditionally. Not everyone loves at all."

"Oh, Roman." She wanted to gather him close then, but he held her away from him.

"I stayed with my father another three years. One night he hit the gin before he got in the cab. He killed himself and his passenger."

"Oh, God." She reached for him, but he shook his head.

"That made me a ward of the court. I didn't much care for that, so I took off, hit the streets."

She was reeling from what he'd already told her, and she could barely take it all in. "At thirteen?"

"I'd been living there most of my life anyway."

"But how?"

He shook a cigarette out of his pack, lighting it and drawing deep before he spoke again. "I took odd jobs when I could find them. I stole when I couldn't. After a couple of years I got good enough at the stealing that I didn't bother much with straight jobs. I broke into houses, hot-wired cars, snatched purses. Do you understand what I'm telling you?"

"Yes. You were alone and desperate."

"I was a thief. Damn it, Charity, I wasn't some poor misguided youth. I stopped being a kid when I came home and found my father passed out and my mother gone. I knew what I was doing. I chose to do it."

She kept her eyes level with his, battling the need to take him in her arms. "If you expect me to condemn a child for finding a way to survive, I'll have to disappoint you."

She was romanticizing, he told himself, pitching his cigarette into the water.

"Do you still steal?"

"What if I told you I did?"

"I'd have to say you were stupid. You don't seem stupid to me, Roman."

He paused for a moment before he decided to tell her the rest. "I was in Chicago. I'd just turned sixteen. It was January, so cold your eyes couldn't water. I decided I needed to score enough to take a bus south. Thought I'd winter in Florida and fleece the rich tourists. That's when I met John Brody. I broke into his apartment and ended up with a .45 in my face. He was a cop." The memory of that moment still made him laugh. "I don't know who was more surprised. He gave me three choices. One, he could turn me over to Juvie. Two, he could beat the hell out of me. Three, he could give me something to eat."

"What did you do?"

"It's hard to play it tough when a two-hundred-pound man's pointing a .45 at your belt. I ate a can of soup. He let me sleep on the couch." Looking back, he could still see himself, skinny and full of bitterness, lying wakeful on the lumpy sofa.

"I kept telling myself I was going to rip off whatever I could and take off. But I never did. I used to tell myself he was a stupid bleeding heart, and that once it warmed up I'd split with whatever I could carry. The next thing I knew I was going to school." Roman paused a moment to look up at the sky. "He used to build things down in the basement of the building. He taught me how to use a hammer."

"He must have been quite a man."

"He was only twenty-five when I met him. He'd grown up on the South Side, running with the gangs. At some point he turned it around. Then he decided to turn me around. In some ways he did. When he got married a couple of years later he bought this old run-down house in the suburbs. We fixed it up room by room. He used to tell me there was nothing he liked better than living in a construction zone. We were adding on another room—it was going to be his workshop—when he was killed. Line of duty. He was thirty-two. He left a three-year-old son and a pregnant widow."

"Roman, I'm sorry." She moved to him and took his hands.

"It killed something in me, Charity. I've never been able to get it back."

"I understand." He started to pull away, but she held him fast. "I do. When you lose someone who was that much a part of your life, something's always going to be missing. I still think about Pop all the time. It still makes me sad. Sometimes it just makes me angry, because there was so much more I wanted to say to him."

"You're leaving out pieces. Look at what I was, where I came from. I was a thief."

"You were a child."

He took her shoulders and shook her. "My father was a drunk."

"I don't even know who my father was. Should I be ashamed of that?"

"It doesn't matter to you, does it? Where I've been, what I've done?"

"Not very much. I'm more interested in what you are now."

He couldn't tell her what he was. Not yet. For her own safety, he had to continue the deception for a few more days. But there was something he could tell her. Like the story he had just recounted, it was something he had never told anyone else.

"I love you."

Her hands went slack on his. Her eyes grew huge. "Would you—" She paused long enough to take a deep breath. "Would you say that again?"

"I love you."

With a muffled sob, she launched herself into his arms. She wasn't going to cry, she told herself, squeezing her eyes tight against the threatening tears. She wouldn't be red-eyed and weepy at this, the most beautiful and exciting moment of her life.

"Just hold me a moment, okay?" Overwhelmed, she pressed her face into his shoulder. "I can't believe this is happening."

"That makes two of us." But he was smiling. He could feel the stunned delight coil through him as he stroked her hair. It hadn't been so hard to say, he realized. In fact, he could easily get used to saying it several times a day.

"A week ago I didn't even know you." She tilted her head back until her lips met his. "Now I can't imagine my life without you."

"Don't. You might change your mind."

"Not a chance."

"Promise." Overwhelmed by a sudden sense of urgency, he gripped her hands. "I want you to make that a promise."

"All right. I promise. I won't change my mind about being in love with you."

"I'm holding you to that, Charity." He swooped her against him, then drained even happy thoughts from her mind. "Will you marry me?"

She jerked back, gaped, then sat down hard. "What? *What?*"

"I want you to marry me—now, today." It was crazy, and he knew it. It was wrong. Yet, as he pulled her up again, he knew he had to find a way to keep her. "You must know somebody, a minister, a justice of the peace, who could do it."

"Well, yes, but . . ." She held a hand to her spinning head. "There's paperwork, and licenses. God, I can't think."

"Don't think. Just say you will."

"Of course I will, but—"

"No buts." He crushed his mouth to hers. "I want you to belong to me. God, I need to belong to you. Do you believe that?"

"Yes." Breathless, she touched a hand to his cheek. "Roman, we're talking about marriage, a lifetime. I only intend to do this once." She dragged a hand through her hair and sat down again. "I guess everyone says that, but I need to believe it. It has to start off with more than a few words in front of an official. Wait, please," she said before he could speak again. "You've really thrown me off here, and I want to make you understand. I love you, and I can't think of anything I want more than to belong to you. When I marry you it has to be more than rushing to the J.P. and saying I do. I don't have to have a big, splashy wedding, either. It's not a matter of long white trains and engraved invitations."

"Then what is it?"

"I want flowers and music, Roman. And friends." She took his face in her hands, willing him to understand. "I want to stand beside you knowing I look beautiful, so that everyone can see how proud I am to be your wife. If that sounds overly romantic, well, it should be."

"How long do you need?"

"Can I have two weeks?"

He was afraid to give her two days. But it was for the best, he told himself. He would never be able to hold her if there were still lies between them. "I'll give you two weeks, if you'll go away with me afterward."

"Where?"

"Leave it to me."

"I love surprises." Her lips curved against his. "And you . . . you're the biggest surprise so far."

"Two weeks." He took her hands firmly in his. "No matter what happens."

"You make it sound as though we might have to overcome a natural disaster in the meantime. I'm only going to take a few days to make it right." She brushed a kiss over his cheek and smiled again. "It will be right, Roman, for both of us. That's another promise. I'd like that champagne now."

She took out the glasses while he retrieved the bottle from the water. As they sat together on the blanket, he released the cork with a pop and a hiss.

"To new beginnings," she said, touching her glass to his.

He wanted to believe it could happen. "I'll make you happy, Charity."

"You already have." She shifted so that she was cuddled against him, her head on his shoulder. "This is the best picnic I've ever had."

He kissed the top of her head. "You haven't eaten anything yet."

"Who needs food?" With a sigh, she reached up. He linked his hand with hers, and they both looked out toward the horizon.

CHAPTER 10

Check-in on Tuesday was as chaotic as it came. Charity barreled her way through it, assigning rooms and cabins, answering questions, finding a spare cookie for a cranky toddler, and waited for the first rush to pass.

She was the first to admit that she usually thrived on the noise, the problems and the healthy press of people that proved the inn's success. At the moment, though, she would have liked nothing better than having everyone, and everything settled.

It was hard to keep her mind on the business at hand when her head was full of plans for her wedding.

Should she have Chopin or Beethoven? She'd barely begun her list of possible selections. Would the weather hold so that they could have the ceremony in the gardens, or would it be best to plan an intimate and cozy wedding in the gathering room?

"Yes, sir, I'll be glad to give you information on renting bikes." She snatched up a pamphlet.

When was she going to find an afternoon free so that she could choose the right dress? It *had* to be the right dress, the perfect dress. Something ankle-length, with some romantic touches of lace. There was a boutique in Eastsound that specialized in antique clothing. If she could just—

"Aren't you going to sign that?"

"Sorry, Roger." Charity pulled herself back and offered him an apologetic smile. "I don't seem to be all here this morning."

"No problem." He patted her hand as she signed his roster. "Spring fever?"

"You could call it that." She tossed back her hair, annoyed that she hadn't remembered to braid it that morning. As long as she was smelling orange blossoms she'd be lucky to remember her own name. "We're a little behind. The computer's acting up again. Poor Bob's been fighting with it since yesterday."

"Looks like you've been in a fight yourself."

She lifted a hand to the healing cut on her temple. "I had a little accident last week."

"Nothing serious?"

"No, just inconvenient, really. Some idiot joyriding nearly ran me down."

"That's terrible." Watching her carefully, he pulled his face into stern lines. "Were you badly hurt?"

"No, no stitches, but a medley of bruises. Scared me more than anything."

"I can imagine. You don't expect something like that around here. I hope they caught him."

"No, not yet." Because she'd already put the incident behind her, she gave a careless shrug. "To tell you the truth, I doubt they ever will. I imagine he got off the island as soon as he sobered up."

"Drunk drivers." Block made a sound of disgust. "Well, you've got a right to be distracted after something like that."

"Actually, I've got a much more pleasant reason. I'm getting married in a couple of weeks."

"You don't say!" His face split into a wide grin. "Who's the lucky man?"

"Roman DeWinter. I don't know if you met him. He's doing some remodeling upstairs."

"That's handy now, isn't it?" He continued to grin. The romance explained a lot. One look at Charity's face settled any lingering doubts. Block decided he'd have to have a nice long talk with Bob about jumping the gun. "Is he from around here?"

"No, he's from St. Louis, actually."

"Well, I hope he's not going to take you away from us."

"You know I'd never leave the inn, Roger." Her smile faded a bit. That was something she and Roman had never spoken of. "In any case, I promise to keep my mind on my work. You've got six people who want to rent boats." She took a quick look at her watch. "I can have them taken to the marina by noon."

"I'll round them up."

The door to the inn opened, and Charity glanced over. She saw a small, spare man with well-cut auburn hair, wearing a crisp sport shirt. He carried one small leather bag.

"Good morning."

"Good morning." He took a brief study of the lobby as he crossed to the desk. "Conby, Richard Conby. I believe I have a reservation."

"Yes, Mr. Conby. We're expecting you." Charity shuffled through the papers on the desk and sent up a quick prayer that Bob would have the computer humming along by the end of the day. "How was your trip?"

"Uneventful." He signed the register, listing his

address as Seattle. Charity found herself both amused and impressed by his careful manicure. "I was told your inn is quiet, restful. I'm looking forward to relaxing for a day or two."

"I'm sure you'll find the inn very relaxing." She opened a drawer to choose a key. "Either Roman or I will drive your group to the marina, Roger. Have them in the parking lot at noon."

"Will do." With a cheerful wave, he sauntered off.

"I'll be happy to show you to your room, Mr. Conby. If you have any questions about the inn, or the island, feel free to ask me or any of the staff." She came around the desk and led the way to the stairs.

"Oh, I will," Conby said, following her. "I certainly will."

At precisely 12:05, Conby heard a knock and opened his door. "Prompt as always, DeWinter." He scanned down to Roman's tool belt. "Keeping busy, I see."

"Dupont's in cabin 3."

Conby decided to drop the sarcasm. This was a big one, much too big for him to let his personal feelings interfere. "You made a positive ID?"

"I helped him carry his bags."

"Very good." Satisfied, Conby finished arranging his ebony-handled clothes brush and shoe horn on the oak dresser. "We'll move in as planned on Thursday morning and take him before we close in on Block."

"What about the driver of the car who tried to kill Charity?"

Always fastidious, Conby walked into the adjoining bath to wash his hands. "You're inordinately interested in a small-time hood."

"Did you get a confession?"

"Yes." Conby unfolded a white hand towel bordered with flowers. "He admitted to meeting with Block last week and taking five thousand to—to put Miss Ford out of the picture. A very minor sum for a hit." His hands dry, Conby tossed the towel over the lip of the sink before walking back into the bedroom. "If Block had been more discerning, he might have had more success."

Taking him by the collar, Roman lifted Conby to his toes. "Watch your step," he said softly.

"It's more to the point for me to tell you to watch yours." Conby pulled himself free and straightened his shirt. In the five years since he had taken over as Roman's superior he had found Roman's methods crude and his attitude arrogant. The pity was, his results were invariably excellent. "You're losing your focus on this one, Agent DeWinter."

"No. It's taken me a while—maybe too long—but I'm focused just fine. You've got enough on Block to pin him with conspiracy to murder. Dupont's practically tied up with a bow. Why wait?"

"I won't bother to remind you who's in charge of this case."

"We both know who's in charge, Conby, but there's a difference between sitting behind a desk and calling the shots in the field. If we take them now, quietly, there's less risk of endangering innocent people."

"I have no intention of endangering any of the guests. Or the staff," he added, thinking he knew where Roman's mind was centered. "I have my orders on this, just as you do." He took a fresh handkerchief out of his drawer. "Since it's apparently so important to you, I'll tell you that we want to nail Block when he passes the money. We're working with the Canadian authorities on this, and that's the way we'll proceed. As for the conspiracy charges, we have the word of a bargain-basement hit man. It may take a bit more to make it stick."

"You'll make it stick. How many have we got?"

"We have two agents checking in tomorrow, and two more as backup. We'll take Dupont in his cabin, and Block in the lobby. Moving on Dupont any earlier would undoubtedly tip off Block. Agreed?"

"Yes."

"Since you've filled me in on the checkout procedures, it should go very smoothly."

"It better. If anything happens to her—anything— I'm holding you responsible."

Charity dashed into the kitchen with a loaded tray. "I don't know how things can get out of hand so fast. When have you ever known us to have a full house on a Wednesday night?" she asked the room at large, whipping out her pad. "Two specials with wild rice, one with baked potato, hold the sour cream, and one child's portion of ribs with fries." She rushed over to get the drinks herself.

"Take it easy, girl," Mae advised her. "They ain't going anywhere till they eat."

"That's the problem." She loaded up the tray. "What a time for Lori to get sick. The way this virus is bouncing around, we're lucky to have a waitress still standing. Whoops!" She backed up to keep from running into Roman. "Sorry."

"Need a hand?"

"I need two." She smiled and took the time to lean over the tray and kiss him. "You seem to have them. Those salads Dolores is fixing go to table 5."

"Girl makes me tired just looking at her," Mae commented as she filleted a trout. She lifted her head just long enough for her eyes to meet Roman's. "Seems to me she rushes into everything."

"Four house salads." Dolores was humming the "Wedding March" as she passed him a tray. "Looks like you didn't need that dynamite after all." Cackling, she went back to fill the next order.

Five minutes later he passed Charity in the doorway again. "Strange bunch tonight," she murmured.

"How so?"

"There's a man at table 2. He's so jumpy you'd think he'd robbed a bank or something. Then there's a couple at table 8, supposed to be on a second honeymoon. They're spending more time looking at everyone else than each other."

Roman said nothing. She'd made both Dupont and two of Conby's agents in less than thirty minutes.

"And then there's this little man in a three-piece suit sitting at 4. Suit and tie," she added with a glance over her shoulder. "Came here to relax, he says. Who can relax in a three-piece suit?" Shifting, she balanced the tray on her hip. "Claims to be from Seattle and has an Eastern accent that could cut Mae's apple pie. Looks like a weasel."

"You think so?" Roman allowed himself a small smile at her description of Conby.

"A very well-groomed weasel," she added. "Check it out for yourself." With a small shudder, she headed toward the dining room again. "Anyone that smooth gives me the creeps."

Duty was duty though, and the weasel was sitting at her station. "Are you ready to order?" she asked Conby with a bright smile.

He took a last sip of his vodka martini. It was

passable, he supposed. "The menu claims the trout is fresh."

"Yes, sir." She was particularly proud of that. The stocked pond had been her idea. "It certainly is."

"Fresh when it was shipped in this morning, no doubt."

"No." Charity lowered her pad but kept her smile in place. "We stock our own right here at the inn."

Lifting a brow, he tapped a finger against his empty glass. "Your fish may be superior to your vodka, but I have my doubts as to whether it is indeed fresh. Nonetheless, it appears to be the most interesting item on your menu, so I shall have to make do."

"The fish," Charity repeated, with what she considered admirable calm, "is fresh."

"I'm sure you consider it so. However, your conception of fresh and mine may differ."

"Yes, sir." She shoved the pad into her pocket. "If you'll excuse me a moment."

She might be innocent, Conby thought, frowning at his empty glass, but she was hardly efficient.

"Where's the fire?" Mae wanted to know when Charity burst into the kitchen.

"In my brain." She stopped a moment, hands on hips. "That—that insulting pipsqueak out there tells me our vodka's below standard, our menu's dull and our fish isn't fresh."

"A dull menu." Mae bristled down to her crepe-soled shoes. "What did he eat?"

"He hasn't eaten anything yet. One drink and a couple of crackers with salmon dip and he's a restaurant critic."

Charity took a turn around the kitchen, struggling with her temper. No urban wonder was going to stroll into her inn and pick it apart. Her bar was as good as any on the island, her restaurant had a triple-A rating, and her fish—

"Guy at table 4 wants another vodka martini," Roman announced as he carried in a loaded tray.

"Does he?" Charity whirled around. "Does he really?"

He couldn't recall ever seeing quite that glint in her eye. "That's right," he said cautiously.

"Well, I have something else to get him first." So saying, she strode into the utility room and then out again.

"Uh-oh," Dolores mumbled.

"Did I miss something?" Roman asked.

"Man's got a nerve saying the food's dull before he's even had a taste of it." Scowling, Mae scooped a helping of wild asparagus onto a plate. "I've a mind to add some curry to his entrée. A nice fat handful of it. We'll see about dull."

They all turned around when Charity strolled back in. She was still carrying the platter. On it flopped a very confused trout.

"My." Dolores covered her mouth with both hands, giggling. "Oh, my."

Grinning, Mae went back to her stove.

"Charity." Roman made a grab for her arm, but she evaded him and glided through the doorway. Shaking his head, he followed her.

A few of the diners looked up and stared as she carried the thrashing fish across the room. Weaving through the tables, she crossed to table 4 and held the tray under Conby's nose.

"Your trout, sir." She dropped the platter unceremoniously in front of him. "Fresh enough?" she asked with a small, polite smile.

In the archway Roman tucked his hands into his

pockets and roared. He would have traded a year's salary for a photo of the expression on Conby's face as he and the fish gaped at each other.

When Charity glided back into the kitchen, she handed the tray and its passenger to Dolores. "You can put this back," she said. "Table 4 decided on the stuffed pork chops. I wish I had a pig handy." She let out a laughing squeal as Roman scooped her off the floor.

"You're the best." He pressed his lips to hers and held them there long after he'd set her down again. "The absolute best." He was still laughing as he gathered her close for a hug. "Isn't she, Mae?"

"She has her moments." She wasn't about to let them know how much good it did her to see them smiling at each other. "Now the two of you stop pawing each other in my kitchen and get back to work."

Charity lifted her face for one last kiss. "I guess I'd better fix that martini now. He looked like he could use one."

Because she wasn't one to hold a grudge, Charity treated Conby to attentive and cheerful service throughout the meal. Noting that he hadn't unbent by dessert, she brought him a serving of Mae's Black Forest cake on the house.

"I hope you enjoyed your meal, Mr. Conby."

It was impossible for him to admit that he'd never had better, not even in Washington's toniest restaurants. "It was quite good, thank you."

She offered an easy smile as she poured his coffee. "Perhaps you'll come back another time and try the trout."

Even for Conby, her smile was hard to resist. "Perhaps. You run an interesting establishment, Miss Ford."

"We try. Have you lived in Seattle long, Mr. Conby?"

He continued to add cream to his coffee, but he was very much on guard. "Why do you ask?"

"Your accent. It's very Eastern."

Conby deliberated only seconds. He knew that Dupont had already left the dining room, but Block was at a nearby table, entertaining part of his tour group with what Conby considered rather boring stories. "You have a good ear. I was transferred to Seattle eighteen months ago. From Maryland. I'm in marketing."

"Maryland." Deciding to forgive and forget, she topped off his coffee. "You're supposed to have the best crabs in the country."

"I assure you, we do." The rich cake and the smooth coffee had mellowed him. He actually smiled at her. "It's a pity I didn't bring one along with me."

Laughing, Charity laid a friendly hand on his arm. "You're a good sport, Mr. Conby. Enjoy your evening."

Lips pursed, Conby watched her go. He couldn't recall anyone having accused him of being a good sport before. He rather liked it.

"We're down to three tables of diehards," Charity announced as she entered the kitchen again. "And I'm starving." She opened the refrigerator and rooted around for something to eat, but Mae snapped it closed again.

"You haven't got time."

"Haven't got time?" Charity pressed a hand to her stomach. "Mae, the way tonight went, I wasn't able to grab more than a stray French fry."

"I'll fix you a sandwich, but you had a call. Something about tomorrow's delivery."

"The salmon. Damn." She tilted her watch forward. "They're closed by now."

"Left an emergency number, I think. Message is upstairs."

"All right, all right. I'll be back in ten minutes." She cast a last longing glance at the refrigerator. "Make that two sandwiches."

To save time, she raced out through the utility room, rounded the side of the building and climbed the outside steps. When she opened the door, she could only stop and stare.

The music was pitched low. There was candlelight, and there were flowers and a white cloth on a table at the foot of the bed. It was set for two. As she watched, Roman took a bottle of wine from a glass bucket and drew the cork.

"I thought you'd never get here."

She leaned back on the closed door. "If I'd known this was waiting, I'd have been here a lot sooner."

"You said you liked surprises."

"Yes." There was both surprise and delight in her eyes as she brushed her tumbled hair back from her forehead. "I like them a lot." Untying her apron, she walked to the table while he poured the wine. It glinted warm and gold in the candlelight. "Thanks," she murmured when he offered her a glass.

"I wanted to give you something." He gripped her hand, holding tight and trying not to remember that this was their last night together before all the questions had to be answered. "I'm not very good with romantic gestures."

"Oh, no, you're very good at them. Champagne picnics, late-night suppers." She closed her eyes for a moment. "Mozart."

"Picked at random," he admitted, feeling foolishly nervous. "I have something for you."

She looked at the table. "Something else?"

"Yes." He reached down to the seat of his chair and picked up a square box. "It just came today." It was the best he could do. He pushed the box into her hand.

"A present?" She'd always liked the anticipation as much as the gift itself, so she took a moment to study and shake the box. But the moment the lid was off she snatched the bracelet out. "Oh, Roman, it's gorgeous." Thoroughly stunned, she turned the etched gold, watching the light glint off the metal and the square-cut amethyst. "It's absolutely gorgeous," she said again. "I'd swear I'd seen this before. Last week," she remembered. "In one of the magazines Lori brought me."

"You had it on your desk."

Overwhelmed, she nodded. "Yes, I'd circled this. I do that with beautiful things I know I'll never buy." She took a deep breath. "Roman, this is a wonderful, sweet and very romantic thing to do, but—"

"Then don't spoil it." He took the bracelet from her and clasped it on her wrist. "I need the practice."

"No." She slipped her arms around him and rested her cheek against his shoulder. "I think you've got the hang of it."

He held her, letting the music, her scent, the moment, wash over him. Things could be different with her. He could be different with her.

"Do you know when I fell in love with you, Roman?"

"No." He kissed the top of her head. "I've thought more about why than when."

With a soft laugh, she snuggled against him. "I'd thought it was when you danced with me and you kissed me until every bone in my body turned to water."

"Like this?"

He turned his head, meeting her lips with his. Gently he set her on fire.

"Yes." She swayed against him, eyes closed. "Just like that. But that wasn't when. That was when I realized it, but it wasn't when I fell in love with you. Do you remember when you asked me about the spare?"

"The what?"

"The spare." Sighing, she tilted her head to give him easier access to her throat. "You wanted to know where the spare was so you could fix my flat." She leaned back to smile at his stunned expression. "I guess I can't call it love at first sight, since I'd already known you two or three minutes."

He ran his hands over her cheeks, through her hair, down her neck. "Just like that?"

"I'd never thought as much about falling in love and getting married as I suppose most people might. Because of Pop's being sick, and the inn. I always figured if it happened it would happen without me doing a lot of worrying or preparing. And I was right." She linked hands with him. "All I had to do was have a flat tire. The rest was easy."

A flat, Roman remembered, that had been deliberately arranged, just as her sudden need for a handyman had been arranged. As everything had been arranged, he thought, his grip tightening on her fingers. Everything except his falling in love with her.

"Charity . . ." He would have given anything to be able to tell her the truth, the whole truth. Anything but his knowledge that in ignorance there was safety. "I never meant for any of this to happen," he said carefully. "I never wanted to feel this way about anyone."

"Are you sorry?"

"About a lot of things, but not about being in love with you." He released her. "Your dinner's getting cold."

She tucked her tongue in her cheek. "If we found something else to do for an hour or so we could call it a midnight supper." She ran her hands up his chest to toy with the top button of his shirt. "Want to play Parcheesi?"

"No."

She flicked the button open and worked her way slowly, steadily down. "Scrabble?"

"Uh-uh."

"I know." She trailed a finger down the center of his body to the snap of his jeans. "How about a rip-roaring game of canasta?"

"I don't know how to play."

Grinning, she tugged the snap open. "Oh, I have a feeling you'd catch on." Her laugh was muffled against his mouth.

Her heated thoughts of seducing him spun away as he dragged her head back and plundered her mouth. Her hands, so confident an instant before, faltered, then fisted hard at the back of his shirt. This wasn't the gentle, persuasive passion he had shown her since the night they had become lovers. This was a raw, desperate need, and it held a trace of fury, and a hint of despair. Whirling from the feel of it, she strained against him, letting herself go.

He'd needed her before. Roman had already come to understand that he had needed her long before he'd ever met her. But tonight was different. He'd set the stage carefully—the wine, the candles, the music—wanting to give her the romance she made him capable of. Then he'd felt her cool fingertips on his skin. He'd seen the promising flicker of desire in her eyes. There was only tonight. In a matter of hours she would know everything. No matter how often he told himself he would set things right, he was very much afraid she wouldn't forgive him.

He had tonight.

Breathless, she clung to him as they tumbled onto the bed. Here was the restless, ruthless lover she had known existed alongside the gentle, patient one. And he excited her every bit as much. As frantic as he, she pulled the loosened shirt from his shoulders and gloried in the feel of his flesh under her hands.

He was as taut as wire, as explosive as gunpowder. She felt his muscles tense and tighten as his mouth raced hungrily over her face. With a throaty laugh she tugged at his jeans while they rolled over the bed. If this was a game they were playing, she was determined they would both win.

A broken moan escaped him as her seeking hands drove him toward delirium. With an oath, he snagged her wrists, yanking them over her head. Breath heaving, he watched her face as he hooked a hand in the top of her shirt and ripped it down the center.

She had only time for a gasp before his hot, open mouth lowered to her skin to torment and tantalize. Powerless against the onslaught, she arched against him. When her hands were free, she only pressed him closer, crying out as he sucked greedily at her breast.

There were sensations here, wild and exquisite, that trembled on but never crossed the thin line that separated pleasure from pain. She felt herself dragged under, deep, still deeper, to windmill helplessly down some dark, endless tunnel toward unreasonable pleasures.

She couldn't know what she was doing to him. He was skilled enough to be certain that she was trapped by her own senses. Yet her body wrapped around his, her hands sought, her lips hungered.

In the flickering light her skin was like white satin. Under his hands it flowed like lava, hot and dangerous. Passion heated her light floral scent and turned it into something secret and forbidden.

Impatient, he yanked her slacks down her hips, frantically tasting each new inch of exposed flesh. This new intimacy had her sobbing out his name, shuddering as climax slammed impossibly into climax.

She held on to him, her nails digging in, her palms sliding damply over his slick skin. Her mind was empty, wiped clear of all but sensation. His name formed on her lips again and again. She thought he spoke to her, some mad, frenzied words that barely penetrated her clouded brain. Perhaps they were promises, pleas, or prayers. She would have answered all of them if she could.

Then his mouth was on hers, swallowing her cry of release, smothering her groan of surrender, as he drove himself into her.

Fast, hot, reckless, they matched rhythms. Far beyond madness, they clung. Driven by love, locked in desire, they raced. Even when they tumbled back to earth, they held each other close.

CHAPTER 11

With her eyes half closed, her lips curved, she gave a long, lazy sigh. "That was wonderful."

Roman topped off the wine in Charity's glass. "Are you talking about the meal or the preliminaries?"

She smiled. "Both." Before he could set the bottle down, she touched his hand. It was just a skimming of her fingertip over his skin. His pulse doubled. "I think we should make midnight suppers a regular event."

It was long past midnight. Even cold fish was delicious with wine and love. He hoped that if he held on hard enough it could always be like this. "The first time you looked at me like that I almost swallowed my tongue."

She kept her eyes on his. Even in candlelight they were the color of morning. "Like what?"

"Like you knew exactly what I was thinking, and was trying not to think. Exactly what I wanted not to think. Exactly what I wanted, and was trying not to want. You scare the hell out of me."

Her lazy smile faltered. "I do?"

"You make too much difference. All the difference."

He took both of her hands, wishing that just this once he had smooth words, a little poetry. "Every time you walk into a room . . ." But he didn't have smooth words, or poetry. "It makes a difference." He would have released her hands, but she turned them in his.

"I'm crazy about you. If I'd gone looking for someone to share my life, and my home, and my dreams, it would have been you."

She saw the shadow of concern in his eyes and willed it away. There was no room for worries in their lives tonight. With a quick, wicked smile, she nibbled on his fingers. "You know what I'd like?"

"More Black Forest cake."

"Besides that." Her eyes laughed at him over their joined hands. "I'd like to spend the night making love with you, talking with you, drinking wine and listening to music. I have a feeling I'd find it much more satisfying than the slumber parties I had as a girl."

She could, with a look and a smile, seduce him more utterly than any vision of black lace or white silk. "What would you like to do first?"

She had to laugh. It delighted her to see him so relaxed and happy. "Actually, there is something I want to talk with you about."

"I've already told you—I'll wear a suit, but no tuxedo."

"It's not about that." She smiled and traced a fingertip over the back of his hand. "Even though I know you'd look wonderful in a tux, I think a suit's more than adequate for an informal garden wedding. I'd like to talk to you about after the wedding."

"After-the-wedding plans aren't negotiable. I intend to make love with you for about twenty-four hours."

"Oh." As if she were thinking it through, she sipped

her wine. "I guess I can go along with that. What I'd like to discuss is more long-range. It's something that Block said to me the other day."

"Block?" Alarm sprinted upward, then centered at the base of his neck.

"Just an offhand comment, but it made me think." She moved her shoulders in a quick, restless movement, then settled again. "I mentioned that we were getting married, and he said something about hoping you didn't take me away. It suddenly occurred to me that you might not want to spend your life here, on Orcas."

"That's it?" He felt the tension seep away.

"It's not such a little thing. I mean, I'm sure we can work it out, but you might not be crazy about the idea of living in a . . . well, a public kind of place, with people coming and going, and interruptions, and . . ." She let her words trail off, knowing she was rambling, as she did whenever she was nervous. "The point is, I need to know how you feel about staying on the island, living here, at the inn."

"How do you feel about it?"

"It isn't just a matter of what I feel any longer. It's what we feel."

It amazed him that she could so easily touch his heart. He supposed it always would. "It's been a long time since I've felt at home anywhere. I feel it here, with you."

She smiled and linked her fingers with his. "Are you tired?"

"No."

"Good." She rose and corked the wine. "Just let me get my keys."

"Keys to what?"

"The van," she told him as she walked into the next room.

"Are we going somewhere?"

"I know the best place on the island to watch the sun rise." She came back carrying a blanket and jiggling the keys. "Want to watch the sun come up with me, Roman?"

"You're only wearing a robe."

"Of course I am. It's nearly two in the morning. Don't forget the wine." With a laugh, she opened the door and crept down the steps. "Let's try not to wake anyone." She winced a little as she started across the gravel in her bare feet. With a muttered oath, Roman swung her up into his arms. "My hero," she murmured.

"Sure." He dumped her in the driver's seat of the van. "Where are we going, baby?"

"To the beach." She pushed her hair behind her shoulders as she started the van. Symphonic music blared from the radio before she twisted the knob. "I always play it too loud when I'm driving alone." She turned to look guiltily back at the inn. It remained dark and quiet. Slowly she drove out of the lot and onto the road. "It's a beautiful night."

"Morning."

"Whatever." She took a long, greedy gulp of air. "I haven't really had time for big adventures, so I have to take small ones whenever I get the chance."

"Is that what this is? An adventure?"

"Sure. We're going to drink the rest of the wine, make love under the stars and watch the sun come up over the water." She turned her head. "Is that all right with you?"

"I think I can live with it."

It was hours later when she curled up close to him. The bottle of wine was empty, and the stars were blinking out one by one.

"I'm going to be totally useless today." After a sleepy laugh, she nuzzled his neck. "And I don't even care."

He tugged the blanket over her. The mornings were still chilly. Though he hadn't planned it, the long night of loving had given him new hope. If he could convince her to sleep through the morning, he could complete his assignment, close the door on it and then explain everything. That would let him keep her out of harm's way and begin at the beginning.

"It's nearly dawn," she murmured.

They didn't speak as they watched day break. The sky paled. The night birds hushed. For an instant, time hung suspended. Then, slowly, regally, colors seeped into the horizon, bleeding up from the water, reflecting in it. Shadows faded, and the trees were tipped with gold. The first bird of the morning trumpeted the new day.

Roman gathered her to him to love her slowly under the lightening sky.

She dozed as he drove back to the inn. The sky was a pale, milky blue, but it was as quiet now as it had been when they'd left. When he lifted her out of the van, she sighed and nestled her head on his shoulder.

"I love you, Roman."

"I know." For the first time in his life he wanted to think about next week, next month, even next year—anything except the day ahead. He carried her up the stairs and into the inn. "I love you, Charity."

He had little trouble convincing her to snuggle between the sheets of the rumpled bed once he promised to take Ludwig for his habitual run.

Before he did, Roman went downstairs, strapped on his shoulder holster and shoved in his gun.

Taking Dupont was a study in well-oiled police

work. By 7:45 his secluded cabin was surrounded by the best Sheriff Royce and the F.B.I. had to offer. Roman had ignored Conby's mutterings about bringing the locals into it and advised his superior to stay out of the way.

When the men were in position, Roman moved to the door himself, his gun in one hand, his shoulder snug against the frame. He rapped twice. When there was no response, he signaled for his men to draw their weapons and close in. Using the key he'd taken from Charity's ring, he unlocked the door.

Once inside, he scanned the room, legs spread, the gun held tight in both hands. The adrenaline was there, familiar, even welcome. With only a jerk of the head he signaled his backup. Guarding each other's flanks, they took a last circle.

Roman cautiously approached the bedroom. For the first time, a smile—a grim smile—moved across his face. Dupont was in the shower. And he was singing.

The singing ended abruptly when Roman yanked the curtain aside.

"Don't bother to put your hands up," Roman told him as he blinked water out of his eyes. Keeping the gun level, he tossed his first prize a towel. "You're busted, pal. Why don't you dry off and I'll read you your rights?"

"Well done," Conby commented when the prisoner was cuffed. "If you handle the rest of this as smoothly, I'll see that you get a commendation."

"Keep it." Roman holstered his weapon. There was only one more hurdle before he could finally separate past and future. "When this is done, I'm finished."

"You've been in law enforcement for over ten years, DeWinter. You won't walk away."

"Watch me." With that, he headed back to the inn to finish what he had started.

When Charity awoke, it was full morning and she was quite alone. She was grateful for that, because she couldn't stifle a moan. The moment she sat up, her head, unused to the generous doses of wine and stingy amounts of sleep, began to pound.

She had no one but herself to blame, she admitted as she crawled out of bed. Her feet tangled in what was left of the shirt she'd been wearing the night before.

It had been worth it, she thought, gathering up the torn cotton. Well worth it.

But, incredible night or not, it was morning and she had work to do. She downed some aspirin, allowed herself another groan, then dove into the shower.

Roman found Bob huddled in the office, anxiously gulping laced coffee. Without preamble, he yanked the mug away and emptied the contents into the trash can.

"I just needed a little something to get me through."

He'd had more than a little, Roman determined. His words were slurred, and his eyes were glazed. Even under the best of circumstances Roman found it difficult to drum up any sympathy for a drunk.

He dragged Bob out of his chair by the shirtfront. "You pull yourself together and do it fast. When Block comes in you're going to check him and his little group out. If you tip him off—if you so much as blink and tip him off—I'll hang you out to dry."

"Charity does the checkout," Bob managed through chattering teeth.

"Not today. You're going to go out to the desk and handle it. You're going to do a good job because you're going to know I'm in here and I'm watching you."

He stepped away from Bob just as the office door opened. "Sorry I'm late." Despite her heavy eyes, Charity beamed at Roman. "I overslept."

He felt his heart stop, then sink to his knees. "You didn't sleep enough."

"You're telling me." Her smile faded when she looked at Bob. "What's wrong?"

He grabbed at the thread of opportunity with both hands. "I was just telling Roman that I'm not feeling very well."

"You don't look well." Concerned, she walked over to feel his brow. It was clammy and deepened the worry in her eyes. "You're probably coming down with that virus."

"That's what I'm afraid of."

"You shouldn't have come in at all today. Maybe Roman should drive you home."

"No, I can manage." He walked on shaking legs to the door. "Sorry about this, Charity." He turned to give her a last look. "Really sorry."

"Don't be silly. Just take care of yourself."

"I'll give him a hand," Roman muttered, and followed him out. They walked out into the lobby at the same time Block strolled in.

"Good morning." His face creased with his habitual smile, but his eyes were wary. "Is there a problem?"

"Virus." Bob's face was already turning a sickly green. Fear made a convincing cover. "Hit me pretty hard this morning."

"I called Dr. Mertens," Charity announced as she came in to stand behind the desk. "You go straight home, Bob. He'll meet you there."

"Thanks." But one of Conby's agents followed him out, and he knew he wouldn't be going home for quite a while.

"This virus has been a plague around here." She offered Block an apologetic smile. "I'm short a housekeeper, a waitress and now Bob. I hope none of your group had any complaints about the service."

"Not a one." Relaxed again, Block set his briefcase on the desk. "It's always a pleasure doing business with you, Charity."

Roman watched helplessly as they chatted and went through the routine of checking lists and figures. She was supposed to be safe upstairs, sleeping deeply and dreaming of the night they'd spent together. Frustrated, he balled his hands at his side. Now, no matter what he did, she'd be in the middle.

He heard her laugh when Block mentioned the fish she'd carried into the dining room. And he imagined how her face would look when the agents moved in and arrested the man she thought of as a tour guide and a friend.

Charity read off a total. Roman steadied himself.

"We seem to be off by . . . $22.50." Block began laboriously running the numbers through his calculator again. Brow furrowed, Charity went over her list, item by item.

"Good morning, dear."

"Hmm." Distracted, Charity glanced up. "Oh, good morning, Miss Millie."

"I'm just on my way up to pack. I wanted you to know what a delightful time we've had."

"We're always sorry to see you go. We were all pleased that you and Miss Lucy extended your stay for a few days."

Miss Millie fluttered her eyelashes myopically at

Roman before making her way toward the stairs. At the top, he thought, there would now be an officer posted to see that she and the other guests were kept out of the way.

"I get the same total again, Roger." Puzzled, she tapped the end of her pencil on the list. "I wish I could say I'd run it through the computer, but . . ." She let her words trail off, ignoring her headache. "Ah, this might be it. Do you have the Wentworths in cabin 1 down for a bottle of wine? They charged it night before last."

"Wentworth, Wentworth . . ." With grating slowness, Block ran down his list. "No, nothing here."

"Let me find the tab." After opening a drawer, she flipped her way efficiently through the folders. Roman felt a bead of sweat slide slowly down his back. One of the agents strolled over to browse through some postcards.

"I've got both copies," she said with a shake of her head. "This virus is really hanging us up." She filed her copy of the receipt and handed Block his.

"No problem." Cheerful as ever, he noted the new charge, then added up his figures again. "That seems to match."

With the ease of long habit, Charity calculated the amount in Canadian currency. "That's $2,330.00." She turned the receipt around for Block's approval.

He clicked open his briefcase. "As always, it's a pleasure." He counted out the money in twenties. The moment Charity marked the bill Paid, Roman moved in.

"Put your hands up. Slow." He pressed the barrel of his gun into the small of Block's back.

"Roman!" Charity gaped at him, the key to the cash drawer in her hand. "What on earth are you doing?"

"Go around the desk," he told her. "Way around, and walk outside."

"Are you crazy? Roman, for God's sake—"

"Do it!"

Block moistened his lips, keeping his hands carefully aloft. "Is this a robbery?"

"Haven't you figured it out by now?" With his free hand, Roman pulled out his ID. After tossing it on the desk, he reached for his cuffs. "You're under arrest."

"What's the charge?"

"Conspiracy to murder, counterfeiting, transporting known felons across international borders. That'll do for a start." He yanked one of Block's arms down and slipped the cuff over his wrist.

"How could you?" Charity's voice was a mere whisper. She held his badge in her hand.

He took his eyes off Block for only a second to look at her. One second changed everything.

"How silly of me," Miss Millie muttered as she waltzed back into the lobby. "I was nearly upstairs when I realized I'd left my—"

For a man of his bulk, Block moved quickly. He dragged Miss Millie against him and had a knife to her throat before anyone could react. The cuffs dangled from one wrist. "It'll only take a heartbeat," he said quietly, staring into Roman's eyes. The gun was trained in the center of Block's forehead, and Roman's finger was twitching on the trigger.

"Think about it." Block's gaze swept the lobby, where other guns had been drawn. "I'll slice this nice little lady's throat. Don't move," he said to Charity. Shifting slightly, he blocked her way.

Wide-eyed, Miss Millie could only cling to Block's arm and whimper.

"Don't hurt her." Charity stepped forward, but she

stopped quickly when she saw Block's grip tighten. "Please, don't hurt her." It had to be a dream, she told herself. A nightmare. "Someone tell me what's happening here."

"The place is surrounded." Roman kept his eyes and his weapon on Block. He waited in vain for one of his men to move in from the rear. "Hurting her isn't going to do you any good."

"It isn't going to do you any good, either. Think about it. Want a dead grandmother on your hands?"

"You don't want to add murder to your list, Block," Roman said evenly. And Charity was much too close, he thought. Much too close.

"It makes no difference to me. Now take it outside. All of you!" His voice rose as he scanned the room. "Toss down the guns. Toss them down and get out before I start slicing into her. Do it." He nicked Miss Millie's fragile throat with the blade.

"Please!" Again Charity took a step forward. "Let her go. I'll stay with you."

"Damn it, Charity, get back."

She didn't spare Roman a glance. "Please, Roger," she said again, taking another careful step forward. "She's old and frail. She might get sick. Her heart." Desperate, she stepped between him and Roman's gun. "I won't give you any trouble."

The decision took Block only a moment. He grabbed Charity and dug the point of the blade into her throat. Miss Millie slid bonelessly to the floor.

"Drop the gun." He saw the fear in Roman's eyes and smiled. Apparently he'd made a much better bargain. "Two seconds and it's over. I don't have anything to lose."

Roman held his hands up, letting his weapon drop. "We'll talk."

"We'll talk when I'm ready." Block shifted the knife so that the length of the blade lay across Charity's neck. She shut her eyes and waited to die. "Get out, now. The first time somebody tries to get back in she dies."

"Out." Roman pointed to the door. "Keep them back, Conby. All of them. There's my weapon," he said to Block. "I'm clean." He lifted his jacket cautiously to show his empty holster. "Why don't I hang around in here? You can have two hostages for the price of one. A federal agent ought to give you some leverage."

"Just the woman. Take off, DeWinter, or I'll kill her before you can think how to get to me. Now."

"For God's sake, Roman. Get her out of here. She needs a doctor." Charity sucked in her breath when the point of the knife pierced her skin.

"Don't." Roman held up his hands again, palms out, as he moved toward the crumpled form near the desk. Keeping his movements slow, he gathered the sobbing woman in his arms. "If you hurt her, you won't live long enough to regret it."

With that last frustrated threat he left Charity alone.

"Stay back." After bundling Miss Millie into waiting arms, he rushed off the porch, fighting to keep his mind clear. "Nobody goes near the doors or any of the windows. Get me a weapon." Before anyone could oblige him, he was yanking a gun away from one of Royce's deputies. With the smallest of gestures Royce signaled to his man to be silent.

"What do you want us to do?"

Roman merely stared down at the gun in his hand. It was loaded. He was trained. And he was helpless.

"DeWinter . . ." Conby began.

"Back off." When Conby started to speak again, Roman turned on him. "Back off."

He stared at the inn. He could hear Miss Millie

crying softly as someone carried her to a car. The guests who had already been evacuated were being herded to safety. Roman imagined that Royce had arranged that. Charity would want to make sure they were well taken care of.

Charity.

Shoving the gun into his holster, he turned around. "Have the road blocked off a mile in each direction. Only official personnel in this area. We'll keep the inn surrounded from a distance of fifty feet. He'll be thinking again," Roman said slowly, "and when he starts thinking he's going to know he's blocked in."

He lifted both hands and rubbed them over his face. He'd been in hostage situations before. He was trained for them. With time and cool heads, the odds of getting a hostage out in a situation of this type were excellent. When the hostage was Charity, excellent wasn't nearly good enough.

"I want to talk to him."

"Agent DeWinter, under the circumstances I have serious reservations about you being in charge of this operation."

Roman rounded on him. "Get in my way, Conby, and I'll hang you up by your silk tie. Why the hell weren't there men positioned in the back, behind him?"

Because his palms were sweating, Conby's voice was only more frigid. "I thought it best to have them outside, prepared if he attempted to run."

Roman battled the red wave of fury that burst behind his eyes. "When I get her out," he said softly, "I'm going to deal with you, you bastard. I need communication," he said to Royce. "Can you handle it?"

"Give me twenty minutes."

With a nod, Roman turned back to study the inn.

Systematically he considered and rejected points of entry.

Inside, Charity felt some measure of relief when the knife was removed from her throat. Somehow the gun Block was pointing at her now seemed less personal.

"Roger—"

"Shut up. Shut up and let me think." He swiped a beefy forearm over his brow to dry it. It had all happened so fast, too fast. Everything up to now he had done on instinct. As Roman had calculated, he was beginning to think.

"They've got me trapped in here. I should've used you to get to one of the cars, should've taken off." Then he laughed, looking wildly around the lobby. "We're on a damn island. Can't drive off an island."

"I think if we—"

"Shut up!" he shouted and had her holding her breath as he leveled the gun at her. "I'm the one who needs to think. Feds. That sniveling little wart was right all along," he muttered, thinking of Bob. "He made DeWinter days ago. Did you?" As he asked, he grabbed her by the hair and yanked her head back to hold the barrel against her throat.

"No. I didn't know. I didn't. I still don't understand." She could only give a muffled cry when he slammed her back against the wall. She'd never seen murder in a man's eyes before, but she recognized it. "Roger, think. If you kill me you won't have anything to bargain with." She tasted fear on her tongue as she forced the words out. "You need me."

"Yeah." He relaxed his grip. "You've been handy so far. You'll just have to go on being handy. How many ways in and out of this place?"

"I—I don't really know." She sucked in her breath when he gave her hair another cruel twist.

"You know how many two-by-fours are in this place."

"Five. There are five exits, not counting the windows. The lobby, the gathering room, the outside steps running to my quarters and a family suite in the east wing, and the back, through the utility room off the kitchen."

"That's good." Panting a bit, he considered the possibilities. "The kitchen. We'll take the kitchen. I'll have water and food there in case this takes a while. Come on." He kept a hand in her hair and the gun at the base of her neck.

His eyes on the inn, Roman paced back and forth behind the barricade of police cars. She was smart, he told himself. Charity was a smart, sensible woman. She wouldn't panic. She wouldn't do anything stupid.

Oh, God, she must be terrified. He lit a cigarette from the butt of another, but he didn't find himself soothed as the harsh smoke seared into him.

"Where's the goddamn phone?"

"Nearly ready." Royce pushed back his hat and straightened from where he'd been watching a lineman patch in a temporary line. "My nephew," he explained to Roman with a thin smile. "The boy knows his job."

"You got a lot of relatives."

"I'm lousy with them. Listen, I heard you and Charity were getting married. That part of the cover?"

"No." Roman thought of the picnic on the beach, that one clear moment in time. "No."

"In that case, I'm going to give you some advice.

You're wrong," he said, before Roman could speak. "You do need it. You're going to have to get yourself calm, real calm, before you pick up that phone. A trapped animal reacts two ways. He either cowers back and gives up or he strikes out at anything in his way." Royce nodded toward the inn. "Block doesn't look like the type to give up easy, and Charity sure as hell's in his way. That line through yet, son?"

"Yes, sir." The young lineman's hands were sweaty with nerves and excitement. "You can dial right through." He passed the damp receiver to Roman.

"I don't know the number," Roman murmured. "I don't know the damn number."

"I know it."

Roman swung around to face Mae. In that one instant he saw everything he felt about himself mirrored in her eyes. There would be time for guilt later, he told himself. There would be a lifetime for it. "Royce, you were supposed to clear the area."

"Moving Maeflower's like moving a tank."

"I don't budge until I see Charity." Mae firmed her quivering lips. "She's going to need me when she comes out. Waste of time to argue," she added, "You want the number?"

"Yes."

She gave it to him. Tossing his cigarette aside, Roman dialed.

Charity jolted in the chair when the phone rang. Across the table, Block simply stared at it. He had had her pile everything she could drag or carry to block the two doors. Extra chairs, twenty-pound canisters of flour and sugar, the rolling butcher block, iron skillets, all sat in a jumble, braced against both entrances.

In the silent kitchen the phone sounded again and again, like a scream.

"Stay right where you are." Block moved across the room to answer it. "Yeah?"

"It's DeWinter. Thought you might be ready to talk about a deal."

"What kind of deal?"

"That's what we have to talk about. First I have to know you've still got Charity."

"Have you seen her come out?" Block spit into the phone. "You know damn well I've got her or you wouldn't be talking to me."

"I have to make sure she's still alive. Let me talk to her."

"You can go to hell."

Threats, abuse, curses, rose like bile in his throat. Still, when he spoke, his voice was dispassionate. "I verify that you still have a hostage, Block, or we don't deal."

"You want to talk to her?" Block gestured with the gun. "Over here," he ordered. "Make it fast. It's your boyfriend," he told Charity when she stood beside him. "He wants to know how you're doing. You tell him you're just fine." He brushed the gun up her cheek to rest it at her temple. "Understand?"

With a nod, she leaned into the phone. "Roman?"

"Charity." Too many emotions slammed into him for him to measure. He wanted to reassure her, to make promises, to beg her to be careful. But he knew he would have only seconds and that Block would be listening to every word spoken. "Has he hurt you?"

"No." She closed her eyes and fought back a sob. "No, I'm fine. He's going to let me fix some food."

"Hear that, DeWinter? She's fine." Deliberately Block dragged her arm behind her back until she cried out. "That can change anytime."

Roman gripped the phone helplessly as he listened

to the sound of Charity's sobs. It took every ounce of control he had left to keep the terror out of his voice. "You don't have to hurt her. I said we'd talk about terms."

"We'll talk about terms, all right. My terms." He released Charity's arm and ignored her as she slid to the floor. "You get me a car. I want safe passage to the airport, DeWinter. Charity drives. I want a plane fueled up and waiting. She'll be getting on it with me, so any tricks and we're back to square one. When I get where I'm going, I turn her loose."

"How big a plane?"

"Don't try to stall me."

"Wait. I have to know. It's a small airport, Block. You know that. If you're going any distance—"

"Just get me a plane."

"Okay." Roman wiped the back of his hand over his mouth and forced his voice to level. He couldn't hear her any longer, and the silence was as anguishing as her sobbing. "I'm going to have to go through channels on this. That's how it works."

"The hell with your channels."

"Look, I don't have the authority to get you what you want. I need to get approval. Then I'll have to clear the airport, get a pilot. You'll have to give me some time."

"Don't yank my chain, DeWinter. You got an hour."

"I've got to get through to Washington. You know how bureaucrats are. It'll take me three, maybe four."

"The hell with that. You got two. After two I'm going to start sending her out in pieces."

Charity closed her eyes, lowered her head to her folded arms and wept out her terror.

CHAPTER 12

"We've got a couple of hours," Roman murmured, continuing to study the inn and the floor plan Royce had given him. "He's not as smart as I thought, or maybe he's too panicked to think it through."

"That could be to our advantage," Royce said when Roman shook his head at his offer of coffee. "Or it could work against us."

Two hours. Roman stared at the quiet clapboard building. He couldn't stand the idea of Charity being held at gunpoint for that long. "He wants a car, safe passage to the airport and a plane." He turned to Conby. "I want you to make sure he thinks he's going to get it."

"I'm aware of how to handle a hostage situation, DeWinter."

"Which one of your men is the best shot?" Roman asked Royce.

"I am." He kept his eyes steady on Roman's. "Where do you want me?"

"They're in the kitchen."

"He tell you that?"

"No, Charity. She told me he was going to let her fix some food. Since I doubt eating's on her mind, she was letting me know their position."

Royce glanced over to where Mae was pacing up and down the pier. "She's a tough girl. She's keeping her head."

"So far." But Roman remembered too well the sound of her muffled sobbing. "We need to shift two of the men around the back. I want them to keep their distance, stay out of sight. Let's see how close we can get." He turned to Conby again. "Give us five minutes, then call him again. Tell him who you are. You know how to make yourself sound important. Stall him, keep him on the phone as long as you can."

"You have two hours, DeWinter. We can call for a SWAT team from Seattle."

"We have two hours," Roman said grimly. "Charity may not."

"I can't take responsibility—"

Roman cut him off. "You'll damn well take it."

"Agent DeWinter, if this wasn't a crisis situation I would cite you for insubordination."

"Great. Just put it on my tab." He looked at the rifle Royce had picked up. It had a long-range telescopic sight. "Let's move."

She'd cried long enough, Charity decided, taking a long, deep breath. It wasn't doing her any good. Like her captor, she needed to think. Her world had whittled down to one room, with fear as her constant companion. This wouldn't do, she told herself, straightening her spine. Her life was being threatened, and she wasn't even sure why.

She rose from where she had been huddled on the floor. Block was still sitting at the table, holding the gun in one hand while the other tapped monotonously on the scrubbed wood. The dangling cuffs jangled. He was terrified, she realized. Perhaps every bit as much as she. There must be some way to use that to her advantage.

"Roger . . . would you like some coffee?"

"Yeah. That's good, that's a good idea." He took a firmer grip on the gun. "But don't get cute. I'm watching every move."

"Are they going to give you a plane?" She turned the burner on low. The kitchen was full of weapons, she thought. Knives, cleavers, mallets. Closing her eyes, she wondered if she had the courage to use one.

"They're going to give me anything I want as long as I have you."

"Why do they want you?" Stay calm, she told herself. She wanted to stay calm and alert and alive. "I don't understand." She poured the hot coffee into two cups. She didn't think she could swallow, but she hoped that sharing it would put him slightly more at ease. "They said something about counterfeiting."

It didn't matter what she knew. In any case, he had worked hard and was proud of it. "For over two years now I've been running a nice little game back and forth over the border. Twenties and tens in Canadian. I can stamp them out like bottle caps. But I'm careful, you know." He gulped at the coffee. "A couple thousand here, couple thousand there, with Vision as the front. We run a good tour, keep the clients happy."

"You've been paying me with counterfeit money?"

"You, and a couple other places. But you're the longest and most consistent." He smiled at her, as friendly as ever—if you didn't count the gun in his hand. "You have a special place here, Charity, quiet, remote, privately owned. You deal with a small local bank. It ran like a charm."

"Yes." She looked down at her cup, her stomach rolling. "I can see that." And Roman had come not to see the whales but to work on a case. That was all she had been to him.

"We were going to milk this route for a few more months," he continued. "Just lately Bob started getting antsy."

"Bob?" Her hand fisted on her lap. "Bob knew?"

"He was nothing but a nickel-and-dime con man before I took him on. Working scams and petty embezzlements. I set him up here and made him rich. Didn't do badly by you, either," he added with a grin. "You were on some shaky financial ground when I came along."

"All this time," she whispered.

"I'd decided to give it another six months, then move on, but Bob started getting real jumpy about your new handyman. The bastard set me up." He slammed the cup down. "Worked a deal with the feds. I should have caught it, the way he started falling apart after the hit-and-run."

"The accident—you tried to kill me."

"No." He patted her hand, and she cringed. "Truth is, I've always had a liking for you. But I wanted to get you out of the way for a while. Just testing the waters to see how DeWinter played it. He's good," Block mused. "Real good. Had me convinced he was only interested in you. The romance was a good touch. Threw me off."

"Yes." Devastated, she stared at the grain in the wood of the tabletop. "That was clever."

"Sucked me in," Block muttered. "I knew you weren't stringing me along. You haven't got it in you. But DeWinter . . . They've probably already taken Dupont."

"Who?"

"We don't just run the money. There are people, people who need to leave the country quietly, who pay a lot for our services. Looks like I'm going to have to take myself on as a client." He laughed and drained his cup. "How about some food? One of the things I'll miss most about this place is the food."

She rose silently and went to the refrigerator. It had all been a lie, she thought. Everything Roman had said, everything he'd done . . .

The pain cut deep and had her fighting back another bout of weeping. He'd made a fool of her, as surely and as completely as Roger Block had. They had used her, both of them, used her and her inn. She would never forgive. She rubbed her hands over her eyes to clear them. And she would never forget.

"How about that lemon meringue pie?" Relaxed, pleased with his own cleverness, Roger tapped the barrel of the gun on the table. "Mae outdid herself on that pie last night."

"Yes." Slowly Charity pulled it out. "There's a little left."

Block had ripped the frilly tiebacks from the sunny yellow curtains, but there was a space two inches wide at the center. Silently Roman eased toward it. He could see Charity reach into a cupboard, take out a plate.

There were tears drying on her cheeks. It tore at him to see them. Her hands were steady. That was something, some small thing to hold on to. He couldn't see Block, though he shifted as much as he dared.

Then, suddenly, as if she had sensed him, their eyes met through the glass. She braced, and in that instant he saw a myriad of emotions run across her face. Then it was set again. She looked at him as she would have looked at a stranger and waited for instructions.

He held up a hand, palm out, doing his best to signal her to hold on, to keep calm. Then the phone rang and he watched her jolt.

"About time," Block said. He was almost swaggering as he walked to the phone. "Yeah? Who the hell's this?" After listening a moment, he gave a pleased laugh. "I like dealing with a title. Where's my plane, Inspector Conby?"

As quickly as she dared, Charity tugged the curtain open another inch.

"Over here," Block ordered.

She dropped her hand, and the plate rattled to the counter. "What?"

He gestured with the gun. "I said over here."

Roman swore as she moved between him and a clear shot.

"I want them to know I'm keeping up my end." Block took Charity by the arm, less roughly this time. "Tell the man I'm treating you fine."

"He hasn't hurt me," she said dully. She forced herself to keep her eyes away from the window. Roman was out there. He would do his best to get her out safely. That was his job.

"The plane'll be ready in a hour," Block told her after he hung up. "Just enough time for that pie and another cup of coffee."

"All right." She crossed to the counter again. Panic sprinted through her when she looked out the window and saw no one. He'd left. Because her fingers were unsteady, she fumbled with the pie. "Roger, are you going to let me go?"

He hesitated only an instant, but that was enough

to tell her that his words were just another lie. "Sure. As soon as I'm clear."

So it came down to that. Her heart, her inn, and now her life. She set the pie in front of him and studied his face. He was pleased with himself, she thought, and she hated him for it. But he was still sweating.

"I'll get your coffee." She walked to the stove. One foot, then the other. There was a buzzing in her ears. It was more than fear now, she realized as she turned the burner up under the pot. It was rage and despair and a strong, irresistible need to survive. Mechanically she switched the stove off. Then, taking a cloth, she took the pot by the handle.

He was still holding the gun, and he was shoveling pie into his mouth with his left hand. He thought she was a fool, Charity mused. Someone who could be used and duped and manipulated. She took a deep breath.

"Roger?"

He glanced up. Charity looked directly into his eyes.

"You forgot your coffee," she said calmly, then tossed the steaming contents into his face.

He screamed. She didn't think she'd ever heard a man scream like that before. He was half out of his chair, groping blindly for the gun. It happened quickly. No matter how often she played back the scene in her mind, she would never be completely sure what happened first.

She grabbed for the gun herself. Block's flailing hand caught her across the cheekbone. Even as she staggered backward there was the sound of glass breaking.

Roman was through the window. Charity landed on the floor, stunned by the blow, as he burst through.

There were men breaking through the barricaded doors and rushing into the room. Someone dragged her from the floor and pulled her out.

Roman held the gun to Block's temple. They were kneeling on the shattered glass—or rather Roman was kneeling and supporting the moaning Block. There were already welts rising up on his wide face. "Please," Roman murmured. "Give me a reason."

"Roman." Royce laid a hand on his shoulder. "It's over."

But the rage clogged his throat. It made his finger slippery on the trigger of the gun. He remembered the way Charity had looked at him when she had seen him outside the window. Slowly he drew back and holstered his gun.

"Yeah. It's over. Get him the hell out of here." He rose and went to find Charity.

He found her in the lobby, wrapped in Mae's arms.

"I'm all right," Charity murmured. "Really." When she saw Roman, her eyes frosted over. "Everything's going to be fine now. I need to speak with Roman for a minute."

"You say your piece." Mae kissed both of her cheeks. "Then you're going to get in a nice hot tub."

"Okay." She squeezed Mae's hand. Strange, but it felt more like a dream now, as if she were pushing her way through layers and layers of gauzy gray curtains. "I think we'll have more privacy upstairs," she said to Roman. Then she turned without looking at him and started up the stairs.

He wanted to hold her. His fingers curled tight into his palms. He needed to lift her against him, touch her hair, her skin, and convince himself that the nightmare was over.

Her knees were shaking. Reaction was struggling to set in, but she fought it off. When she was alone, Charity promised herself. When she was finally alone, she would let it all out.

In her sitting room she turned to face him. She would not, could not, speak to him in the intimacy of her bedroom. "I imagine you have reports to file," she began. Was that her voice? she wondered. It sounded so thin and cold, so foreign. Deliberately she cleared her throat. "I've been told I'll have to make a statement, but I thought we should get this out of the way first."

"Charity." He started toward her, only to be brought up short when her hands whipped out.

"Don't." Her eyes were as cold as her voice. It wasn't a dream, she told herself. It was as harsh and as brutal a reality as she had ever known. "Don't touch me. Not now, not ever again."

His hands fell uselessly to his sides. "I'm sorry."

"Why? You accomplished exactly what you came to do. From what I've been able to gather, Roger and Bob had quite a system going. I'm sure your superiors will be delighted with you."

"It doesn't matter."

She dug his badge out of her pocket, where she had shoved it. "Yes." She threw it at him. "Yes, it does."

Struggling for calm, he pushed it into his pocket. He noted dispassionately that his hands were bleeding. "I couldn't tell you."

"Didn't tell me."

There was a faint bruise on her cheekbone. For a moment all his guilt and impotent fury centered there. "He hit you."

She ran a fingertip lightly across the mark. "I don't break easily."

"I want to explain."

"Do you?" She turned away for a moment. She wanted to keep her anger cold. "I think I get the picture."

"Listen, baby—"

"No, *you* listen, baby." Her composure cracking, she whirled around again. "You lied to me, you used me from the first minute to the last. It was all one huge, incredible lie."

"Not all."

"No? Let's see, how can we separate one from the other? A convenient flat." She saw the anger in his eyes and shoved a chair out of her path. "And George, good old lucky George. I suppose it was worth a few thousand dollars to get him out of the way and leave you an opening. And Bob—you knew all about Bob, didn't you?"

"We couldn't be sure, not at first."

"Not at first," she repeated. As long as she kept her brain cold, she told herself, she could think. She could think and not feel. "I wonder, Roman, were you so sure of me? Or did you think I was part of it?" When he didn't answer, she spun around again. "You did. Oh, I see. I was under investigation all the time. And there you were, so conveniently on the scene. All you had to do was get close to me, and I made it so easy for you." With a laugh, she pressed her hands to her face. "My God, I threw myself at you."

"I wasn't supposed to get involved with you." Fighting desperation, he paced his words carefully. "It just happened. I fell in love with you."

"Don't say that to me." She lowered her hands. Her face was pale and cool behind them. "You don't even know what it means."

"I didn't, until you."

"You can't have love without trust, Roman. I trusted you. I didn't just give you my body. I gave you everything."

"I told you everything I could," he shot back. "Damn it, I couldn't tell you the rest. The things I told you about myself, about the way I grew up, the way I felt, they were all true."

"Do I have your word on that? Agent DeWinter?"

With an oath, he strode across the room and grabbed her arms. "I didn't know you when I took the assignment. I was doing a job. When things changed, the most important part of that job became proving your innocence and keeping you safe."

"If you had told me I would have proven my own innocence." She jerked out of his hold. "This is my inn, and these are my people. The only family I have left. Do you think I would risk it all for money?"

"No. I knew that, I trusted that, after the first twenty-four hours. I had orders, Charity, and my own instincts. If I had told you who I was and what was going on, you would never have been able to keep up a front."

"So I'm that stupid?"

"No. That honest." Digging deep, he found his control again. "You've been through a lot. Let me take you to the hospital."

"I've been through a lot," she repeated, and nearly laughed. "Do you know how it feels to know that for two years, *two years*, people I thought I knew were using me? I always thought I was such a good judge of character." Now she did laugh. She walked to the window. "They made a fool out of me week after week. I'm not sure I'll ever get over it. But that's nothing." She turned, wrapping her fingers around the windowsill. "That's nothing compared to what I feel when I think of how I let myself believe you were in love with me."

"If it was a lie, why am I here now, telling you that I do?"

"I don't know." Suddenly weary, she dragged her hair away from her face. "And it doesn't seem to matter. I'm wrung dry, Roman. For a while today I was sure he was going to kill me."

"Oh, Charity." He gathered her close, and when she didn't resist he buried his face in her hair.

"I thought he would kill me," she repeated, her arms held rigidly at her sides. "And I didn't want to die. In fact, nothing was quite so important to me as staying alive. When my mother fell in love and that love was betrayed, she gave up. I've never been much like her." She stepped stiffly out of his hold. "Maybe I'm gullible, but I've never been weak. I intend to pick up where I left off, before all of this. I'm going to keep the inn running. No matter what it takes, I'm going to erase you and these last weeks from my life."

"No." Furious, he took her face in his hands. "You won't, because you know I love you. And you made me a promise, Charity. No matter what happened, you wouldn't stop loving me."

"I made that promise to a man who doesn't exist." It hurt. She could feel the pain rip through her from one end to the other. "And I don't love the man who does." She took a small but significant step backward. "Leave me alone."

When he didn't move, she walked into the bedroom and flipped the lock.

Mae was busily sweeping up glass in the kitchen. For the first time in over twenty years the inn was closed. She figured it would open again soon enough, but for now she was content that her girl was safe upstairs in bed and the coffee-guzzling police were on their way out.

When Roman came in, she rested her arms on her broom. Mae had rocked Charity for nearly an hour while she'd cried over him. She'd been prepared to be cold and dismissive. It only took one look to change her mind.

"You look worn out."

"I . . ." Feeling lost, he glanced around the room. "I wanted to ask how she was before I left."

"She's miserable." She nodded, content with the anguish she saw in his eyes. "And stubborn. You got a few cuts."

Automatically he lifted a hand to rub at the nick on his temple. "Will you give her this number?" He dropped a card on the table. "She can reach me there if— She can reach me there."

"Sit down. Let me clean you up."

"No, it's all right."

"I said sit down." She went to a cupboard for a bottle of antiseptic. "She's had a bad shock."

He had a sudden mental image of Block holding the knife to her throat. "I know."

"She bounces back pretty quick from most things. She loves you."

Roman winced a little as she dabbed on the antiseptic, but not from the sting. "Did."

"Does," Mae said flatly. "She just doesn't want to right now. You been an agent for long?"

"Too long."

"Are you going to make sure that slimy worm Roger Block's put away?"

Roman's hands curled into fists. "Yes."

"Are you in love with Charity?"

He relaxed his hands. "Yes."

"I believe you, so I'm going to give you some advice." Puffing a bit, she sat down next to him. "She's hurt, real bad. Charity's the kind who likes to fix things herself. Give her a little time." She picked up the card and slipped it into her apron pocket. "I'll just hold on to this for now."

She was feeling stronger. And not just physically, Charity decided as she jogged along behind Ludwig. In every way. The sweaty dreams that had woken her night after night were fading. It wasn't nearly as difficult to talk, or to smile, or to pretend that she was in control again. She had promised herself she would put her life back together, and she was doing it.

She rarely thought of Roman. On a sigh, she relented. She would never get strong again if she began to lie to herself.

She *always* thought of Roman. It was difficult not to, and it was especially difficult today.

They were to have been married today. Charity veered into the grass as Ludwig explored. The ache came, spread and was accepted. Just after noon, with the music swelling and the sun streaming down on the garden, she would have put her hand in his. And promised.

A fantasy, she told herself, and nudged her dog back onto the shoulder of the road. It had been fantasy then, and it was a fantasy now.

And yet . . . With every day that passed she remembered more clearly the times they had spent together. His reluctance, and his anger. Then his tenderness and concern. She glanced down to where the bracelet shimmered on her wrist.

She'd tried to put it back in the box, to push it into some dark, rarely opened drawer. Every day she told herself she would. Tomorrow. And every day she remembered how sweet, how awkward and how wonderful he'd been when he'd given it to her.

If it had only been a job, why had he given her so much more than he had needed to? Not just the piece of jewelry, but everything the circle of gold had symbolized? He could have offered her friendship and respect, as Bob had, and she would have trusted him as much. He could have kept their relationship strictly physical. Her feelings would have remained the same.

But he had said he loved her. And at the end he had all but begged her to believe it.

She shook her head and increased her pace. She was being weak and sentimental. It was just the day . . . the beautiful spring morning that was to have been her wedding day.

What she needed was to get back to the inn and keep busy. This day would pass, like all the others.

At first she thought she was imagining it when she saw him standing beside the road, looking out at the sunrise over the water. Her feet faltered. Before she could think to prevent it, her knees weakened. Fighting her heart, she walked to him.

He'd heard her coming. As he'd stood in the growing light he'd remembered wondering if he came back, if he would stand just there and wait for Charity to run to him.

She wasn't running now. She was walking very slowly, despite the eager dog. Could she know, he wondered, that she held his life in her hands?

Nerves swarmed through her, making her fingers clench and unclench on the leash. She prayed as she stopped in front of him that her voice would be steadier.

"What do you want?"

He bent down to pat the squirming dog's head. "We'll get to that. How are you feeling?"

"I'm fine."

"You've been having nightmares." There were shadows under her eyes. He wouldn't make it easy on her by ignoring them.

She stiffened. "They're passing. Mae talks too much."

"At least she talks to me."

"We've already said all there is to say."

He closed a hand over her arm as she started by him. "Not this time. You had your say last time, and I had a lot of it coming. Now it's my turn." Reaching down, he unhooked the leash. Free, Ludwig bounded toward home. "Mae's waiting for him," Roman explained before Charity could call the dog back.

"I see." She wrapped the leash around her fisted hand. "You two work all this out?"

"She cares about you. So do I."

"I have things to do."

"Yeah. This is first." He pulled her close and, ignoring her struggling, crushed his mouth to hers. It was like a drink after days in the desert, like a fire after a dozen long cold nights. He plundered, greedy, as though it were the first time. Or the last.

She couldn't fight him, or herself. Almost sobbing, she clung to him, hungry and hurting. No matter how strong she tried to be, she would never be strong enough to stand against her own heart.

Aching, she started to draw back, but he tightened his hold. "Give me a minute," he murmured, pressing his lips to her hair. "Every night I wake up and see him holding a knife at your throat. And there's nothing I can do. I reach for you, and you're not there. For a minute, one horrible minute, I'm terrified. Then I remember that you're safe. You're not with me, but you're safe. It's almost enough."

"Roman." With a helpless sigh, she stroked soothing hands over his shoulders. "It doesn't do any good to think about it."

"Do you think I could forget?" He pulled back, keeping his hands firm on her arms. "For the rest of my life I'll remember every second of it. I was responsible for you."

"No." The anger came quickly enough to surprise both of them. She shoved at his chest. "*I'm* responsible for me. I was and I am and I always will be. And I took care of myself."

"Yeah." He ran his palm over her cheek. The bruise had faded, even if the memory hadn't. "It was a hell of a way to serve coffee."

"Let's forget it." She shrugged out of his grip and walked toward the water. "I'm not particularly proud of letting myself be duped, so I'd rather not dwell on it."

"They were pros, Charity. You're not the first person they've used."

She pressed her lips together. "And you?"

"When you're undercover you lie, and you use, and you take advantage of anything that's offered." Her eyes were closed when he turned her around to face him. "I came here to do a job. It had been a long time since I'd let myself think beyond anything but the next day. Look at me. Please."

Taking a steadying breath, she opened her eyes. "We've been through this already, Roman."

"No. I'd hurt you. I'd disappointed you. You

weren't ready to listen." Gently he brushed a tear from her lashes. "I hope you are now, because I can't make it much longer without you."

"I was too hard on you before." It took almost everything she had, but she managed a smile. "I was hurt, and I was a lot shakier than I knew from being locked up with Roger. After I gave my statement, Inspector Conby explained everything to me, more clearly. About how the operation had been working, what my responsibilities were, what you had to do."

"What responsibilities?"

"About the money. It's put us in somewhat of a hole, but at least we only have to pay back a percentage."

"I see." Roman laughed and shook his head. "He always was a prince."

"The merchant's responsible for the loss." She tilted her head. "You didn't know about the arrangements I've made with him?"

"No."

"But you work for him."

"Not anymore. I turned in my resignation when I got back to D.C."

"Oh, Roman, that's ridiculous. It's like throwing out the baby with the bathwater."

He smiled appreciatively at her innate practicality. "I decided I like carpentry better. Got any openings?"

Running the leash through her hands, she looked over the water. "I haven't given much thought to remodeling lately."

"I work cheap." He tilted her face to his. "All you have to do is marry me."

"Don't."

"Charity." Calling on patience he hadn't been aware he possessed, he held her still. "One of the things I most admire about you is your mind. You're real sharp. Look at me, really look. I figure you've got to know that I'm not beating my head against this same wall for entertainment. I love you. You've got to believe that."

"I'm afraid to," she whispered.

He felt the first true spark of hope. "Believe this. You changed my life. Literally changed it. I can't go back to the way it was before. I can't go forward unless you're with me. How long do you want me to stand here, waiting to start living again?"

With her arms wrapped around her chest, she walked a short distance away. The high grass at the water's edge was still misted with dew. She could smell it, and the fragile fragrances of wildflowers. It occurred to her then that she had blocked such small things out of her life ever since she'd sent him away.

If it was honesty she was demanding from him, how could she give him anything less?

"I've missed you terribly." She shook her head quickly before he could touch her again. "I tried not to wonder if you'd come back. I told myself I didn't want you to. When I saw you standing in the road, all I wanted to do was run to you. No questions, no explanations. But it's not that simple."

"No."

"I do love you, Roman. I can't stop. I have tried," she said, looking back at him. "Not very hard, but I have tried. I think I knew under all the anger and the hurt that you weren't lying about loving me back. I haven't wanted to forgive you for lying about the rest, but— That's just pride really." Perhaps it was simple after all, she thought. "If I have to make a choice, I'd rather take love." She smiled and opened her arms to him. "I guess you're hired."

She laughed when he caught her up in his arms

and swung her around. "We'll make it work," he promised her, raining kisses all over her face. "Starting today."

"We were going to be married today."

"Are going to be." He hooked his arm under her legs to carry her.

"But we—"

"I have a license." Closing his mouth over hers, he swung her around again.

"A marriage license?"

"It's in my pocket, with two tickets to Venice."

"To—" Her hand slid limply from his shoulder. "To *Venice*? But how—?"

"And Mae bought you a dress yesterday. She wouldn't let me see it."

"Well." The thrill was too overwhelming to allow her to pretend annoyance. "You were awfully sure of yourself."

"No." He kissed her again, felt the curve of her lips, and the welcoming. "I was sure of you."

The thrilling conclusion to Nora Roberts's #1 *New York Times* bestselling Lost Bride Trilogy

where two women—one dead, one alive—
prepare for a terrifying final showdown.